MW00338211

Bring Her Home

CROWN OF PROMISE

BRING HER HOME

HANNAH CURRIE

WhiteCrown
PUBLISHING

This is a work of fiction. All characters and events portrayed in this novel are either fictitious or used fictitiously.

WhiteCrown Publishing, a division of WhiteFire Publishing
13607 Bedford Rd NE
Cumberland, MD 21502

ISBNs:
978-1-941720-97-4 (paperback)
978-1-941720-99-8 (hardcover)
978-1-941720-98-1 (digital)

To those praying for their prodigals.
Keep praying.
The road is long, the road is heartbreaking, but please, don't give up.
Keep fighting to show them the way home.

You walked away so certain
So sure you had it all
So sure you needed nothing more from me
You had to find your own way
I had to let you go
Even though it broke my heart in two
My daughter, my child
The road you take is long
You'll fall more than you'll walk
And fall again
I would have walked it with you
If you'd have only asked
I would have given everything for you
Was it love to let you go?
Should I have made you stay?
Could I have saved you from the pain you face?
Do you know how much my heart aches
As I pray each day for you?
And search in hope of seeing you again?
Know this, I'll keep the light on
Through every darkest night
I'll love you, no matter how you come
You might have walked away
But you will never leave my heart
I'll always be your father, on your side
Be it hours or be it decades
I'll wait and watch and pray
I won't give up the fight
To bring you home

Raedonleith, 1423

Sobs wracked his body as King Lior fell on his knees, the missive clutched to his chest as if it hadn't already imprinted its message on his heart.

We've found her.

Four years of searching. Four years of waiting. Four years of hoping she was even still alive. He'd never once been bested in battle, yet three hastily written words had brought him to his knees.

His reply was as short as his knight's letter had been. Three simple words.

Bring her home.

CHAPTER 1

There were tapestries on the walls. The windows. The cottage's door. Enough to keep out the light and prying eyes, but not the screams. No amount of tapestries could dampen the screams. They came, again and again, piercing the night air and shredding Darrek's heart.

"Put down your sword. You can't go in there."

Darrek gritted his teeth against the quiet words of the man who'd become more of a father to him than his had ever been. Manning's hand on his arm might have been gentle, but Darrek knew the strength behind it.

He gripped his sword tighter. "I can't take it anymore."

"Stay with the plan."

The sound came again, through the trees to their makeshift campsite. Terror-filled, like that of a child, instead of a grown woman. Darrek wanted to block his ears, but even if he did, he'd still hear it. In his head. Etched in his soul. It was too much. They'd come to rescue Lady Evangeline, not listen to her scream. "What if I can't?"

"Then you should leave."

"Without her?" Unthinkable. She was the reason they were here.

"Lord Cavendish is a dangerous man, as well you know. Until we find out precisely what the relationship is between him and Lady Evangeline, we wait. I won't lose good knights to poor preparation."

Wait and watch. Day in, day out. Wait and watch. The years of searching, empty leads, disappointment, and frustration had nothing on this. Sit. Wait. Watch. While Lady Evangeline screamed herself hoarse.

They'd thought the sound was an animal being attacked the first time they'd heard it—and kept their swords close to their sides all night. Three nights later, when it had come again, they'd been closer to the castle and recognized it as that of a woman. It had sickened Darrek that night too, though he'd not known yet whose screams they were.

"What if it's not a nightmare?" Darrek asked. "What if she's in pain? What if she's being attacked?"

"Craig would have told us if she was."

For the first time in his life, Darrek felt a spark of jealousy toward a squire. A spark growing quickly into a wildfire. Oh, to be small and inconsequential enough to be all but invisible sneaking about the castle grounds. Darrek, with his height and bulk, would have been spotted the instant he walked through the gate, but a barely teenaged boy? No one paid him any attention.

While Craig walked about freely, gathering information, Darrek and the other knights hid in the forest. Waited for their chance. A chance Darrek was starting to think would never come.

Curse common sense.

Darrek had been the one to spot Lady Evangeline when they neared Cavendish Castle five days ago. They'd searched the castle twice before—the week she'd gone missing and then two years later—but found neither her nor any sign she'd been there. They likely wouldn't have found her this time either, if not for Adam's hunger for meat and the rabbit he and Darrek had chased. It had led them to a cottage tucked into the edge of the forest and so covered in vines and leaves that it blended in with the trees.

The large lock on the door had been the first hint of the treasure within. The two guards who'd scurried over to unlock it before hurriedly moving aside, the second. Darrek and Adam had whispered wonderings over who might live there for several minutes before the door opened and a girl stepped out. It had been their first glimpse of hope in almost two years.

Lady Evangeline.

She might have been garbed in the clothes of a peasant and far changed from the girl he'd once known, but there was no mistaking those features. Red hair. Blue eyes. A beauty, just like her mother.

The guards had moved several more steps back, eyeing the girl as if she were a wild animal about to rip out their hearts instead of the cowed woman shuffling along with her gaze on the ground. It had taken every bit of Darrek's self-control—and Adam's vice of a grip on his arm—to stay hidden in the trees and not throw her onto the closest horse and take her home. The image of her had wavered then, tears marring his view as he imagined that day. Lady Evangeline's homecoming. He'd had to clear his throat before whispering.

"It's her."

Nervousness had tempered the thrill of their find. They knew how hard a mistake was to live with. None of their small group wanted to be the one who made it. And yet, they'd never stopped looking, riding the length and breadth of the country, and even across seas, certain their king's youngest daughter had to be somewhere. Sooner or later, someone had to find her.

If only it had been somewhere other than here.

"Darrek."

Anywhere but here.

"Sir Darrek."

Manning's voice was louder this time, breaking through Darrek's frustration. He turned to see not only his mentor but all three of the other knights' gazes focused solely on him. Wary. They'd fight him, if they had to.

"You must wait. There is nothing we can do tonight."

Darrek lay his sword back on the grass beside the threadbare blanket he called his bed and pulled on a thick brown cloak. Manning was right. He couldn't save Lady Evangeline. Not tonight. There was too much they still didn't know. But that didn't mean there was nothing he could do.

"I'm going to her."

The men's protests were instant. Darrek brushed them aside

and tucked one knife into his belt and another into his boot. He couldn't rescue Evangeline, not from Cavendish or the nightmares that plagued her, but he had no intention of letting her face them alone.

"Darrek," Manning tried one more time.

Darrek paused, turning back slightly to look at Manning. "I have to—"

"Be careful. Cavendish won't show mercy if he finds you, and neither will his guards."

Darrek nodded once, before moving away. His steps were quick but certain as he walked through the darkness to the tiny cottage. He'd take every care possible, but he *would* get to Evangeline.

Screams filled his ears again. He wondered, not for the first time, how the forest patrols and the men guarding the castle each night could so easily ignore the agony of the woman just outside it. Were they truly so heartless? Or did they, like so many others within Cavendish Castle, believe her to be cursed? Crazy, even. Darrek had laughed when Craig relayed that rumor. The Evangeline Darrek remembered might have driven *men* crazy with her beauty, but she was far from touched herself.

Of course, the Evangeline he knew had also been missing for four years. And now screamed like a demon fought for her soul.

He slowed as the cottage came into view, careful to keep his steps light and his mind alert. His breath fogged the air, mingling with the sound of another childlike scream. Darrek rubbed his chest and forced out another breath.

Think. Focus. Breathe. Getting himself captured wouldn't help Evangeline.

The screams played with his mind as his gaze silently tracked the area around the cottage, searching for guards. According to Craig's reports, the patrols stayed clear of the cottage once it was locked each night, but Darrek had been a knight for too long not to be wary. He forced himself to stay still for a minute before creeping forward.

The lock on the door was heavy, solid, and tightly closed. As expected. He wouldn't be entering through there without far more noise than even the screams could cover. But—he walked around the cottage—*there*. A window. It would be a squeeze, but he'd do it. For Evangeline. He'd do anything for the daughter of his king. Darrek hesitated only a moment, considering Evangeline's honor, before climbing through. The girl was in pain. Propriety be hanged. He almost hoped there was a guard inside just so he'd have someone to fight.

Eyes already adjusted to the dim light, it was a simple task to find the woman he sought. She lay curled in a blanket on the floor of the one-roomed cottage, every muscle tensed as she screamed. Two other people were in the room, though neither of them were guards. One was an older woman dressed in the same simple garb as Evangeline. The other, a young, sleeping child she carefully stood in front of. He didn't blame her—not for that, not for the glare she set on him. Certainly not for the iron pot she grabbed in lieu of a weapon.

Darrek held up his hands. "Please. I'm not here to hurt any of you. I only want to help."

When the woman didn't throw the pot at his head, he lowered his hands and slowly moved to Evangeline's side, kneeling beside her. A gentle but firm shake of her shoulder did nothing to wake her. He tried again. "Evangeline."

"I don't know who you are or what you're doing here in the middle of the night, but she won't wake. She never does when the terrors come. Not until morning, when she's limp from the fight."

Darrek looked up, surprised to see the woman had sat down. The pot was still in her hand, and she was still hiding the child, but she seemed more wary than threatened by him. Had she decided to trust him after all? He nodded to her before trying again to shake Evangeline out of the nightmare. The woman was right. Evangeline wasn't waking. Was it like this every time the terrors came? What fears held her so tightly in their clutches? "Evangeline," he said again, more force behind his words this time. "Evangeline." Again and again he said her name, shaking her shoulder. "Evangeline!"

Her screams lessened, but now her whole body shook. Darrek wanted to pick her up and cradle her in his arms, like one would an upset child, rocking her against his shoulder until she calmed. But she was no child. More, she was the daughter of his king. He'd already come into her room in the middle of the night—something he hoped her father would understand, given the circumstances. He didn't need to compound that by embracing her. Even if the older maid could vouch for his honor.

He reached for Evangeline's hand instead, stroking his thumb up and down the back of it.

Lord Almighty, give her peace.

Lord Most High, calm her heart. Banish the terrors and fill her mind with beauty.

"Shh… Sleep, lass."

A tear ran down her cheek, caught for a moment in the moonlight before disappearing into her hair. Darrek held her hand tighter, his whispered prayers becoming a jumble of more sentiments than sense. If only they'd found her sooner. Might they have been able to save her from the terrors that claimed her mind?

"Shh…" he said again. "Sleep now. No harm will come to you tonight. You're safe here."

His voice caught as her screams turned to whimpers.

"There's a good lass."

It was a wonder they'd found her at all and even more that they'd recognized her. They'd been searching for a flighty teenager. This was a woman, not only in looks but in temperament. It was Evangeline, yet so different from the one he'd known.

The girl he'd last seen was slim, always ready with a smile, confident to the point of being arrogant, and certain of her effect on men and women alike. The men were drawn to her, the women envious.

This woman—and she definitely had the body of a woman—was quiet. Cowed, almost. It wasn't just the clothes—the brown and white servant garb she donned each day. It was the way her shoulders drooped forward when she stood. The wariness in her eyes. A shuffle of a walk where once she strode. Even her hair, once the vibrant red of fiery autumn leaves, now seemed dull. Trailing her this past week had brought an ache to his chest and an overwhelming longing time and time again to swoop her into his arms and carry her away from this place.

He'd foolishly admitted as much to the other knights two days ago. Adam and Landon had laughed, joking that he was a besotted romantic who'd been deprived of the fairer sex for too long to fall so hard for a woman like her. Even Spencer, always ready with a word of affirmation, had tried to stifle a grin. Only Manning had seemed to understand, nodding quietly as he whittled a piece of wood by the fire. It wasn't a romantic love at all but a fierce sense of loyalty. Of protection. She was hurt, and he wanted to save her. He had to save her. This was why they'd come. Why they'd given up four years of their lives.

"You've a gift, sir," came the quiet voice of the older woman. "Who are you?"

"A friend," Darrek said quietly. He daren't give his true name, not so near the castle of his king's greatest enemy, not until he knew who his friends were. The woman nodded, not seeming to mind. Would she be friend? Foe? Would she tell her master he'd been here tonight? She hadn't gone running yet, so perhaps not. Perhaps, she might even become an ally, if she cared as much about Evangeline as it seemed.

"Well, friend. I thank you." She smiled at him before closing her eyes. "Perhaps we'll get some sleep this night after all. I can't say I wouldn't welcome it."

Darrek sent a nod of his own back to her. If he'd been the one whose sleep was interrupted by a screaming roommate several nights a week, he'd likely welcome anyone who calmed the screams also.

Evangeline was quiet, her breathing steady, her muscles lax in sleep again. He should go. With a final prayer, Darrek eased his hand out of hers. She whimpered. He stood, gently shaking his feet to bring back circulation. Her whimpers turned to cries. He bent back down to take her hand again. She instantly stopped.

"Maybe ye should stay," came the sleepy voice of Evangeline's fellow maid.

"'Twouldn't be right." Much as he wanted to.

"I'm a light sleeper, friend. There's not much trouble you could get into with the boy and me in here. Still, 'tis your choice. Do what you think best."

His choice. *Almighty, would it be right?* He was a knight, honor bound to King Lior. He'd already crossed the line of impropriety simply by coming into her room. Would he eradicate it altogether if he stayed?

Darrek eased his hand out of Evangeline's again, testing. Again, she whimpered. He couldn't leave her, not like this.

He sat beside her pallet, stretching his legs out across the stone floor, careful not to touch any part of Evangeline other than her hand.

Leaning back against the wall, he tipped his head to the ceiling and settled in to pray.

"Friend, you must wake."

A shake of his shoulder had Darrek instantly alert, if completely disorientated. Where was he? Inside a house, given the tapestry-lined walls and stone floor. But whose house?

"You have to leave. Now."

Darrek looked from the loudly whispering woman to the hand clasped within his, following it up an arm to—

Evangeline. He'd come to help Evangeline. He must have fallen asleep. The room was still dark but, based upon the panicked expression of the woman still shaking his shoulder, he guessed it to be close to morning. In a half hour or less, the servants would all be up and the nearby castle buzzing with preparations for the new day.

"She won't take kindly to your presence. Nor will the master if he finds you here. Go, now, before they wake."

She pushed at his shoulder, urging him to move. Darrek needed no more incentive. Taking one last look at the soundly sleep-

CHAPTER
2

A troupe of entertainers had arrived at the castle and set up tents near the front gate. It had been all any of the servants could talk about. Entertainers wouldn't normally have caused such a stir, especially when a wealthy lord and his retinue were expected in several days. Only these entertainers were a very small troupe, and all of them particularly handsome.

Or so the gossip went.

Eva threw a handful of flour on the table, followed by the dough she'd been tasked with kneading, and tried to block out the noise. It was mindless work, making bread. Peaceful, in the mornings when she started before anyone else. Not so much late in the afternoon when the kitchens sweltered with the heat of too many pots, too many people, and too many unfounded opinions. The chatter was endless, grating on Eva's tired nerves. Perhaps it might not have been so bad, if she'd been part of the conversations. But no one spoke to Eva. They only spoke about her.

Usually.

Today, every conversation had been about the three men.

She hadn't seen them herself yet, nor was she likely to, but it seemed every other servant in the castle had.

A washer woman had been the first to come back with the tale, bustling into the kitchen to tell her friend about one of the men coming to her rescue when she tripped on a rock walking back from the river. According to her, he was the strongest, most handsome, and most chivalrous man she'd ever seen. Which, of course, had every hapless, romance-minded maid in the keep finding a reason to wander the troupe's way to judge for themselves. As if they'd never had a troupe of traveling entertainers visit before.

The healer's apprentice suddenly needed more herbs despite Eva bearing witness to the fact that she'd gone into the forest yesterday and come back with two baskets full. The apprentice returned an hour later with no herbs but plenty of matrimonial illusions.

Two kitchen maids went out next in search of mushrooms. They too came back empty-handed. Convenient given that they needed their hands to giggle behind.

A housemaid was next to come back with a story, telling anyone close enough to listen that she'd claimed the tall, blond one who looked far more like a knight than a jester. As if saying such a thing would stop any other maids from wanting him. The girl should have kept her mouth shut. Making such a bold claim would only lead to fighting and foolery.

Not long after that, a squire ran into the kitchen to request lunch for the stablemaster and told a story of his own about the men's horses. This sent three more twittering maids running to fill water buckets, which they'd none-too-subtly kicked over ten seconds before.

And they thought Eva was the crazy one.

There were three men, according to the gossip. The tall blond and two with light brown hair. A jester, a bard dressed like the blue-faced sprites he spun tales of, and a minstrel. All three big men, muscled and strong. And all the handsomest men in the land.

Of course, to many of these women, that could have simply meant that the men had all their limbs, teeth, and faculties intact. Give or take a few teeth.

Eva pushed back her red hair with her arm, careful not to brush flour into it. Handsome men. On the castle grounds. Once, that would have excited her too. She would have been first to primp her hair and tie her belt a little tighter around her waist to show off her figure to the best advantage. They would have noticed her too. She would have made sure of it. Now, she was more than happy to stay in the shadows. Intent even, in doing so. It had been a long time since she'd wanted to show off her figure to anyone. A long time since she'd *had* a figure to show off.

She might have even wondered, once, if they'd come to rescue her. Wondered if they weren't entertainers at all, but rather her father's knights disguised, come to save her from a life of drudgery. She shook her head and let out a bitter laugh. Foolish thought. She'd given up that hope around the same time she'd lost her figure.

Eva pounded the dough into the table, reminding herself for the millionth time that this had been her choice. She'd been the one to walk away. This wasn't what she'd been thinking when she did it, but there was no going back now. The time for second thoughts had been four years ago. These days, her regrets were as well known to her as her shortened name. And almost as comfortable.

Two more minutes of kneading and the dough was ready. Eva rolled it into a neat ball and placed it in a tin. Her arms shook as she pulled another mass of dough out of the bowl and began the process all over again. How was it possible that a body could ache so? It was as if her bones had melted into nothing and all that held her up was her stubbornness. Nineteen years. It was all the life she could lay claim to. She might as well have been ninety, the way her joints creaked.

Shuffling tired feet, she took a step backward, yelping when her foot hit something that hadn't been there before. Half turning, half falling, she caught herself just in time to spot her little boy, hands tucked behind his back. Wiping her hands on a piece of cloth, she crouched down.

"Arthur, what are you doing here? I thought you were helping Maeve make the beds."

One hand came out from behind his back. He opened his fist to show her a crumpled flower.

"You brought me a flower?"

He nodded.

"It's beautiful. Thank you."

She took the yellow flower—likely a weed—and held it between her thumb and forefinger. It was pretty, even if it was missing several petals. And a stem. One day Arthur would realize that flowers were far easier to hold when they still had their stems attached. Of course, he was only three. Plenty of time to learn how to woo a lady. Until then, she remained his one and only love. And he hers.

Arthur's other hand came out, this one holding a tattered piece of cloth that might have been white at one point. Long, long ago. Where had he gotten that piece of fabric? Eva wanted to know but thought it better not to ask. She'd hate to find out someone's undergarments were missing a square of fabric from them. Tattered as it was.

She smiled. "It's…nice."

He frowned before pointing to the flour-coated table she was kneading on. His head tilted, eyes asking the questions his mouth wouldn't form.

"You want to help?"

He nodded. Eva cringed inside. That piece of cloth could do nothing except make people ill. Perhaps if it had been dry, she might have taken it from him to place beside hers, but Arthur's hands must have been wet when he picked up the dirty cloth because they were also muddy and needed to be washed.

"Thank you, kind sir." Arthur smiled at the salutation. "But I still need that flour. It stops the dough from sticking to the table. But, let's see—" She brushed back a piece of straw-colored hair from Arthur's eyes, trying to think of something he could help with that wouldn't add too much more work to her already full day. "Would you like to help me get more water?" The kitchens could always use more water. Especially since the maids kept forgetting to fill their buckets today. Distracted as they all were. "Or I'm certain Maeve would love to see you."

Arthur shook his head.

"You don't want to help?"

He shook his head again.

"You don't think Maeve wants to see you?" She should have learned by now only to ask Arthur one question at a time.

This time he nodded, to Eva's relief, before pointing toward the castle gate.

Ah. Maeve had gone into the forest, beyond their cottage garden. It wasn't safe for Arthur, so she'd sent him to the kitchens. At least, that's what Eva assumed had happened. Widowed almost twenty years ago and still holding her husband tightly in her heart, Maeve didn't seem the type to be trying to catch the attention of a group of men likely half her age.

Young men. Handsome. Strong.

Eva hated how quickly her mind switched back to them. Her days of swooning over a man were long past. No good man would ever look at her as anything more than a ruined servant girl, and thinking any differently was only torture.

But what if they were her father's knights disguised as entertainers? Raedonleith was only two days' journey away. It wasn't inconceivable that they might have come. But why now?

If they had come for her, they might as well go home. She wasn't leaving. Even if she'd wanted to, she couldn't. Not without Arthur—and he didn't have the option. Not while his father lived.

Eva smiled at Arthur, dabbing him on the nose with her floury finger. He was a good boy, if exasperating at times. Not mischievous, or bad, just there. Always there. Wanting to help. Trying to help, even when that caused more work for Eva. She wanted to give him the chance—it was what a good mother would have done—but she already struggled to get all her work done before the sun set each day. Arthur's help could add hours to it, and the truth was, she just didn't have the energy.

"Maybe you could play until she gets back?"

With a sad nod, the boy walked over to the corner of the kitchen. Back to his stool. Back to the sticks and rocks he played with day in day out while she worked to keep him safe. She'd had dolls and jewels and balls to play with when she was a child. Arthur had rocks and two small somewhat-sword-shaped sticks. But no one his age to play with. No one to laugh with. So little reason to smile. It broke Eva's heart. Over and over again. If the Almighty was real, he'd made a mistake with her.

She turned back to the table, one hand landing on the dough while the other swiped at the tears she refused to let fall.

Perhaps the entertainers were knights, and perhaps they were strong. Perhaps, by some miracle, the men would look more than once at one or two of the besotted maids and take them far away from the life they'd fallen into. But one of those maids wouldn't be her. Bread, brooms, dust, and chamber pots. That was her lot. She'd be a fool to wish for anything more.

CHAPTER
3

"**I**t's time."

Darrek stilled, the blanket he'd been rolling dropping to the dirt in front of him as he turned every bit of his attention to Manning and the words he'd been waiting to hear.

Finally.

"Lord Dickerson, his daughters, and a full retinue of knights arrived at the castle this morning."

They had? How had Darrek missed that? He opened his mouth to ask before a look from Manning had him closing it again. Oh. Darrek had been sleeping. He'd slept through Landon and Spencer sneaking back to the camp too. Manning must have sent word for them to return long enough to hear the rescue plan. The arrival of so many people would have caused enough ruckus for the two of them to slip away for a half hour or so, leaving Adam behind to cover for the troupe. Or so Darrek assumed. His mind was still a little foggy from a lack of sleep.

Darrek had gone to the cottage again last night. Just like the first time, he'd simply sat and held Evangeline's hand, praying over her while she fought the clutches of her night terrors. He'd left as quietly as he'd come, before the sun could cast a shadow, and returned to the camp to sleep for an hour or two before Manning prodded him awake again.

He should have felt guilty about the way he crept to Evangeline's side and stayed without her knowledge. Instead, he only felt called. This was why they'd come. To protect the daughter of their king. He wasn't doing anything wrong. The maid, the boy, and the Almighty could all vouch for that.

But he was becoming lax in his duties. A lord, ladies, and full retinue of knights? That was no small group of travelers. And he'd not only slept through the group's arrival but missed its presence altogether. He wasn't on the castle grounds and in the heart of the gossip like Spencer, Landon, Adam, and Craig were, but failing to notice such an event was unforgiveable.

"The kitchen is already astir with preparations for a welcome feast tonight. It's the perfect time to take Lady Evangeline away from here. With so many extra people milling about the castle and grounds, two or three more shouldn't be noticed."

A thrill of anticipation swirled around the group of knights at Manning's declaration. They might have agreed with their leader's plan to wait and watch, but none of them were good at sitting still. Neither were Spencer, Adam, or Landon enjoying their tenure as entertainers. The sooner they freed Evangeline, the sooner the knights could put away their juggling balls.

"The feast will go until late, keeping most of the maids and guards occupied. Whether by choice or order, Lady Evangeline never enters the Great Hall. She will come out of the kitchens once the last of the food is prepared. Spencer, you and Adam will meet her then. Though there will be guards about, they seem to believe the rumor that she's cursed and rarely stay close to her. Use that. Use your charm. Use the crowd. Use your disguise. Whatever it takes to get Lady Evangeline out the gate without being seen.

"Landon, you'll wait with me at the gate. Darrek, you'll watch from the stables. Craig will have the horses ready at the edge of the forest. We'll ride through the night to get as much distance between Cavendish and Lady Evangeline as possible before he's alerted to her absence. It'll be a rough ride, but if luck be on our side, two days hence, we'll have our lady back safely within the walls of Raedonleith Castle."

Spencer and Craig nodded from where they sat. Darrek should have been doing the same. It was exactly what he'd been telling Manning they needed to do since the day they'd found her. Except for one thing.

"Spencer can watch from the stables. I'll go with Adam to meet Evangeline."

Manning shook his head immediately. The small bit of compassion in his eyes was almost eclipsed by the stubbornness of his chin. "You'll watch from the stables. You're too close to her already."

"Exactly why it should be me. She trusts me." A part of her did, at least. The part that calmed each time he took her hand.

Darrek ignored the smirking from the younger knights. Let them think what they wanted. He and Manning knew his actions were nothing more than a knight protecting his charge.

"She barely knows you," Manning argued.

"But the two nights—"

"She was unaware of your presence. Unless you've lied about that?"

"No, sir." Manning was right. Darrek had always known Evangeline—she was one of the king's daughters, so everyone in Raedonleith knew her—but knowing a person and trusting them were two entirely different things. Though Darrek had been loyal to King Lior since his squire days, he likely was only one of many such men to Evangeline. The two times he'd conversed with her in the past, she'd been so drunk he doubted she remembered talking to anyone at all, let alone that it was him. Drunk, stubborn, and nobody's fool. Such a stark contrast to the broken woman who now needed to be rescued.

"Since we've not had Cavendish or his men attack us yet, we can assume the maid you spoke of hasn't told anyone of your presence—Lady Evangeline included. However, I won't take the risk.

"I'm sorry, Darrek. I realize you care. You always have. But, in Evangeline's case, you care too much. I won't have you being too distracted by her to see what dangers may be around you."

Darrek frowned, offended Manning would think he could be distracted from such a task after having it be his life for the past four years. "I'm a good knight."

"Which is why I want you watching from the stables. You said the stablemaster was someone Evangeline trusts? Stay with him. The more men on our side, the better."

"I said I *thought* he may be." In the scant few interactions Darrek had witnessed between Evangeline and the older man, the stablemaster had neither leered at her, steered clear of her, or ignored her presence, as every other male in the castle seemed to do in various measures. "He may just as quickly turn me in to Cavendish." Darrek doubted it, but if it helped his cause, he'd throw in whatever doubt he needed.

"Regardless, Spencer and Adam will be the ones to escort her."

It didn't help. Darrek opened his mouth to protest again, but the challenge on Manning's face stopped him. Manning was his superior, the position gained not only by the fact that he was twenty years their senior, but that he'd had twenty years more experience and training than the rest of their band. The man had well earned the knights' respect. And their trust.

"What does Lady Evangeline think of this plan?" Spencer asked.

"I haven't spoken to her yet, but I'm hoping she'll approve of it. Regardless, we have to take the chance given us. We'd be fools not to."

Darrek kicked at the grass near his feet, tempted to throw a tantrum despite his age and training. The plan made sense. It was good and solid. But he didn't like it. He'd been the one to find Evangeline, the one to hold her and calm her when terrors overtook her dreams. Manning aside, he was the oldest of the four knights. Spencer and Adam were good knights, but they were still young, with all the enthusiasm of fighting without having faced the reality of it. They thought all this a grand game, a treasure hunt, with Lady Evangeline being the prize. She was a prize, but she was also a woman. And a broken one at that.

He'd watched her this past week while Spencer and Adam had hunted rabbits and sharpened their wits alongside their swords. She was fearful. She only spoke to two other servants—the older maid who shared her cottage and the stablemaster—both of whom were also the only ones who treated her like a person instead of a plague. She kept her head down when passing anyone else. She stayed well clear of all Cavendish's knights. What made Manning think she'd trust Spencer and Adam? It wasn't as if they'd be in Raedonleith's colors to prove their allegiance. They'd be dressed as a juggler and a minstrel. Hardly trustworthy.

It should have been him who rescued her instead of being relegated to guard duty while Spencer and Adam went in. She might not have known him, but something inside her recognized him. Even in the clutch of a nightmare, she calmed at the sound of his voice and his touch on her hand. He had far more chance of convincing her to trust him than they did.

"You're angry."

Darrek looked up, surprised to find he and Manning were the only two left in the clearing.

"They've gone back to the castle," Manning answered, anticipating Darrek's question. "Something you would have heard them say if you hadn't been sulking."

"I'm not sulking."

Manning looked at him.

Very well, he was sulking. Temper tantrums and sulking. He might as well have been a two-year-old instead of a man of twenty-six.

"Darrek, I know you want to be the one to rescue her but, in terms of strategy, sending Spencer and Adam is the better choice. They've been inside the gates for three days already. They won't be noticed."

Darrek doubted that.

"They're tall, strong men dressed in colors so bright they'd have to climb inside a rainbow to hide themselves. They'll be noticed."

"But not as a threat."

"And you think I would?"

"Aye. That I do. You look too much like a knight, even dressed as a peasant. When Cavendish hears Evangeline is missing, every one of the servants will be questioned. It would be safer for them if the servants think strangers took Evangeline or that she simply walked away rather than that one of her father's knights rescued her.

"You're a good knight, Darrek. You always have been. You're strong, quick, loyal, protective, and see what others miss. I'm counting on every one of those traits to get Lady Evangeline home safely, but getting her from the castle to the horses will be Spencer and Adam's job. If I see you anywhere other than the stables, you'll be playing the role of squire until we get home."

Darrek bowed his head. "Yes, sir."

"I do have one other task for you, though, if you think you can keep that pride of yours in check long enough."

Darrek straightened. "I can."

"We need to convince Lady Evangeline to come with us. I told the others we'd take her no matter what, but it's going to be difficult if she's not willing."

"I'll talk to her."

"We both will," Manning said, leaving no room for argument. "Keep watch and alert. We'll wait in the trees near the well. When next she goes to fill a water bucket, the castle's newest entertainers will cause a stir. We may have minutes, or we may have mere moments."

A moment to change a life forever. It was tight, but it would work.

It had to.

"Yes, sir."

CHAPTER 4

"Lady Evangeline."

Evangeline looked up, her wide-eyed gaze landing on Darrek and Manning for barely a second before lowering back to the bucket she was filling. Her busy hands continued their work. "You have the wrong woman."

Her voice had a rasp to it, but Darrek had been expecting that, given her screaming. What he hadn't been expecting was the bitterness coating the pain of her words.

Not Evangeline? Of course she was Evangeline. Though her figure had changed, and her words claimed otherwise, there was no mistaking those eyes, as pale and bright as if they were made of glass. Or magic. Queen Caralynne's eyes were blue, along with those of her oldest daughter, Rose, but neither of them had the same light shade as Evangeline's. Paired with her coppery hair, the effect was both unusual and breathtaking.

A trill of laughter came from the other side of the square, followed by a gasp loud enough to draw stares and several more people to the group captivated by Adam and Spencer's tumbling antics. Exactly as they'd planned. Their part, at the very least. Manning wasn't having quite so much luck with his own.

"Lady Evangeline," the older knight tried again, "third daughter of King Lior and Queen Caralynne of Raedonleith."

This time, she didn't say anything, though her movements slowed just enough to give Darrek hope. She might not want to acknowledge them, but she was listening. They had to hurry.

"I am Sir Manning, and this is Sir Darrek, knights in your father's service."

"I know who you are."

"Then you know why we've come."

"You shouldn't have."

Darrek had heard the same phrase from other women in the past but never with such bitterness. They'd said it with a coy smile, eagerly taking whatever he or his friends had offered, their actions belying their words. There was none of that in Evangeline's tone. No coyness, no smile, no gratitude. Only bitter resignation. He wished he could see her eyes again. Would they hold the same?

"Lady Evangeline, for the past four years, we've been searching for you. We've come to bring you home."

"You've been searching for a woman long gone."

The wooden bucket sloshed against the side of the well as she dropped it before pulling it back up again to fill a second larger bucket. Though she seemed focused on the task, she did it with an ease that made Darrek certain she didn't have to. The bucket was getting the attention she was determined not to give them.

But why?

"We've been searching for you, Lady Evangeline, and here you are," Manning tried again.

"Barely."

The word was said so quietly, Darrek would have missed it had he not been staring at her face. What did she mean by that? She was here. Clearly alive, even if she were different.

She dropped the bucket in the well for a final time before turning to pick up the one she'd filled. Darrek moved to carry it for her but stopped when she held up a hand, finally looking him in the eye. Her sorrow-filled expression shaved another few strips off his heart.

"You shouldn't have come, you and however many others King Lior sent. If you value your life at all, you'll leave before Lord Cavendish hears of your presence. You're not welcome here."

No. Darrek wouldn't accept this. She might have been different from the Lady Evangeline he'd known four years ago, but no one chose to live a life of pain and terror when they had another option. She was bluffing. She had to be.

"We shouldn't have come?"

Manning placed a calming hand on Darrek's arm. Darrek shrugged it off. She was being foolish. No matter what she said or felt, the woman standing before them *was* Lady Evangeline, and she didn't belong in this place. It was breaking her. Tearing her apart. Tearing him too, just seeing her like this. She was a princess, not a servant, and he refused to let her stay like this. "We came for you. We came to bring you home."

For the tiniest of moments, a wistful expression crossed Evangeline's face, but it was gone as fast as the rabbit Landon had hoped to catch for dinner, covered over with the same wary indifference on her face that Darrek had seen so often during the past week of watching her.

"You've wasted your time. Whatever plan or scheme or mission you have prepared, call it off. I'm not leaving."

"Lady Evangeline—"

"Eva, if you must call me by name. Evangeline is—" She pursed her lips, holding back words. Or was it memories? Could it be regret? "Evangeline is gone."

She took two steps in the direction of the castle before Darrek caught her arm, pulling her to a stop.

"You'll always be Lady Evangeline to me. Please, don't walk away. Talk to me. Us. We came to help."

"Darrek—"

Darrek heard the warning in Manning's voice, telling him to stand down, step back, that time was running out, and they'd find another way. Manning was wrong. They were here now. Who knew when they'd get another chance like this? They had to take it. Had to take Evangeline, even if they trussed her up and carried her away. Apologies could come once she was safe.

Evangeline settled her glare on Darrek, as if Manning weren't even there.

"What if I don't want help?" she questioned him. "What if I'm content here? It was my choice to come. My choice to leave Raedonleith. You think you know me so well. You'll know, then, that no one forced me out. I left under my own strength and of my own accord."

"It wasn't your choice to become a servant. You're tired, Lady Evangeline. Come home."

Evangeline bristled. If her eyes truly had been magical, Darrek would likely have been a bug by now, given the way she glared.

"You're right, Sir Darrek. I am tired but not of this. I'm tired of people talking about me and giving their opinions about who I am and what I should do. I'm tired of people thinking they can make my decisions for me. Why should I go home? So King Lior can marry me off to a man I have no intention of wedding? So I can see the disappointment in his eyes when he sees how far the girl he once called his daughter has fallen? Your king may have sent you to rescue me, but I don't need to be saved. The sooner you accept that, the better."

"King Lior is—"

"No longer my father. Now, please leave." She said it more forcefully this time, though it had no more effect than it had previously. Without waiting for a reply, she walked away, buckets swaying by her sides.

Darrek watched her go, anger of his own rising. Didn't need to be saved? *Didn't need to be saved?* She might as well have told them they were fools who'd wasted their time. Well, she was the fool if she thought they would leave without her. Not after four years of searching. Tonight's plan would have to be called off, but they'd make another. And another. And, if need be, another. They'd come to bring Lady Evangeline home, and that was what they were going to do.

Eva's hands and arms had long ago become accustomed to the weight of the full water buckets. She had calluses on top of calluses, which served her well. She knew how to hold the buckets steady so the water didn't spill, and she knew how to balance them against the wall while she opened the door with her hip. Doing so came as a second nature these days, which left her mind with far too much freedom to contemplate the men she knew wouldn't take her advice and leave.

Her father had sent his knights to rescue her. Or so they'd claimed. She believed they'd come to take her, but a rescue? That might have been stretching the truth. If they'd come to take her home, it wouldn't be back to the lavish one she'd known. No, it would be to the dungeon, with the rats. At least, thanks to her years of servitude, she'd become accustomed to vermin. Evangeline the princess would have screamed at the sight of a rat. Eva the servant merely kicked them aside or grumpily swiped them out of her flour.

She hadn't been lying when she told the men Evangeline was long gone.

"Oh good, the water."

Maeve took one of the buckets from Eva, placing it on one of the wooden tables they used to prepare food. Eva put the other under the table, noting the rushes sitting beside it. She still needed to soak those before the end of the day. Arthur sat in the corner, out of the way of the rest of the bustle of the kitchen, a piece of straw in his hand as he drew lines in the dirt. She often took him with her to get the water, but with Lord Dickerson's arrival and so many extra people milling about the castle grounds, she'd thought it best to keep the boy out of sight. If only she could send Arthur to Raedonleith with her father's knights and ensure his safety and welcome on the other side. But they didn't even know he existed and, if all went to plan, never would.

Arthur looked up for a moment when she tapped him on the shoulder but quickly dropped his head back down, hiding in on himself. Though it saddened her, Eva could understand why. The maids were cruel to him, calling him all sorts of names, assuming that because he couldn't speak, neither could he hear. Or perhaps they simply didn't care that he heard them. They did the same to her, though they *knew* she could hear.

Cursed. Broken. Crazy. Demon.
Cursed. Broken. Crazy. Demon.

She heard the accusations whether the words were spoken aloud or not, long ago having admitted the truth of them.

"Who are they?"

Eva pushed hair away from her face with the back of her hand and threw a handful of flour across the wooden table before taking a mound of dough from Maeve to knead. She'd never been so happy to have something to pound.

Raedonleith knights. Inside Cavendish Castle. Because of her. And not just any knights either—Sir Manning Beckett and Sir Darrek Drew. Loyal, determined, and stubborn.

"Eva?"

She should have known Maeve wouldn't let the matter of Eva speaking with two men go without question. She should have been more careful. Ignored them entirely, if not sent them away right at the start. Although, she'd tried that. They hadn't gone.

"No one important."

Maeve slid four loaf tins onto the fire, wiping her forehead with her apron. She crossed her arms and turned to face Eva. "They spoke to you with respect. They can't be that unimportant."

Eva kept kneading, doing her best to ignore the way her pulse seemed to skitter faster than usual. Sir Darrek Drew. He looked... good. The past four years had been kind to him. Far more than to her. "How would you know how they spoke to me? You weren't there."

"I could see it in their faces. You knew them."

"Were you spying on me?"

"I don't call it spying when two men pull ranks around my friend. I call it keeping an eye on you. Now, who were they?"

"Knights." She whispered the word, still trying to believe it herself.

Maeve didn't seem surprised by her admission. She nodded as if she'd suspected as much. "Whose knights?"

"How would I know?"

"Because you called one of them by name."

Had she? Darrek, no doubt. He'd irritated her so much with his high-handedness and assuming he knew what was best for her that the name had probably slipped out. He always had been good at rising her ire—likely because he thought himself so far above her despite the fact that she was the daughter of the king and he only a knight. She'd always felt as if she came off second-best to him.

But Maeve had heard that? Had she heard it all?

No. She couldn't have. She wouldn't have been asking so many questions if she already knew the truth of the knights' quest. Or, more likely, she *would* have asked as many questions as possible, but they would have been very different. First and foremost, what Eva was still doing here.

Cursed, remember. Broken. Crazy. Ruined.

Her father wouldn't have sent the knights to rescue her if he knew what she'd become. Only a fool would choose a broken pot to proudly display when he could have perfection. He might have loved her once, but King Lior was no fool.

"Who is he, Eva?"

"A man I once knew."

Sir Darrek and Sir Manning. Her father's most trusted knights. Here. For her. It was as ridiculous as it was humbling. Had they really spent the past four years searching for her?

Sir Manning had always treated her well, even when she'd given him no reason to, twittering her way through the knights' early morning drills, thrilling at the attention the younger ones gave her. His hair was more silver than she remembered, his face a little more drawn. Had age been the cause? Or had she? She didn't want it to be her, yet somehow she knew it was. Another layer to add to the weight of guilt she carried.

Sir Darrek, on the other hand, looked stronger and fiercer than she'd ever seen him. Not that she'd been looking. Or admiring. It was more that he was an impossible man to miss, big as he was. At least, that's what she would tell herself.

"Once?" Maeve asked. Eva didn't have to look at her friend to know the woman would be narrowing her eyes, suspicion roaring to life. In the three years Maeve had known Eva, she'd never once asked where Eva had come from, content, as most servants were, to leave the past exactly where it was. In the past.

Until today. Stupid knights.

"A long time ago."

"It can't have been so long ago. You're only just scraping nineteen. Hardly old enough to be claiming old age."

"I feel it."

"Not too old to notice the way that handsome young knight was looking at you, I hope?"

Eva rolled her eyes. Sir Darrek was handsome, without a doubt. Broad across the shoulders from a lifetime of training, dark hair that touched his shoulders when it wasn't tied back with a scrap of leather, a beard she'd thought ridiculous when he'd first grown it but suited him now, eyes that strange mix of green and gray that changed with the skies above him. He was taller than she remembered, the lines on his face more pronounced, the skip of attraction she'd once felt when seeing him more of a thud against her stomach.

Yes, she'd noticed him.

But none of that mattered because he was one of her father's knights. Maeve always believed the best of everyone, even when she shouldn't have. It was because of that belief that she'd taken Eva into her house and heart when everyone else pushed her away.

"Perhaps you should have come closer to spy. Your eyesight isn't what it used to be."

"I don't think so. That man thinks you're something special. And I'll wager he is too."

Eva threw the ball of dough at the table with enough force to send flour all over her apron and into her eyes. Maeve handed her a damp cloth and waited in silence while Eva wiped her face clean. She was still waiting when Eva set aside the cloth, the gentle expression on her face neither deserved nor desired.

"You're not a servant, Eva."

"Of course I am."

"I may be old, but I'm no fool. You dress like one and act the part, but you'll never truly hide the fact that you weren't born one of us. Was he your intended?"

Eva's cheeks heated. She blamed it on the fire. Maeve, she hoped, would do the same.

"Who, Sir Darrek? Heavens, no."

"Guard then? Protector?"

A glance over her shoulder ensured the rest of the kitchen maids were still busy, their giggles loud as they chatted and prepared food, uncaring of the conversation going on near the fire. There was that to be thankful for, at least. The last thing she needed any of those gossips knowing was her true identity or that of the entertainers they still mooned over. She didn't know for sure, but two of the three entertainers looked familiar enough that she was almost certain they also were Raedonleith knights in disguise.

Knights she'd rather forget.

"Sir Darrek was no one to me. He's still no one."

"You're not fooling me."

She wasn't fooling herself either.

"The bread is going to burn," Eva said.

"It is if you don't tell me what I want to know."

"Take it off the fire."

"After you tell me. Who are they? Who is that man to you?"

Fire licked the bottom of the thick pan. An acrid scent began to rise from it. Maeve put floury hands on her hips and stared at Eva. Eva sighed.

"He's one of my father's knights."

"I see." Grabbing a cloth, Maeve lifted the bread off the fire. "And your father is…"

"King Lior."

The bread pan dipped in Maeve's hand, almost joining Arthur and the reeds on the ground. This time, when she looked at Eva, Maeve's eyes were wide. "You're the princess?"

"I *was* a princess."

"You're the daughter he lost. That's why the knights are here, isn't it? They've come to rescue you."

"They've come a long way for nothing. I'm not leaving."

"Because you believe the lie that you're cursed?" Maeve shook her head. "It's not true. I know it, and those men do too. They know worth when they see it. Trust them, Eva. Go with them. Go home. You don't belong here."

Eva had to look away, the passion in Maeve's claim hurting almost as much as the other maids' jeers. She let her gaze stray to Arthur instead, sitting in his little corner. He'd stopped drawing with the straw and was now playing with three rocks, trying to balance them on top of each other. Neither of them belonged here, but that didn't matter because they didn't belong in her father's house either. Maeve was wrong. The knights she so fiercely defended too. Eva couldn't go home.

Cursed. Broken. Crazy. Demon.

"Don't tell the knights about Arthur."

Though Maeve nodded and went back to her work, Eva knew the conversation was far from over. When Maeve got an idea in her head, she went after it with a passion that defied defeat. She'd probably only stopped talking now because she was scheming a way to befriend the knights and offer whatever she could to help them complete their quest to get Eva away from here. She wouldn't accept Eva's answer any more than Sir Manning and Sir Darrek had.

Arthur's rock pile toppled. Eva continued kneading dough, wondering with every pound whether she'd made the right choice. Whether there was even a choice to make.

She was still wondering hours later, when the feast they'd spent the day preparing for was over and she was in Maeve's little cottage, brushing hair back from Arthur's sleeping face. Her own pride and foolishness aside, should she have agreed, for Arthur's sake? If only her son didn't have to pay for her mistakes. She sighed into the darkness.

It was foolish, staying up every night when she was already bone weary from the long day simply to stare at her son. But every night she did it anyway. He was so peaceful in slumber, long eyelashes brushing his smooth, slightly flushed cheeks. Now and then, his lips pursed, as if he were thinking about something, only to relax again. His hair would need to be cut again soon, long as it was getting.

Eva brushed another strand away from Arthur's closed eyes, careful not to wake him. Not that he would have. It was strange, how deeply he slept, given how wary he was while awake. She could have dropped a kettle beside his head, and he wouldn't wake. She knew because, once, she had. He'd slept through it all—the crash, the clanging as it rolled around the floor, her shout of fright, Maeve's shriek, and their subsequent conversation assuring each other that they and the kettle were fine.

She leaned over and placed a kiss on his cheek. Then another, just because. And another because, somehow, no matter how many times she told him she loved him and kissed him—awake or asleep—it never seemed enough. She'd made so many poor choices during the course of her life, but the Almighty had still given her this precious boy.

She wasn't enough for him and never would be. Eva didn't need the knights to remind her of that. She should have begged Lord Cavendish to foster Arthur with a family like so many nobles did. It would be so much better for him than growing up here. Yet she'd never begged. Never demanded. Never even asked. The thought of her son being taken away from her, even for a few months, was too much to bear. So he stayed by her side, silent and cowed.

But loved. Infinitely loved.

With one final kiss, Eva pushed herself to her aching feet and lumbered the few steps to bed. She had to sleep, whether she wanted to or not.

CHAPTER 5

The screams came again that night, wrenching Darrek from a sleep he'd barely found. Manning didn't even glare this time when Darrek said he was going to her. He just told him to be careful.

"I'll cover your watch later," Craig said before rolling over on his pallet and letting out a snore.

Darrek looked again at Manning, comradeship warring with his need to protect Evangeline. He was letting down his men and putting extra responsibility on the young squire, but she was the reason they were here at all. Her welfare had to come first, didn't it?

Manning swished a hand through the air. "Go. You'll keep us all awake if you stay."

Still, Darrek hesitated. Was he doing the right thing by going to her? It felt right, but then, feelings couldn't be trusted. It was one of the first lessons he'd learned as a child. Logic, action, strength—those could be trusted. Emotions were too fickle to be of use to anyone.

Another scream came, louder this time.

Hang logic. The woman was in pain. That was all he needed to know.

"I'll be back before sunrise," he assured his captain.

"See that you are."

Low branches tugged at Darrek's legs as he picked his way with more haste than care through the trees. They moved their camp each night for safety, so this path wasn't familiar, but the forest was. Not eager to draw attention to their little band, he and the other men had spent many nights these past four years sleeping under a ceiling of boughs, tucked away in the forests that stretched the length of the land. It had become second nature to them all. As had traveling by darkness.

The almost-full moon washing the grass in a silvery glow lent a shadow to his steps as Darrek crept his way across the small clearing behind the cottage. A guard's voice to his left had him ducking out of sight. The patrols were close tonight. Darrek waited almost a minute before chancing rising, making his way to the window he'd used before.

His entrance was as quiet and unhurried as he could make it, which wasn't much of either. Evangeline's screams felt as if they'd taken up residence in his soul. He would have slayed a thousand men to get to her if that's what it took. Though he was thankful, again, that he hadn't had to.

The moon's light came through the window at just the right angle to illuminate Evangeline and the tears smudged across her face. Darrek's knees buckled as he fell to the hard floor beside her, completely ignoring the room's other two occupants.

Almighty—

The prayer caught on the crack her tears had wrought open in his heart. What could he say? What could he ask? There were no words. Kneeling there beside this lady who was so broken, so changed by the terrors that haunted her nights and whatever had caused them in the first place, his heart simply bled.

I won't leave you, he silently promised her. *You're not alone. I'm here. I will be here for as long as you need me. Forever, if it comes to it. I'll fight this. We'll fight this. Together. I'm not leaving, no matter what.*

Darrek brushed a shaking hand across Evangeline's head, the calluses on his hands catching on her sweat-soaked hair. He had no right to make such a promise. She was the daughter of his king. She'd marry, be bound to another man. Likely the man her father had hastily betrothed her to the day before she left Raedonleith. Though, four years on, Darrek wondered if the betrothal still stood. He'd heard no word otherwise, but four years was a long time to wait for a bride no one was sure was even alive. Of course, they knew now. Was King Lior once again preparing for Evangeline's wedding?

Darrek had dreamed of marrying too, one day, when his king's daughter was home and the task set of him and the other knights complete. Yet despite that long-held hope, Darrek meant every word of his promise to Evangeline. He would give it all up to protect this woman for as long as she needed him. He would give up anything to see her smile again.

Evangeline's screams turned to cries and then to whimpers as Darrek knelt there, making promises in his heart as he stroked a hand across her hair. She couldn't hear his promises—no one could—but he meant them no less than if he'd declared them in the presence of his king and a thousand witnesses. He would protect this woman. Even if it was only from her own mind.

What caused her terrors every night? The servants claimed demons were purging her soul. Or, worse, that Lady Evangeline herself was the demon. Superstitious fools. Darrek could far more easily believe Lord Cavendish or another man in the castle had abused her, though he'd not know for certain unless Lady Evangeline told him. Assumptions only led to error. Would she ever trust him enough to share her pain?

Moreover, why did he care?

He'd never felt such a burden of protection toward any other woman, including Lady Rose and Lady Mykah, King Lior's two other daughters. He admired and respected them—always had—and would have fought for their honor too, if it was asked of him, but he would have also happily stood aside while another knight took on their battle. Five years ago, the same would have been true of what he felt toward Lady Evangeline. Admiration, protectiveness, but little else. He certainly wouldn't have given up sleep to sit beside her bed and hold her hand through the night. Especially when she had no idea he was even here.

Yet here he was. Making promises that he always would be. Ready to fight anyone who came near her, his own comrades included.

What was it about this woman who brought about such strong emotions in him?

And why hadn't she wanted to leave? The noise of the feast earlier would have easily covered their escape. They could have been hours away from this place by now. Was it fear of Lord Cavendish—a man closer to her father's age than her own—that held her here? Respect? Darrek swallowed hard, hating the next thought that came. Could she *love* him? Or was it something—or someone—else she feared? Why would she choose squalor over the life of a princess?

Quieter now, Evangeline rolled onto her side, one hand tucked under her head, the other stretching out past the edge of her pallet, as if reaching for something. Darrek pulled the thin blanket she'd kicked away back up over her, tucking it around her shoulders as he'd taken to doing, before moving from his knees to the floor. Though she was quiet and likely would stay that way, it felt wrong to leave when minutes ago he'd promised her he wouldn't. He took her outstretched hand instead. A snore came from the other woman in the room and heavy breathing from the child, but otherwise all was silent.

Blissfully so.

Darrek stroked his thumb along the back of Evangeline's hand, finally finding words to pray. No, not words. One simple phrase, over and over, sent the way of the Almighty.

Thank you.

His thumb brushed against a piece of rough fabric wrapped around Evangeline's wrist. A bandage? He leaned forward to better see it in the streak of moonlight, tugging her arm out of the blanket's warmth just enough to see.

It was a bandage. Darrek frowned. Had it been there this morning when he and Manning confronted her at the well? With the long sleeves of her tunic, it would have been mostly covered and easy to miss. Especially with how confused and frustrated he'd been at her refusal to leave this place. Or had she been injured after? She worked in the kitchens. Perhaps she'd been as befuddled by their meeting as he'd been and slipped while cutting vegetables.

Or had someone hurt her? One of the other maids, perhaps?

Darrek closed his eyes against the pain that thought caused him. Strange that a tiny cut on someone else would affect him in such a way, when he'd dealt with far worse to his own person in battle.

It was the stillness of night, that's what it was. Everything always seemed bigger and more intimidating at night. Or closer and more intimate. These puzzling emotions would disappear with the light of day, much as the mist did each morning.

His gaze moved to Evangeline's face. Tears no longer wet her cheeks, nor did her breathing catch. By all accounts, she simply slept, which meant it was time for him to go. Comforting her, holding her hand, brushing hair from her face as she fought the terrors, that he could justify. But watching her as she peacefully slept? Only a husband had that right.

With a final prayer that her peace would remain, Darrek slipped between the pallets and out of the window.

"Ho there! You!"

A guard's shout sounded as his feet hit the ground. The patrol. With no chance of hiding, he ran instead, his mind racing as quickly as his feet. He couldn't go back to the campsite, nor take his pursuers anywhere near the other knights. The river was too exposed at its narrowest and too wide and deep elsewhere to cross.

Footsteps pounded behind him forcing him nearer the castle wall. They were close. Too close. He needed to hide. But—

The door. There. In the castle wall. Between the cottage and the castle. Craig had mentioned it once. Though not where it led. Was it a servants' entrance? A garderobe exit? Darrek didn't let himself think anything beyond getting away from the guards as he swerved and ducked inside.

A whinny sounded. Then another.

Not a garderobe. A stable. Full of horses and—

Hiding places. Darrek breathed out another prayer of gratitude as he threw himself behind a large pile of hay. A puff of dust went straight into his nose, the inevitable sneeze coming right as the first of his pursuers pushed through the opening.

He tucked himself as deep inside the hay as he dared. Had the man heard the sneeze? Seen him come in here? Manning would be furious if Darrek's carelessness destroyed their mission.

The man stood no more than a body's length from where Darrek hid. Darrek only hoped the man's labored breathing concealed his own.

"I know you're in here, scum."

Footsteps came from the other end of the stable, along with the groan of a ladder and more whinnying of horses. "There, now," crooned the voice of the stablemaster to the horses, before turning the full force of his irritation on Darrek's pursuer. "Scum, am I? I suppose you have an excuse to be stumbling in here in the middle of the night, rousing me from my bed? It had better be a good one."

The guard took a half step backward. "There's a man in here."

"Yes. Me. And I'm running short on patience. Get out before I make you." Darrek lifted his head just enough to see the stablemaster pick up a pitchfork. The man mumbled something about green guards. It wasn't complimentary.

The young guard, now bracketed either side by two more, shook his head.

"Not you, fool. Another man. He was in the cursed girl's room. I saw him climb out her window and chased him in here."

The stablemaster huffed. "As you can see, I am the only one in here. So unless your man looks like a horse, you're looking in the wrong place."

"If you're the only one here, you won't mind if we look around."

"If it makes you leave faster. Hurry up."

The stablemaster stood aside while the three men walked up and down the stable. Was it by chance that the older man sat himself down on the pile of hay Darrek hid behind? Somehow Darrek doubted it. The man knew he was here. The question was, what would he do once the guards were gone? Could he be trusted, as Darrek had hoped?

"He was here," the first guard said. "I saw him."

"Well, he's not here now," the stablemaster grizzled, "and if it's all the same to you, I'd like to get some sleep this night. Something you're making impossible with all your noise. Out, the lot of you."

The guards obeyed, though the first grumbled about how he was certain a man had been in here. The stablemaster waited a full minute after they'd left to rise.

"You can come out now."

Darrek pushed himself to his feet, brushing straw off his clothing.

"Who are you?" the man demanded.

He could have hidden the truth, but something inside Darrek was too proud to do so. For better or worse, this man had protected him from being tossed into the dungeon tonight. He deserved the truth.

"Sir Darrek Drew, knight of King Lior of Raedonleith."

The man nodded, seeming unsurprised by Darrek's declaration.

"Were you in the maids' bedchamber?"

Too shocked by the man's calm acceptance to think up anything else, Darrek again went with the truth. "Aye."

The man considered Darrek's answer for a time before speaking. Darrek refused to squirm like a page before a knight, forcing himself to stand tall.

"You weren't there for your own amusement."

"No, sir. Evang—Eva. Her terrors. I—"

"You calmed her."

The stablemaster had noticed? How many others had? Was that what had alerted the guard also? How many months must Evangeline's screams have torn through the night for people to notice the silence?

"I held her hand. 'Tis all."

"'Tis a lot, when most won't go near her. You care for her?" the man asked.

Darrek nodded. "Aye, but not as—"

"Doesn't matter how. You calmed her. 'Tis more than any of us have done. If she trusts you, I do too."

Trust him? Evangeline? Not likely. "She doesn't know I was there."

"I suggest you keep it that way." He pointed back to the straw. "Sleep there."

"Sir?"

"You want to be close to her? Protect her? You can't do that from the dungeon. Work for me, sleep here. It's the best offer you'll get."

"The guards will see me."

The man shrugged. "Not if you hide when they come."

"The squires, then."

"We'll tell them you're simple-minded. Keep your head down, do your work, and they won't question it. Wouldn't be the first stray I've taken in. They're barely here most the day anyway, following round the knights like they do."

Darrek looked toward the opening he'd come through as he considered the man's offer. "The door?"

"Should have been locked. You owe the squire who forgot. I'd say it won't happen again, but it will now. As long as you're watching over her."

It was either proof of Darrek's desperation or pure brilliance on the man's part that Darrek thought the plan might work.

"Why are you helping me? I'm your enemy."

"My master's, not mine. I have no quarrel with your king. Work hard, and I'll have no quarrel with you neither."

It was more than Darrek could have hoped and the answer to the prayer he hadn't yet found the time to ask.

"Thank you, sir."

"George."

The man nodded once then walked away, no doubt back to his pallet in the hope of a few more hours' sleep before dawn woke him. Darrek sat down on the straw and watched him go.

"Thank you, George."

CHAPTER
6

The stables smelled of horses, dirt, manure, and sweat. It would have disgusted most people, bar those like Darrek who'd all but grown up in one. It had been a while since he'd been the one to shovel manure and clean out stalls, but the place felt as much like home as anywhere.

It hadn't taken more than a few hours to learn that George was a man of few words but great respect—for those he deemed worthy of it. Lord Cavendish did not number among them, something that gained Darrek's respect. That and the fact that George spoke well of Evangeline. As far as, "She's a good 'un," was well.

George seemed pleased with Darrek's work. The squires had been happy too, given that Darrek could shovel three times as much as them in a single hour. As George had predicted, they hadn't even questioned his supposed simple-mindedness. Manning had accepted the plan too, claiming it an answer to prayer. After he'd finished berating Darrek, via Craig, for almost getting himself caught.

Mundane, even demoralizing, as the work was, Darrek was thankful for it. Not only because it came with a place to sleep and gave his hands something practical to do, but because it gave him a reason to be closer to Evangeline.

He heaved another shovelful of manure from the stall, adding it to the pile behind him and sneaking another look out the window at the woman he'd come to find.

Evangeline was getting water again, hand over hand on the rope as she pulled the bucket from the well. It was no wonder her hands were so rough. It had surprised him, the first night he'd held them. It didn't anymore.

Darrek spun at the sound of a shuffle behind him, expecting to see one of the pages trying to sneak up on him again, as they'd taken to attempting. But it wasn't a page. Nor a squire. The tiny boy who stared up at him was the same one who shared the cottage with Evangeline and the older maid. Was he the older woman's son? Grandson? He couldn't have been more than three or four years of age, hardly old enough to be out of his nurse's care. Perhaps the older woman was his nurse. Darrek checked to see that he was alone before crouching down.

"Hello there."

The boy looked at him but didn't reply. Just stood there, as quiet and as still as a statue, his hair the color of straw in the shaft of sunlight he stood under.

"Where's your mother, young sir? Or your nursemaid?"

Silence.

"Are you lost?"

More silence.

"Did you come to see the horses?"

That got a flicker of interest though still no reply. The boy must have been terribly shy.

"Well, I can show you the horses. Which one would you like to meet first?"

Darrek put down his shovel and held out a hand to the young boy, surprised when he took it. Not so surprised this time that he didn't speak. Darrek went on as if the boy had. "This black one here is my favorite, although you mustn't tell the others. They may get jealous, and the last thing you want in a stable is a jealous horse."

He tugged the boy gently over to Storm, careful to stand between him and the horse lest the child be more afraid up close than he was at a distance. Should Darrek pick up the boy so he could greet the horse face-to-face?

"His name is Storm, which comes from the white stripe on

his nose, I'll wager. Looks a bit like a lightning strike, don't you think? What's your name, young one?"

Again, no answer. Ah well. Darrek could appreciate a man of few words. They'd get along well enough. Though he should probably see about returning the boy to his nursemaid. No doubt he'd run off and she was frantically trying to find him.

"Let's go find your nurse, shall we?"

With the nameless boy's hand still tucked inside his much larger one, Darrek led him to the door of the stables. The only person to notice them was Evangeline.

"Arthur!" Dropping her water buckets, she ran over to them, wrapping the boy in a tight embrace. "What are you doing in the stables? You were supposed to stay in the kitchen. You know you can't wander off. It's not safe."

"He's a boy. They do that," Darrek said, winking down at the boy before turning his attention to Evangeline. "*You're* his nurse then?"

A flicker of emotion Darrek couldn't identify shot across her face before she raised her chin and answered. "Yes."

Nursemaid, kitchen maid, housemaid, chambermaid—was there anything Evangeline wasn't responsible for? It was no wonder she always looked so tired. The poor woman worked from dawn till long after dusk and had responsibility for a young child as well. Was the child the reason she was reticent to leave? Darrek could understand becoming attached to a child, and the boy was sweet, but surely another maid could care for him in her absence. There were enough of them around, and if the amount of time they spent collecting flowers and gossiping by the river indicated their workload, they had little work to do.

"Well, he's welcome to visit me in the stables any time. Although," he looked directly at the boy, "you make sure you let Miss Eva know where you're going next time, so she won't worry. Better yet, bring her with you. A pretty face in the stables is always welcome."

The boy—Arthur, she'd called him—ran back to the kitchen without so much as a nod to Darrek or his nurse. Evangeline picked up her buckets but didn't follow him, frowning at Darrek as she considered him instead. Though he didn't know what he'd done to garner such a reaction, it was no great task to let her, those blue eyes of hers trying to peer past his soul. He could have stared happily into them for hours, marveling at that unusual color.

"You're a knight," Evangeline finally said, enough accusation in those three words to bring down the whole castle.

"I am."

She narrowed her eyes. "What are you doing in the stables?"

"Shoveling manure."

It wasn't the answer she was looking for, that much was certain. If she sharpened that glare any more, she wouldn't be able to see him. He was already missing her stunning eyes.

"I told you to leave me alone."

"I told you we're not leaving without you."

"I can't—"

"Yes, you can. You don't belong here, Lady Evangeline."

Her eyes flashed with annoyance and something else. Longing? Or did he just wish it to be? When she spoke, all the fight had gone from her. All that was left was sadness.

"I don't belong there either."

Darrek took the buckets and placed them on the ground, her struggle hitting him like it was his own. She did belong at Raedonleith. It was not only her birthright but her life. So long as King Lior ruled Raedonleith, his daughters would always belong there. She couldn't walk away from her name.

"Is this really what you want? To live each day as a servant, working from sunup past sundown, calluses on your hands, hiding who you truly are?" he asked.

"You think I have a choice."

"You do."

Evangeline shook her head. "I *did*. There's a difference."

"You can come home."

"No, I can't. Whether or not I want it, this is the life I chose."

"You were a child. You made a mistake."

"Aye," she said, dropping her gaze along with her voice. "And every day of the rest of my life, I'll pay for it."

It was too much—her sadness, her regret, the way her fingers trembled as they clutched at her ragged skirts. In so many ways, Evangeline had grown up, yet before him, she was a child. Longing for what she didn't have. Too stubborn to realize it was already hers.

"Come home."

"So I can be a servant there instead? So I can have people who knew me once look on me with disdain and pity? Thank you, but I'd rather stay where no one knows my past."

"I know it. And one day, likely they will too. You can't hide forever."

"I can certainly try."

"They wouldn't look down on you."

Darrek watched helplessly as Evangeline picked up the buckets again, their weight pulling her shoulders down in a weariness she couldn't hide.

"They already do."

Eva put a hand to her back, supporting it as she bent to sit on the low stool. She might have been only nineteen, but the perpetual aches made her feel much older. She should have become accustomed to the work and the toll it took on her body, but it never seemed to get any easier. Every day was another minute-by-minute fight to keep going. Every night she sank into bed and finally let her weary body relax, almost crying with the joy of not having to hold herself up any longer. She almost wished she could lie in bed and savor the feeling, but the nights were short, and morning always came long before she was ready. If the terrors let her sleep at all.

The milk bucket clanged against the hard floor as she dropped it into place, startling Flora. Eva pressed her forehead against the cow's flank, stroking her side as she crooned an apology. It wasn't the cow's fault Eva was tired.

Would it really be so bad to go home?

The thought whispered in Eva's mind, tantalizing her with the hope it left behind.

Home.

Her parents. Her sisters. Her friends. Clothes that fit instead of the rags she wore. A room to herself, luxurious enough to lose herself in. Sleep that came without fear. People who looked on her with awe rather than derision. Safety.

Arthur would love the castle's towers. She could just imagine the look of awe on his face when he saw the view from the top of them, the mountains stretching out to the east and forest to the west. The particular group of trees that looked like a trio of knights sword fighting when they lost their leaves every winter. She could teach Arthur to read in the same room she'd learned. Introduce him to Father Douglas, the cleric who'd taught her the Holy Scriptures and told her one day he'd do the same for her children. She'd laughed then, too young at the time to even consider children of her own.

Eva shook her head, gritting her teeth as she pushed aside the memories. They were dreams—taunts—and nothing more. Arthur would never know the view from Raedonleith's turrets, nor would he sit at Father Douglas's feet. A child like him wouldn't even be welcome in the chapel, conceived as he was. Even if she did go home, nothing would be the same, despite Darrek's assurances. It couldn't be. Her chest ached with the pain of it. She'd brought Arthur into the world, yet she could give him nothing. She'd failed him before he'd even drawn a breath.

"Lady Evangeline—"

Eva groaned inwardly while outwardly she bestowed the best glare she could on the man who refused to leave her alone. Everyone else had been. The past two days would have been bliss, if not for Darrek. Even Rhea and Flaire, whose greatest enjoyment came from taunting Eva, had been too busy twittering over Lord Dickerson's arrival—or, more accurately, trying to catch the attention of his "finely proportioned" guards—to waste more than a word or two on Eva. But the stables, the well, the servants' entrance to the castle? Everywhere she looked, Sir Darrek was there. Waiting for her. Trying to convince her of what she could never have.

He'd even introduced himself to Maeve yesterday when she came to the stables in search of Eva, charming the older woman with tales of sunsets over the heather-filled moors of the homeland she hadn't seen in thirty years. Eva had stood in silence and tried not to care. He'd gained a fast ally in Maeve, who'd spent much of the day praising the man's superb qualities. As if Eva hadn't already noticed.

That he was handsome was never in question. That he was persistent wasn't either. Eva stood and carried the full bucket past him to the door. She should have left the milking to the milkmaids, but two of them were ill, the kitchen needed cream, and Eva needed to get out of the kitchen.

Darrek took the bucket from her hand without asking and walked beside her, hunching as if to hide his height. She almost wished he would be caught. At least then he'd stop irritating her. She crossed her arms and moved slower. She would have gone faster, except Maeve was in the kitchen, and Eva was in no rush to hear more about how Darrek's eyes were the same dark brown as Maeve's beloved late husband's or how you could tell the true strength of a man by the respect he had for a woman.

"You're a knight," she said, trying—and failing—to keep the frustration out of her voice. "Shouldn't you be out fighting battles instead of following me around?" It was so much easier to convince herself she was content here when the option to leave wasn't staring her in the face. *Leave, Darrek. And take your impossible hope with you.*

"You are my battle."

Eva frowned. "What?" That didn't make any sense. Her? His battle?

"Your father chose me and the other knights to find you and bring you home. It's all we've done for the past four years."

"All? But Sir Manning was his wisest and most trusted knight, and you're one of his best. My father could spare you all for four years?"

Darrek stopped. "You still don't understand, do you?" He tilted his head. Eva wanted to look away but something in his gaze wouldn't let her go. Compassion? Pity? Surprise? "He would have spared us for a decade. Two decades. Forty years, if that's what it took. He would have given whatever it took to bring you home."

"Why?"

"Because you're his daughter."

"His prize, you mean. The mar on the record he wants to perfect."

"His love." Darrek lifted a hand, as if he were reaching for her, before dropping it back to his side. Eva tried not to think about how much she wished he'd followed through. Foolish thoughts. "His cherished daughter."

"He has two others."

"But he doesn't have you."

"He doesn't want me."

"Nothing could be further from the truth." Darrek pulled a piece of rolled parchment from his belt and held it out. "Perhaps this will show you how much."

Eva eyed it warily. "You wrote me a letter?"

"No. Your father did."

Eva clutched a hand to her chest, feeling as if Darrek had thrust a knife into it rather than hold out a piece of parchment. A letter? From her father? Why hadn't he started with that? "What does it say?"

"I didn't read it."

Of course not. Darrek was too honorable to read someone else's communication. Which meant she had no option but to read it herself. But—

"You don't need to fear it," Darrek said quietly. His voice—or perhaps his words?—did something to her heart. Something she pushed aside immediately.

"I'm not afraid."

Not afraid, but she certainly was wary. Words said in passing could be forgotten, misconstrued, misheard altogether. Words on paper? They had power. The last words her father had said to her had been yelled in anger. What if these were too? Or not anger but, worse, disappointment. She'd held on to enough disappointment for them both. She didn't need more from him.

"Take it. Even if you choose not to read it until you're ready."

Still, Eva hesitated before daring to ask the question that held her back. "What if I'm never ready?"

Darrek gently pressed the parchment into her hand, taking the option from her. "Few of us are. But if we waited till we were, we'd never take a single step."

CHAPTER
7

Darrek swung his arm at a tree branch, strangely satisfied with the way it cracked under the pressure and fell to the ground. Sure, it wasn't the man he wanted to swing at, the one whose treatment of Evangeline had her so terrified she dared not leave, but it was something. He swung at another, wishing he held his sword. But no, he'd left that behind with Manning in an attempt not to frighten Lady Evangeline any more than she already was.

Frightened yet defiant. Humbled yet still proud. Somehow, she was all those things, though they defied each other. She'd been shamed, taunted, and frightened, but beneath the cowering—at least with him—the lady who'd grown up in privilege was still there. She might not have shown it to anyone else, cowed as a servant must be, but he saw it. Was it because he'd known her before?

They had to get her out of here. But how? She didn't want to leave.

Darrek swung at another branch.

It wasn't supposed to have been this difficult. Lady Evangeline was supposed to have been thrilled to leave, looking upon Darrek and his fellow knights as her saviors, and going with them without a backward glance at the castle that had been her prison. Instead, she'd told them to leave. Without her. Refused to read her father's letter welcoming her home.

No, he hadn't read it. He'd been honest in that. But it wasn't difficult to guess what it would say. The king had stalked the palace towers day and night waiting for her, barely eating out of grief over her disappearance. All King Lior had wanted for the past four years was to have his youngest daughter home. There was no doubt the letter would say as much. If she'd read it. By the defiant look in those eyes of hers, she'd rather burn the thing. Maybe she already had.

Darrek stomped his way through the trees toward the small clearing they'd made today's camp in. He'd fix this. Solve it. Fight his way through. It was what he did. It had to be Cavendish holding her back. But why? How? What did the man have over her? Surely she knew her father and his army could protect her once she was home. Now, even, if Manning gave the word. Two days, fewer if they traveled through the night, and every single one of King Lior's knights could be here. Protecting her.

Darrek hoped Manning didn't do that. He wanted to be the one to save Lady Evangeline. Prideful? Likely. Did he care? No. She'd been their whole life for the past four years. Every decision they'd made had been with her in mind. Every choice of where to search next, which lead to follow, whether they slept or raced toward the next clue, the skirmishes they avoided, the ones they didn't.

The years had been long and draining in a way that battle never could be. Battles had an end, a purpose, a thrill. It was almost always obvious who was winning. Their quest hadn't had that. Every day had been a challenge to keep searching. Keep hoping. Keep believing that there even was reason to hope. That somewhere, Lady Evangeline was alive and waiting to be rescued. They'd kept on, putting their own dreams of marriage and family and great feats on hold. For her.

Everything had been about Evangeline. And now they had her. He wasn't letting her go. Nor was he going to let the king's men swoop in and save her. Too much blood would be shed—possibly even hers. It wasn't worth the risk.

At least, that was what he told himself.

Darrek hit another tree. Harder this time. A streak of pain shot up his arm and into his shoulder when the tree didn't move. He hissed back a gasp of pain and hit it again. And again, pummeling it in his frustration.

Evangeline didn't know what was best for her if she insisted on staying. She might have left her father's house in a fit of childish anger, but that didn't mean she had to stay away. One decision didn't make a life. The future could be rewritten. He just needed to convince her.

Something tapped Darrek's shoulder. He spun around to see Manning standing behind him, wooden sword raised.

"Good to see you're alert to your surroundings," Manning said drily.

Darrek clenched his teeth, hating himself for being caught unaware. More, for Manning having caught him. He was better than this.

"Care to take that frustration out on me rather than a defenseless tree?"

Manning held up a second sword, the same as the first. Training swords quieter than the real ones. Far less balanced too. Darrek hadn't even fully grasped the hilt before Manning attacked. Without thought, Darrek blocked before pushing an attack of his own. Manning easily defended it. He might have been twenty years Darrek's senior, but the older man wasn't by any means weak nor slow. He fought as if he could read Darrek's mind. Likely, he could, having been both the one to train Darrek in sword fighting all those years ago and the one he practiced most against still. Manning knew Darrek's weaknesses as well as his strengths and unashamedly abused them both.

"You're not thinking, boy," Manning said as he pulled back a breath from delivering a killing blow. Darrek side-stepped, tripping on a tree root and cursing under his breath as he dropped to the ground. If this were a real sword fight, he'd be dead.

Manning sat down beside him. "You can't save her."

"Of course I can. That's why we're here."

"No. We're here to give her the chance. She has to make the choice."

"Then I'll convince her."

"And if you can't?"

"I will."

Manning was silent. Irritatingly so. The words he wasn't saying were almost louder than if he'd spoken them outright. *You can't save her. She's not a puppet. She has free will. She's not a child. You have to let her go.* He'd said them before. About another woman. Darrek had listened then. The woman had died. He wasn't making that mistake again.

"She's not your mother," Manning said quietly. Darrek's defenses raised higher. It was as if Manning could read his mind. Perhaps he could. To Darrek's current frustration.

"I know that."

"Do you?"

"Of course."

"And you know that your mother's death wasn't your fault?"

"You don't know what you're talking about."

"You couldn't have saved her."

"You weren't there."

Like the years had turned back before his eyes, Darrek's mind went back to that day. He'd been nine. Older than every other page at Raedonleith by at least a few years, but it had taken his mother that long to let him go. His father had been dead three years already, killed on the battlefield, a valiant knight to the end. His father's death had changed his mother. It had made her weaker. She'd leaned on Darrek like he was her savior rather than her son. It had been fun at first, making him feel like the man he'd already been trying to be.

But it hadn't taken long for her continual attention to grow tiresome. He wanted to be a brave knight, like his father had been, not cooped up doing "women's work" in a manor house. So, he'd begged. And begged.

And she denied him and denied him. "How could I let you go?" she'd said. "You're all I have. My reason to live."

Darrek had been too young to realize how literally she meant that.

An illness had swept through their village a month after Darrek left to foster at Raedonleith. He'd been proudly polishing a helmet when Manning told him his mother had succumbed.

He'd wondered ever since if his mother might have lived had he stayed. Everyone else in the village recovered. As an adult, looking back, he knew she might have died regardless, but fifteen years of guilt were difficult to let go. And the truth was, he didn't know. Maybe she would have tried harder to get well if he'd stayed.

Her reason to live.

It was foolish thinking because who but the Almighty could know for certain, but in many ways, he'd never grown past that nine-year-old polishing armor and feeling like he'd finally gotten his dream at the expense of hers.

He couldn't live with himself if he considered doing the exact same thing again.

"I'm not leaving Evangeline," Darrek said. "Her father—our king—asked us to bring her home, and I intend to do just that."

"I pray it is so."

Darrek got to his feet, passed the wooden sword to Manning and, without another word, stalked back in the direction of the castle. Manning could pray. Darrek would too. Prayer was good. Powerful. Essential. But so was action. He *would* convince Evangeline to come with them. And if she refused? He'd pick her up and carry her all the way home himself.

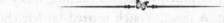

> *Evangeline,*
>   *You cannot imagine the joy I felt when I received word that you'd been found. My beautiful daughter, alive and well. It is all I have hoped for since the day I woke to find you gone.*
>   *We have much to discuss but nothing that can't wait until you are home again. I eagerly await the day.*

Her father's seal sat beneath his words, pressed into burgundy wax. Eva ran a finger over it as she read the missive again. And again.

Sunlight burned against her back, heating her hair as she sat on the rock behind the stables. She'd been too distracted by her father's letter to be of any use in the kitchens. Maeve had ordered her away before she injured herself. Or someone else. The perch wasn't anywhere near as comfortable as the time-smoothed rock she used to claim as her throne in Raedonleith's hills, but it was hers. With the way the stables folded around the space and the overwhelming stench from the nearby manure pile, no one else ever came here. It was the perfect place to think.

Only, she still didn't know what to think about her father's letter.

He sounded happy. Delighted, even, talking about his joy and eagerness. But what if they were only words? He hadn't said anything about forgiving her, only that he wanted her home. She, Evangeline. His daughter. His pristine, perfect, beautiful daughter. Not Eva, the scarred, broken servant girl with an illegitimate son in tow. What would her father say when he saw her? When he saw Arthur? Would he still welcome her home with open arms?

"Lady Evangeline."

Eva started. Sir Darrek, back again. After he'd only just left. Was he following her? Stalking her, to have found her here? Still, maybe it was for the best. He'd seen her father more recently. She looked up at him, surprised to see his clothing dusty and hair matted with sweat. A raised scratch marred his left cheekbone and— Was that a twig stuck in his hair?

She lifted her hand to tug it free before thinking better of it. Touching him, no matter how innocently done, was not a good idea. Far better to get her mind back on the letter crumpled in her hand. She smoothed it out across her knees.

"You read it."

She nodded.

"And?"

And she didn't know what to think of it.

She watched in silence as Darrek lowered himself to the ground and leaned back on his hands, again, surprising her. He was a knight, forever at attention, forever prepared for whatever foe might come against him. But sitting there in the dirt, he seemed just a man. One she just might be able to trust.

"What happened after I left?"

It wasn't what Eva had intended to ask. She'd meant to give Darrek the letter and ask him what he thought, but somehow the question that came out seemed more appropriate. Even if it had made her sound more vulnerable than she wanted to.

Darrek tipped his head, considering her quietly before answering.

"The castle was in uproar. No one knew what had happened or how you'd disappeared. When questioning every servant and guard in the castle shed no light on where you'd gone, your parents determined you'd been abducted. Within minutes of coming to that conclusion, your father was suited up in full armor and calling on every knight, guard, and willing servant to join him in the search for you. We all went, with your father leading the charge.

"For the rest of that day, all through the night, and long into the next day, we searched. Some of the servants went back to sleep through the night and prepare for the next day, but so long as our princess was missing and our king on his horse, the knights continued on."

He paused as if testing his words before saying them. Eva leaned forward, desperate for him to continue.

"I remember thinking I should have felt weary, but it was as if the urgency of finding you kept weariness at bay. We first searched the castle, then the town, and finally the outer villages. We were combing the forests for signs of you or a carriage or anything— even animal tracks—when one of the servants brought to your father the note you'd left.

"I was close enough to the king to see the expression on his face when he read it. He'd been filled with fierce determination until that moment, but all that changed as he crushed the note in his hand. It was as if life itself had been taken from him, though he still sat astride his mount.

"I was never privy to what you wrote. King Lior never spoke

of it. But whatever it was, it broke him. He called off the search and ordered us home, though he didn't return himself until much later that night."

Four years filled with a lifetime of regret after writing the note, Eva could still remember what it had said. Every horrible word of it.

> *If you cared about me as much as you claim,*
> *you'd let me live instead of caging me in this prison*
> *of a life you call privilege. Your people might love*
> *you, but I know the truth. You're a tyrant who wants*
> *nothing more than to elevate himself no matter how*
> *many lives he destroys in the process. I refuse to stay*
> *and let you destroy any more of my life. Don't come*
> *looking for me. I have no wish to be found by you*
> *nor ever to see you again. You might as well be dead,*
> *for that is what you are to me.*

"Your father was distraught for months. He barely ate on those few occasions he left the tower walls long enough to come to meals. He spent every day, and many nights when he should have been sleeping, pacing the castle walls, searching the distance for you. It wasn't until he collapsed one day that the queen finally convinced him to rest. He'd lost so much weight by that time that he was hardly recognizable."

She'd almost killed her father. Darrek hadn't said it in those words exactly, but then, he hadn't needed to. The grief of those memories was written across his face. She'd told her father she wished him dead. She'd almost gotten her wish.

"I didn't know. I was—"

He shrugged. Smiled, though it was sad. "Young. You were young and angry. Your father knew that. He never blamed you for leaving, nor was it you he was angry with. As far as I could see, he heaped that all on himself."

"I told him I wished he was dead."

Darrek nodded, though he couldn't possibly understand her pain or forgive her for it. He was right. She'd been a child, but that was no excuse. She should have given her father the respect he deserved as her king, even if she didn't appreciate him as a father.

Had he really become so ill? Because of her?

"I shouldn't have said those things. If only I'd appreciated then how good my life was."

"The ability to see what we should have done is a wonderful thing. But Evangeline"—Darrek placed his hand over hers—"so is forgiveness. It's not too late to come home."

Eva pulled her hand away, shaking her head. "You keep saying that."

Darrek moved over to kneel before her, humbling her with the intensity of his gaze as he stared up at her. Did he truly care so much? Or was it simply his allegiance to his king that had him kneeling here in the manure-infused dirt? Surely it was the latter. Sir Darrek Drew didn't seem like the kind of man who took failure well.

"I mean it," he said. "This isn't where you're meant to be. You're the daughter of a king."

"I used to be."

Darrek took her hands again, grasping her fingers in his, holding tight when she tried to pull away. "No, not used to be. You *are*. Nothing you do can change your birthright. Not what you wear, not where you live, not what you've done. You *are* your father's daughter. You always will be."

Eva clenched her teeth against the wave of pain that came with his words. *Not what you've done.* If only he knew.

But no, he could never know. Not her father and certainly not this knight whose steady, compassionate gaze had her insides trembling. Darrek couldn't know. Not about Arthur's true parentage. Not about her scars. Not about the nightmares. Never how weak she truly was. He'd never look at her like that again if he knew.

Eva tugged her hands out of his, standing to put a few feet distance between them. She didn't need his pity. She was strong. At least on the outside.

"Is he still unwell? My— The king?"

Darrek stood, but, to Eva's relief, didn't come any closer. "I haven't seen him in two years, but from all reports, he's improved and almost back to his former self."

"Almost?"

"His body has recovered, but he's not the same man he was before you left. It's as if part of him is gone. Some say it's his heart. He still patrols the tower walls each night, wanting to be the first to welcome home his youngest daughter."

Her father wanted her. Forgave her. If Sir Darrek could be believed. Would it really be so bad to go home? Leave this place? Lord Cavendish's dominance? Asking her father's forgiveness would be bitter and painful, but was staying here any worse? Knowing at any moment that Cavendish might snap and destroy the pitiful piece of respect she still held on to. Or take Arthur from her forever. Her father might refuse to accept Arthur as her son, but he'd never physically hurt a child.

As to her scars, she could hide them. Her whole life, if need be. No one need ever know. She'd dress in the dark, away from the other maids, claim an over-abundance of modesty. Intimacy with a husband would never be a problem because the idea of any man wanting to marry her after all she'd done was ludicrous.

She wouldn't be the daughter she'd once been—she didn't deserve that—but she and Arthur would be happy enough as servants. Her father had always treated his servants well. She'd be safe there. Far safer than here.

"You'd take me home?"

"It's what we came to do."

Eva nodded.

"Very well then."

"You'll come?" His gaze collided with hers, excitement and relief in his expression.

"Yes." She'd likely regret it a thousand times in the two days' journey home and wish she'd stayed a million more, but it was time.

"I'll tell the others. We'll meet you at the east corner of the castle tomorrow at dusk."

Eva blinked, the knight's words stopping her heart. "Tomorrow? We're not leaving today?"

"The sooner we depart this place, the better, but we can't risk getting caught. There's another feast tomorrow, I understand?"

"Aye." Lord Dickerson and his daughters were determined to get Lord Cavendish besotted enough—or, alternately, drunk enough—to marry one of the girls. They were wasting their time. Lord Cavendish wasn't the marrying kind. Still, he and his men were happy enough to let the nobles try.

"Tomorrow then. Will that be enough time for you?"

To pack the few pitiful possessions she and Arthur owned and say goodbye to the one person who'd befriended them? "Yes."

"Good. Dusk, then."

CHAPTER
8

Eva spotted her father's men instantly, waiting at dusk, as Darrek had told her, beside the east corner of the castle. Though they'd swapped their jester costumes for the far more nondescript garb of a servant, their faces were fierce, expressing none of the weariness that came from day after day, year upon year, of servitude. She clutched Arthur's hand tighter while they walked toward the knights, her stomach churning with uneasiness over whether she'd made the right choice. The thought of *her* being thrown in her father's dungeon or surrendering herself to a life of servitude brought with it only resignation. It was what she deserved. But Arthur didn't.

"You're bringing a child?" the taller of the two men asked as she ducked into the shadows with them. "Manning said nothing about a child."

As she'd hoped. "Sir Manning didn't know."

"I don't—"

"The boy comes or I stay. I'm not leaving without him."

Though quiet, her voice rang with command. In this, she would not be swayed. There was no way she was leaving Arthur here for Cavendish to destroy. She'd find a place for the boy. Somewhere. But not here.

The men looked at each other, seeming to converse silently. Eva waited, heart racing. Yesterday, she'd been determined to stay. Only moments ago, she'd had doubts. Yet the idea that the knights might change their mind and leave without her had her hand sweating in Arthur's. It hadn't even been her father's letter that had changed her mind. It had been Darrek's hope. He'd made her believe she might have a chance. That Arthur might.

"Very well."

Eva let out a slow breath, feeling her heart follow. They'd agreed.

A cheer rose from inside the Great Hall, followed by shouts of drunken laughter and the clattering of goblets. Eva pulled Arthur closer, tucking the cloak Maeve had given her around them both, more eager with every minute to get away.

"Ready?"

Eva nodded. To leave, at least. Beyond that—

No. She wouldn't think beyond tonight.

The two men flanked her and Arthur, one on each side, as they skirted the castle's deserted courtyard. It was strange to think she was leaving this place she'd once thought of as her salvation—before she'd realized it to be quite the opposite. She'd thought she would live out her life and die here. Arthur too.

She looked down at the boy walking quietly beside her, his hair shining even in the dimming light of dusk. Arthur glanced up as if sensing her gaze. His blue eyes were so serious. When was the last time she'd heard him laugh? Too long. Far too long. Could she introduce Arthur as a deceased friend's child instead of her own? His eyes were the same shade as hers, but his hair, height, and features came from his father. Not enough, yet, that people might suspect his parentage, but enough that she had no doubt Arthur would come to look more like the man in the future. She could tell others he wasn't her child, but could her heart take the pain? Even if it was for Arthur's good?

Eva's heart battled with her mind as the four of them secreted their way across the courtyard. She really was doing this. Leaving Lord Cavendish. Leaving this place. Returning to the life she'd once known but would never know again. Had she made the right choice?

Their little group was only a few steps away from the castle gates when a shout rang out. Eva gasped. Her two escorts pushed against her sides, crushing her and Arthur between them as they raised swords they'd pulled from somewhere beneath their cloaks.

"Run."

She didn't know which of the two men said it. She didn't wait to find out, pulling Arthur along as she did exactly as ordered.

She made it seven steps before a gloved hand seized her arm and held tightly. Her heart almost stopped when she looked back.

Knights. Fifteen, maybe twenty, of them. And none of them the kind she was trying her best to trust.

Black ravens on green shields. Cavendish's men.

She pushed Arthur behind her as Lord Cavendish strode into view. He'd caught her. Of course he had. Because hope was for fools. No one escaped their past. No matter what her father or Sir Darrek said.

"Leaving, Eva?"

Stalking forward, Cavendish grabbed a handful of Eva's hair and wrenched her backward. Eva couldn't help the scream that ripped from her throat. Her head was on fire. Through a haze of more fear than pain, Eva watched as her father's two knights tried to fight, but—outnumbered ten to one—were quickly subdued. Arthur's tiny hand was pulled from hers. She wished she could turn her neck enough to see where he had gone, but Cavendish's hold on her hair was too tight.

Her attention, and Cavendish's, was arrested by a single knight stalking forward. He wore her father's coat of arms across his chest and, although Eva couldn't quite make out his face through the helmet he wore, she was certain Sir Manning was beneath it. His sword remained by his side, but his hand clutched it tightly, at the ready.

"By order of King Lior of Raedonleith, I demand you release this woman at once," the knight declared. Eva had been correct. It was Sir Manning. Though, what hope she might have felt at his claim was dashed at Cavendish's laugh.

Still holding her by the hair, Cavendish wrenched her back again. This time, she lost her footing and would have fallen if not for the chunk of hair still holding her up. Cavendish twisted it around his fist, pulling her close to his face until she could feel the bristles of his beard against the side of her neck.

"No, I don't believe I will. She's mine. And she'll not be leaving this castle. Men?"

Manning's low-throated growl had Eva wondering what was happening behind her. And then, as two of Cavendish's knights came forward, Arthur's skinny arms pinned between them, she wished she couldn't. The boy was terrified, though no sound came from his mouth. Nor was there a single tear dripping down his face.

"Arthur!"

Evangeline's terror-filled scream would have been heard for miles. Darrek moved to leave the stable, only to have Manning gesture for him to stay hidden. Fury blurred the edges of Darrek's vision, leaving only Evangeline and her captor in perfect clarity.

Cavendish was going to kill her. That much was clear. His tight grasp on her hair, the way he swung her about so effortlessly, the glib amusement on his face. He didn't care about Evangeline any more than he would a rabbit in the forest. At any moment, her neck would snap, and they'd be returning a body to King Lior rather than the daughter he'd waited for all these years. It didn't matter what Manning said. Darrek would never forgive himself for that.

He stepped forward again, only to have a hand clamp on his shoulder.

"You don't want to do that, boy."

The grisly stablemaster stood behind him with his hand on Darrek's shoulder. Darrek tried to shake it off, but George held fast.

"I have to."

"You're outnumbered. You'll never save her."

"I can try."

"And be captured along with the rest of them, never able to

show your face here again. You want to help her? Be here tomorrow when the others are sitting in that man's dungeon."

"She'll be dead tomorrow."

George huffed, though there was no amusement in it. "He's not going to kill her. He would have done it years ago if she weren't important. Whoever that maid is, Cavendish needs her. And she needs you. She and the boy. Stay. Pray. It's the best you can do for her."

Stay? Pray? While the woman he'd been tasked to find and protect whimpered in the hold of that man, tears running down her face as she tried to reach for the boy.

The guards held Arthur mere inches from her fingers, as if to taunt her. It was working. On her *and* on Darrek. He wanted to storm out there, sword blazing, and cut every one of Cavendish's men down where they stood, even if he died in the process. He wanted to do far worse to Cavendish himself.

But pray? Still his heart when his head pounded with righteous anger and his hands shook with the need to act? "I don't know if I can."

"Then you'd better figure out how, boy, because the Almighty is the only one who can save her right now."

Dusk was fading into night, but not quickly enough to mask the satisfaction on the faces of the guards who held Arthur. Eva was certain it would be mirrored in Lord Cavendish's face if she could have seen it. He always had enjoyed his power. Once, she'd reveled in that. Found it attractive, even. Alone and penniless, with no other recourse but to return home and beg her father's servants for a place to stay, she'd been thrilled to find a powerful man like Cavendish looking on her with pleasure. It had been beyond what she'd hoped for.

Now, it sickened her.

"Please, not Arthur," Eva whimpered. "He's just a boy."

Cavendish pulled her tighter against his face, his beard scratching her cheek, ale-soaked breath assaulting her almost as much as the hold on her hair. "You truly thought you'd leave me? You *and* the boy?"

"We'll pay you kindly for her board and food," Sir Manning said.

Cavendish laughed. "How magnanimous of the good King Lior. Nothing has changed, I see. Still throwing money about, thinking a few coins could make up for the pain he causes. The girl, perhaps, could be bought. Broken and thoroughly ruined, she's worth naught to anyone now. But what amount of gold would he give me for my son?"

Shock—a mix of laughter and gasps—rippled through the gathering of men as Cavendish's words registered. Manning reached for his sword, only to find himself held fast between two guards. The other two of her father's knights were the same. Eva couldn't see Sir Darrek. He'd said he'd be here so he must be behind her. Her face burned with shame at what he must think. Of all the knights, it was his reaction to the news she feared the most. He was so upright, and she was so…not.

Broken and thoroughly ruined. Her life and worth summed up in a mere four words. She knew it, always had, but with Cavendish's words, the knights did too.

"She didn't tell you?" Cavendish's tight hold brought tears to Eva's face, but it was his words which tore her heart. "She spent many a night in my bed before I cast her aside. The proof stands before you." He pointed at Arthur, so there could be no mistake. "Her son is mine."

"No!"

Evangeline cried out in pain as Cavendish threw her against the castle wall. Fire seared across her middle, nausea overwhelming her thoughts and vision. She tried to push herself to her feet, reach out an arm for help, anything. But the pain held her fast. The last thing she saw before blackness took her was Cavendish hauling Arthur away.

CHAPTER 9

is fellow knights were gone, rounded up and taken to the dungeon as George had predicted. The boy, too, had been carried off by the man who claimed to be his father. Cavendish's slew of guards had returned to the feast not long after, laughing as they left, thinking this all some wonderful joke. Only the broken figure of Lady Evangeline remained, silent and still at the base of the stone wall she'd landed beneath.

And Darrek had stood by and watched, so incensed he couldn't even find the words to pray, as George had charged him to do. It was enough to make a man ill.

George's hand finally lifted from Darrek's shoulder. "Go to her."

Gladly. He wasn't sure whether he was more furious with the stablemaster, Manning, Cavendish, or himself—likely the latter—but he wasn't waiting a moment longer to go to Evangeline. If guards still watched, so much the better. He'd be more than happy to take out his anger on any and every man who'd played a part in this woman's ruin.

No one—knight, guard, servant, or otherwise—stopped him on his way to Evangeline. He reached her at the same time as her friend. Maeve had brought a cup of water. It was more than he'd thought to bring.

"Eva, honey?" Maeve said. "Can you wake?"

A moan came from somewhere deep inside the girl. Maeve touched her shoulder, attempting to rouse her as gently as possible. "Eva?"

Evangeline's eyelids fluttered, loosing tears down the side of her cheeks.

"Ar—thur."

Of course her first thought would be of her son. *Her son.* Darrek's breath caught again, his stomach dropping much as it had the first time he'd heard the news. The boy—Arthur, who'd stood in the stable that day and been fascinated by the horses—wasn't just a boy she cared for. He was her son. Lady Evangeline had a son.

With Lord Cavendish.

No amount of blood, guts, manure, or bile had ever nauseated him as much as that did. His stomach roiled with the thought of it. Were they married? Had they been? Or had the boy been conceived by more nefarious means. Having seen the delight on Cavendish's face at Evangeline's pain, Darrek could easily believe it. However the birth had come about though, the fact remained—if Lord Cavendish truly was the boy's father, he wouldn't give up Arthur without a fight.

"He's fine," Maeve assured her. "Scared but unharmed."

"Where—"

"The room beside his."

Evangeline blanched—if that were even possible, given her already pale face. Her eyelashes wavered as if she struggled to hold on to consciousness. She'd struck the wall hard. Was she cut? Bleeding inside? *Almighty, let it not be so.*

"Guards outside the door," Maeve said. "Likely to stop anyone from rescuing him rather than the poor mite escaping. I'll send a maid to check on him. The master won't deny us that."

"Do—now—" Evangeline bit out between gasps.

"After I see to you."

"No—now—"

Maeve ignored her. Darrek was glad. From what the maid said, Evangeline was in far more danger than her son at the moment. He didn't like the way she still hadn't moved more than her eyes or the way she struggled to breathe. Being winded was inevitable—he'd felt the pain of that himself more than once, and the way it stole one's ability to draw breath—but it should have begun to ease by now.

"Darrek."

Landon. Darrek held back a growl as his friend knelt beside him. "Where have you been?"

"Manning ordered me to stay back."

Of course he had. Just as he'd ordered Darrek. And, like Darrek, Landon had obeyed. Did he regret it as much as Darrek himself did?

"Craig?" Darrek asked of the squire.

Landon shook his head. "I don't know. But he wasn't taken."

"Find him. Get him and the horses away from here. I'll come for you both when I can."

"Is she—"

"Alive," Darrek answered. "But—"

He couldn't finish the sentence. Didn't want to admit how much fear that she might not be for much longer was twisting his thoughts and insides. Certainly not in Evangeline's hearing. Landon placed a hand of support on Darrek's shoulder for a moment before running off into the darkness.

As gently as possible, Darrek reached a hand under Evangeline's head, feeling for bumps, relieved when he didn't find any. The fullness of her hair must have protected her. *The fullness of her hair.* It was so soft. Warm, almost, against his wrist.

Her hair was what had first given her away when they'd been searching. Her face had changed, as had her body and her demeanor, but not the golden-red hair that had captivated his dreams far more often than appropriate. In more than one of those dreams, he'd run his hands through the length of it.

He stroked his thumb along the side of her head, captivated by the feel of her hair, which was so much softer than he'd ever imagined hair could be.

Maeve cleared her throat. He pulled his hand away. *Mind on the task.*

"Can you sit?" Maeve asked Evangeline. Darrek was glad for her brusqueness. It helped clear his head and gave him something to focus on other than his own fears and failure. They had to get Evangeline back to her cottage. The longer they stayed here, the more attention they'd draw. Both the noise of the feast and the darkness were on their side. The closest torch was ten or more yards away, and whether by the Almighty's grace or pure luck, no one had come into the courtyard while they'd been here.

Evangeline came forward a few inches before letting out a cry of pain and clutching her middle. She turned her head just enough to miss him and Maeve as she retched, tears streaming down her face. Her whole body shook with the effort.

"There, there, my sweet girl. It will all work out well in the end."

Darrek wondered if the girl believed the older woman any more than he did. Nothing that had happened in the last hour or what Cavendish had insinuated was good, nor could Darrek see how any good could come from it. Fortunately for Evangeline, he doubted she could hear much over the sound of her retching other than the crooning tone of her friend. At least her bile held no blood, as far as he could see. That was something to be thankful for.

When she finally stopped, Evangeline lay back against the wall, tears continuing to course down her cheeks, though she made no sound.

"I know you're hurt, but we can't stay here," Maeve said. "Can you walk?"

This time it was Darrek who growled. Walk? The girl couldn't even rise. And even if she had been able to, he wasn't taking any chances on her injuring herself further. He'd carry her.

If only he could have carried her right away from Cavendish Castle. Away from the pain. Away from the hurt. Away from the mess of the life she'd found herself in.

But she'd never leave the boy.

Her son.

Almighty—

No. He'd deal with that news later. Right now, Evangeline needed him.

Darrek locked one arm behind Evangeline's back, another under her knees, and forced himself to ignore the cry of pain she let out as he lifted her. It wasn't what he wanted, but Maeve was right. They couldn't leave her here.

"Where to?"

"Bed," Maeve said, leading the way to the cottage she and Evangeline shared. They passed three guards at the gate on their way there and another two near the cottage. Darrek kept his head lowered, but none of them seemed in any hurry to raise the alarm. Perhaps because he followed the maid they knew so well. Perhaps because he held a broken woman in his arms and—no matter who she was—they all felt the horror of that. Perhaps because they thought her already dead and were glad they weren't the ones having to dispose of the body. Whatever their reasons, he was thankful Evangeline had succumbed again to oblivion. The ribs he suspected were broken had to be excruciating. And that on top of fear for her son? Unconsciousness seemed kind.

Darrek lay Evangeline on her pallet, settling a blanket over her as Maeve lit a candle.

"Darrek—"

Her gasp mirrored his own agony. "I see it." Though he wished he hadn't.

Evangeline's left shoulder. It was—wrong. Out of alignment. Lower or…something. Broken ribs, a shoulder pulled from its place, and a possible head injury. How many other wounds would they find?

"I'll get the healer," Maeve said.

"I'm staying," Darrek replied. He expected Maeve to argue. That she only nodded said a lot for her state of mind.

Darrek looked down at Evangeline, his throat tightening. He hadn't cried for decades. Not when his arm had been almost severed in battle, not at the grave of the friend he'd called brother, not when he heard his mother had died, not when years of searching had left him struggling for hope. But in this moment, by this fragile woman's side, a tear escaped. First one then another. Anger stopped a third.

He'd allowed this to happen. He might not have been able to stop it—no doubt he *would* have ended up in the dungeons along with the other three knights—but at least he could have tried. It would have made him feel better instead of feeling like the coward he was. If anyone deserved to be fighting pain for each breath, it was him. He deserved this. Not Evangeline, daughter of the king.

Almighty, why? Why didn't you stop it? Why did you let her get hurt?

Darrek reached out a hand to take Evangeline's, needing to touch her even in the smallest way, needing to feel she was real. Still breathing, even though he could hear breath rasping through her.

Almighty—

The healer came in then, bustling over to Evangeline's side, filling the room with a burst of herbs. Darrek was relieved, not only that she was here to fix Evangeline but for the interruption. He hadn't known what to pray anyway.

She ordered Darrek from the room, bristling when he refused. A quiet word from Maeve satiated her enough that she allowed him to stand on the other side of the room with his back turned. Darrek didn't know what Maeve had told the healer, but he was thankful. He wasn't leaving Evangeline behind. Not again. Certainly not tonight while she lay broken on that pallet.

He only hoped the healer could fix her.

Because the Almighty didn't seem to care.

--•❦•--

Darrek stayed with Evangeline that night. He expected the nightmares but, whether due to the tonic the healer gave Evangeline or the physical pain that made her groan every time she attempted to move, they never came. Darrek should have been thankful for that small grace. Instead, all he felt was fury.

He was glad when Maeve ordered him away from Evangeline's bedside sometime in the last watch before dawn. Physical torture would have been preferable to the mental battle he waged. With a final glance at the broken woman he'd barely taken his gaze off all night, he moved to leave. Maeve's hand stopped him.

"This way," she whispered, "and stay quiet."

They walked out the door.

Past sleeping guards—who might have locked the cottage door but never once had checked to see whether the woman inside still lived or question the man by her side—along the castle wall, through the door that led to the stables. Darrek opened his mouth to thank Maeve, but she shook her head and gestured him forward. "This way."

Along the shadows, through the courtyard, in one of the castle's many side doors that Maeve unlocked with a key. It wasn't until she pointed to the long staircase leading down that Darrek realized where she'd led him.

"My men?" he whispered.

"I can't give you long. Five minutes. Maybe more, likely less. You'll be able to talk to them, naught else, but—" She shrugged. Darrek shook his head, feeling as if, for the first time during this seemingly unending day, something had gone right.

"Thank you."

She nodded. He wondered what this would cost the maid if either of them were caught. More than he was willing to let her pay.

"Thank you," he said again, this time silently promising her his protection as he did so.

The dungeons were dark, the few candles lit along the passageway barely worth their sacrifice.

"Manning?" Darrek whispered. Even that felt too loud in this solemn place. He'd been in dungeons before but had never needed to hide the fact.

"Darrek, what are you—"

Darrek moved toward the gruff voice he knew so well. There, in the last cell. They'd put the three of them together. Maybe Cavendish's guards were hoping the knights would turn on each other.

Manning's first words weren't promising. "You shouldn't be here."

There was little point in answering that they shouldn't have been there either.

"How are you?" Darrek asked instead, looking first at Manning then to the other knights. It appeared as if they'd been well beaten for their rescue attempt. Manning clutched at the bars like they were the only thing holding him up. Spencer let out a hiss of pain as he tried to rise before leaning back against the wall, hand pressed to his side. Adam had yet to move at all.

"Fine," Manning said, waving aside the pain as Darrek could have predicted he would. He'd have to be dead before he'd admit to weakness. "Landon and Craig?"

"Laying low for a few days." He hoped. He'd find them tomorrow. Ensure they were safe. Come up with a new plan.

"Lady Evangeline?"

"Alive, barely. The healer believes she'll recover—at least from the physical injuries—but it'll take time we don't have."

"Cavendish has the boy?" Manning asked.

"Yes."

"Then she won't be going anywhere."

Darrek growled. That wasn't the plan. "King Lior ordered us to bring her home."

"He also wants her to be in one piece when she does. I sent word it may take time. He understands."

King Lior might have approved the delay, but Darrek didn't. He'd watched Lord Cavendish throw her to the ground with such force that she'd broken a rib and wrenched her shoulder out of its socket. Darrek had had to hold her still while Maeve and the healer pulled it back into place. Almost ill himself, it wasn't an image he'd banish from his mind any time soon. The longer they delayed, the more danger Evangeline would be in.

"We have to get her out of here."

"We will. But it will take patience and planning. Angering Cavendish will do none of us any good, least of all Lady Evangeline and her son."

Her son. Darrek hadn't yet had time to process the fact that Evangeline had a son. Or perhaps it wasn't so much that he hadn't had *time* to process it, as that he'd been purposely trying not to think of it. Evangeline had a son. With Lord Cavendish.

"Do you believe Cavendish is the boy's father?" Darrek asked Manning.

The older man shrugged. "Evangeline didn't refute it."

"She was thrown against a wall before she could say anything."

"What reason would Cavendish have for making up such a claim? It affects him as much as it does Evangeline."

"He wants the throne of Raedonleith. If this is true—"

Manning shook his head, stopping Darrek. "Whether or not it's true doesn't matter so much right now as keeping Evangeline safe. *That* is the task set us by King Lior."

A task they were failing to complete. A rat scuttled across the far edge of the cell, eyes catching just enough light to glow eerily. Spencer groaned and clutched at his stomach as he rolled over.

"Why does Cavendish hate King Lior? I know they're enemies and that Cavendish is determined to steal the throne, but why? He holds no claim."

"He thinks he is owed it."

"Owed?"

"'Tis a tale too long for here, but he's not wholly unjustified. Promises were made, and broken, to the detriment of Lord Cavendish and his family. Many men would have chosen to let it go. Cavendish wasn't one of them. I only pray Lady Evangeline doesn't pay too dearly for his pain."

Darrek couldn't help thinking she already had.

"What do you want me to do?" he asked Manning.

"What you've been doing. Watch over her. Protect her."

"I failed her."

Manning shook his head. "We all did, but that doesn't mean we're done. We will see her home. What you see today isn't the end. Remember that."

The sound of male voices drifted down the stairs. Bleary, as if they'd had too much to drink, but there all the same. Even a drunk guard could shout an alert. Darrek needed to go.

Manning grasped his hand through the bars, having come

to the same conclusion. With a solemn nod, Darrek clasped his mentor's hand tight before taking two stairs at a time back out. He didn't see the guards, and neither did he wait to see how close a call it had been.

Thoughts pulled at his mind as he slipped back into the bed he'd made in one of the stable's empty stalls. Evangeline was in danger. Evangeline had a son. He'd failed them both.

He pushed the roiling thoughts aside, every one of them, and focused like an arrow on why he'd come:

Find Evangeline.

Protect Evangeline.

Bring her home.

CHAPTER 10

Eva hadn't seen her son in more than a week. That hurt far more than the ribs holding captive every one of her breaths or the dull ache in her shoulder. Maeve said he was being treated well and that Cavendish hadn't been near him even once since confining Arthur to that room—the one which had once been Eva's—but Eva still worried. He wasn't with her, and while she knew the maids who cared for him, they weren't her. They weren't his mother.

After five days confined to her sickbed, Eva had summoned enough will to drag herself to Cavendish's solar and beg him to let her see Arthur. He'd laughed in her face. "And have you try to take him from me again?" he'd taunted. "He's mine."

He'd walked up to her, placing a single finger on the ribs he must have known pained her. "Need you another reminder?" She'd faltered back a step but not before he pressed the ribs. She'd cried out, almost fainting from the pain.

"You've never showed any interest in him before," she'd said when she could breathe again.

"What use would I have for a weakling boy who doesn't even speak?"

"Then why—"

"Because he's mine, Eva. And, weakling though he be, he holds a claim to the Raedonleith crown. And a hold on you. And those are two things I have no intention of giving up."

He'd smiled before telling her that, if she behaved, *maybe* he'd give Arthur back to her.

Behave. Another word for "do everything I demand."

She'd hobbled out of there before he demanded any more than he already had. Maeve had found her gripping a wall, too faint to walk the rest of the way to the cottage. A guard had been summoned to carry her. She'd lain in her bed for the rest of the day and alternated between misery, fury, and reluctant acceptance. Much as she wanted to kick and scream and make some demands of her own—first and foremost getting back her son—doing so would only taunt Cavendish into hurting someone. She couldn't take the risk that that person would be Arthur.

She'd risen from bed the next day determined not to spend another day with only her miserable thoughts to keep her company. No matter what the healer said.

Along with Arthur, her father's knights were gone, and with them, the last of the hope she'd momentarily held of being rescued. According to Maeve, the men had spent five days in the dungeons starved of food and given only what little water Maeve had managed to smuggle in. They'd been escorted a day's journey away by Cavendish's knights, warned they'd be killed if they were sighted on Cavendish land again. Eva had been surprised at Cavendish's mercy until Maeve mentioned their battered faces and how they limped where normally they strode. Eva knew Cavendish well enough to guess the rest. The men hadn't been sitting idle in that dungeon for five days. Nor had they been blissfully alone.

Eva closed her eyes and focused on breathing, like she'd done every time the nausea became too much. She wasn't sure anymore what was causing the nausea—the injuries to her body or the guilt-ridden blow to her heart. The knights had done this for her. Been tortured and likely scarred for life for her. And she'd failed them. She couldn't help but believe that if she'd told Sir Manning and Sir Darrek about Arthur and her relationship with Cavendish the first time they'd spoken, this all would have turned out differently. The men would have left, no doubt, but they wouldn't have been tortured on her behalf before doing so.

"Evangeline."

A deep whisper had Eva turning to find the source, even

though there was only one man who called her that. Surely her hopes were playing tricks on her. Sir Darrek had been banished with the others.

But no. There he was. Impossibly. Standing just inside the door of the stables, beckoning her inside.

She rushed over as fast as her fiery ribs would allow, uncertain whether relief or anger was causing the hitch in her heart. He shouldn't be here. He couldn't be. It was foolish and reckless and dangerous and—

Why was she so relieved he was?

"Evangeline."

Darrek's brow furrowed as he spoke her name again, his voice catching on the single word despite the way he stood tall. Was this strong knight as shaken by the events of the past week as she was? Surely not. Yet those had been his friends who'd been beaten so badly they could barely walk before being threatened with their lives.

Why hadn't Maeve mentioned Darrek was still here? Or had Eva only asked what had become of the knights in the dungeons, assuming all her father's knights had been sent there. Perhaps Maeve thought Eva already knew.

Eva ran her gaze over Darrek's face, wondering at the lack of bruising. Had he escaped the torture? She'd thought he'd merely been beyond her line of sight when it all happened. Had he not been in the square at all?

And if so, should she feel relieved? Or furious?

Why did this man evoke such strong emotions in her?

Whatever the answer, he needed to go. Today. Now. Yesterday, even, if that could have been possible.

"What are you doing here?" Eva chanced a glance behind her. No one was watching, not that she could tell, so she ducked a little farther into the stable. She'd be out of sight here. For better or worse.

"Working. George hired me."

Darrek crossed his arms. Eva tried not to notice how much bigger that made them seem. Had Darrek always been this strong?

Not that it mattered. Cavendish would hang him if he saw Darrek here, if not worse. Eva's ribs ached, and she pressed a hand to her stomach. She didn't want to think about worse. "I told you to leave."

He stared at her, unblinking. "I asked you to come."

Exasperating man. "I'm not coming."

"Then I'm not leaving."

"You have to."

"Not without you."

Pressure built in Eva's chest, cutting her breathing. Her hands started to shake. She closed her eyes and told herself to calm down. She couldn't let the panic take her, not here. Not in front of him. He was a knight, one of the best in her father's service. She needed to convince him she was not only fine but strong. She had to appear strong. He would never leave otherwise.

And she couldn't have him stay. Even if Cavendish never discovered Darrek was here, she would know. And she had far too much to hide. He knew about Arthur, but he couldn't know the rest. The shame was too much to bear.

"I can't."

Picking up a spade, he shoveled a clod of dirt into the rapidly growing pile of muck behind him. His shoulders strained against his shirt as he did so. Eva looked away. She didn't need any more distractions.

A week ago, when Darrek and Manning had first confronted her at the well, it hadn't taken more than a glance for Eva to remember Sir Darrek.

He'd been the most devout of her father's knights. Morning and night he was found in Raedonleith's chapel saying his prayers. For what, she didn't know. She'd never seen him do anything wrong. Though he wasn't the strongest of the knights back then, he was fast, his speed more than making up for his lack of brawn.

But that had been four years ago.

His eyes were more shadowed than she remembered, his shoulders were twice as large, and his hair—once worn loose to the middle of his back—was tied back with a strip of leather or something of the sort, but there had been no mistaking the man in front of her. Sir Darrek Drew.

She'd liked him once. Even considered asking her father to arrange a marriage between them.

For all of two minutes.

Before Sir Darrek had called her a child and sent her back to her mother's solar.

He'd been right—she could see that. But four years ago, she'd been furious.

Now, she couldn't imagine anyone she'd rather have come and save her.

If only he could.

"Please, Sir Darrek, if not for your own sake, leave for mine and Arthur's. Lord Cavendish isn't known for his mercy."

"I won't let him hurt you."

"He already has."

Darrek's reaction was swift. He threw the spade down, growling at it. Or her? Eva couldn't tell. His gaze when it turned back to her was as wild as she'd ever seen it. But then it gentled. Softened, to the point of almost seeming as if he was about to weep. A ridiculous thought. He was a man, a strong man, a knight. Knights didn't cry. They fought.

Eva jumped as his fingers brushed against hers before landing on the edge of her wrist. Staying there, light as they were. Could he feel her pulse racing to meet his fingers? She wanted to pull away but couldn't find the strength.

"Evangeline," Darrek said, his voice deep, quiet, but strong. "I wish I could take back what Cavendish did to you. It makes me ill to know he hurt you as he did. No man should ever treat a woman like he did you. But I promise you, he won't do it again. I won't let him."

"You can't stop him." Eva's words were a mere shake of a whisper, terror holding them as captive as they held her.

"I can and I will. I told you I wouldn't leave you. I swore an oath to your father to find and protect you. Now, I swear one to you."

Eva watched in shock as Darrek knelt on the dirt-strewn ground before her and took her right hand between both of his. His expression as he looked up at her was fierce, and certain.

"Lady Evangeline, on my honor as a knight, I swear I will not leave Cavendish Castle without you. I will not leave your side until the day I bring you home. You have my word."

Eva tugged her hand out of his, shaking her head. His words were a boon to her heart, but she couldn't accept them. Doing so would be wrong. And dangerous.

"You have to go." She gestured behind him. "You may carry a shovel and smell of manure, but Cavendish will never believe you're a simple stable boy."

"George gave me a job. He's the stablemaster and Cavendish pays him to make wise choices. I'll be fine. I'll stay in the stables. Play the fool they all think me to be."

Eva looked behind her, certain any second the call would go out that there was an imposter here. "It won't be enough."

"I'm not leaving you unprotected."

Darrek didn't know Cavendish at all if he thought staying in the stables would keep him safe. George might have trusted the man, but she could guarantee none of Cavendish's other men did. Strangers were rarely welcomed around here, especially ones strong enough to challenge Cavendish's leadership. Or who looked like they might be. Cavendish might have been arrogant, but he was shrewd about it.

"I can handle myself." She crossed her arms and stared Darrek down, willing him not to see how much his presence here had shaken her. Had he watched his men leave, paraded through the jeering crowds, stumbling on their own feet from weakness and pain? Knowing they'd done it for her had almost broken her, and they'd been all but strangers. Sir Darrek, she knew. She couldn't watch him be killed for trying to protect her.

"You can't hide forever," Eva said.

"Not forever. Only until I get you home."

"I told you I can't leave."

"You wanted to a week ago."

Yes, and she'd paid for it. As had everyone she loved. "Wanting and having are two very different things."

"You'd have me go back to your father without you?"

"Surely you've done it before."

She looked again behind her, the quietness of the courtyard making her uneasy. Lord Cavendish and his guests had gone hunting, but other guards still should have been patrolling. Knights training. Servants gossiping. The only time it was ever this quiet was the morning hours after a banquet when all but the greenest of knights slept off their drinking. Those mornings were bliss.

This was not one of them. The silence made her nervous.

"Not when he's expecting you. Not when he knows you're alive."

That got her attention.

"He thought I was dead?"

Darrek stood. His hand reached out again, as if he'd wanted to cradle her cheek, before dropping to his side. His sigh was pure frustration with a side of disbelief.

"Your father hadn't heard from nor seen sight of you for four years, despite us searching the length and breadth of this land. None of us wanted to believe it might be true, but we had to prepare ourselves for the fact that it might have been."

"Maybe it would have been better if I was."

The hand that took hers was warm and strong. "Don't ever say that. And don't tell me to leave either. I'm staying. We're not leaving without you."

"The others did. You should have gone with them."

"They're still here."

"Cavendish's men escorted them away. Maeve told me. She saw them walk from the dungeon, through the courtyard, out along the road home. I saw the men return without them a day later."

"It's two days' journey to Raedonleith," Darrek said, waiting a beat before pointing out what Eva didn't dare allow herself to believe. "Cavendish's men left them halfway, assuming the beatings were warning enough for them not to return. They weren't. The knights waited only long enough for Cavendish's men to be out of sight before trailing them back. You won't see Manning or the others, but they're out there in the forest. All of them. Safe and well.

"Don't fret," Darrek said before she could put words to the panic rising within her. "They'll stay out of sight, same as I will. We can protect ourselves, and we *will* be here to protect you. If you won't come home, then home will come to you. You're our lady, no matter what your role here or who these people think you are. You, Lady Evangeline, are the daughter of our king."

"But Arthur…"

"We'll protect him too."

It was too much to hope for, that someone here cared about her and her son. Maeve did, of course, but she held little more power than Eva. The knights, though, could fight. Protect her and Arthur.

But they'd tried that already. And almost lost their lives for it. She couldn't bear to watch it happen again.

"I wish you'd go."

"Truly?"

Eva opened her mouth to say yes before closing it again. She should send them away. That much was clear. They risked everything to be here, and there was no way she was worth the sacrifice. Yet she couldn't deny her relief when Darrek had called her name or that the other knights were still there. Protecting her, even if it was from a distance.

Though the sound didn't have enough force to be called a word, Eva knew Darrek was watching her closely enough to see her lips form the sigh of an answer. The truth that escaped despite every bit of logic telling her to lie.

"No."

CHAPTER
11

"**C**ome inside."

King Lior rubbed gritty fatigue from his eyes and rolled his shoulders. His feet ached, his stomach reminded him he'd missed dinner again, and his back screamed with the pain of ten hours walking the tower wall. His wife's gentle request was tempting—very tempting—but what if he left and that was the very moment Evangeline came home? Sleep wasn't worth missing that. Nothing was.

"Two more hours."

"She's not coming tonight."

"She may. And if she does—" His voice caught roughly on words he was unable to speak.

"You want to be waiting."

Lior looked out over the wall again, blinking away the wetness in his eyes. Always so close to the surface when it came to thinking about his youngest daughter and the way he'd failed her.

"I have to, Cara. I know I can't change the past, but I have to believe there's a future for us. And that starts with being here, waiting for her, when she comes home. It was my anger that drove her away. I want my love to be the first thing that welcomes her home. Don't you see?"

Caralynne gave Lior a sad smile before putting a hand on his arm and leaning forward to kiss his cheek. "Don't drive the guards crazy with your stalking."

He placed a hand over hers, taking in her strength and acceptance. "Thank you."

She nodded again before walking toward the steps to the lower floors. She stopped at the top and turned back for a moment. "Lior." She waited until he faced her. "I want her home too. You're not alone."

"Sire!"

Both monarchs turned at the sound of the guard's shout.

"A letter has come. Delivered just now."

Lior swallowed hard, afraid to hope, afraid not to. "From Evangeline?"

He'd opened the missive and skimmed half of the page before the guard answered. Not Evangeline but Sir Manning, though it was regarding Lior and Caralynne's daughter. Lior tilted the page so Caralynne could read over his shoulder.

She wasn't coming home. Not tonight, at least. Maybe not for weeks. He began again at the start, determined to read every word.

> Our attempt at a rescue was thwarted, and several of our group were escorted from Cavendish's lands, our lives threatened should we return. We returned anyway, though we remain hidden. Sir Darrek, per my order, stayed out of sight during the melee—though you can imagine how much it irked him to do so—and has now taken a position shoveling muck within the stables to be close to and better protect Lady Evangeline.
>
> The ties between Cavendish and your daughter are more complicated than we thought. He holds great power over her, and convincing her to leave again will be difficult. I believe Sir Darrek is up to the task, though it may take time.
>
> Be assured, we have not given up nor will we.

Thwarted. Banned. Threatened.

There was more to this story than Manning had written, though it didn't surprise Lior that Manning had glazed over the morbid details. Victories were so much sweeter to report than defeat, and Lior had no doubt those threats had come in the form of more than words. He silently thanked the Almighty that his men still lived.

He'd handpicked the five knights for this task.

Sir Manning was the obvious choice to lead the mission. The oldest and most experienced of Lior's knights, Manning not only had the experience to spearhead an attack but the level-headedness to see it through.

Sir Adam and Sir Landon, on the other hand, had been knighted only days before Lior chose the group. Though they were green, they'd well earned their titles and had the strength, vigor, and determination to face whatever came. The fact that they were considered the most handsome of his men—according to several of the blushing maids he'd asked—may have also come into consideration. Of his three daughters, Evangeline had always been the one most swayed by a pretty face. If infatuation could bring her home, he'd be a fool not to use it.

Sir Spencer, though also brave, strong, and fierce, had been chosen for his gift of encouragement. Every team needed someone who held tightly to hope and encouraged others to do the same. Men like that, though irritating at times, were often the difference between victory and defeat.

And Sir Darrek. He'd been chosen for his heart. He was skilled, for certain, and loyal to a fault, but as Lior returned with his men to Raedonleith that horrible day Evangeline's note had been found, Darrek was the one who'd caught his attention. The pain in his eyes had matched the ache in Lior's heart. Darrek had been the first to suggest they regroup and go back out. That Evangeline couldn't have gotten far. When others had grumbled under their breath about warm beds and hot ale, Darrek had sat taller on his horse, all but begging Lior to agree.

Darrek wouldn't give up on Evangeline. The promise etched in his expression overwhelmed the weariness there. Until she was found, he'd keep looking. He *would* bring her home.

It seemed Lior had been correct in his assessment that day.

Any knight who would humble himself to the level of squire that he might better protect another was worthy. That he'd done it to protect Lior's own daughter rose the king's estimation of him even higher.

"Ties? I wonder what he means by that," Caralynne mused beside him.

Lior shook his head. He didn't know, and neither did he want to.

"Ties can be broken."

"What if she loves him?"

His daughter? Love their enemy? When she knew their families' history?

"She doesn't."

"But if she does?"

"I won't allow it."

"Lior—"

"Come. Let us retire."

CHAPTER
12

The chapel was quiet, hushed, as if to speak or even breathe would break the reverence. It was only a building. The Almighty certainly wasn't chained to it, and yet, heaven and earth seemed to meet within its stone walls, as if hundreds of prayers from scores of worshipers throughout the decades had thinned the veil.

Yes, the Almighty was here—and for the first time in his life, Darrek didn't know what to say to him.

Evangeline's nightmares hadn't gone away. Arthur was still locked in a room inside the castle. And, though she'd told him he could stay, Darrek could see how much the admission had cost Evangeline. She might have allowed him to stay, but she'd lost all hope of leaving herself.

Nothing he'd asked for had changed. The Almighty hadn't stepped in and saved Evangeline or any of his faithful servants. Her situation had worsened following their failed attempt to save her.

The slowly dipping sun illuminating the stained-glass window at the front of the chapel showed a shepherd holding a lamp. Darrek turned away from it, instead running his fingers along the rough stone of the chapel walls, following their track with his gaze. Stone was cold, timeless, reliable. It didn't change with the seasons or on a person's whim. It didn't promise protection, only to pull back when danger came.

"You come here every morning at dawn and every evening."

A cleric so old he could have built the chapel himself walked into the building. With the shuffling steps of someone who'd taken too many in his lifetime, the man moved from candle to candle, lighting each of them in turn. He stopped under the stained-glass window—rapidly dimming now that the sun had dipped too far to reach it—and bowed his head in respect before moving on to the next candle.

"It's quiet," Darrek finally said.

"I'll wager your mind isn't."

What did this man know of Darrek's inner thoughts? He likely hadn't ever picked up a sword, let alone failed in battle. Who was he? Darrek had never seen him in the chapel before, though Darrek came as often as the man said. A traveling friar?

"What is it you seek, young man?"

Answers rushed through Darrek's mind too quickly for him to capture even one of them, not that it mattered because he didn't plan on sharing more than a few words with this stranger. "Nothing."

"If that were true, you wouldn't be here."

"Perhaps I like the silence."

"You think this place silent?"

Darrek looked around the chapel again, from stone to candle to one empty bench after another.

"Yes."

"Then it seems you haven't yet learned to listen."

❦

The man's words stuck in Darrek's head as he walked the long way back to the stables. The chapel had been silent. It was the reason Darrek went there every morning and evening. Situated as it was, little noise penetrated the stone walls. Not the noise of the servants preparing for the day nor the knights drilling with sword and bow. No shouts, no children shrieking with laughter, no maids chattering about which herbs would make the men they fancied fall in love with them.

Just silence.

Did the man have exceptional hearing? Or was he speaking spiritually? Clerics were supposed to be the voice of the Almighty to the masses. Was that the voice he heard? Was he, like the prophet Samuel, able to hear the voice of the Almighty out loud? In which case, he was either well worth talking to, or completely crazy.

Still, his words wouldn't leave Darrek alone.

It seems you haven't yet learned to listen.

Darrek had spent his life listening. It was what made him a good knight. He'd long ago learned to quiet his breathing so he could listen—the hitch in the breath of his opponent the moment before the sword swung, the whisper of a doe in the forest, the sound of a creek when he was tracking or being tracked. He'd swear he even heard Lady Evangeline's heartbeat thudding in terror as he held her hand last night through yet another nightmare.

Listening wasn't his problem. No matter what the cleric said.

Unless it was.

A hiss of frustration burst from Darrek's mouth. The cleric could say what he wanted. That didn't make it true.

Darrek looked up at the darkening sky. The sun had dropped below the horizon while he'd been keeping a watch out for Cavendish's guards. Night would be here soon. Finally. Darrek had been itching to wash at the creek all day, but going in daylight hours wasn't an option anymore. Too many maids found him interesting for him to risk it. Not that he thought all that highly of his own appearance. Not when compared to men like Landon and Adam, who he'd heard maids back in Raedonleith had swooned over—whether or not those tales from Landon could be believed. But the fact remained that he was a male, and they were eager young females.

No, he'd wait till night well and truly fell before creeping his way out there.

A solitary figure walked toward the wall gate. Even in the dimming light, Darrek could tell it was Evangeline. What was she doing leaving at this time of night? Was she even well enough to be walking? Despite how strong she'd tried to act yesterday, her eyes had given her away. That and her trembling hands.

He stepped out into a clearing, ten steps from where she

walked, but with her head down, she didn't see him. Should he follow her?

Find my daughter. Keep her safe. Bring her home.

He couldn't do that if she were lost in the forest.

Darrek ducked inside the stable, quickly grabbing the sword he'd hidden there along with his cloak. With the darkness came the cold. Whether he wore the cloak or gave it to Evangeline, it would be foolish to leave it behind. And it covered his sword.

She'd disappeared by the time Darrek made it outside the gates, but he knew she couldn't have gone far, especially not injured as she was. He headed toward the creek, the most likely place she would have gone. The way she'd been walking—purposefully yet distractedly—she'd had something on her mind. He wouldn't disturb her, only ensure she was safe. It wouldn't be the first time he'd tracked a wounded creature.

The creek was empty, save Landon sitting at the edge of it. Landon hadn't seen her. Neither had Manning, Spencer, Adam, or Craig.

"She wouldn't leave without her son," Manning reminded Darrek. It didn't help. Too many things could happen to a woman alone in the forest at night for Darrek to be comforted by it. He opened his mouth to say something more, but Manning and the others were already strapping on their swords. Darrek winced along with them as the men tried to hide the pain of their beatings.

"We'll find her."

<hr />

The silver knife shook in Eva's hand as she pulled it free from the pile of dead leaves and unwrapped the fabric protecting it. She'd told Maeve she was going to wash at the creek. Instead, she'd come here. To the hollowed-out tree that had become her haven and her downfall.

The knights had stayed. No, not stayed. They'd *come back*. To the realm of the man who'd almost killed them for trying to save her. They'd come back to try again. What if this time they died? Her father's best knights.

She wasn't worth it. If only they knew how much. If only they saw her now, huddled in the hollow just big enough for her to sit comfortably within—or lie a sobbing mess, as it far more often saw her—knife clutched in her fist.

She shouldn't be doing this. Sir Darrek would be horrified. Sir Manning would look on her with disappointment. Maeve would tell her she was stronger than this. Lord Cavendish would likely laugh, unsurprised in the least at further proof of just what a failure she was. It wasn't right, wasn't healthy, wasn't even safe, though she did her best to keep the knife clean. And yet—

Yet.

It was the only thing keeping her together.

One little cut. The pain just enough to remind her that she was still alive. Still fighting. Something to bandage. Something to watch heal and prove healing was possible.

She barely winced as the knife cut across the inside of her forearm. Not her wrist—she wasn't desperate enough to go too close to her wrist, and it would have been too hard to hide anyway—but in the middle. A single cut across the soft, white skin of her arm.

Blood pooled, bringing tears to her eyes. Not at the pain but at the failure. Her failure. She kept doing this. Even though she knew she shouldn't. Because it helped.

She was like a pot full of stew. Steaming, bubbling up inside. Keep the lid on and it boiled out over the edges, scalding anything and everything in its way. But open the lid, the smallest amount, let out some steam, and all was well.

There was no lid to take off the pain boiling inside her. The feelings of failure, the terrifying darkness, a future devoid of hope, the suffocating reminder of all she'd given up, all those moments she could never get back. The fact that she'd doomed her innocent son to the same.

The overwhelming, never-ending, heart-crushing guilt.

They boiled and bubbled inside Eva until she wanted to scream from the agony. Or burst. Or do something—anything—to make it stop.

But she couldn't. Had no way to take it away or make any of it stop. She'd tried. Over and over, she'd tried. There were days she found the strength to face her demons head on and thought she'd won, only to have them come back harder the next day when she was too exhausted from the fight to try again. It was easier to live with the pain than hope and hope again only to see defeat.

It had been an accident, the first time.

She'd been slicing carrots. Her knife had slipped. She'd stared at the blood welling across the palm of her hand for likely close to a minute before Maeve spotted it and whisked a bandage around it, cautioning Eva to be more careful. Asking if she was okay.

Her hand had throbbed beneath the bandage. But the raging darkness inside her, the pain so overwhelming yet so untouchable, had dulled, just the tiniest amount. Barely noticeable but enough. The tears hadn't come that day. The self-loathing dimmed by the cut on her hand.

It hadn't been an accident the second time.

Eva could still hear Lord Cavendish's laugh as he'd pulled the serving girl into his lap that night at the feast and kissed her to the cheers of a hall full of guests. She should have been sickened by his actions and what he so willingly, so unashamedly, took from the maid. Instead, she'd been jealous. Of a flushed, slightly embarrassed but clearly flattered maid. Eva had been that girl once—one delighted by the public attentions of a man so formidable. She'd reveled in his attention, his kisses, his claim. She, too, had blushed while secretly loving the power that came from knowing *she* was the one he wanted.

Eva had fled from the hall that night, sobbing at all she'd lost. At the fact that she'd wanted it in the first place. At the fact that she still wanted it now. Not Cavendish's attention—the girl could have that—but someone's. At the fact that the girl could laugh while all Eva managed was tears.

Beyond the walls of the castle, the forest had swallowed her into its darkness. Barely able to see through her tears, she'd stumbled and fallen against a rock. It hadn't hurt, and even if it had, she doubted the pain would have registered. What was a mere scratch compared to the swirling storm inside her? Arms wrapped around her knees, she'd sat there, letting the tears pour out of her, willing the guilt and despair to go with it.

But they didn't. If anything, the more she cried, the more the feelings grew until she was certain her body would explode into more pieces than anyone could ever hope to put back together. Her ears rang with the voices taunting her.

You think you deserve any better?

You're nothing. You have nothing. You never will.

He doesn't want you. No one does.

This is all you'll ever be. A maid. A slave. His throwaway.

The scream had welled up in her throat like that of a wild animal caught in a trap and writhing to be free. The sharp rock she picked up sliced across her arm almost before she could think better of it. But, like the first time, along with the physical pain, came an instant lull to the voices. The inward pain. The boiling over of emotions.

She'd torn a scrap from her apron, bound the wound tightly, and sat there until the sounds of the feast turned to silence, the throbbing pain of her arm all she felt.

It had been two hours of bliss.

When she'd returned, Maeve had asked where she'd been, of course, and how she'd torn her apron. It had been easy enough for Eva to tell her friend that she'd gone for a walk in the forest and snagged it on a bush. Her sleeve covered the bandaged arm. No one need know the truth.

It hadn't been until the next morning that the guilt hit.

Eva had promised herself she'd never do it again. And she'd kept that promise.

For a whole week.

She'd found the hollowed-out tree. Stolen a knife. Hidden it there.

And just like that, the cycle was started, and she became just what she'd tried so hard to escape. The scars on her arms were proof. Every single one of them, however many of them there were. Two score? Three score? She'd long ago stopped counting. It didn't matter anymore how many scars there were. Only that they were there. And would be, forever. Etched into her skin. Their silent testimony to her struggle louder than any word could be.

Eva swiped a hand across her eyes, wiping at tears which had already dried, before wrapping a cloth tightly around her arm and pulling back down her sleeve.

She might as well have scored the word into her arm with a knife, for that is all she'd ever be.

A failure.

CHAPTER
13

Darrek sat beside Evangeline's bed, stroking sweat-soaked hair back from her face and holding her hand while she screamed. The terrors had begun early tonight. The nightmares were getting worse—unsurprising given that not only had Cavendish almost killed her, but he still held her son captive. That night played over in Darrek's dreams too, and he'd merely witnessed her pain. It hurt too much to imagine what she must have felt.

Slowly, her screams turned to sobs then whimpers.

She never spoke any words when the nightmares came, so he had no idea what terrors plagued her. She never spoke about the nightmares during the day either. Darrek was almost certain she'd change the topic if he asked. One day, he might feel he could. First, he had to earn her trust.

Something he'd never do if she knew he was here while she slept.

Every time he came, he risked her waking to see him there, and every time he came anyway. Because she needed him. He might not have earned her trust in her waking hours, but something about his presence calmed her nights.

Darrek moved his feet out from under him, wincing as blood flowed back into them.

"There now, love, rest. You're safe. I'm here. Naught will harm you."

He wished he could pick her up and cradle her in his arms as one would a child, as he'd done that night he carried her in here. He'd almost given into the urge many times already. But that was a line he was unwilling to cross. So, he stroked her hair, held her hand, whispered prayers and comfort. Hoped, somehow, they'd help.

The long sleeves of her sleeping shift rose as she rolled onto her side and tucked a hand under her head. Even in the dim light, it was impossible to miss the scars crisscrossing her arm. Thin, healed for the most part, but permanently etched in her delicate skin. Had Cavendish done this to her? After what Darrek had witnessed the night they'd tried to escape, he could easily believe it of the man.

Evangeline...

Anger mixed with disgust as Darrek held back a cry of his own. What had she been through in this place? Was the rest of her body covered in scars too? What if it were? The healer had only mentioned excessive bruising when Darrek had been allowed to turn around and ask how Evangeline was that night, but she might have assumed he knew the rest. What if whoever did this to her had gone that tiny bit further and left her for dead? He and the other knights had rejoiced when they'd found her. How close had they come to finding her grave instead?

Evangeline...

Moving to his knees beside the low bed, Darrek placed a hand on her arm and began again to beseech the Almighty on her behalf. This time, it wasn't freedom from the terrors he begged for. It was for her protection.

The sooner he got her away from here, the better.

He didn't sleep that night, too angered by the scars and what they might mean to let himself, so he was still awake when Maeve stirred. Reluctant as he was to leave Evangeline, the time had come. Most times, Maeve thanked him with a nod, before closing the window behind him. This time, when he reached the window, she stopped him.

"She does it to herself, you know."

Darrek, who'd thought the maid was restraining him to avoid a guard from spotting them, turned back. She couldn't mean—

"The scars. She thinks I don't see, but I do."

"Evangeline cuts herself?"

"Aye. I've tried to get her to stop, but she just laughs it off as clumsiness."

Darrek thought back to the scars covering Evangeline's arm. There had to be twenty or more. Was her other arm the same? He considered the bandage he'd felt on her wrist, trying to remember which arm it had been on. Surely the maid was mistaken. Evangeline would never do that. No one in their right mind would. But why would Maeve lie? She cared about Evangeline. She had to be telling the truth. But if she were, then—

Oh, Evangeline...

"They've never become infected?"

"She's careful. Binds them immediately, from what I can tell."

Darrek's stomach clenched, bile clawing at his throat. She did this to herself. Marred her own skin. What must she have been through to have found solace in such pain? He didn't want to even consider it, let alone believe it to be true.

What if she took it too far? He'd seen too many men bleed out from cuts or die from infection not to know how easy it would be.

But what could he do? How did one fight the mind? He couldn't take out his sword and slay it, nor challenge it to a duel. He could stay with Evangeline every minute of every day and still not be able to help her fight the demons that caused this, even if he wanted to. Which he did. More than he should have. More than was wise. Because no matter what happened—whether she lived with the scars or died from them—he would blame himself.

"Don't tell her I know," he told Maeve.

"Heavens, no. She doesn't even know I do. You think I want to be the one blamed for your anger toward her?"

"I'm not angry."

"No? Then you're not the man I thought you were."

Spotting a guard at a distance, Darrek hurried back to the relative safety of the stables. Though she closed the window behind him, Maeve's challenge followed him the whole way there.

CHAPTER
14

Darrek missed his sword, his friends, and the sun.

True to his word, he hid in the stables during daylight hours, staying out of sight whenever anyone but George or the stable boys came in. And when Cavendish had come to request horses that he might use when he took Lord Dickerson's oldest daughter for a ride. The two of them returned less than an hour later, Cavendish furious and the girl crying. Whatever enticement she'd tried to gain a proposal hadn't worked. Lord Dickerson and his entourage had left Cavendish Castle at first light the next morning. The drama of it all had fueled the servants' gossip for hours.

It had been a nice change from hearing the servants muse about the ever-darkening circles under Evangeline's eyes and how the way her voice rasped proved she was a demon. Their superstitions were pure foolishness, but Darrek too had noticed the darkness of her eyes. Deep, like bruises. From her terror-broken sleep? Or something else?

What if she were ill?

She does it to herself, you know. The scars. She thinks I don't see, but I do.

Was that where she'd gone that time when Darrek had lost her in the forest?

She'd been gone for an hour that night. Though Darrek and the other knights had searched, they hadn't spotted her until she was almost back to the gate. She'd seemed surprised to see them. Surprised and wary. She told them she'd been washing at the river.

None of them pointed out that she was dry or that the river had been the first place they'd looked. Darrek had been so relieved to find her well that he hadn't pushed her for the truth. He'd wondered ever since if that had been a mistake.

Darrek hefted another shovel-load of manure into the ever-growing pile. Had he ever felt so helpless?

Instead of sparring each morning with Landon or Adam in the forest, or running, or climbing trees to keep up his strength, Darrek shoveled manure. Instead of talking strategy with Manning and Spencer as Manning sat whittling sticks, Darrek shoveled manure. Instead of joking and laughing with the men he counted as brothers, Darrek shoveled hay. And manure.

It was a dull, demeaning, and unending cycle, but it meant he was near Evangeline, and that was the only thing that mattered.

As if anything he was doing was making even a drop of difference.

You're not the man I thought you were.

With a hiss of frustration, Darrek punched the brick wall beside him. Hard. The shock of pain down his arm barely helped the anger. Near wasn't good enough. Evangeline's nightmares were getting worse. She was scarring her own body. He almost wished he'd been sent away with Manning and the others. At least they had the option of running until they couldn't hear the screams anymore.

Day by day, hour by hour, Evangeline was losing herself. Soon, if she weren't already, she'd only be a brittle shell of pain, and no amount of scar tissue would be able to hold her together when the shell cracked.

Cavendish had done this to her.

Darrek punched the wall again. And again.

What gave men like that the right to live?

Almighty, I—

What? What was he even asking? *Almighty, I hope you smite him? Kill him in one fell swoop?* Unlikely from a deity who claimed to be love. Then again, a deity who claimed to be love would protect the helpless too, and Darrek hadn't seen any evidence of that lately. Quite the opposite.

Every muscle in Darrek's arm shuddered as he clenched his fist and slammed it into the wall again. The wall didn't even move an inch.

"If you can stop pounding that wall long enough to listen, I have something to say."

George stood behind Darrek. How long had he been there? Long enough to see Darrek's temper tantrum. Darrek refused to be embarrassed. So what if he got angry over the mistreatment of a woman. Shouldn't every man?

"What is it?"

His voice came out gruffly, bordering on rudeness. George acted as if Darrek hadn't even spoken.

"Lord Cavendish ordered me to accompany Eva into the village. She needs supplies. We'll be taking McIntyre, Storm, and Bay."

"Evangeline hates horses."

"I know."

No doubt, so did Lord Cavendish. Was he so cruel that he would make her ride one for his own satisfaction?

Unfortunately, Darrek could believe it.

"I thought she could ride with you. She may be less afraid that way. 'Tis clear she trusts you."

"Ride with—" Darrek frowned. "Cavendish would sooner run me through than allow me to escort his prize out of here."

"I assured him one of my stable boys would accompany us also, to assist with her purchases. He need not know the boy's identity. Or his age. Garrett, a guard well-paid to turn a blind eye, will also accompany us."

If a stable boy and guard were both going, then Darrek didn't see where he— *Oh.* "I'm the stable boy."

"Do you have a problem with that?"

Surprisingly, no. He didn't. Not if it gave him time with Evangeline. Uninterrupted time at that. The village was a good twenty-minutes ride away at least.

"No, sir. Not at all. If you trust the guard, then so do I. When do we leave?"

"As soon as you prepare the horses."

Darrek grinned then did what any good little stable boy would do—he prepared the horses.

CHAPTER
15

When Maeve had sent word to Lord Cavendish that the kitchens were running low on spices, Eva had started thinking through what she would need to do to cover Maeve's work while the older woman was gone. She hadn't expected Lord Cavendish to order her to go in Maeve's place. And she certainly hadn't expected Sir Darrek to take her. Admittedly, George and Garrett were with them too, two full horse lengths ahead. But Darrek's arm braced her back, and Darrek's breath whispered across her neck, stirring her hair and her heart.

If only her ribs would stop throbbing long enough for her to enjoy it.

Eva took in a breath as deeply as she dared before slowly letting it out into the breeze. They were traveling at barely more than a walking pace, yet every step the horse took sent shards of pain across her middle. She shifted slightly before moving back when that position was worse. At least she was in too much pain to care that she sat helpless atop an enormous animal with a mind and will of its own.

Halfway to the village. Maybe if she held her breath as much as possible, the piercing pain wouldn't hurt so much.

"May I?"

Darrek was asking her permission for something, but Eva didn't realize for what until he cupped her elbow and gently urged her to lean against his broad chest. His arm wrapped around her. Eva only then noticed the way he'd moved both reins to one hand so he could do so.

"Riding with bruised ribs is torture. I know. But if my hold doesn't frighten you, it may lessen the impact."

Eva nodded. It was better—on her ribs. And a million times worse on her heart as she sat cradled against Darrek the same way she'd held Arthur so many times as she shared stories with him under the stars. But though the hold was the same, the feelings it stirred were entirely different.

With Arthur, her heart swelled, filled to overflowing with a love that couldn't be contained, tinged with grief she could never quite find words for. It was peace, and hope, and love, and rightness, and regret, and fear all tucked into the body of her son curled against her stomach almost as if he wanted to find his way back inside it.

Here, with Darrek, she was the one being held. She was the one being comforted. Protected in the embrace of his arms. His heart racing against her shoulder. His breath mingling with hers, making her want—

What was it she wanted? Not Darrek, surely. There was no chance he'd ever look at her in any way other than as the wayward daughter of his king. She'd given up hope of marrying a respectable man the day Cavendish threw her aside. She'd thought the two of them had a future, but in one heartbreaking moment, that had been dashed. Cavendish hadn't wanted her, and because of him, no one else would now either.

Especially not an honorable knight like Sir Darrek.

Care. That was what she wanted. To be cared for, cherished, protected. To be loved.

She'd thought Lord Cavendish loved her. How foolish she'd been to think so. He hadn't loved her. She doubted he'd ever loved anyone but himself.

"Better?"

"Yes." Sir Darrek was protecting her, that was all. Protecting her just like he'd vowed to. "Thank you."

Love was for fools. Or saints like her parents. Not for mistakes like her. Sir Darrek Drew had a job to do—to protect her and bring her home. Everything he did was simply that. No more. No less.

"Lord Cavendish knows who you are, doesn't he?" Darrek's voice rumbled along the arm pressed up against him.

Eva sighed. "Yes."

"And his guards? The other servants? His knights?"

"Some of them."

"George?" Darrek asked quietly, nodding toward the man three horse lengths in front of them.

Eva considered the stablemaster for a few moments.

"I don't know. He's always been kind to me and shown me respect, but he's like that with everyone. I don't believe he'd treat me any differently if he knew my parentage."

"He's a good man."

"Aye."

They rode in silence for some time after that, only the hushing of the trees and the sounds of the horses' steps breaking it. Evangeline shook with the strength it took to hold herself upright, even with Darrek's support.

"Almost there."

Darrek was a good man too. Strong enough to trust, if she dared.

Which she wouldn't.

She'd trusted the wrong man once before. It had gotten her a broken rib, aching shoulder, and a scalp so tender she'd not been able to brush her hair for more than a week without clenching her teeth from the pain.

The horse stopped. Caught in her mind, Eva hadn't even noticed the time passing. Darrek slid to the ground behind her. Eva bit back a cry of pain as he reached up to help her down.

"Forgive me, my lady," Darrek said. "There was no other way."

Her pain seemed to hurt him even more than it did her. She looked at his hands, still at her waist. Blood smeared across the right one. She picked it up.

"Darrek, you're bleeding!" She wiped it with her apron, promising herself she'd find water to properly clean and bandage the cuts as soon as possible. "Who did this to you? How could they?"

"I did it."

Her hands stilled. "What?" He'd done it? To himself?

"I punched a wall."

"By...accident?"

"No. I was angry. It was the wall or Cavendish's head."

"Why?"

"He hurt you."

Her mind was too full of emotion to think a single thought. She let go of his hand, watching as it fell to his side. Darrek had done this for her.

"I'd fight them all if I thought it would get you home."

His words were quiet yet full of intensity.

He'd done this for her. He'd fight for her. Bleed for her. He'd said as much, but here was proof. The knowledge was too much. She looked into Darrek's eyes. His gaze was soft, gentle, yet as certain as his claim had been. And something else, something... more. Something she hadn't seen in a long time. Something that beckoned her in and promised hope. Promised acceptance. Protection. Love. Without meaning to, she swayed toward it. Toward him. Those eyes. That mouth...

"Lady Evangel—"

"Spices." Tearing her gaze from his, Eva stepped backward, out of Darrek's reach, away from whatever it was that made her ache to move closer. "Maeve needs spices."

Darrek closed his mouth, a single blink shuttering whatever had been in his gaze. When she looked again, in time to see his nod and offered arm, nothing was there except calmness. "Spices we shall find. This way, my lady."

She ignored his arm. She was no lady. Not anymore.

•◦⬥◦•

The ride to Cavendish Castle was as tortuous as the ride from it had been. Evangeline trembled where she leaned up against him. Darrek didn't know whether it was out of fear, pain, discomfort, or something else entirely. Neither did he know how to help her. She'd told him Maeve needed spices and hadn't said a single word since. Not to him, George, Garrett, or any of the vendors they visited. She simply pointed to the things she wanted, passed over the coins, and nodded her thanks before moving on to the next person. While Darrek didn't mind the silence, the thought that he'd done something to offend or hurt her further left him uneasy.

Especially after the way she'd leaned toward him, the expression on her face so lost and confused he'd wanted to sweep her back into his arms then and there and promise everything was going to be fine. Maybe he should have. Except she was skittish enough already.

Spices. Maeve needed spices.

He'd almost laughed at her abrupt change in topic and the way she'd so purposely put distance between the two of them. Was she afraid of him? Or herself? Because he wouldn't have been the one to pull away. Not when every part of him ached to hold her.

Like he was doing now, only differently. Less horse involved. And far less fear. Not that he wasn't enjoying this. If anything, the opposite proved to be true.

Evangeline shifted in front of him.

It was easier to ride with his arms on either side of her. It kept her secure atop the horse, rattled her ribs less, and kept them both warm. But he was enjoying it far more than he should have. The poor woman was injured, terrified, and here against her will, yet all he could think was how he never wanted the ride to end. Her hair smelled of lavender, and her neck begged for a kiss. And her form between his arms? Perfection. Guilt warred with desire in a battle for which there could be no winner.

The path to Raedonleith loomed. It would be so easy to take Evangeline and run. George wouldn't stop them. He could fight Garrett if need be. They'd have to return for Arthur, but at least Evangeline would be free. From her captor, at least.

She shifted again.

"Easy now, love, you're safe. I'll not let anyone hurt you again." The endearment came as easily as the words of comfort. They were the same ones he told her every night. She calmed like she did then.

The road forked with Raedonleith to the left and Cavendish Castle to the right. Darrek followed George and Garrett down the right path. Evangeline would never leave without Arthur.

"What about you?" she asked after some time.

"Me?"

"Will you hurt me?"

Darrek bristled at the question, hurt she'd even ask. "Never."

He missed her whispered answer when George stopped. It didn't take more than an instant for Darrek to understand why and halt his own horse.

They weren't alone.

Riders were approaching.

Less than a minute later, ten riders crested the hill. Cavendish's guards.

"Stay back," George ordered. "But don't run."

Eva clenched her teeth in an attempt to hold herself together. Her jaw hurt with the effort but at least she looked calm to the guards surrounding them. Darrek was eerily still behind her. Wary? On guard? Or terrified. None of them boded well. Ten guards. Was this one of Cavendish's normal patrols? Or something more?

"We received word that Raedonleith's knights have been seen back on Cavendish land. You haven't seen them in your travels, have you, stablemaster?"

George shook his head. "No, sir. We encountered none but a few peasants."

"You would report them, if you did."

"Of course."

The man narrowed his eyes, his gaze moving past George and Garret to lock on the man sitting behind Eva. With a flick of the leader's head, the circle of knights closed in.

"And this man?"

Eva gasped. Darrek's hand tightened across her middle—to calm her? Or out of fear? George merely shrugged. "A stable boy. Too simple-minded to get work elsewhere but good enough at shoveling manure. Lord Cavendish ordered me to accompany the maid here to purchase supplies. I brought him to assist. She doesn't ride horses often, and I didn't fancy having her topple off and injure herself."

"Bit big to be a mere stable hand, don't you think?"

"Shoveling manure day after day will do that to a person."

"As will sword play. He has the look of a knight."

"And yet, as you can see, he has no sword nor knife on his person. I have known and served many knights in my life, and not one of them was ever without the protection of a weapon or two."

The tip of a sword was against Darrek's neck before Eva had the chance to gasp. A scream ripped from her mouth as she was pulled roughly off the horse and thrown aside. Darkness pulsed her vision as pain radiated from what felt like every muscle in her body. Darrek fell to the ground beside her, immediately surrounded by four knights, swords drawn.

"No—"

"Quiet, wench," one of them said as they kicked her out of the way. Eva clutched arms around her middle and tried as hard as she could to keep quiet, a near impossible task with everything going on around her.

Two of the men held Darrek's arms while another pulled the shirt over his head, exposing a back lined with muscles and scars. She closed her eyes against the horror when another began to beat him, the sound of fist meeting flesh more than she could take. Would he die, here and now? While she stood witness?

No, not stood. Cowered. Whimpered.

Eva opened her eyes, determined to at least give him the respect of that. He didn't fight back, didn't even say a word as the men continued to strike at him. A trickle of blood ran from his lip down his chin. His cheek was already swollen.

Movement at the edge of the trees caught Eva's attention. There one instant and gone the next, Eva wondered if she imagined it. More guards? Come to finish what these had started?

A whistle came—almost birdlike—and Darrek finally reacted, his gaze going to the direction the noise had come from. One shake of his head and he let it drop again.

"Enough," George said, walking his horse forward. "You've proven he is unarmed. Stop before you kill him. Lord Cavendish approved this man's presence with me here today. Unless you plan on explaining to him why you've detained us, I suggest you allow us and the supplies we carry to return to the castle."

"Perhaps he's merely disguised as a peasant," the leader countered.

"And perhaps I'm the lord of the manor," George replied, clearly running short on patience. "I appreciate your concern, Sir Robert, and wish you success on your mission to find the knights you seek, but this man is not one of them. My man, if you please."

Sir Robert waited an endless moment more before calling off his knights with a jerk of his head. Eva didn't dare move until all ten of them were back on their mounts, in formation, and at least half a mile down the road. Darrek, having already risen and reclothed himself, held out a hand to help her up. She jerked her head around at a noise behind her.

Sir Manning. It was him. And the other knights. Darrek hadn't been trying to appease her when he said they'd returned. With barely a nod in Darrek's direction, Sir Manning went to talk to the stablemaster. Eva watched in fascination as the two men clasped hands with a respect far beyond what she'd expected, given George had stood there while Darrek was beaten. The three other knights—whose names she'd already forgotten but faces she never could—missed the exchange, too busy grinning at their comrade.

"About time you took a beating," the tallest of them teased. "Fair's fair. We took our share."

Darrek shook his head, his attention still focused on Eva. He winced when she took his hand but helped her to her feet. Her ribs protested the sudden movement, and she almost crumbled back to the ground. Would have, if not for Darrek's hold on her arms.

"All right?" he asked after a moment. She nodded. Only then did he glance at the other knights. "Make yourself useful and help her onto the horse, won't you? Gently. She's taken a beating too."

Darrek mounted the horse again with far more agility than Eva would have thought possible after seeing the beating he received.

"Ready?"

Her attention captured by the man who now sat proudly atop the big horse and effortlessly looked the part of every maid's dream of a dashing knight, Eva started to see one of the other knights kneeling at her feet.

"Steady now," the knight said, as if she were the restless horse. "Use my knee as a mount. Darrek will help you from there."

Though getting back on the monstrosity of a horse was the last thing Eva wanted to do, breathing hurt too much for her to even consider walking the rest of the way, and she'd die before she allowed one of these men to carry her. She looked up at Darrek. He smiled. The burst of confidence that smile gave her was—

Something she would consider later. When there weren't men around who'd read far too much into her blushing cheeks. Before she could reconsider, she stood on the man's knee and allowed Darrek to lift her the rest of the way onto the horse. Blackness swirled her vision again. Her ribs felt like someone was reaching into her chest and wrenching them out one by one. Strong hands pulled her in against an even stronger chest. Pain mixed with peace as Eva let herself fall.

She'd passed out in his arms. The realization brought with it a wave of relief. Darrek had known getting Evangeline back on the horse would make the pain worse, but there hadn't been another option. At least, passed out as she was, the ride back to Cavendish Castle would be easier. Little mercy as it was.

The beating the men had given him hadn't even come close to

breaking him, but the terror and pain on Evangeline's face almost had.

George brought his horse up beside Darrek's. "Forgive me," he said. "There was no other way."

Darrek nodded. "You protected the maid. That's all that matters."

"She's more than a servant, isn't she."

Evangeline's face was flushed where she lay heavily against his chest, her cheeks soft like flower petals. Her hair smelled like them too, despite all she'd been through in the past hour. He'd never felt more burdened with a person's care than he did in that moment as he stared down at her. Evangeline's life was, quite literally, in his hands.

"Aye, she is."

"And she is?"

Beautiful. Broken. Precious. Lost. A treasure he would take many more beatings to protect. The courageous woman he'd found while searching for a helpless girl.

George waited. Darrek turned his attention to Manning, who nodded once, before slipping along with the others back into the forest. It was just the four of them on the dusty road now—him, the guard, the stablemaster and—

"Lady Evangeline. The daughter of the king."

CHAPTER
16

Eva lay on her bed. Body aching with weariness, she should have fallen asleep within seconds. Instead, she stared into the darkness, her mind too conflicted to rest. Most nights, regret or fear kept her awake. Tonight, it was simply one man.

Sir Darrek. The man she kept trying to banish from her thoughts only to have him keep pushing his way back in. Heat rushed into Eva's cheeks along with the memory of Darrek's arms around her on the horse. Of their almost kiss and the way the world around her had ceased to exist when he whispered her name.

Darrek had fought for her today, even without drawing a sword. Allowed himself to be beaten and demeaned, that he might stay free to watch over her. Even when doing so meant shoveling manure day after day. What possessed a knight to lay down his sword in favor of a shovel?

None of the other knights had done so. They'd fought, been beaten and banished, and returned—as she'd seen proof of today—all on her behalf, but none of them put themselves through the menial labor every day that Sir Darrek did. Her silent protectors, ready the moment she gave the order to leave but not coming any closer until then.

But Sir Darrek, he'd left his sword behind. Left his armor, left his pride. For what? Her? Surely not. Everyone, Darrek included, knew she was a lowly servant. She might have been a princess once, but she'd thrown that title and everything that came with it away the day she walked out of her father's palace, jewels in tow.

So why did he stay? And, more aggravating than any of that, why did she care?

It wasn't love nor a deep affection of any kind, but Eva couldn't deny any longer that she was drawn to her father's knight. Her reaction to him on their ride today merely proved what she'd tried so hard to ignore. Against her stubborn will, he rose higher in her estimation every day. She respected his opinion. Trusted his judgment. It had been years since she'd allowed anyone that respect, let alone a man, but here she was wondering about him when she should have been sleeping.

Was he being well treated in the stables? Did he have a blanket to cover him these cold nights? Was he getting enough food? Had he or someone else seen to his injuries? Did he need bandages? A cold cloth for the bruises?

Eva rolled onto her side, curling up her legs as she tucked both hands under her chin. She had to sleep. Morning came too soon on the nights when she did get rest.

But no matter which way she turned, sleep wouldn't find her. Finally accepting it was not to be, she rolled her blanket into a ball, clutched it against her chest, and crept outside.

Darrek woke at the sound of footsteps in the stable. He rarely slept deeply at the best of times and even less so since finding Evangeline. A hand clasped the sword beside him as he rose on his haunches and leaned into the shadows. The person's steps were light, but until he knew who it was, he'd best be on his guard.

The copper hair was his first clue and all he needed to step back into the half-moon's dim light. His breath caught somewhere between fear and awe. She was beautiful, which was all the more reason she shouldn't be traipsing about the grounds alone so late at night. He'd lowered his guard, thinking her safe inside that locked cottage.

"Evangeline, how are you here? And what are you doing here? You should be sleeping."

She took one tentative step toward him but came no farther.

She held something bundled under one arm. A coat? A gown? A blanket?

"I climbed through the window. I wanted to see the horses."

For a second, Darrek let his mind be amused by the fact that Cavendish's guards locked the door each night, when he—and Evangeline herself—could escape so easily through the window.

"You hate horses."

"Do not."

"You walk, even when a mount is available. Your voice trembles talking about them. And, when forced to ride one, you alternate between breathing so fast it's a wonder you don't pass out from the effort and holding your breath so long you actually do."

Evangeline didn't bother gracing him with an answer. They both knew he was right even if she was too stubborn to admit it. There was a good reason her father rarely let her ride alone.

"Did someone hurt you?" His sword rose before he'd realized what he was doing.

"No." She eyed his sword. He put it behind him, covering it with straw. She seemed to breathe a little easier with it out of sight despite the way she still clutched the doorway like it would protect her from the world.

"Then you came to see me?" He couldn't believe it of her, but there was no other reason he could think of why she'd be here in the middle of the night.

"Of course not."

He nodded. Waited. Watched her fiddle with a loose thread at the edge of the fabric she was holding. She seemed more uncertain than anxious, which tugged at Darrek's heart in a way it had no right to. He hated seeing her like this.

"I wasn't sure whether you had a blanket," she finally said, shoving the fabric into his arms. He caught it before it fell, warmed by not only the gesture—uncertainly as it was offered—but also by the blanket itself. She must have been holding it for some time for it to have absorbed so much of her body's warmth on a cool night like tonight.

He thought she'd flee then. She didn't. He considered returning the blanket so she'd have something to do with her fluttering hands.

"You know, I've been told I'm a good listener," he told her.

She blinked like a new foal. "That's…nice."

"If there's anything you wanted to talk about."

"What makes you think I want to talk?"

"You hate horses, yet you're standing in a stable in the middle of the night. I'd say that's a cry for help."

She frowned. "I don't need help."

"No. You're strong, independent, wise…and completely alone."

"Not completely."

Even in the dim light, Darrek could see the way Evangeline pursed her lips together, as if she wished she could take back those two words. She looked around the stable, taking in every part of it and, if the continued uncertainty on her face was anything to go by, none of it. She might have moved her gaze around in an effort to look at ease, but her thoughts were a long way from leather and straw.

"I have Maeve and—"

Darrek waited while Evangeline swallowed. "Arthur," he said quietly when she didn't continue.

"Yes, Arthur. My son."

"And Cavendish's."

"Yes."

Her admission was followed by a silence so loud it throbbed inside Darrek's head. Her son. Cavendish's son. Though he'd known it for two weeks now, it was still so hard to believe.

"I'm surprised Lord Cavendish hasn't named Arthur as his heir."

"To be his heir, Cavendish would have to claim me first as his wife, and he'd never do that."

"Why not?"

"He doesn't want me."

"Would you want him?"

Evangeline was silent long enough that Darrek wished he'd

not asked. Cavendish and this beautiful, fragile woman? It went against everything Darrek believed. Cavendish would crush her—and likely already had if her nightmares indicated her history with him.

In lieu of the words he couldn't find to speak, he walked toward her, telling himself to ignore the way she shied away from him when he wrapped the blanket around her shoulders. She'd been hurt. But it wasn't by him. Her fear wasn't of him. The fact that she'd come here tonight spoke volumes of how much she trusted him, even if she didn't want to admit it.

With as much of a smile as he could manage, Darrek sat on the straw, reclining against the rough wood of the stable wall. He patted a space a foot away, on the other side of the doorway, holding his breath as he realized how much he was hoping she'd stay.

He let it out in a gush when Evangeline sat. Legs bent to her chest, arms wrapped around them, she looked like she'd run a mile if he so much as breathed in her direction. But she stayed. It was more than he could have hoped for.

Darrek picked up several pieces of straw and began mindlessly twisting them together into a flimsy rope. The number of questions he had for Evangeline could have kept her talking until dawn, but something in him cautioned him to wait and give her the gift of silence. He'd twisted together almost a foot of rope before she began to speak.

"I didn't come here straight from home. I wandered some towns first, enjoying their festivals and the freedom that came with being just another girl rather than the daughter of a king. I ate whatever I wanted, danced with as many men as I chose, and slept in the finest of inns. It was bliss—or so I thought.

"When my coins ran out, I paid with jewels instead. People were more than willing to take them, only too happy to give me their finest in exchange. Then, one day, I went to pay for my room, only to find the few jewels I had left gone. Including my crown."

Her voice hitched. It took all the strength Darrek had not to reach out a hand to touch her. Though he'd never seen it, he knew what crown she meant. Everyone in Raedonleith did. One had been made for each of the king's daughters to celebrate their births and be given to them on the day they married. Their birthright, as such, unique to each of them. Their claim to the throne, should it be required. He knew Evangeline had taken many of the royal jewels when she'd fled, but King Lior had never mentioned that her crown had been among them. What would he think if he knew it had been stolen from her?

Darrek gritted his teeth to keep from speaking. He had to let Evangeline tell her story. Even if her words broke them both.

"When the innkeeper found out I had no way to pay for the room, he threw me out, claiming the rest of my gowns and the necklace I was wearing his due. I had nothing else to give him, so allowed it. I thought to stay with some friends I'd made, but they had no time for me either. Without the proper clothing and jewels, I was no better than the beggars on the street.

"Before long, I grew hungry and thought to take an apple from a tree. The man who owned the tree caught me before I could and dragged me to the magistrate. I spent six hours in the stocks. I suppose I should have been thankful he caught me before I could take it, or I may have lost my hand instead.

"I left that town as soon as I was released."

She paused.

"And came here?" Darrek asked gently.

"I was going to come home." Evangeline picked at a piece of straw. "I didn't want to and hated that it was my only option, but I didn't know what else to do. Had I not come across Lord Cavendish that day, I would have been home after only a few months away." She looked over at him, sadness in her eyes. "You could have been too."

"'Tis no matter."

"No, Darrek, it is. And for what it's worth, I'm sorry."

This time, Darrek did reach out his hand. Though he wanted to hold hers, he contented himself with a simple brush of his fingers against her arm. Wishing he could erase the pain in her voice. The pain she'd caused herself yet so clearly regretted. "It's been an honor to serve my king in this way. The only greater honor would be to sacrifice my life for his. I must say, I prefer this option."

She didn't laugh, which saddened him, because Darrek remembered well what a beautiful laugh Evangeline had. It had been so long since he'd heard it.

"Cavendish rescued you only to make you his servant?"

Evangeline started, obviously having been caught up in the memories. Darrek watched as she blinked a few times before shaking her head.

"No, not then at least. He complimented me first and asked where I was going. When I said I was on my way to Raedonleith, he offered his manor as a place to stop for the night. Tired and hungry after having walked so far and not looking forward to another night under the stars with the bugs and dirt, I accepted."

"But you didn't stay for a night."

"No."

Somewhere in the distance an owl hooted, its call breaking the silence left in the wake of Evangeline's simple admission. As much as Darrek wanted to press for details, he didn't, forcing himself to wait. She'd talk when she was ready, even if it wasn't tonight. She'd already shared far more than he'd expected of her. He could be patient. He'd certainly learned how to be during the past four years.

"Lord Cavendish offered me kindness when everyone else had offered only scorn. When you have nothing, anything—even the tiniest courtesy—seems grand. When he heard my crown had been stolen, he even sent men to search for it and bring it back."

"It was found?"

"Yes. Cavendish has it—or so he claims."

"You've not seen it?"

"He keeps it locked away, as I should have."

For safety, no doubt Cavendish had told her. Darrek knew better. That crown—and the woman it belonged to—gave Cavendish a part claim to the throne of Raedonleith. Marry Evangeline, and he'd well be able to challenge Lior for the crown and power Cavendish had always wanted. So, why hadn't he? Why was Evangeline a servant in his household rather than the queen of it?

Surely he didn't believe the lies that she was cursed. Was he simply biding his time? Waiting for the right moment to take what he felt was owed to him?

"I was surprised," Evangeline continued, oblivious to Darrek's confusion. "I'd been told all my life to be wary of Lord Cavendish. That he and those loyal to him weren't to be trusted. Yet, that day, Lord Cavendish helped me onto his own horse, gave me a place to rest, as much food as I could eat, and clean clothing to wear.

"I'll admit, part of me thought going with him would spite Papa—because I knew how much Papa despised the man—but, mostly, I was just a tired, hungry, lonely girl who took the first kind hand offered her. The fact that it was a Cavendish one meant far less than that it was a hand at all.

"And he truly was kind. For three months, I thought myself the luckiest girl in the world. Cavendish can be quite charming when he wants to be. He called me all manner of beautiful names, clothed me in gorgeous gowns, and turned my head with compliments. His musicians wrote songs about my beauty and sang them while we feasted each night."

"He knew who you were."

"Aye. Though he told few. He simply presented me as his lady. I wonder now if that was to keep word from reaching my father about where I stayed, but at the time, I thought it just another charming thing Cavendish did. To claim me as such.

"It didn't take more than a week of being here to think myself wholly in love with him. When he asked me to be his, I agreed without even a second thought."

Darrek dropped the straw rope.

"His wife? You're married? I thought—"

"No. There were never any words or commitments like that spoken between us. Not even a handfasting ceremony. Small mercies, I suppose."

Very small. "Yes."

"I knew he had other women, but he told me I was the one he loved. He lavished jewels and banquets on me, gave me the best of the food each night from his plate, shared his cup with me."

"But—" Darrek didn't know how to ask the question at the forefront of his mind.

"But I'm a servant."

Darrek nodded. Not only a servant but the lowest of the low. Cast aside. Looked down on by all but Maeve and George. Her clothes were one step up from rags, and the coarse blanket she held was the only one she owned. He knew. He'd seen her cottage. She might have been the lord's love once, but it was clear that was no longer the case.

"What happened?"

He asked the question quietly, knowing he had no right to ask but wondering if the answer would be too personal for her to share.

"I found out I was expecting."

Arthur. Of course. A child would change everything.

"He didn't want the boy?"

"He didn't want me." She leaned back her head, looking up as if she saw right through the ceiling to the stars beyond. This time, Darrek did take her hand, letting his thumb caress the back of it. Though she started, she didn't pull away.

"I thought he'd be happy when I told him. I was wrong. He was furious. His anger is no small thing, as you've seen."

"He hurt you."

"Not intentionally. At least, I don't believe so. He roared like a man who'd lost everything and pushed me aside in his rush to leave. I may have kept my feet if I'd not been unwell from the babe. Instead, I fell. Maeve says I must have hit the edge of his table or chair as I fell. All I remember is waking in Maeve's cottage with a head that ached to move.

"A day later, I came back to the bedchamber Cavendish and I had shared to find everything of mine removed. It was as if we'd never even been together. That night, when I went to the Great Hall for the feast, another woman sat by his side. He'd told his guards not to even allow me into the room.

"Maeve took pity on me and gave me a bed and one of her

gowns. I cleaned my first chamber pot the next day and burnt my first loaf of bread the day after. I've been here ever since."

"You could have come home."

"When, Darrek?" she asked, a tinge of emotion in her voice for the first time this night. "When I was large with child? When the pains of childbirth took over me? When I held in my arms the proof of my infidelity? When the terrors began? Or the rumors that I'm cursed?"

Her father would have taken her back. Darrek knew that without a doubt. Even if she walked in with a child and the worst rumors a servant could conjure drifted among the crowds. King Lior would have taken her in an instant. It was all he'd yearned for since the day she left. But Evangeline didn't know that. Not in her heart.

"So you stayed, all these years."

Evangeline shrugged. "I made my choice four years ago."

"You were a child. You didn't know what you were doing."

"What does it matter? I did it."

"You matter."

"Not anymore."

"Evangeline—"

"Please, Darrek. The choice was made. Whether it was the right one or not doesn't matter, nor whether I'd make the same choice again. This is who I am and where I am today. If you can't accept that, then—"

"I do." He didn't like it, but he accepted it. Everyone's journey started somewhere. If this was hers, then so be it. He just wished he could convince her that this wasn't its ending too.

"You do?"

"Aye. But do you?"

"I—" Slowly, as if she weren't sure whether she wanted to or not, Evangeline pulled her hand from his and tucked it beneath the blanket. She nodded, shook her head, and dropped it. "I should go."

Standing, Darrek offered a hand to help her to her feet, ignoring the scars shining across her arm when her sleeve fell back upon taking it. So many questions. So many more things he wanted to know. She hadn't even mentioned the scars.

"Evangeline—"

She looked at him, enough wariness in her gaze to hold his tongue. It was late. She was worn out. And she'd already shared far more than he knew what to do with. *Patience, Darrek. She'll run if you rush her.*

"Thank you for telling me your story."

CHAPTER
17

It was strange to miss the presence of a boy who didn't talk. With the exception of those few times a day when Eva left Arthur with Maeve to go wash or see to personal needs, he was always there. Behind her. Beside her. Her silent shadow.

A shadow she hadn't seen for nigh on fourteen days. It was as if a part of her heart was locked away in that room along with her son. Living was difficult without it. She would have offered every one of her ribs to Cavendish to break if doing so meant she could have kept her son. Not even telling Darrek her story—something she'd regretted from the moment she walked out of the stable—had been able to distract her from the fact that Arthur wasn't in the room when she returned. Nor that he was in the room that had once been hers. The room she'd been in when she first realized she held a child within her.

Eva blinked back emotion she couldn't afford as Maeve placed an apple beside the small loaf of bread on the tray of food she was preparing for Arthur. She'd cut the fruit into slices so thin they were almost transparent, and then she'd put it all back together as if it had never been cut. Arthur's favorite.

"Maeve, tell him—"

The words stuck in Eva's throat.

Maeve patted her hand. "He knows. But I'll tell him you love him all the same."

Eva nodded and clasped her hands together. Behave, Cavendish had said, or he'd take Arthur for good. It was that threat alone that stopped Eva from grabbing the tray and key from Maeve's hand and rushing to her boy's side to smother him with all the love she had to give.

He knows.

Eva sighed as she placed loaves of bread on a tray to take into the Great Hall for dinner. Did he, though? Did he really know she loved him? Would saying the words ever be enough when all she could give him was heartache?

Arthur didn't talk. Hadn't made a noise since the day Lord Cavendish hit him in the throat and knocked him over not long after Arthur's first birthday. The fall broke the tiny boy's arm. Cavendish had been shouting at Eva at the time. Eva hadn't stayed long enough to know if it had been an accident or not. Cavendish had ordered she and Arthur go to the healer and never mentioned it again. The arm had healed, but the boy hadn't spoken since. Eva didn't know whether that was because he couldn't or because he was afraid to.

Much as she hated the thought, she hoped it was the latter. Fear, he might one day overcome. But what future could there be for the mute, illegitimate son of a servant girl? He'd be naught but a pawn in Cavendish's hand. Not a son—never a son—but a bargaining tool. At least if Arthur learned to speak, he might one day escape this place and his past—her past—to start again. New town. New name. New history. It had been done before and no doubt would again, many times over. But if he remained mute?

Almighty, if you care, save my son.

She wouldn't ask for herself. She'd willfully defied the Almighty too many times during the past four years to ever lay claim to his favor for herself, but for her son, she'd ask. Beg. Beseech until she was mute herself. The boy was innocent of her faults. Even if, daily, he paid for every single one of them.

It wasn't long—yet still, somehow, felt like an eternity—before Maeve returned with an empty tray. Fighting too many emotions to talk, Eva beseeched Maeve with her gaze. She'd know what it was Eva wanted to know. It was the same thing she asked morning, noon, and night when Maeve came back from Arthur's room with an empty tray. *How is he?*

Maeve placed a gentle hand on Eva's wrist. "He's well. He's been practicing the game Lord Cavendish gave him. He's getting quite good at it."

"A...game?"

"Didn't I tell you? Lord Cavendish gave Arthur several toys and games to play with. He's been working hard to master the games. I wonder if several of the guards have been helping him with the more difficult ones—or even Lord Cavendish himself."

"Lord Cavendish? But—" Eva shook her head. "He wouldn't do that."

"Cormac Cavendish has more heart than he shows."

"I doubt that."

"I've known him since he was a child, Eva. He's let bitterness get the best of him and made more bad choices than I could count, but don't doubt that he has a heart beneath the pain. I can only pray one day he'll open it again. Perhaps Arthur will be the change."

"No." Arthur was everything good in her life. And Lord Cormac Cavendish all but the root of everything bad. "I won't allow it. All Cavendish does is destroy, and I won't let him take my son."

Eva flung out her arm in frustration. The loaves she'd been piling on the platter scattered across the table, several falling on the floor. She groaned. All that work. For nothing. Cook would be furious. Eva already was. Could this day get any worse? All she'd had to do was take those loaves into the Great Hall before she would have finally been finished for the day. Now, she'd be spending the night doing whatever penance Cook doled out.

"Go," Maeve said before Eva could pick up a single loaf. "There are enough. I'll take them. Wash at the river, listen to the minstrels, look at the stars. Rest, if you can. Arthur will be back at your side soon enough."

The loaves mocked her from their place on the flea-ridden floor. *Failure*, they cried. Eva balled her hand into a fist and stalked outside. She couldn't do anything right.

No. The darkness wouldn't get the better of her this time. She'd fight it. She'd conquer it. She wouldn't give in. She was stronger than the emotions.

Ten minutes later, she lay sobbing in the bottom of the hollowed-out tree—a new bandage on her arm and a new tear in her heart.

Even Cavendish was a better parent to Arthur than she was. He gave Arthur games. All Eva had to give was brokenness.

The sound of a woman crying stopped Darrek, his senses on high alert. He'd waited until he could speak with Manning alone to tell the man Evangeline's story. Mindful of her trust in him, he'd only shared what the other knights needed to know—Evangeline and Cavendish had been together for a time but weren't married, she'd confirmed that Cavendish was the boy's father, all her money and jewels were long gone, and Cavendish had her crown. Manning had nodded, whittled, and nodded some more, far less affected by the facts than Darrek had been. He'd told Darrek to continue as he had been, protecting Evangeline. He'd send an update to King Lior, something Darrek didn't envy in the least. If Darrek felt Evangeline's pain so deeply, how would her own father feel?

Spencer had returned while he and Manning were speaking and challenged Darrek to a foot race. Darrek had accepted, relieved to be able to take out his irritation on something tangible, even if it were only the forest floor his feet pounded. He'd lost the race, something Spencer would no doubt be crowing about for weeks—if not forever—but it had helped.

He'd walked away slightly out of breath but smiling.

Until he heard the sobs.

"Hello?" he called into the trees, searching for any sign of a person. Few came this far into the forest, which was why the knights had made camp here. No one called back, though the cries grew more muffled.

There. Two feet to his left. A flower trod into the dirt. A half a footprint several paces on. Too small to be a man's, not that the crying sounded masculine, but at least the woman hadn't been carried here.

"Let me help you," he called again. "Please. I'm not here to hurt you."

He walked slowly through the trees, following his instincts as much as his sight and hearing. Whoever it was hadn't been trying to cover their tracks, nor hide them at all. A distinct handprint in a muddier part of the ground showed the woman had fallen at least once as she stumbled through the trees.

"Miss?"

A scrap of white caught his attention through the leaves. A few more steps and—

"Evangeline?"

She was huddled against a large tree, mud smudged across her face where she'd tried to wipe tears with a dirt-covered hand. She pulled down her sleeve but not before he glimpsed a new bandage on her wrist.

Evangeline. No...

Almighty—

Words failed Darrek before he could finish the prayer. He'd thought listening to Evangeline scream through nightmares was heart-wrenching. But this? Seeing her so broken, so crushed, when she was awake and alert? She had no control over the nightmares.

"I—fell."

He nodded, as if either of them believed her blatant lie. If it helped her to think he believed it, so be it.

For now.

"I'll walk you back."

His words were flat, the anger and helplessness he felt too big to allow for anything more.

CHAPTER
18

avendish enjoyed his feasts. On most nights he was home, the hall rang for hours with the sound of them. Tonight was no different.

"You don't attend?"

Though Eva started at the sound, she was unsurprised to see that Darrek had joined her. He'd walked her back to the castle, as promised. He'd left her at Maeve's side and, though he hadn't said a word about where or how he'd found her, somehow it seemed as if Maeve had known anyway. She'd given Eva enough tasks to fill her hands and mind, and almost smothered her with care. Eva had only escaped when the feast begun, and Maeve had been required to serve.

As usual, Eva hadn't been invited.

"One of the privileges of being despised by the lord of the castle. It 'embarrasses' him to see me. I haven't attended a feast since before Arthur was born."

"But you wish to."

Was it so obvious? Eva sighed. "Sometimes."

Darrek sat on the other end of her bench—close enough to talk comfortably but far enough away not to make her feel crowded. Did he do it purposely? She suspected he did.

"And so you sit out here?" he asked her.

"I like the music."

The minstrels were playing tonight. Cavendish had a circus of entertainment at his beck and call—acrobats, jugglers, jesters, and even a bard, but the minstrels were her favorite. Though the acrobats made her gasp and the jesters made her smile, the music of the minstrels soothed her soul. Shared emotion—albeit the sadness of heartbreak, the captivation of a ballad, or the depth of a hymn—drew her in and made her feel as if she wasn't alone.

"I used to attend the feast every night. Right beside Lord Cavendish himself at the head table. It's difficult to believe that I was once proud of that position."

"You were in love."

Eva leaned her head back against the rough brick of the wall behind her and considered Darrek's comment. Was it love she'd felt for Lord Cavendish? She'd thought so once. Would have claimed it adamantly to any and all who asked. But looking back—

"I don't know if it was ever love. Infatuation, perhaps, but to be honest, I think it was more that he'd noticed me that turned my head more than anything I felt for him. It's a heady thing to be wanted."

"You are wanted."

Eva smiled sadly. "If only that were true."

"Evangeline—"

She shook her head. "Please, Sir Darrek. Don't tell me again of my father's love. It hurts too much to hope right now."

"But it's true. He loves you more than you could ever know."

"Then why hasn't he come for me?"

The question was out before she could think better of letting it. Frustration brought tears to Eva's eyes. She'd tried so hard to push the question aside, but ever since the day she left, she'd wondered. It was like a burning ache in her heart that no salve could soothe. She hated that it hurt so much. Hated that it bothered her at all. She'd been the one to leave. She'd told him she never wanted to see him again, that she wished he was dead. Why should he have come?

Yet, still, why hadn't he?

"He sent us," Darrek answered.

Eva wished it were enough. "Aye, he did," she said quietly. "But he didn't come himself, did he?"

He'd said he loved her and always would. But the last words they'd shared had been shouted loud enough for half the castle to hear. The words in the letter she'd left him were merely a record of what she'd already told him to his face.

I hate you. You're a terrible father. I wish you were dead.

She'd thought herself so justified in saying such.

He'd turned away a suitor, the third in as many days. "They're not worthy of you," her father had said. Evangeline had accepted it the first time, coyly waving goodbye to the man from behind a pillar when she was supposed to have been in the solar. The second time, she'd pouted for a few hours but given it up when a new gown was delivered. She'd barely known the man anyway.

The third time, it had been Sir Wick, a neighboring knight. He'd been their guest for a week, if one could call the shouting matches between her father and the noble "guest-ly." Evangeline had never bothered to pay attention to what they were shouting about, but she had paid attention at dinnertimes to the handsome man sitting near her father. And he'd paid attention to her too. She'd made certain of it, wearing her brightest jewels and gowns, along with the smile that had left many a young man tongue-tied in her presence. Sir Wick hadn't been tongue-tied. He'd been captivated. He'd told her as much behind the chapel later that night, seconds before he'd kissed her.

She'd still been reeling from the bliss of her first kiss when her father found them and ordered Sir Wick to leave. Wick had asked if she'd come with him. There had been no time to consider his offer before her father roared his displeasure, had ten guards escort the knight out of the palace grounds, and walked her to her chamber.

He'd announced her betrothal to Baron Waddingham that night.

She'd left the next evening, determined to enjoy a few days of freedom at least before her father ordered her home again. The two of them had always had explosive tempers.

He'd never come. By the time Cavendish found her, she'd stopped expecting him to.

"My father is more powerful than Lord Cavendish. He could wield that power and demand my release and that of my son. Perhaps he didn't know where I was before, but I have no doubt he does now. You found me. You came for me. Why didn't he? Why doesn't he now?"

"He's a powerful king, but that didn't come from taking away the free will of his subjects."

"No. Just from ignoring his daughter."

"You'll never feel free if it's not your choice to come. Love is giving you that choice. But it's wrecking him. You have to un—"

She shook her head, swiped the foolish tears from her eyes before they dared to fall. "Don't."

"But, Lady Ev—"

"What is there to understand? He could come, and he doesn't. Anything else is simply an excuse."

"But—"

"I don't want to talk about it. If you must stay, let us talk of something else."

She shouldn't have said anything. He was the one who didn't understand. She'd been foolish to think he would. Darrek was one of her father's knights, sworn of fealty to him no matter what. Of course, he'd defend her father. After all, it wasn't him who faced rejection so often in his nightmares that hope felt like torture.

Eva jumped when Darrek laid a hand on her arm. His touch was gentle but right over the bandage she'd wrapped around her newest cut. She made the mistake of meeting his gaze. There was too much compassion in his expression for the gesture not to have been done purposely.

"Will you tell me about your scars?"

Jerking her arm away, Eva pulled her sleeves over her hands.

"What scars?"

"The ones you're trying to hide."

She looked down at her hands, which she'd tucked deeply in her sleeves, fighting a terror that stole her breath and made her heart race.

Scars. He'd said scars. Plural. He'd seen the bandage this afternoon. She'd known as much from the way he'd looked at her—his face equal parts anger and disappointment. But how had he known there were more? Her stomach swirled with uneasiness as she hunted for an answer for this man who saw far too much. What should she say? What could she say?

With a laugh that was forced—and sounded it—Eva pulled up her right sleeve just enough to show an inch beyond the bandage.

"Oh, these? They're nothing. I was clumsy with a knife when I first started in the kitchens." Even in the darkness, on her most unmarred arm, the scars looked unsightly. Like threads on the back of a tapestry, only etched into her skin. It took every bit of courage Eva had to bare even this small part of her arm to him. What would he say if he knew how far up her arms the scars stretched? If he knew she hadn't been the victim at all but the perpetrator?

"I don't think so."

Darrek didn't believe her, which came as little surprise to Eva. No one was that clumsy. At least, no one *still* allowed in the kitchen. But she wished he'd at least pretended to. On the long list of things she didn't want to discuss with anyone, he'd struck upon the top two.

"They're scars, Sir Darrek. Nothing more, nothing less. They healed a long time ago. Let it go."

Eva pulled the sleeve down, her stomach roiling, heart thudding in her ears as she sat there in silence, waiting to see what Darrek would do. Silently begging him with every heartbeat not to push her further. She'd leave. She'd have to. To talk about her scars tonight, admit what she was certain he'd already guessed, would shatter her. Darrek had picked her up off the ground once today. She didn't have the strength to let him again.

"Do you still like to dance?"

Eva breathed out a gush of air. He'd done it. Changed the subject, just as she'd wished. She was so thankful it took two swallows to clear the lump in her throat enough to speak. "You remember that?"

"How could I forget? I asked you once."

He had? She tried to recall Sir Darrek asking her, but—whether due to the passing of time or the relief coursing through her body—Eva's mind remained blank. "Did I agree?"

"No," he said with a wry smile. "You called me one step up from a peasant and laughed at my assumption that you'd consider me before returning to your sister's side."

Though Darrek smiled as he remembered the moment, Eva couldn't do the same. Had she truly treated him so poorly? If only she'd seen then the man before her now, the man who was ten times more noble than she'd ever be. She wished she could take back those horrible words, but all she could do was apologize. "I'm sorry."

"It was a long time ago."

"Even so, I truly am sorry."

"Perhaps one day, I may ask you again."

"Sir Darrek—"

"Fear not, my lady. I won't ask tonight."

A loud trill of the minstrel's finale breaking through the night stopped Eva from needing to answer. Darrek didn't seem to mind, tilting his head up to stare at the stars just beginning to glitter.

"Unless you wish me to?"

Something in Darrek's voice had Eva turning to face him. No laughter nor confidence laced his tone. He'd always been so certain of himself, even tonight as he talked about her father's affection for her and asked about her scars. He hadn't shied away from either topic. But now—

His gaze met hers. "Lady Evangeline, do you wish to dance?" A muscle jumped in his cheek, right near the edge of his beard. "With me?"

Another song started inside the Great Hall along with the deep thunder of scores of feet walking from table to empty floor. Three claps, a swoosh of skirts, another clap. The dance began.

She should have been angry at Darrek for his questions. Disgruntled, at the least, for the way he'd inserted himself into her life and refused to move. But all she could think about was how much she wanted to touch Darrek's cheek where that muscle had moved. How she wished she could brush away his concern and uncertainty as easily as she brushed a hand through Arthur's hair each morning.

He'd seen her at her worst today, asked questions that crossed the line of personal, reminded her of how self-centered she'd once been. Yet here, instead of running from him, she yearned to draw closer.

Dancing was out of the question. Not because she didn't want to but because she did. The yearning clawed like hunger inside her—to lay her head against his chest and breathe in the steadiness of his heartbeat, to feel his arms so solid around her, to believe that, even for just a moment, she was cherished.

But Darrek hadn't offered any of that. Just a dance.

Just a dance would never be enough.

"Not tonight. But—" Eva bit her lip, wondering already if what she was about to say was a mistake. But she had to give him something. He'd given her so much, and she'd given him so little in return. "Another time?"

Darrek smiled. "I shall look forward to it."

Darrek waited until Evangeline was safely back in her cottage before he escaped to find Manning. The older man sat studying a piece of parchment. No doubt yet another plea from King Lior to bring his daughter home. The familiar clash of wood on wood and the occasional shout of glee gave away the presence of the other three knights and their squire sparring farther in the forest, making the most of the blanket of noise from the feast. Though this affected them all, Darrek was happy to find Manning alone.

"Tell me Cavendish's story," he asked without preamble. "You said he thinks the throne owed him. Why?"

Tucking the letter into his belt, Manning motioned for Darrek to sit on the log beside him. Darrek remained standing, too much tension in him to even pretend to relax. He'd never considered how King Lior's actions—or apparent lack of—might look to Evangeline. That she'd take it as proof he no longer cared.

Darrek knew as well as everyone in Raedonleith about the tension between Lord Cavendish and King Lior. The two powerful men had been enemies as long as Darrek had been alive, but he'd always thought that merely due to Cavendish's desire to be king. Manning had insinuated there was more that morning in the dungeon. Darrek had been willing to wait on an explanation until this moment. Why *hadn't* King Lior come to rescue his daughter?

"Manning?"

"Patience, patience. I'm trying to decide where to start."

"How about the beginning." The words came out far more tersely than Darrek planned. He bit out an apology and began pacing back and forth, slowing when Manning began.

"The two families were friends once. So much so that a marriage was planned between Lord Cavendish's grandmother and King Lior's grandfather. From what I understand, a few weeks before the wedding was to occur, King Felix called it off. He'd fallen in love with another woman."

Darrek stopped. Looked incredulously at Manning. "All this over a woman?"

"Not one woman—*two* women."

"I don't—"

"Do you want to hear this story or not?"

"Yes."

"Then be quiet and listen. Cavendish's grandmother—Alycea, I believe her name was—was upset by Felix's decision but not as much as her father. King Felix had broken their trust and his daughter's heart—something unforgiveable, in his opinion. His daughter should have been royalty. Instead, she was quickly married to a lesser nobleman to save face.

"Grieved but with his mind unchanged, King Felix gave the Cavendish family a great deal of wealth to make up for being the one to break the engagement. The money, and likely the fact that Alycea found love herself with the nobleman, eased the tension between the two families and all was well again. Until it happened again."

Darrek sat then, too surprised by Manning's story to continue pacing.

"Two women?"

"Two women," Manning confirmed. "Alycea *and* Lord Cavendish's sister, Lady Sunny."

"I didn't know Cavendish had a sister."

"A brother too, though few have seen either of them in years."

Darrek stared at Manning, his mind too captivated by these new facts and what they might mean to Evangeline to do anything else. Why had he never questioned the enmity between the two men before? "She too was spurned?"

"Aye. By King Lior.

"Sunny, Cavendish, and Lior were close as children and into their youth. It came as little surprise to anyone that a marriage was agreed upon between Sunny and Lior. However, as you know, they didn't end up marrying. Lior met and quickly fell for Caralynne several weeks before the wedding was to occur and, though upset at the thought of breaking his commitment to Lady Sunny, could not make himself go through with the wedding when his heart was already committed to Caralynne.

"For the second time, the Cavendish family was promised a royal title only to have the promise rescinded. Lord Cavendish was unwilling to forgive the same offense a second time, especially when it concerned his beloved sister. He determined to avenge her honor, and one day claim the crown of Raedonleith for his family. Though he's tried several times and failed, I wonder if this time, he may have the leverage it takes."

"Arthur," Darrek said.

Manning nodded. "Arthur."

Both men froze at the rustle sounding from their left. A rabbit hopped out of a bush and, seeing them, bounded away. Darrek watched it go, in no rush to stop it. He might have to shovel manure every day, but George—by way of the castle kitchens—fed him well in the stables. With fresh bread and cheese and the occasional venison on his plate, he didn't miss the monotony of stale bread and rabbit meat. Although he probably should have made an effort for the other knights. He pushed aside the thought. Manning hadn't moved either.

"What happened to Lady Sunny? And their brother?" he asked.

"The brother is quite a few years younger than Sunny and Cavendish. Closer to your age than that of his siblings. He fostered with a family in the far north when he was a child and has traveled widely since. Lady Sunny fled Raedonleith after the engagement was broken. She, like her grandmother, married quickly to avoid gossip. She's rarely been seen at Cavendish Castle in the years since."

"She's happy?"

"Content, at least."

Darrek waved aside a bug buzzing near his ear. A fire would have been nice and kept the bugs away, but they couldn't risk both fire *and* training the same night. One was risky enough, even with a feast going on. Although the noise of wooden swords clashing had now stopped. Darrek heard Spencer laugh and wondered if that meant he'd won. It was rare, but not unheard of, for Spencer to beat either of the other two.

"King Lior regrets his decision?" Darrek asked, determined, for Evangeline's sake, to understand the men's enmity. One was her father. The other, the father of her child. It was little wonder she felt her allegiance so torn between the two.

"Not the decision itself but certainly the effect it had on the two families."

"They truly were once friends?"

"Aye. Which is likely why the feud has continued so long. It is far easier to forgive a stranger than the betrayal of a friend."

An all too familiar scream broke through the night. Darrek ran a hand across his eyes as the cry seared across his heart. Evangeline must have fallen asleep quickly tonight. The nightmares didn't usually come for another couple of hours. He pushed himself to his feet.

"Darrek, be careful."

He nodded and let the sound of Evangeline's screams lead him back through the forest to her side.

"There now, lass," he began, the words becoming as familiar as her screams. "You're safe. No one's going to hurt you tonight."

He gripped her hand, willing peace into her. Into himself too. Because, as much as he preferred being here with her than listening from afar, he'd choose a siege over nightmares every time.

He'd be getting no sleep tonight.

CHAPTER 19

Someone was touching her arm. Eva froze, nightmare banished as she became alert. It wasn't Arthur. He would have climbed in beside her. Cavendish would have done the same, though for a far different and more sickening reason. Maeve knew better than to touch her while she thrashed about. She'd ended up with a black eye once for her trouble.

Had she imagined it?

Eva moved her arm the tiniest bit, swallowing back fear. No. She hadn't imagined it. Someone's hand lay across her arm. Her heart thudded in her throat, deafening her in the silence of the night.

"Who's there?" she squeaked.

The deep rumble of a snore was her only response. Eva's heart raced, her breath coming in unsteady rasps. A man, in her cottage. His hand on her arm while she slept. How long had he been there? What other liberties had he taken before falling to sleep beside her?

Her mind told her to scream. She couldn't even find the courage to whisper.

The man let out a loud snort, startling himself in the process. His hand dropped. Eva pulled her arm away before he could take it again. She held her breath, waiting for him to wake. Ten seconds felt like an hour. He didn't move again. She let out her breath. Then counted.

One minute, two, three. Eva counted out five whole minutes before she dared to roll over to face him. Even that was painfully slow, lest she make a noise and wake the man. It took every bit of courage she had to open her eyes.

"Darrek?"

He didn't wake. His snoring, which must have woken her, filled the little room. He must have been exhausted not to have roused when she did or when she whispered his name. She should wake him. Should order him from the room before Maeve saw him. But what was he doing leaned up against the wall fast asleep? What was he doing in their little cottage at all? A man in her chamber while she slept? It wasn't right. Yet—

The instant she'd realized who it was, peace washed over her, banishing the terror. Her heart still raced but for an entirely different reason.

Sir Darrek Drew was in her room.

Sir Darrek Drew who had, however many hours ago it was now, walked her back to Maeve, talked with her under the stars, asked her to dance.

Sir Darrek Drew who had no idea how close she'd been to agreeing.

"Darrek," she whispered again, more to herself than the man himself. She knew he'd never take advantage of her or hurt her in any way, so had he come to protect her? From Cavendish?

He'd vowed he'd protect her no matter what. Apparently, that meant even at the risk—or rather *cost*—of his own reputation. If Cavendish or his guards caught Darrek in her room, a forced marriage would be the kindest of the punishments offered him. Death was far more likely.

She should definitely wake him and send him away.

Only—

His beard had a slight curl to it, something she'd never noticed before. His eyelashes, flush against his cheeks, seemed longer too. Back at Raedonleith, he'd been one of the few knights she'd not bothered to flirt with, and here at Cavendish Castle, she'd always either avoided his gaze or been too far away to draw out features. It was nice to simply look, much as it made her heart thunder and her stomach roll with guilt.

His hair, as per usual, was tied at his nape, though a long piece had fallen free. Her hand jumped to brush it back before she thought better of it—for the second time tonight. She couldn't touch him, for so many reasons. Not even his hair.

He looked younger in sleep, not quite so fierce. Though she'd never been afraid of him. Darrek had always been too kind for her to be afraid of his brawn. He might have been a giant, but he was a giant sworn to protect her. Even from her nightmares, it would seem.

He stretched out his legs. Evangeline started then quickly looked away. Her cheeks flamed in the darkness. Was he waking? Had he noticed her movement? Was he watching her? No. He wouldn't do that. Would he?

He was moving again. She didn't blame him. The floor was not the most comfortable place to sleep, especially when sitting upright against a wall. He let out a sigh. Eva steadied her breathing. She almost—*almost*—wished she'd kept watching. At least then, she'd know what he was doing.

A big hand brushed against her fingers before clasping her hand. It was all Eva could do not to screech with fright, so unexpected was the touch. His hand was warm around hers. Warm and welcome. She focused again on her breathing—in-two-three-four, out-two-three-four—determined he think her still asleep.

The practical voice in her head told her again that she should send him away. Her comfort and peace weren't worth his life.

Soon, she promised herself. She'd allow herself just a few more minutes to enjoy the peace he brought with him, and then she'd send him away. It was for the best.

Eva woke before the sun. Darrek was gone. Had he even been there? Or had he simply been a sweet interlude of dreams between the nightmares?

"Sleep well?" Maeve asked as she rose to dress.

It had to have been the doubts flooding Eva's mind that made her pause at her friend's question. Maeve would have seen Darrek if he'd come. It was impossible that he could have come into their room without Maeve knowing. Wasn't it? Although, Eva hadn't known. Still didn't know for certain.

"Maeve, was—"

Was there a man in our room last night?

Eva closed her mouth, the question seeming too foolish to even ask. Of course there hadn't been. The cottage was locked. Maeve was ever on alert. And everyone knew to avoid Eva.

Cursed. Broken. Crazy. Demon.

Darrek slept in the stables. Not beside her. A dream. That's all it was. A foolish, broken girl's hope that one day someone might love her enough to stay.

"Eva, honey? Are you well?"

"Yes. Fine." Her voice crackled, words catching on her scream-roughened throat. "Slow this morning, I suppose. But I'll be well."

Maeve's sympathetic smile was a welcome boon to Eva's racing mind. "I'll see you in the kitchen soon."

No word of a man in their room. She must have dreamed it then. After all, Darrek would never go into a lady's room while she slept. He was far too honorable to do such a thing, even to a peasant.

Still, as Eva forced herself through her morning chores, she couldn't help but feel as if he'd truly been there. Watching him had felt so real. The curl of his beard. The eyelashes resting against his cheeks. The warmth and weight of his hand on hers.

"Is it my head you imagine etched into those tapestries you're pounding so hard?"

Eva spun, the stick she'd been using flying a yard away, barely missing Lord Cavendish where he stood. She blanched, stomach rolling at the thought of what punishment he'd force upon her this time, before—

"Arthur!"

She held out her arms, all thoughts of Darrek, Cavendish, and punishment flung from her mind as she rushed to embrace the boy she'd missed so much. Her ribs screamed with pain as Arthur landed with a thud against her chest, but it was worth every bit of agony to hold him again. She clutched him against her, breathing in the smell of his hair, kissing his cheeks, reveling in the feel of his heartbeat against hers.

"Thank you," she said, looking up at the man watching them. The expression on Cavendish's face was difficult to decipher through the tears blurring her eyes, but he seemed almost sad.

For all of a breath of a second before his usual coldness returned.

"Forget not, *Lady Evangeline*, that he is my property to do with whatever I wish. Try to leave again, and you will *both* pay the price. Doubt not that I can find you, wherever you go. And I won't be so lenient next time. Do we have an understanding?"

It wasn't a request or even a question. He didn't even need an answer, given the way the man stalked away. Cavendish knew the threat of taking Arthur away from her was enough to make her do anything he wanted. It had always worked before. The only reason she'd taken the chance to leave was because the foolish hope of the knights had her convinced happy endings existed for people like her.

They didn't.

Eva pressed another kiss to Arthur's head.

She had her son back. That was all that mattered.

Three and a half hours later, Eva was ready to scream with frustration, even if it tore her already aching throat to pieces. Arthur wouldn't leave her alone. She wanted to be near him too but not so near that she tripped over him or endangered his life. She'd almost knocked him into the fire when she'd turned with a pot to find him on the wrong side of it. That after dropping a bag of flour when he'd bumped her elbow and sent a bottle of ale flying in an arc across the room when he'd walked in front of her.

Twice.

He'd always been her shadow, but today it was as if that weren't close enough. He wouldn't even leave her the few minutes it took to relieve herself, insisting on keeping a hold on her sleeve. The whole time.

"Arthur, just—" She looked around the kitchens for somewhere close but safe for him to sit, groaning with frustration when she couldn't find somewhere suitable. "Stay there!"

Her regret was instant. She'd shouted at her son. The hurt in his eyes made her sick. She'd hurt him when all she'd wanted was one minute of space to take a breath. What kind of a horrible mother was she?

He'd been away from her side for more than two weeks, locked in that room, probably as terrified as she was to know that Cavendish was right next door. She'd ached to see Arthur and hold him again, but it had also been almost a relief not to have him underfoot while she worked. What kind of a mother did that make her that she'd preferred those moments without him?

Guilt rose like bile in her throat. A terrible one. That's what kind of mother.

She watched, unable to find words to apologize or even the strength to call him back, as he picked his way through the busy kitchen to a corner by the scrap pile.

"Cook needs more spices."

Eva turned to Maeve, shaking her head with disbelief. She had to swallow twice before the self-hatred in her throat moved enough to speak. "So soon? I only just went to the village for more."

"We've used them all."

Maeve fiddled with the edge of the cloth beside her. Though she was always busy, Eva got the impression her friend was trying to avoid her gaze.

"We bought enough for a month."

"Some spilled."

Some. Had Maeve purposely thrown the lot of them out with the scraps?

"I need you to get more. Take Arthur."

Eva looked to where her tiny son cowered in the corner. She could barely see him over the bustle of the kitchen maids cutting and stirring between them. Maybe if she took him with her, he'd forgive her for her harsh words. Maybe she'd feel as if she had the right to ask Arthur's forgiveness. If nothing else, going into the village would get the two of them out of the overwhelming bustle and heat of the kitchens.

"Lord Cavendish won't like it. He'll think we're running."

"In the wrong direction?" Maeve harrumphed. "Hardly. Go on with you. If Lord Cavendish asks questions, send him to me."

Eva shook her head but did as she was told. There was little point arguing. It wasn't as if Maeve would change her mind.

"Come on, Arthur."

She took her son by the hand and led him toward the stables, heart feeling as skittish as the foals she'd seen there once. Darrek was in the stables. Darrek, who might also have been in her room last night. Would he say something? Should she? Heat sprung into her cheeks like she'd been staring into a fire at the mere thought. If he *had* been there, the last thing she wanted was for him to know she knew. And had let him stay. That fact was far more mortifying than him being there.

If he had been there. Which she might never know for sure.

And what would he say about Arthur?

He'd been kind to Arthur the first time he'd met the boy, but that was before he knew Arthur was her son. Would that change now that he knew?

Eva raised her hand to knock on the stable door only to have it fly open before she could.

"Evangeline. Is everything—"

Darrek stopped, his gaze falling to Arthur, who stared up at him. Eva was still trying to figure out how to speak when Darrek crouched down to Arthur's height.

"Arthur, wasn't it? You came to visit me a few weeks ago. A pleasure to formally meet you, young squire."

Darrek nodded to Arthur, as if bowing before royalty. Eva looked away, pain tearing at her heart to see the knight offer her boy such respect. Arthur might have been the son of a lord, but unless Cavendish saw fit to marry Eva, Arthur's claim was useless.

As far as Darrek—and anyone else—was concerned, he was the mute, young son of a poor peasant. Cows were more valuable and gave more to society. Rabbits too. At least they gave their life for food and fur.

"Have you come to visit Storm again? He's been missing you, you know. Tells me every night when I tuck him in. 'Where's my friend, Arthur?' he says."

"We need more spices," Eva responded, stopping Darrek's kindness before she burst into tears. It should have charmed her and otherwise would have. His treating Arthur with respect was everything she dared not hope. But it was also more than she had to give Arthur and only made the fact more obvious. Darrek took the time to talk to Arthur when all Eva had done was yell at him. Guilt piled on top of guilt.

"Spices, you say? Different to the ones we purchased two days ago?"

"The same."

Would Darrek know enough about the running of a castle to know how ridiculous a statement that was? Eva hoped not. She couldn't bear to think that he thought she was trying to get his attention. Or spend time with him. Both of which, a part of her didn't want to acknowledge, were true.

"Well then, spices we shall find. Arthur, I believe I'm in need of a young squire to assist me. Might you be the one to assist me?"

Arthur's eyes widened as he looked first from Darrek to Eva. Eva could only imagine what he might have said or what his squeal of excitement might have sounded like if he hadn't been mute. She nodded her permission and smiled, gesturing for him to take Darrek's hand and follow the knight. He all but skipped away. She slipped into an empty stall instead of following them, tears threatening with every breath as failure pounded bruises into her heart.

Don't cry, don't cry, don't cry.

If she let one out, there would be no stopping the torrent that followed. She had neither the privacy, nor the time, nor the energy to deal with a torrent.

Push it aside. Deal with it later.

"Eva?"

Eva swallowed back the tears, shaking her frown into a smile as George poked his head into the stall. "I'm here."

"We're ready to go."

"Thank you."

"Are you?"

"Excuse me?"

"Ready. Are you ready? Forgive me. But you look—" He stopped, scrubbed a hand across his beard, and grimaced, obviously not wanting to finish the observation. Eva brightened her smile.

"I'm fine."

"Are you certain? You don't have to be, you know."

Perhaps he thought so. Perhaps if the world were fair, and just, and loving, and accepting, his words might be true. But Eva knew differently. Life didn't stop because she wasn't well or because she wasn't strong enough to fight the demons inside. It didn't stop for anything. Cavendish's kitchens needed spices. She would get spices.

"Perfectly fine."

"Another maid could—"

"Thank you for your concern, but I am well."

She brightened her smile and walked ahead of George to the horse Arthur stood beside.

Fine? What a lie. One need only count the scars on her arms to know that. She hadn't been fine for a long time. If she'd ever been.

The horse neighed beside her, and Eva jumped.

"Easy girl," Darrek said quietly.

Eva wasn't sure whether he was trying to calm her or the horse.

CHAPTER
20

Eva spent the next two hours as they rode into the village, purchased spices, and started back to Cavendish Castle doing everything she could to distract herself from the torrent of tears so close behind her eyes. The two men hadn't even asked her opinion before lifting Arthur onto George's horse and her in front of Darrek. She was thankful for that. And that they seemed content to ride in silence. She was uncertain whether that was normal or not, considering that all the men she'd spent time with before had been happy to fill the silence with compliments and flatteries. But then, she'd been flirting with them, and in turn they'd been trying to impress her.

She was long past having any chance of impressing Darrek, and George had been widowed for almost as long as she'd been alive.

"Are you married?"

Eva could have clawed her throat open as the thought she'd never meant to voice dissipated into the air. Darrek choked behind her. Or was he laughing? It was difficult to tell when she couldn't see him and when she was far too focused on trying to turn back time to care. Her cheeks flushed. The curse of the red hair.

"Married? Me?"

"Never mind," Eva grizzled, pressing a hand to her burning cheek.

Trees passed beside them, the sound of the horses' hooves pounding like drums as they continued down the well-traveled road. The clouds from the morning had cleared, leaving a bright blue sky. Days like these made for brilliant star-gazing nights. Eva hadn't done any proper stargazing since Arthur had been gone. It hurt too much to think of doing it without him. Would he want to watch the stars with her tonight? Hear their stories?

"If I were married, would I do this?"

A shiver of surprise—and something more—went through Eva as Darrek put his lips beside her ear and whispered the question. She was trying to figure out what he meant when he brushed her hair aside and bent to place a gentle kiss on the side of her neck.

"I—you—" Words failed her, jumbled up in a river of confused sensation. His silence had fooled her into thinking he'd let her mistaken outburst go. Instead, Darrek had kissed her. Not on her mouth. The simple kiss he'd given her could just as easily have been given to a sister or friend or— No. A man didn't kiss his sister like that. Not like he had. But then—what? He cared? Found her as attractive as she found him?

Unlikely. He was tall, broad, strong, and had hair that begged for tousling and eyes that promised safety. She was just…her. A scarred and broken princess. Less, to vast majority of the castle who had no idea she'd once worn a crown.

"I'm not married."

The news shouldn't have pleased Eva as much as it did.

"Though I hope to be, one day."

Conversation ceased for a time after that. At least, out loud. Eva's mind was far from silent, more questions than she could ever answer—or dare to ask—vying for dominance.

He wished to marry. Did he have someone in mind?

And if so, why had he kissed her like that? Unless he were thinking of her.

But that couldn't be right because no one wanted her. Lord Cavendish had made certain of that, and she'd etched it into her own skin to remind herself of it.

Then again, what if he did? What if it *were* her Darrek had alluded to marrying? And if, by some miracle of wonders, he could forgive her Arthur and see her as whole, what would he say when he realized that her brokenness went so far beyond what the eye could see? Could she dare let him, or any man, close enough to find out?

Becoming a man's wife had been her dream once, back when she was naïve enough to think marrying meant simply having someone fawn over you and give you gifts and call you beautiful every day of your life. She'd adored the attention of every knight she'd flirted with and every nobleman she'd danced with. She'd even kissed a few of them, giggling at their stupefied expressions afterward and the way they muddled up their words. Just as she had, only moments ago. She'd thrilled at the power she'd had over men.

Now, she wasn't sure she wanted any of it.

Marriage meant so much more than having a man fawn over her. It meant having a man know her. *See* her.

Only a fool would believe someone could love her after that. She'd stopped being a fool the day Cavendish called her unlovable.

Darrek's hand brushed against Eva's as the horse took a step sideways.

Were you in my room last night?

The question begged to be asked but, for the hundredth time, Eva let the embarrassment of asking it push back the words.

"George?" Darrek asked.

Caught in her delusions, it took Eva a few seconds longer to notice what Darrek had. George had turned his horse off the road and was leading it along a smaller path. Strange, since Cavendish Castle was in view—directly ahead. They weren't escaping after all, were they? Panic clawed at Eva's throat. They couldn't. Not now. She'd only just gotten Arthur back.

George looked over his shoulder just long enough to throw out an order. "Follow me."

Darrek hesitated for only a moment before turning their horse to follow. Eva fought to hold her fear at bay. If the two men's plan—and likely Maeve's too, given her strange request—had been to help Eva and Arthur escape, they wouldn't have wasted time purchasing spices in the opposite direction. They would have gone away directly. And they would have met up with the rest of her father's knights by now.

She thought.

The path was so overgrown that they had to duck under several branches. A bird flew upward, almost hitting Eva in the face. She wasn't sure which of them was more startled.

George had already tethered his horse to a tree and helped Arthur to the ground when Darrek and Eva finally caught up to them. Eva slid to the ground, stumbling slightly when the drop was farther than she expected. Darrek would have helped her, gentleman that he was, but she'd almost kissed him last time that had happened, something she'd never forget but was loathe to repeat. Especially not while she was still reeling from the kiss he'd already given her today. The slight twinge in her ankle was preferable to landing in his arms again.

Or so she told herself.

She looked around the place they'd stopped, seeing nothing remarkable. Had George meant to stop here? Perhaps he'd thought to take a shortcut and gotten himself turned around. Although George knew these forests better than anyone, so she doubted that was the case.

A tree full of bold red flowers was to her left, the blooms giving off a scent as sharp as their hue. A perfect spiderweb graced the area between the red-flowered tree and the one beside it. George walked toward it. Eva wondered if that was why he'd stopped here until he moved past the flowers and used a stick to brush aside the web.

"Is this—"

Darrek broke off the question when George grinned and gave a single nod. Darrek shook his head, a smile tugging at his own mouth. Eva was too confused already to try to figure out whatever had passed between the two men.

"Follow me," George again threw back over his shoulder. "We walk from here."

Darrek offered a hand to Arthur. Arthur reached for Eva's

hand, wrapping it tightly around his before taking Darrek's in his other. Anyone would have thought they were a family.

How easy it was to fool people.

"Shall we?" Darrek asked her, gesturing with his free hand toward the path George had taken. Eva nodded, unsure what other option she had. Stay with the horses? Take Arthur and try to make it back to Cavendish Castle on her own? She didn't recognize any of this part of the forest. She'd only succeed in getting the two of them lost.

Darrek ducked under several branches, holding them back as he waited for the two of them to follow. She did so warily, Arthur tightly beside her as they stepped around stones and thick roots. The air was muggy and smelled of dead leaves, in such contrast to how clear the day had felt only minutes ago at the road. Much as she wanted to call out and ask George where he was leading them—or ask Darrek what was happening—she kept her mouth shut. She wasn't certain she wanted to know.

They hadn't gone far before George slowed and turned with a smile on his face. "We're here."

Eva stopped. Looked around. Trees, roots, dirt, rocks, more trees. No flowers but a few scattered budding weeds. No spiderwebs that she could see. One of the trees had grown a little skewed, making almost a tunnel with its branches, but that was common enough. Whatever it was George had brought them out here to see, he'd have to be more specific than that. This particular sight, she could have seen anywhere in the forest.

George held out a calloused hand to her, tugging her gently toward him. When she was so close beside him that she could feel the heat radiating off his clothing, he moved a final branch and pushed her forward.

"Oh—"

Words failed Eva as she stared at the sight the old stablemaster had brought her to see.

There, in the small clearing in front of her, must have been hundreds of tiny white butterflies. They were like gently falling snow, flying in all directions and landing only to rise again. Never in her entire life had Eva seen so many butterflies in one place. They floated and flew through the dappled sunlight the trees made at the edges of the clearing and all but danced along the brightness of the middle. It was breathtaking.

"Darrek…"

"I know."

His voice held the same air of wonder that filled her mind. Eva vaguely registered George walking back the way they'd come. He was gone before she could thank him.

"He'll wait with the horses. Said to take as long as we needed."

"I—they're beautiful."

"George found them this morning on his ride. He told me about them when he got back, musing how the unusual weather lately had caused them to multiply. I wondered aloud if you'd ever seen such a thing. He said I should take you to see them, but I didn't know where they were."

"So he brought us both."

"Good thing the kitchens ran out of spices."

They hadn't run out of spices. But right now, watching a million butterflies fly without the slightest care, Eva didn't mind. Maybe she'd accidentally lose the spices they'd just purchased before they reached Cavendish Castle so that she could have the excuse to see the butterflies again. It was a foolish, whimsical, even scandalous thought, but something about the butterflies made her feel free. Want to smile, even. Strange, when only moments ago she'd been fighting back tears.

"Thank you." She turned her head to face Darrek, forgetting for a moment how close they stood. He was right there, already watching her. He was smiling, a soft smile that barely tipped the edges of his mouth but was there all the same. Not a joyful smile but a contented one. A happy one. Her reaction had caused that. It was a heady feeling.

His lips parted as if he were about to speak, but no words came out. Eva leaned closer, wondering how those lips might feel against hers.

She reeled back. Kiss Darrek? Her? No. She couldn't. That would—that would—

She bent down to pick up Arthur instead, needing a moment to compose herself. "See the butterflies?" she asked him, hating the tremble in her voice she knew Darrek would hear. "Aren't they beautiful?"

Arthur reached for the butterflies. Eva stayed silent, wondering if one might land on her son's arm. Anything to distract her from how close Darrek stood beside her and his touch on her shoulder.

"Evangeline."

It didn't take more than a gentle push for her to turn and face him. The hand he laid on her burning cheek felt equal parts soothing and terrifying.

"Don't call me that," she whispered, desperate for…something. For him to move away? Or did she wish him closer? Arthur wiggled in her arms. She let him down, but her gaze never left Darrek's. It was as if he'd put a spell on her. Or perhaps it was this clearing filled with butterflies. There was a sense of magic here. Of wonder. That anything could happen. Even two people as different as them falling in love.

"Evangeline? But that is your name."

"It's who I used to be, but it's not who I am. Not anymore." Someone had to remind her of that. Her heart was struggling to remember it with Darrek's hand still on her cheek. His thumb stroked down her nose, his gaze following it.

"I won't call you Eva. 'Tis a servant's name, and that's not who you are either. I must call you something."

"Perhaps you could simply call me friend."

"Aye. You are that. But you are something more. Princess. That is what I shall call you. For you are, and always will be, my princess."

Eva wrenched her gaze from Darrek's, looking into the distance, barely seeing the butterflies through her pain. "Please don't." He couldn't know how much that word hurt. It was what her father had called her when she was a child. He'd come into the room she shared with her sisters, often long after they'd all said goodnight, and kissed them each on the forehead. "Sleep well, my princess," he'd whispered over them each in turn. Many a night Eva had forced herself to stay awake for that kiss and the four words that followed. Her father's love had been her last thought each night as she drifted into sleep.

"Any name but princess."

Darrek tugged her gaze back to his. Eva closed her eyes, all too aware of his thumb brushing across her cheekbone.

"You cannot escape who you are. Perhaps you are Eva, perhaps Evangeline, but no matter what name you call yourself nor what you answer to, you will always be the beautiful, honorable, kind-hearted, self-sacrificing woman I know you to be. 'Tis not your name that makes you, but your heart."

"My heart is broken."

"Perhaps it is merely dormant, like the caterpillars in their cocoons. Perhaps it is simply waiting for its turn to fly."

Eva took a step back, only just catching her balance when her foot hit a rock.

"We need to go. Now." She looked around, spotting Arthur, calling him over.

The three of them were silent on the short walk to George and the horses. Darrek lifted Arthur onto George's horse before turning to Eva. She gritted her teeth before shaking her head and stepping away. They were close enough to the castle. She'd walk. With a shrug, Darrek followed her, leading the horse behind them. The butterflies had been the most beautiful sight she'd ever seen, yet with every step her mantra echoed.

Don't cry. Don't cry.

Sometimes it was better to live without beauty than to know it and walk away.

"May I— Will you— If you—"

Eva stayed silent while Darrek searched for words, already forming a reply in her head. No. Whatever he was asking, the answer was no. It had to be. He took a deep breath and tried one more time.

"Lady Evangeline, I don't know how long the butterflies will be there, but if you want to see them again, I'd be honored to escort you."

"Escort me?" The words pulled forth images of courting couples arm in arm parading about the marketplace. Eva's face grew warm at the thought. Her and Sir Darrek. Courting.

"The path is overgrown and rarely traversed. I would hate for you to fall or injure yourself with no one to find you."

She laughed bitterly inside at her own foolishness. This strong knight felt nothing for her. He was protecting her. As always. As per his king's orders.

"Thank you, but I don't need your protection."

"How about my friendship?"

"Friendship?"

"Everyone needs friends, Lady Evangeline. Even princesses in hiding." He tipped his head, studying her, much as he'd done at the edge of the clearing. "Especially princesses in hiding."

The castle gates loomed. Eva opened her mouth to answer before closing it again and fleeing. Through the gates, past busy servants and bustling vendors, and into the kitchen where Maeve simply raised her eyebrows in question. Eva shook her head and tried to catch her breath.

She'd left the spices with Darrek. Arthur too. Running hadn't solved anything.

But she'd had to run. If not, she might have said or done something she regretted. Like kissing the knight who offered her friendship. Or letting herself believe that they might have a future.

She was never going back to that clearing.

CHAPTER 21

King Lior stood at the window of his bedroom, staring out into the night. Though it was too dark to see beyond the torch-lit walls of the castle, he watched all the same. Evangeline was out there, beyond the forests, beyond the next town. So close yet still beyond his reach. Was she being treated well? Had the knights he sent tried again to free her? Was she even now on her way home?

He heard a rustle behind him moments before arms came around his waist. Caralynne's head rested against the middle of his back.

"Come back to bed."

She didn't ask why he was standing at the window nor why he didn't sleep. She'd found him in this exact place so often that she didn't need to. Instead, she made the same simple request she did almost every night.

The offer was tempting. The night was cold and his bed warm and inviting. But he'd only toss and turn if he did. "Not yet."

"You have to sleep. You have a kingdom to rule, a castle to oversee, two daughters to parent—Rose and Mykah need their Papa, after all—and a wife who's missing the warmth of her husband on this cold night."

Lior pulled Caralynne around to his front and tucked her firmly against his heart. He breathed in the scent of her hair, which still smelled of lavender from when she washed it earlier. She was right, as always. He had too many responsibilities to stand watch night after night. Too many he'd let go astray already. His guards had orders to wake him the instant Evangeline came into view. He wouldn't miss her arrival.

But what if he did? What if, right this very minute, Evangeline and the knights were only steps away from cresting the hill leading to Raedonleith? They might have pushed through the night to get home.

"One more—"

"Please, Lior. You'll make yourself sick again, and I can't—" Caralynne pressed her forehead to Lior's chest, taking in several steadying breaths. "I can't lose you too. I—" She shook her head before swallowing and trying again. "Please?"

Lior dropped a kiss on his wife's forehead before walking her back to bed, cradling her against his side as he tucked the heavy blankets around them both. Though it took only a few moments for her breathing to steady out in sleep, Lior was far from settled. His body was weary, but his ears strained with every beat of his heart to hear the cry of a guard saying his daughter was home.

Evangeline, my precious girl. Why did I ever drive you away?

It didn't seem to matter how many times Caralynne reminded him it wasn't his fault Evangeline had left. He was her father. He should have made her stay. At the very least, he should have gone straight after her and demanded she come home. Maybe she would have hated him forever, but at least she would have been safe. Who knew what she'd gone through in the past four years, what pain he could have saved her from if he'd only been humble enough to apologize instead of too stubborn to see how much his words hurt her.

He lay in bed until the sky turned from pitch to charcoal and quiet footsteps signaled the servants rising to another day. Sleep wasn't coming.

Lior wrapped a thick cloak around him before stepping out into the cold chill of barely morning. The path to the battlements was well-known to him. He could have walked it in his sleep, and likely would have, if he'd been able to slumber. He walked it every night. He knew the guards in each watch and rotation, their names, their families, their weapons, their proficiencies, and—

likely to their later regret—weaknesses. Of course, they knew his weaknesses too. Everyone in the castle did. Their names were Caralynne, Rose, Mykah, and Evangeline.

"Any word?" he asked Britt. It was the same question he asked the guards every morning. The guard changed, but the question didn't. Unfortunately, neither did the answer.

The man shook his head. "I'm sorry, my king. Perhaps today will be the day."

Lior nodded, clapping Britt on his shoulder. It was foolish to place such hope in the rising of another day, yet one of these days, she would be here.

One day, the answer to the question Lior asked his guards would be different.

One day, she'd come home.

Dust on the horizon had Lior's heart skipping a beat. Was that—

He sighed as the cloud came into focus. Not dust. Just a cloud dusky with morning light.

"Papa?"

"Rose, what are you doing up here so early?"

Lior held out a hand. His oldest daughter walked to his side, tall and slim in her wine-colored gown. She took after him in so many ways—his dark hair, wide face, serious expression, and tendency to rise with the sun. Or before it.

"I knew you'd be here."

She didn't face him, instead looking out over the castle walls much as he did every morning. The slight wind blew her hair into his face before she could tug it back behind her shoulder again. A golden circlet sat atop the braided half of her hair, catching the first rays of the day. He remembered fondly the days when she'd come bounding to his study, long before anyone else was up, barefooted and still in her nightdress, hair a mess of strands. It had been a long time since he'd seen her in any way but dressed to perfection. Even this early in the morning.

"My birthday is next month."

Caralynne had reminded him of it last week. He'd have to remember to thank her for that. "That it is."

"I wondered if you may announce my betrothal at the ball."

Lior's head whipped around. "Your betrothal?"

Rose frowned. "Yes. You told me you'd see to my marriage."

"In time for your twenty-second birthday."

"Aye, next month."

Twenty-two? How had she— When had she— No, surely she was mistaken. His Rose was only twenty, wasn't she? Still older than most girls to marry, but with the upheaval of Evangeline's leaving and his subsequent illness, Rose had understood his need to postpone the negotiations. As his daughter and heir, his Rose couldn't just marry any man. That was Lior's reasoning for giving himself until her twenty-second birthday to find the right one. Which, somehow, was next month.

"Are you certain?"

"Papa!"

The hurt in her voice cut Lior. He wanted to pull her into his arms and apologize as well as wipe it away at the same time. What he didn't want to do was admit to this precious daughter beside him that two years of her life had passed, and he'd barely even noticed.

Was this what Caralynne had meant last night? What else had he missed?

"You haven't made negotiations yet," Rose said. Though she tried to keep the emotion out of her voice, a tiny shake gave her away. Was it disappointment? Anger? Regret? Resignation? Lior couldn't read her like he'd once been able to. That closeness too had gone astray.

He looked back at the cloud over the hill, searching for an answer that wouldn't come. He could lie. How difficult could it be to find a nobleman willing to marry his oldest daughter and one day inherit the kingdom of Raedonleith? One month was plenty of time to see to it. He could have hundreds of potential suitors at his door in only a day. But this was his daughter. His firstborn.

He'd need at least three months, if not twelve—if not all of eternity—to find a man worthy of her.

"I've been—" Lax. Wrong. Missing one daughter so much he'd forgotten about the other two. A terrible king and an even worse father. "Forgive me."

Rose nodded, returning her gaze to the horizon.

"I can— I will—" Sharp rock bit into his palms as Lior gripped the wall. "I'll see—" The words weren't there. What was the point in making another promise to his daughter when he'd already broken the first one? And that was only the one she'd brought to his attention. How many others had he broken that she'd simply let pass? "I'm sorry, Rose."

Rose nodded again before turning and walking away. He didn't see her face, nor did he call her back, but when he let his gaze drift sideways, there was a drop of moisture where she'd stood. A drop that could only have been a tear.

With no care for the guards or anyone else who might see him, Lior dropped to his knees. Sobs shook his weary shoulders as he began to pray.

For forgiveness.

For wisdom.

That, somehow, despite the way he'd already failed them, he wouldn't lose Rose and Mykah too.

CHAPTER
22

Eva woke before the sun. There'd been no nightmares that night. Instead, she'd dreamed of the butterflies. Though she'd promised herself she wouldn't go back to the clearing to see them—and kept that promise for two full days—the pull was physical. She needed to see them fly again. Free. No responsibility pulling them down, no regrets holding them back, no scars marring their perfect wings. She should have hated them for it. Instead, she wanted—no, needed—to bask in them. She was drowning, and they carried hope on their wings. Perhaps if she stood still enough, close enough, a little of that hope would fall on her.

It was a fanciful thought, ridiculous in its foolishness, but it had Eva pulling a cape around her. The butterflies likely wouldn't have even woken yet, let alone been flying, but she had to go anyway. She had to try. She brushed a kiss against Arthur's hair and silently promised both him and the sleeping Maeve to be back soon.

A rush of cold air at the window warned her against leaving. Tugging the cape tighter round her shoulders, she crept through the window anyway. The air was like ice against her face, her breath coming out in clouds. Smoke rose from the ashes of a fire a patrol must have lit, but otherwise, the morning was still.

She made it almost to the edge of the forest before realizing she was being followed.

The man didn't hide, as anyone nefarious might have, when she turned around. She recognized him in an instant.

Darrek. Of course. Did the man ever sleep?

He caught up quickly, stopping a few steps short of her side. Eva glared at him.

"I don't need your protection."

He shrugged. "Perhaps I require yours."

"Darrek—"

"It's dark, you're alone, and you're going into the forest with little more than a cloak to protect you. So unless you have a sword strapped to your back and a knife tucked in your boot, I'm coming. I can walk beside you or follow at a distance, but I'm not letting you go alone."

"I've gone into the forest alone many times, Sir Darrek."

"Not while I've been here."

Eva shook her head and stalked down the path, pretending she was alone though every thudding heartbeat reminded her she wasn't. She didn't want Darrek following her. She didn't want him here at all. But she wanted to see the butterflies, and convincing him to stay behind would take too long.

Birds called to each other as Eva walked, their melodies as varied as the shades of green in the trees or the wildflowers forming a timid guard of honor along the path. They'd show their true faces when the sun touched them.

Ten minutes and two wrong turns later, the path began to grow narrower. Low-sweeping tree branches clutched at her skirt, forcing her to stop and free herself several times from their clutches. When she came across an orange-flowering bush, she was certain she was almost there—until several more showed up around the next corner.

Eva gritted her teeth and stared at the tree in front of her.

She'd been so certain she knew how to find her way to the clearing but, as much as she didn't want to admit it to Darrek, who was staying back just far enough to drive her crazy, she was lost. Much more pressing forward and she wouldn't be able to find her way home. Maeve would watch over Arthur and cover for Eva for as long as possible, but the old woman couldn't do it indefinitely.

"Darrek?"

He was by her side without hesitation.

"Where are the butterflies?"

He gestured with his chin over her shoulder, not even a hint of condemnation or laughter in his expression. "That way."

He didn't reach for her arm, as he needed both hands to hold branches out of the way so they could walk. It didn't take Eva more than a few steps to be thankful he'd come despite her protestations. The path that had been challenging to find in the afternoon light was all but invisible in the soft haze of dawn.

Eva was just starting to wonder if Darrek was as lost as she was when he, like George had, moved aside a final branch. And there was the clearing. He held the branch above her head as she stepped through.

Her breath caught in her throat at the beauty of the sunbeams lighting up the mist, streaks of pure gold stretching from heaven to earth.

There weren't as many butterflies this morning. Perhaps, like most of the world, they still slept. The score that flew around the clearing still managed to hold Eva captivated. They were a moment of peace in Eva's world that felt anything but. Morning to night, and even in her sleep, the voices of failure and despair that held her mind captive didn't stop. But here, for this stolen moment in time, they did.

"I've always had a great respect for butterflies," Darrek said. His voice was hushed, as if he too felt the wonder of the moment. "They seem delicate, but they have an incredible strength.

"They hatch from an egg then spend half of their life crawling along leaves or the ground, trying to avoid birds and stay alive long enough to progress to their next stage of life, which is pretty much death. Think about it—they're closed tightly in what must seem like a grave and left there in the dark for weeks. Do they think that's the end? I would."

Eva frowned. "You've thought about this a lot?"

"There's a bush behind the stables at Raedonleith that seems to attract caterpillars. I'm not sure what it is about the little bush, but it's always covered in them—in every stage. Since my squire days, they've intrigued me.

"Just imagine. You've spent your life crawling around the ground, eating leaves, being free—or what you think is free. And then one day, you crawl up a branch to rest only to be covered in a hard, dark shell you can't break free of."

Eva could relate only too well. She'd thought herself free once before discovering she'd walked into a prison.

"But then, one day, light breaks in, and as you push toward it, you discover you're not only breathtakingly beautiful, but you can fly. The whole world has changed. It's brighter and bigger than you could have ever imagined. Where once you crawled, now you dance. When once you thought your life was over, now you discover it's only just begun."

"You tell a fine tale. Perhaps you should have been a storyteller rather than a knight."

"Your life isn't over, Evangeline."

Eva's breath made tracks in the mist as she breathed out a sigh.

"I fill the same water buckets every single day. Stoke the same fires, clean the same pots, knead the same dough. It's fine. It's my life, but—" She shook her head. "It's my life. Nothing ever changes. The buckets keep needing to be filled, no matter how many times I fill them, the fires in need of stoking, dinner made and served and cleaned and made again the next day. Every day, the same. You say my life isn't over, but it certainly feels like it."

"'Tis like a knight's training. Repetitive."

"Aye, except for one thing—you train *for* something. *Toward* something. You grow stronger through it. You learn new skills, take on new challenges. You go from page to squire to knight. My work never changes. More, anyone could do it. Even a child. Is this all I have to look forward to for the rest of my life?"

"You have—"

"Arthur? Yes, I do. The son I love with all my being but can't look at without seeing my own failure. Him, me, my own family—I've failed us all. I'm not the mother he needs. I have no time to spend with him, no toys for him to play with. No hope for him. He's silent because I let him be hurt. Sad because I can't find a smile to share with him. None of this is his fault, which makes me feel even worse for feeling like it is.

"Maybe I should have let Cavendish take him away from me when Arthur was a babe. At least then I could have blamed him for failing the boy. But I have no one to blame but myself. I'm not enough. I never will be."

Eva let out a sigh.

"But then, the moment I wish him away, overwhelming guilt floods my soul. He won't always be here bringing me flowers or wanting to help. He'll grow and leave, and I really will be alone. I'll have wasted all these years with him, wishing him away when all I want is for him to be happy. Be well. Be more than I could ever make him."

Tears dripped down Eva's cheeks despite her fight to hold them back. She hadn't meant for those words to come out either. What did Darrek know of her pain? He was a knight, not a mother. Even Maeve didn't understand how much Eva struggled.

Eva looked around the clearing. The sunbeams were fading, along with the morning mist, leaving dew in their wake. She took breath after breath and tried to compose herself. Though the tears stopped, the voices in her head didn't.

Fool. Disappointment. Unlovable. Unworthy.
Broken. Cursed.
Failure.

And then, somehow, another voice broke through. Deep. Patient. Kind.

"You have a future, Evangeline. Right now, your life looks dark and bleak, but one day, you'll come through it, and you'll fly."

"People don't fly."

"You will. Not only will you fly; you'll soar. Far above all this. So far it'll all seem a dream."

"I wish I could believe you."

It was sheer will alone that kept Darrek from pulling Evangeline into his embrace. A yearning she didn't often show tinged her voice. He settled for tugging the edge of her cape a little tighter round her shoulders, his hand stalling near her chin for a moment with a yearning of his own before he dropped the hand back to his side.

"I wish you could too," he said with a small smile. "Perhaps, for now, it'll simply have to be enough that I do. Because I do, my little caterpillar. I truly believe, one day, that all this pain will be behind you and that you will smile with abandon."

She was beautiful in the morning light. The sun caught the edges of her unbound hair, giving her a golden halo. He could have easily believed she was an angel.

"How is it so easy for you to believe?"

Darrek forced his gaze away from her hair and back to the clearing.

"It's not always. But if one doesn't have hope, what is the point in living? All those years searching for you? It seemed impossible we'd find you and even more that you'd be alive. It was hope alone that kept me going. I would picture in my mind, over and over, the joy on your father's face when we would crest that last hill and he would finally hold you in his arms again. I knew that would be worth every frustration along the way."

"Do you still picture that?"

Darrek thought for a moment, wondering how to answer. He did. After four years of holding tightly to that image, it was impossible not to. But for the past several weeks, he'd been picturing something more.

Beyond that meeting of Evangeline and her father. After that day. He and Evangeline, together. Married. Happy. Him smiling as he held Evangeline's child-swollen stomach in his hands. Her glowing with love and peace. Arthur's laughter drifting through the window as he played chase with the other children.

It was a bittersweet image because the chance of it ever coming true was infinitesimal. She was promised to another. And even if that betrothal was broken, there was no guarantee King Lior would choose Darrek for his daughter. Not when so many other wealthier, older, worthier titled men to choose from were available.

During the nights when he sat beside Evangeline, her hand tucked in his as he begged the Almighty to take away her nightmares, the image of them together was so clear it might as well have been a vision. He foolishly clung to it like it was.

Evangeline waited for his answer. A butterfly flew past her face. She neither flinched nor turned to look at it, her attention focused solely on his answer. He gave the best one he could.

"Yes. Every day. I look forward to that moment when you and your father meet again, and he cannot contain his joy at having you home."

"You truly think that will happen?"

"Aye, Caterpillar, I do."

CHAPTER
23

King Lior wearily ran a hand over his face. His sigh rustled the list on the table in front of him. Twenty of the finest, most respected men in the land, and not one of them was right for Rose.

Sir Cass was wealthy and scholarly but too reserved. Rose—and future Raedonleith— needed someone strong, someone who would fight for them if need be, not hide in his books at the first sign of trouble. Sir Jones was wealthy and strong but arrogant. He'd trample Rose in his need to rule. Masters Denton and Griffith were amusing but too impulsive. Gustaveson was a man of great faith and even greater action, but he made no secret of the fact that his future plans lay in distant lands. Wade might have been an option, if not for the rumors of his declining health. Baron West was—

Lior sighed again. Wealthy enough. Strong enough. Wise enough. Loyal, humble, and always ready with an amusing tale. West was probably fine. But was fine enough for his Rose? He wanted so much more for his firstborn. And after all this time, fine seemed…not fine enough. She needed someone more than that.

A prince. Rose needed a prince. Raedonleith too. A prince would know how to oversee a castle, provide for its people, and support the future queen who one day would rule them. Yes, a prince would do well.

But a prince came with his own kingdom, and Rose was already heir to this one.

A second-born prince, perhaps? Did any neighboring kingdoms have a second-born prince? Manning would know. But Manning wasn't here.

A knock interrupted his thoughts. Lior pushed aside the list and stood. His guest had arrived.

"Baron Waddingham, welcome."

"King Lior." The man bowed low, sweeping the feathered hat from his head as he did so. The baron was thinner than last time Lior had seen him, but worry could do that to a man. "You have news?"

"Aye, but first, eat. Drink." Lior gestured toward the seats by the fire and the food and wine the servants had laid out. "You've traveled far."

"No. Please, tell me now. I cannot wait another second."

Lior nodded, understanding. "Lady Evangeline has been found."

"She's returning to Raedonleith?"

The answer stuck in Lior's throat, caught behind the hope welling in his soul. Yes. She was coming home. He had to believe that. It was the anchor he'd clung to for the past four years. He couldn't let go of it now when she was so close. "Yes." His knights would find a way.

"That is excellent news, sire. We shall be married at last."

"You still wish to marry Evangeline?"

"Of course. I would not have waited all these years if I did not."

"You would marry her even if—" Lior broke off, the words of Manning's latest missive coming back to him.

She is much changed. Stronger, in some ways, though she would not call it such. Years of servitude have not been kind to her nor have those she serves alongside.

"Even if?"

And then there was her son. Arthur, Manning had said the boy's name was. His daughter had a son. Would the baron still wish to marry her if he knew? Could Lior ask it of the man? He had to ensure Evangeline's safety and future upon her return, but was this the way to do it?

"I assure you, my king, there is nothing that would stop me from marrying your daughter."

"Why?"

"Why, sire?"

Lior stalked toward the fire, staring into it as he tried to figure out the man behind him. The flames swayed in a dizzying dance of color.

"Why have you waited all these years?"

"Because you asked me to. And a man's word is worth nothing if he breaks it, sire."

My word is worth nothing if I break it. Waddingham had said the same thing every time Lior had offered to let him out of the betrothal.

The day after Evangeline disappeared.

The first time the knights had come home without her.

A year after she'd left.

Two years later. Then three. Six weeks ago, when Waddingham had come by to ask after Evangeline again. Every time, the same words with the same certainty. The man was either particularly loyal or had an ulterior motive. Lior spun back around, needing to know the truth about the man he'd pledged his daughter's life to.

"Evangeline has a child," he said, not cushioning the words at all.

"A—child?"

"Aye," he confirmed, watching the man carefully. "A son."

Waddingham smiled. "An heir. How wonderful."

It was the smile that turned Lior's suspicions to certainties. Waddingham was hiding something. No bridegroom would smile to hear the woman he'd waited to marry had already been with another man. And would bring the proof of it into their marriage. A good man might still be willing to marry her and even take the child in as his own, but the acceptance wouldn't come so easily. Nor so quickly.

"A child is a wonderful gift," was all Lior said in reply.

Waddingham glanced at the door, his eagerness for the meeting to be over evident. Lior didn't blame him. The food and wine went untouched as Lior bid him farewell.

As soon as the man was gone from the room, Lior called for one of his guards.

"Follow him," the king ordered. "I want to know what he's hiding."

CHAPTER
24

Noise swirled around Eva. Laughter, music, shouts, the clattering of knives against trenchers. Muffled by the rushes on the floor and the doors closed to her, but there, nonetheless. Familiar and comforting despite the distance.

She leaned against the wall at the back of the blacksmith's shop and tucked Arthur more securely against her, relishing his warmth in an otherwise cool night. Last night, the clouds had mostly hidden the stars. One or two would peek out between the clouds if one waited long enough but that took patience, something Eva had been in short supply of yesterday. She and Arthur had eaten dinner and gone to bed.

Tonight, though, was perfect. Cloudless sky, no moon, a million stars. This was her favorite part of each day—when the work was done but the nightmare of sleep still hours away. When the stars came out, sprinkling their way across the vastness of the black sky, and she and Arthur crept to their place behind the blacksmith's shop. A stolen moment of peace amid the slug of monotony.

Arthur pointed at the sky. Eva knew what he wanted. It was the same thing he asked for every time they sat here—the stories of the stars.

She wished she knew the real ones, but she'd been far more interested in the view of knights training out the window of the schoolroom than the tales her teacher told. Still, Arthur never seemed to mind her made up ones.

"Those ones?" she asked, pointing toward a particularly bright cluster to their left. He nodded. Eva studied them for a moment, trying to make something out of them. An animal? A vessel of some kind? A table set for the feast? They were her usual topics but—no. None of them seemed right this time.

Perhaps it was the fact that Darrek, and her attempted avoidance of him, had taken up far too much residence in her thoughts, but those seven brightest stars looked like a knight raising his sword. Did she dare?

Arthur looked up at her, likely wondering what was taking so long. She smiled down at him, glad he couldn't see her thoughts. *Don't mind me. I was just thinking about a handsome knight I have no right to be thinking of. You know, the one who treats you like a son rather than a bother? The one who steals a little more of my heart each time he talks to you, as if the two of you are holding a conversation instead of him holding up the entirety of it. The one who's taken to sneaking into my dreams and turning them from nightmares to—*

"Forgive me." Taking a seat on the cold ground, she pulled Arthur into her lap, wrapping her arms around him. He snuggled in against her shoulder and pointed, again, up at the stars. "I know. I'm taking a long time. I want to get the story right."

He tilted his face toward her, his eyes big as they searched out hers.

She kissed his cheek, so soft against her lips. "Once upon a time…"

Arthur's gaze went back to the stars.

"Once upon a time, there was a knight named Sir—" *Darrek.* "—Helmsley. Henry Helmsley. He was—" *Tall, broad-shouldered, with wavy dark hair he pulled back with a leather.* "—short and lean, with hair the color of straw."

If Arthur noticed her slight hesitations, he didn't react, which relieved Eva. She needed to get her mind off Sir Darrek if she was going to give this story the proper diligence it was due.

"Sir Henry wanted to be brave. His father had been known as the Hunter of Helmsley, and his older brother Sir Harold the Pure Heart. They'd earned their names with great feats, and he wanted to do the same. But, though Henry trained from sunrise to sundown, he lived in fear that when the time came to fight his greatest battle, he'd cower with fright.

"The day of Sir Henry's first big battle finally came. He rose at dawn to saddle his—"

"Carrot."

Eva started as Darrek pushed off the wall he'd been leaning against and sat down beside Eva and her son. Though he left a respectable distance between them, the fact that he was sitting there, relaxed in the dirt as they were, felt far more intimate than it should have. At least he was relaxed. Eva, suddenly, was much the opposite. Had he been there long? How had she missed a man that big? Admittedly, she'd been staring up at the stars, but had she really been so focused on dispelling the man from her mind that she'd missed him standing there altogether?

And why on earth was he talking about carrots?

"Excuse me?"

"Sir Henry. His mount's name was Carrot. And it wasn't a horse. He rode a pig."

Either the smell of horse manure was turning Darrek's mind, or he was just plain crazy.

"Sir Henry was a brave knight," Eva pointed out, unsure why she was bothering. After all, it was just a story. But it was her story. Not his. "Brave knights don't ride pigs into battle."

"You don't think it would take a mightily brave man to ride a pig into battle?"

"I don't believe bravery is the word I would use, no."

Darrek let out a dramatic sigh. "Very well then. What did Sir Henry ride?"

"A horse."

"Did this horse have a name?"

"I don't know."

"A horse *must* have a name. Don't you agree, young Arthur?"

Arthur nodded. Eva stared down at him. He'd nodded. She couldn't remember the last time he'd interacted with a person.

Darrek went on as if such an occurrence were normal. Perhaps he thought it was.

"Well then, a name, if you please, Great Storyteller." He winked at her before tilting his head and waiting, a smile tugging at the edge of his mouth despite his attempt to remain serious. He was being ridiculous, yet she couldn't deny the way she wanted to smile back at him.

"O—"

"Ophelia? O'Malley? O'Callaghan? O'Hanley? Oh-help-us-this-horse-needs-a-name?"

Arthur giggled. Eva lost every bit of concentration she'd had as she looked, astounded, at the boy sitting in her lap. Had she imagined the sound? It wouldn't have been the first time she'd yearned so much for Arthur to speak that she'd tricked her mind into believing he had. But no. Darrek had heard it too. It was there in the triumph on his face.

"Oh-when-is-Arthur's-mother-going-to-give-this-knight's-poor-horse-a-name?"

Arthur giggled again. The sound was like the music of the minstrels to Eva.

"Omega."

It was the first word that came into her mind. She didn't even know where she'd heard it. Neither did she care. Arthur had made a noise!

"Very well. Omega. Not quite as interesting as Carrot, but at least he has a name." Darrek pulled up his knees, resting his forearms across the top of them. "What happened next?"

Eva couldn't even remember what they'd been talking about. "Next? Uh…" She stared at Darrek. Between his presence making her heart beat twice as fast as it should have and Arthur's giggles turning her mind to something the consistency of pottage, Eva couldn't put two words together. After a few moments of panicked silence, Darrek turned to face her.

"Because *I* think Sir Henry rode Omega boldly into battle and realized as he fought that he was every bit as brave as his father and brother. Because courage doesn't come from the mind but from the heart, and the moment he saw what they were fighting for, all his fears ran away. He knew he would fight as long and as courageously as it took to win the battle."

Eva's heart pounded in her throat. Surely Darrek could see it. Surely the whole world could, even though they sat in the darkness tucked up against a blacksmith's shop. Darrek was telling a story to Arthur. A silly made-up story about a silly made-up knight who rode a horse called Omega—or was it a pig named Carrot?—into battle. That's all it was. Yet the way he looked at her said there was more to it. More than a simple story. Like he was trying to tell her she was the prize. The one worth fighting for.

Which was ridiculous. It was a story. Just a story. There was no deeper meaning. He hadn't even said what the prize was.

So why couldn't Eva look away? Why did her heart thud like he'd wrapped her in his arms when he still sat a respectable distance away?

"I—"

Arthur wriggled in her arms. She winced as he pushed her leg against a stray stone. For a moment, she'd forgotten he was even there. She needed to get him to bed before he fell asleep in her arms. He was getting too big for her to carry in such a way.

When Eva looked back at Darrek, he was looking at Arthur. She couldn't tell what he was thinking any more than she wanted him to know what she was. It was better this way, she reminded herself as she pushed herself off the wall and stood, helping Arthur to his feet.

As she smiled a gentle goodbye to Darrek and ambled off in the direction of her cottage, she couldn't help but stop and look back one last time. He was still standing there, watching them. Protecting, as always.

Why was she finding it so difficult to remember that's all it was?

"You care for her."

Darrek startled awake at Manning's voice beside him. It wasn't the first time the man had tried to sneak up on him. It was, though, the first time Manning had succeeded. When had Darrek fallen asleep? He'd sat down outside the blacksmith's shop after Evangeline and Arthur had left and stared up at the stars as he'd found them doing.

He and his mother had done the same many years ago. His mother had told him stories too, although hers were more traditional—gods and battles and tales of broken hearts marked by the stars. Not pigs. Or horses with unusual names. Of course, he'd been the one to add the pigs. It had been worth it to see Evangeline smile and the expression of wonder on her face when Arthur laughed.

Darrek scowled at the older man when he sat down, annoyed at his presence.

"You're supposed to stay far away from Cavendish Castle," he told Manning. "It's not safe for you here. Unless you've come with a plan to take Evangeline and her son home, in which case, tell me, so we may take them and put this whole quest behind us."

Manning didn't leave, nor did he offer a grand plan of escape. Instead he stretched his legs and made himself comfortable.

"You didn't answer my question," he said.

Darrek rolled his shoulders back. "You didn't ask one."

The walls of the blacksmith's shop were still warm even hours after work had finished for the day. No wonder Evangeline chose this place to stargaze from. A cool breeze had picked up during the time he'd been asleep, but his back and hair were warm where they leaned up against the wall.

He knew what Manning was asking—he was no fool—but he also wasn't fool enough to admit it.

"I watched you for nigh unto ten minutes before waking you just now," Manning said in that quiet way of his. "What if I'd been someone else? George may have stopped Cavendish's guard from taking you that day on the road, but don't think they're convinced of your loyalty.

"You have to make a choice—caring for Evangeline or doing the task your king sent you to do. Training, working in the stables, keeping watch over her day and night. It's commendable, to be sure. But it's too much for one man. You're tired, and a tired knight is a danger to everyone around him."

Darrek rubbed a hand across his eyes, wishing he could ignore the truth of Manning's words. He couldn't do it all. He was tired. But then, the thought of not being there for her when she needed him? It was unthinkable.

"What if Evangeline is my task?"

"Then you have your answer," Manning said. "But you weren't sent to rescue her alone, Darrek, nor does anyone expect you to do so. No man moves a mountain on his own."

"George said the same thing."

Manning laughed quietly. "I'm not surprised. Our mother used to say it all the time."

"*Our?* You're brothers?" Why had neither Manning nor George mentioned it before? It wasn't as if they hadn't had the opportunity.

"Foster, but yes. We were squires together."

"Yet you didn't know he was here?" Darrek asked.

"No. I couldn't believe it when I saw him with you that day on the road. I hadn't seen him in twenty years. We parted ways not long after my nineteenth birthday. I wished to become a knight, and he claimed a different calling, always talking about how dark places needed the light too. The last time I saw George, he was leaving for one of those dark places. For all these years, I thought he meant joining the clergy in far off lands or being a traveling friar. I never imagined he was here shoveling horse manure."

Darrek laughed. "Actually, that's my job."

"And don't you do a fine job of it," Manning said, a grin in his eyes despite his straight face.

"The squires appreciate me. Or rather, my strength."

"Of that I have no doubt."

"So George has been here all these years? A mere two days' journey away?"

"Aye. It makes you think, doesn't it?"

"About what?"

"His purpose. George was adamant when he left Raedonleith

that the Almighty had a task for him elsewhere, and no amount of coercing or arguing could convince him otherwise. But instead of traveling, or joining the church, he came here. Stayed all these years. Worked his way up to the position he holds today. I wonder if the reason he came was so that he may be here when Lady Evangeline arrived. Before she was even born, the Almighty knew she'd need an ally, and he sent George."

Darrek covered a yawn, too tired to share Manning's wonder over the workings of the Almighty.

Sometime while Darrek had been sleeping, the feast had come to an end. The revelers, full of ale and delight, had departed for their rooms, or homes, or wherever else they'd come from. Darrek had heard none of it. Only the occasional hiccupping of a nearby drunk could be heard now, and Darrek was too tired to even make out which direction the hiccups were coming from. He rubbed a hand across bleary eyes and let out another yawn. Manning was right. He was a danger.

"Get some sleep," Manning said with a nod toward the stables. "I'll guard her tonight."

Guard her. As if that was all Darrek was doing.

It didn't bother the other knights as much as it did him. To them, Evangeline was simply broken. The once desirable, now shattered, daughter of their king. Someone to be pitied, at best. But to Darrek, she was everything. Beautiful, desirable, fragile certainly, but no less whole than him or anyone else.

But then, to the other knights, she was just the daughter of their king.

To him, she was the woman he loved.

He wasn't sure when it had happened. Perhaps during the watches of one night when she lay asleep or when she'd beaten by the battle. Perhaps when he'd stood with her in the clearing or held her on his horse. Or perhaps when she told him about her past, and he'd been overwhelmed by her courage. But it had. What had begun as brotherly protection had grown into respect before welling into a love and affection so deep—and so not brotherly— that it took all the control within him not to smother her with it.

He wanted to kiss her. In fact, he wanted to do far more than that. He wanted to marry her, and hold her, and make her his in every way. He wanted to love her until the fear was gone from her eyes and she realized what a precious gift she was. To him. To Arthur. To her family. To Raedonleith and beyond.

But he couldn't. Not now. Maybe not ever. She wasn't his to claim.

Still… "I love her."

Manning didn't even flinch at Darrek's words. "I know. But she's betrothed to another."

One of the blacksmith's hammers pounding against his chest would have hurt less than Manning's reminder.

"It still stands, then? Baron Waddingham still waits?" Perhaps the man had walked away. It had been four years. And such a strange match to begin with.

"Aye. I've not heard otherwise. I'm sorry, Darrek."

Darrek sighed. "No more than I."

CHAPTER
25

Manning was gone when Darrek woke, to Darrek's relief. The extra sleep had been appreciated. The reminder that Evangeline was betrothed—and that he needed to be far more careful—was not. It was becoming all too easy to brush away the fact that she was betrothed when he was with Evangeline.

Or perhaps, Darrek admitted to himself as he knelt at the chapel's altar, his mind far from silent, he'd simply hoped she might choose him instead. Betrothals had been broken before.

Forgive me, Almighty.

He'd come to bring reverence, and all he'd managed was aggravation. He'd best be getting to his work anyway. The squires would be wondering where he was. With another prayer for forgiveness and an extra one for wisdom, Darrek slipped out of the chapel and back to the stables.

Baron John Richard Waddingham, second son of Lord Christoph Waddingham—widower, childless, and far too uptight for Evangeline.

The betrothal had surprised everyone when King Lior announced it. It had come about quickly, and Evangeline was the first of the king's daughters to be betrothed despite her being youngest of the three.

Darrek had thought it unusual at the time, though not much beyond that. He'd been happy for her. He'd also been relieved that his fellow knights would be able to focus better on their tasks without Lady Evangeline distracting them with her constant flirting. He hadn't thought Baron Waddingham a poor choice for Evangeline, seeing only the man's steady countenance and maturity. Exactly what the childish Lady Evangeline had needed in a husband.

He didn't think so now, nor did he believe anymore that Evangeline had thought so then. She'd left Raedonleith the day after the betrothal was announced. She'd said she and her father argued. Was that what it had been about? And if so, did Darrek stand a chance?

No. Darrek shook his head, annoyed at the direction of his thoughts. It didn't matter whether Evangeline liked the man—or even knew the man—King Lior had announced the betrothal. She and Lord Waddingham were as good as married.

And, as Manning had so bluntly said, Darrek needed to remember that.

Darrek ran a hand through his hair, pulling out several pieces of straw that had lodged in it before tying it back with a piece of leather. He didn't bother to dust too much of the dirt off his clothes. They'd be filthy again soon enough. The work of a knight—or squire—was not known to be clean.

Evangeline drew two buckets full of water from the well.

Darrek shoveled manure.

Evangeline beat dust out of a rug.

Darrek shoveled manure.

Evangeline tipped a bucket of muck out a window.

Darrek shoveled manure.

Evangeline drew more water, Arthur by her side this time.

Darrek shoveled manure.

He didn't mind the work. It was something to occupy his hands, and it gave him reason to keep watch over Evangeline. But he couldn't keep doing it. *She* couldn't keep doing it.

Her arms trembled when she lifted the buckets out of the well. Her forehead had a smudge of dust across it where she'd leaned her head against the tapestry to catch her breath. She'd stumbled, almost falling, twice on her way back to the kitchen.

The work had made her stronger than she was when she'd left Raedonleith, but day by day, hour by hour, it was killing her.

But convincing her to leave? She'd never do it. Not without Arthur.

Eva swiped a hand across her forehead, wishing she could wipe away the ache in her head as easily as the sweat pooling there. She shivered outside, but back in the kitchens, she was so warm she felt faint.

Her father had sent her another letter. The young squire, Craig, had slipped it to her as she left the cottage this morning. She'd pulled it from her sleeve and read it so many times in the early morning light that she almost had it memorized. It was still tucked into her sleeve—right beside the bandage she'd wrapped around her arm not ten minutes after first reading the letter. A tiny spot of blood had dropped onto the paper. A tear had smeared two words into one beside it.

> *Evangeline,*
>
> *I love you. If you read no more of this missive, know that. I love you, and that will never change, no matter where you've been these four years past or what you've done.*
>
> *I hope you come home soon. I pray it by the hour as I watch for you from the tower walls. But if, as Sir Manning tells me, you need more time, know this: You will always have a place at my table. You are my daughter, and I will always be proud to call you that.*

A place at his table. No matter what she'd done.

Eva shook her head, as desperate for the words to be true as she was certain they couldn't be. He wouldn't have said them if he knew.

"Even if he is as simple as the guards say, he's still the handsomest man I've ever seen," Flaire said from the table beside Eva.

"Darrek." She drew out the middle, making the name sound far more dramatic than it was. "Even his name is strong."

Flaire's friend, Rhea, laughed. The sound was closer to a bird's screech than anything particularly joyous. "You said the same thing about Sir Pilar four months ago."

"I meant it just as much then. Sir Pilar *was* the handsomest of them all. But now, Darrek is."

"Who will it be next month, I wonder?" Rhea asked with a scoff.

"Darrek, of course. Don't know why he's wasting his time in them stables when he's big enough to be a guard, but it keeps him close, and I, for one, am not going to be complaining none about that."

Eva blinked against the dizziness, trying to clear her gaze. Her head felt twice its usual size. She reached out a hand to steady herself, gasping at the way her arm throbbed with pain when she did so. A bandage had stuck when she'd tried to remove it yesterday. Maeve had come upon her before she'd had time to redress it properly, so she'd simply lowered the sleeve over it. At least the pain gave her something besides the dizziness to focus on.

"You think he'd notice you? A maid?"

"Why not? He notices Eva. I saw the two of them coming out of the forest the other morning when I came to the kitchen. And then he tried to carry the water bucket for her yesterday. He must be simple if he's following around the demon girl. Still handsome though, so I'll take him. Show him what a *real* woman is like."

Eva stirred the jelly she'd been tasked with boiling and tried to ignore the gossiping maids. Impossible, when they were standing close to her and speaking loudly enough to ensure she heard them.

"He only follows her because he pities her. He'll move on soon enough. Why would any man want Eva? She's cursed. Her and the boy. She's as good as dead. And even if she weren't, it's not like she's worth anything. She couldn't even keep Lord Cavendish happy, and we all know how much *he* likes his women. As soon as Darrek realizes that, he'll turn his attention elsewhere. No man wants a cursed woman."

Eva clenched her teeth together and smiled down at Arthur, hoping he was too busy stirring water in the little pot she'd given him to pay any attention to the gossiping maids. They thought Darrek pitied her. They were probably right.

"Yes, well, if he keeps her quiet—"

The spoon tumbled from Eva's hand. She bent to pick it up before slowly turning to confront Flaire. "What do you mean by that?"

Normally, she would have ignored the gossiping maids. Doing so had served her well the past three years. But not knowing if Darrek really had been in her room that night or if she'd merely dreamed him had been frustrating her for days. She had to know.

She pointed the spoon at Flaire. "Tell me."

Eva didn't miss the glare Maeve shot Flaire. Nor the way Flaire debated whether or not to answer anyway—tossing up between the secret she held and whether it was worth Maeve's wrath. Eva's stomach rolled. She pushed an unsteady hand against it and silently begged the scant breakfast she'd eaten to stay.

"Maeve?"

"'Tis nothing. Go back to work." Maeve looked at Flaire and Rhea watching Eva with interest. "All of you."

The two maids did as they were told, though they continued to whisper to each other, sending the occasional look over their shoulder in Eva's direction. Discussing her, no doubt. She should let it go. She'd brought more attention to herself with her questions than was wise, given the way gossip spread amongst the servants, but she had to know.

When Maeve walked outside to get more water, Eva picked up a bucket of her own and followed her out. "What did Flaire mean, about Darrek keeping me quiet?"

The square was almost empty, but Eva still kept her voice low. When Maeve didn't answer, Eva wondered if she'd spoken too quietly. She was about to ask it again when Maeve answered.

"It's nothing." Bucket full, Maeve started to walk away.

Eva stepped in front of her. "No, it's not. I command you to tell me."

"You're not the princess here, love. And I ain't your servant to command."

Maeve's gentle admonishment knocked the fight out of Eva. She braced a hand against the well, shaking her head more at herself than the other woman. "No. Forgive me. You aren't, but you are my friend. The only one I have here. Please, Maeve?"

She had to know. She couldn't keep going like this—second-guessing every movement Darrek made or word he said, doing the same for herself. She'd barely slept a fitful hour these past three nights. She blamed Darrek. It was easier than blaming the butterflies and the hope so close yet out of reach.

"You won't like it."

"I imagine not."

Eva could tell the moment Maeve decided to tell her. The woman's expression changed from determined to compassionate. Too compassionate. Eva braced herself, already guessing at the truth before Maeve said it.

"When your night terrors come, so does your knight. He holds your hand and prays over you. And it works. You calm down. Go back to sleep."

A second hand went to the edge of the well. It took every bit of Eva's self-control to remain standing, and even then, her legs shook.

"He comes most every night. I thought I was the only one who knew why you calmed, but if Flaire knows, then someone—maybe a stable boy—must have seen Darrek and told her. Or she's simply guessing. That girl is as jealous as they come, and she's clearly taken a liking to your knight."

It was worse than Eva had thought. So much worse. Flaire, she could deal with. But Darrek? He hadn't been protecting her or merely watching over her as a guard might. He'd seen—

Too much. She closed her eyes. Willed away the darkness threatening to send her to the ground.

"Every time?" The question was barely a whisper, the pain too much to put into words. "Darrek sees me like…that?"

Screaming. Terrified. Sobbing like a child, Maeve had said once.

Weak. So weak.

"There's more." Maeve put a hand on Eva's, her voice quiet. Apologetic. "He's seen your scars, lass. He knows."

The shaking in Eva's legs stopped. Her heart might well have too given that her breath certainly had. A hundred knights could have stormed the gates of Cavendish Castle not five feet from where Eva stood, and she wouldn't have noticed them nor cared if she had. Eva closed her eyes. Forced herself to draw in a breath before letting it out in a rush.

"How long?"

A pause. Then, "Since the day the knights came."

Eva gripped the edge of the well like it was the only thing keeping her upright. Likely, it was.

"Why didn't you tell me? Why didn't he?"

"Only he can answer his part of that. As to me, you were happy. You calmed with him there and, selfish though I felt, I got a mite more sleep when you were calm."

"I'm—sorry." She knew her terrors were bad. They were why she'd been banished to the cottage with Maeve rather than sharing a room in the castle with the other kitchen maids. They were why others believed she was cursed—everyone except for Maeve.

Maeve and—

Darrek.

Every time, Maeve said. *Every time*. When the terrors came, so did Darrek. He held her hand. Heard her scream. Saw her scars.

"He asked me about my scars," she said.

"What did you tell him?"

"Nothing. He let it go."

Maeve smiled that sad smile again. "He won't always. He cares about you, lass. Don't throw that away out of pride."

But that was the thing. It wasn't pride. It was kindness. He didn't deserve the curse that was a woman like her. No man did.

With a sigh born of weariness, Eva picked up her bucket—

empty though it was—and walked back into the kitchen. Back to the fire. Back to Arthur, still making whirlpools in his pot.

Maids gossiped, pots boiled, knives hit wooden boards in an endless rhythm, life went on. Nothing had changed, yet for Eva, everything had.

Darrek had been there through her nightmares. Darrek had seen her scars.

When he'd asked her about them that day, he hadn't been guessing. He'd known.

When he'd stroked her cheek with his thumb, and called her beautiful, and asked if he might call her his friend, he'd known.

All this time, she'd thought if he only knew, he'd run. As fast and as far away from her as an honorable man could get. And yet, he'd done the opposite. More, he'd found ways to make her smile. To make *Arthur* smile.

The question was, what did she do now?

CHAPTER 26

"Sire?"

Lior dropped his sword to his side, irritated not by the interruption but how relieved he was for it. Once he'd been able to train for hours on end. Illness and worry had stolen his strength along with his physique, but no more. He would be strong again. For his daughters. His people. Evangeline's son. This morning's training had been brutal, but he'd lasted twice as long as he had the week past and three times as long as the week before.

He nodded his thanks to the knight he'd been sparring against and assured the man he'd be back this afternoon to train again. Right now, he had something more important to see to. The guard he had sent to trail Baron Waddingham had returned.

"You found something?" he asked the guard.

"I did."

The man's face was serious. Too serious. And though he stood before his king, he couldn't quite meet Lior's gaze. Lior gripped the handle of his sword and braced himself. Whatever was to come, it wouldn't be good. But then, little news had been since the day he'd found his youngest daughter gone.

Almighty, give me strength.

"Tell me."

CHAPTER
27

A single candle sat lit atop the altar inside the chapel. Its feeble light danced in a circle around the altar's base. Eva was surprised to see one lit so early in the morning and was tempted to blow it out so the darkness might hide her better. But doing so would require her to walk to the front of the chapel, and she'd already used up all her courage merely walking through the door.

Cursed. Broken. Failure. Ruined.

The words throbbed inside Eva, pounding their mark on her heart. She sighed and pressed a fist against her mouth. She shouldn't have come. She'd been a fool to think she might find peace here, as Darrek did. He was good and upright, exactly the type of person this magnificent chapel had been built for. But her? The awe and splendor of the place only proved again how far she'd fallen. If the wrath of the Almighty didn't kill her for daring to enter, the shame would.

She turned to leave, only to see someone standing between her and the door. Though her mind instantly skipped to Darrek, the man was too short to be him. Only when he shuffled a few steps forward did she see he was also far too old.

"Eva, isn't that what they call you? I haven't seen you here before."

His voice was soft, as faded with time as his body had become. His clothing too. Yet his gaze was kind. Too kind for a woman like her.

Cursed. Broken. Failure. Ruined.

"I'm sorry. I'm leaving," she told him quickly.

"Why? You're as welcome here as anyone."

"You wouldn't say that if you knew."

"Knew what?"

Eva dropped her gaze. "Who I am. What I've done."

He shuffled back a step. Eva didn't blame him. If she could have escaped herself, she would have. She turned again to leave. She had bread to make, water to draw, a child to protect, a certain knight to avoid...

"What do you think of the windows?" The cleric's question stopped her for a second time.

"The windows? They're—" Eva let her gaze rise to the stained-glass windows, their colors just beginning to show in the feeble morning light. It would be nice to see them when sunlight streamed through, making the colors truly vibrant, but she'd be gone long before then. Still, even now, she could appreciate their workmanship. "They're beautiful."

"They're broken."

"What?" Eva looked again, harder this time, straining her eyes through the dim light to find a crack or missing piece, but couldn't see what the man was talking about. They appeared perfect to her. Perhaps his sight was going along with his hair.

"Every piece of the glass that makes up those windows is broken. Some are crushed. All of them are ruined."

"But they're—"

"Beautiful? Aye, 'tis as you say. But only because the creator took those broken pieces and made them into something beautiful. That's what the creator does."

Eva shook her head. Though she appreciated the man's comparison, it wasn't the same. "I'm not a window."

"No, child. You're far more valuable."

CHAPTER 28

Evangeline hadn't been exaggerating when she'd told Darrek that Lord Cavendish liked his feasts. Tonight's had to have been the fifteenth—at least—since Darrek and the knights had arrived six weeks ago.

But this one was different from the rest. The feast spread outside, beyond the sight of the Great Hall filled with nobles, so the servants could have their own dance. The servants' steps might have been less intricate, and their clothing might be less elaborate and far more worn, but their joy was greater.

Maids made up for the lack of jewels by weaving flowers into their hair. Laughter made them beautiful in a way no number of cosmetics ever could. Did the servants do the same at Raedonleith? Darrek didn't know. He'd always been inside the Great Hall, one of the privileged ones. Watching the servants now, he wondered if the title was as much a privilege as he'd thought.

"Dance with her."

Darrek didn't need to ask Manning who he was talking about. The instant he'd spotted Evangeline spinning with Arthur at the edge of the crowd, it was as if none of the other dancers existed, except to make her shine brighter.

He'd never seen her dance before. Not like this. Court dances, a gentle sway to the music of the minstrels as she sat at the high table, certainly. But not like this. Free. Light. Beautiful. Her laugh could have lit the heavens.

"I shouldn't."

"Nor should she be a servant, but she is. Life isn't always as black and white as we make it."

"Two weeks ago, you told me to stay away from her."

"A lot can happen in two weeks."

Darrek looked sharply at his mentor. "What do you know? Did King Lior send another missive?" He hadn't seen a messenger come, but then, he was sleeping and working in the stables. It wasn't beyond the realm of possibility that someone had come while he'd been working.

"He did."

"And?"

"Lady Evangeline is no longer betrothed."

Darrek frowned. "Waddingham broke the betrothal? Why now, when he's waited four years for her already? Was another month or two too much for him to take?"

"He would have waited, if it had been only for Lady Evangeline."

Understanding came swiftly. "King Lior told him about Arthur."

"He did."

"And Waddingham didn't want the boy?"

"Not as a son. Neither did he want Lady Evangeline, apart from the riches or status she would have brought him."

Scoundrel. Darrek had never liked that pompous man, but he'd been willing to grudgingly give Waddingham the respect he deserved for waiting patiently for Evangeline the past four years. Apparently, Darrek's first impression of the man had been correct.

"According to the guard King Lior had follow Waddingham, the first stop the baron made after leaving his meeting with the king was to a tavern to see a man about buying poisons to rid himself of an unwanted wife—while still keeping her riches he so desperately needed."

Cold fury washed over Darrek. His hands clenched at his sides. The man planned to wed then kill Lady Evangeline? Because she came with a child?

No, Darrek saw the truth in Manning's barely veiled anger. Because she'd been with another man. Because Baron Waddingham, even though he was a widower, wanted a woman untouched.

"King Lior gave Waddingham the option of breaking the betrothal himself and going away quietly, never to return, or having King Lior announce to everyone in Raedonleith that it was broken along with the truth of why. Waddingham chose the former."

Darrek would have thrown the man in the dungeon. And likely left him there. King Lior had given Waddingham far more grace than he deserved. Imagine, planning to kill a woman because she'd been with another man. It was sickening.

Yet even as Darrek thought it, shame came over him. Killing anyone outside of battle went against everything he stood for as a knight, but ten—even five—years ago, he too would have looked with scorn on a woman who'd given herself to a man outside of the sanctity of marriage. He would have gone as far out of his way as he could to avoid being marred by her presence.

Ten—five—years ago, he'd been as much a fool as Baron Waddingham.

Being with Evangeline this past month, hearing her pain, seeing the proof of it on her arms—she was broken, certainly, but not beyond grace. Not beyond love. She'd made mistakes, but who among them hadn't? Perhaps she was the bravest of them all—she faced them, every day, while others hid them from the world and pretended they weren't there at all.

She was a woman to be admired, not one to be scorned and brushed aside as Baron Waddingham had done.

Though Darrek would have to thank him one day for that.

When he stopped being so incensed on her behalf.

"Does Evangeline know?"

"Not yet."

"She has to know."

Manning nodded. "Aye. But I thought you might be the one to tell her."

"Why?"

"She trusts you. Moreover, she listens to you."

"All the more reason I should stay away."

"Is that what you want?"

Darrek huffed. Of course it wasn't, as Manning well knew.

"It isn't unheard of that a knight marry the daughter of his king."

Darrek almost choked on the hope welling in his chest. "Me? Marry Lady Evangeline?"

"You speak as if you think it ridiculous."

"Two weeks ago, you did too."

Manning shrugged. "Call it the sentimentality of an old fool, but I think everyone deserves a chance at love. Even—especially—those who've given up on it. I'm not telling you to marry the girl, Darrek, though I'm certain you would find the will to do so if I did. Just ask her to dance. Show her you're worthy of that trust she's given you. And if her trust grows to love, don't run from it."

"King Lior—"

"Believes you are the man who will bring his daughter home."

Darrek swallowed. Home. The image it brought to mind was enough to steal every other thought. Evangeline and him. Together. Her arms around him. His child under her heart. Her smiling, no longer afraid. The picture he'd thought an impossible dream. Evangeline, his wife.

"I'm starting to think he's correct. Dance with the girl, Darrek. Before you lose your chance. That's an order."

Dance with Evangeline. It didn't even come close to what Darrek wanted. But it was more than he'd hoped.

"Aye, sir. As you wish."

"May I have this—" Darrek stopped mid-question, stunned at the tears wetting Evangeline's face. His smile dropped to a frown as he bent to better see her. "Evangeline? What is it? What happened? Are you hurt? Who hurt you?"

His hand reached for his sword out of habit before remembering he'd left it behind. He clenched his fist instead. George would tell him to be still or pray. Manning would tell him to watch and listen. Darrek would have rather hit a wall.

"Evangeline?"

Her lips moved, but the music and sound of laughter were too loud for Darrek to hear. He looked around for Maeve, Manning, anyone to help her, but the crowd of dancers obscured any chance he had of finding them. Arthur was gone too. Was that why she wept?

"Come," he said, making the decision for them both. Placing her hand on his arm, he led her across the square to the empty bench beside the blacksmith's shop. Bracketed with walls on either side, the music was quieter here, the moon alone lighting up the sky. "Where's Arthur?"

"With—Maeve."

Darrek looked back to the dancers, spotting the boy and older woman right away. They'd come to the edge of the crowd. Maeve, as always, watched over Evangeline like a guardian angel. When she saw Evangeline with Darrek, she nodded to him before taking Arthur's hand and disappearing back into the throng.

"Please, tell me what the matter is." If it weren't Arthur, was it someone else? Had one of the maids been cruel? More cruel than usual? "What has you weeping? You were so happy. I heard you laugh, even from a distance, with all the other people around. I knew it was yours. I came to ask you to dance and instead saw your tears. Did someone hurt you?"

Evangeline shook her head, tears falling on the hands clasped on her lap. He placed a hand over them, willing strength into her.

"Did they say something? Disrespect you?"

Again, she shook her head. Her shoulders hunched forward as a sob burst out of her throat.

Almighty, what do I do?

"Caterpillar…"

She swallowed twice but couldn't stop the sobs that followed the first. He looked from her hair to their clasped hands to the dirt darkening the bottom of her skirt, as if something in her appearance might help him understand. She'd been so happy as he talked with Manning. What had changed in the half a minute it took to walk to her side?

Pray. George's voice echoed again in his mind. He pushed it aside. What good was prayer when he was right here? He'd fight for her, battle a thousand armies for her, do whatever it took to fix whatever ailed her, if only he knew what she needed.

"Hold me?"

Her whisper broke him. Without another thought, he wrapped his arms around her, holding her against his chest as he'd done that day on the horse. As he'd wished to do a million times over as he'd held her hand through one nightmare after another.

Her hair brushed against his nose. He breathed it in as she wet his shirt with tears. This was good. This was right.

This was torture.

But a torture he'd happily take, if it helped the woman sobbing in his arms.

"I'm s-so t-tired of fighting."

"Then stop."

"And g-give in?"

"Maybe it's time to surrender."

She swallowed audibly before scoffing. "To the v-voices? The darkness? The doubts? The f-failure?" She shook her head before pulling back to swipe the tears off her face. Darrek felt the cold between them immediately. It took another minute of her gritting her teeth—and him wishing there was something he could do—for her to claim back control.

"Darrek, if I gave in to them, I'd throw myself off a cliff. Despite my poor choices, I don't want to die. I don't want to listen to the voices. They're wrong. I know that, deep at the heart of me. But knowing and accepting are two very different things, especially on the days when it's all too easy to believe them. I have to fight. I can't give in to them.

"But the fight never ends. Every day, every minute, the voices are there, telling me how much of a f-failure I am. How the world, Arthur, my family, you even, would be better off without me. How I can never atone for what I've done or change the past. They're always there. And I want to fight them. I do. But it's just so exhausting fighting all the time when I never win."

Though she'd gained control of her words and breathing, tears continued to drip down Evangeline's cheeks.

"I thought if I fought long enough and hard enough, the battle would end. But it doesn't. It never goes away, and I never get any closer to winning. All I can manage is to hold it all together just enough. Enough to keep going, enough to force a smile, enough to get through another day.

"I could scrub linens for five days straight and still not be as exhausted as I am from battling the voices in my head."

Darrek didn't wait for Evangeline's permission this time, pulling her into his arms, tugging her in as close to his heart as he dared. He needed the embrace as much as she did.

The music from the dance still played, laughter and shouts mingling among it. Evangeline wept against his chest, sagging as the tears—or perhaps admission—stole what was left of her strength. How long had she been holding the pain in for it to gush out in so many words? All this time, she'd been fighting. And he'd had no idea.

"I'm so sorry," he said, after a time, hating that he couldn't find any better words to comfort her with. "I didn't know."

"No one does."

"You told me."

She sat up, pushing away from his arms as she swiped a hand across her face and straightened her gown. Every movement evidenced she was already putting back up her walls. He couldn't let her succeed.

"Let me help. Let me fight with you."

Evangeline shook her head, as he'd known she would. Although there was no defiance in the denial, only sadness. "I don't know if you can."

"Would you at least allow me to try?"

"Why?"

Because I love you.

The words came instantly to Darrek's mind, solid in their certainty. He loved Evangeline. But he couldn't tell her. It was too soon, and Evangeline was too vulnerable. She'd never believe he hadn't said it just to woo her through this moment.

"Because I care about you."

It was the truth, if not the whole of it.

"You shouldn't."

"Why? Because you're broken? We're all broken, Caterpillar. But most of us just aren't brave enough to let the pieces show."

"No. Because I couldn't bear to let you down too."

Darrek wrapped an arm around her shoulder, tugging her back in against him. It was more than he should have done. And far less than he wanted to do. Evangeline tucked her head in against his chest. He held his breath lest she hear how ragged it had become, not letting it out until he knew he had himself back under control.

This was why he had become a knight—to fight and protect women like Evangeline.

No. Not for women *like* Evangeline.

For Evangeline herself.

All those years of training, cleaning stables, following the other knights around, of fights and battles and sleeping in places he'd sooner forget—it was all for this moment. This woman. To be here when she was weary of the battle and needed to be reminded that she didn't fight alone.

He kissed the top of her head. "I'll be here."

There was more to what he wanted to say. Far more he wanted to promise her. But if there was one thing he'd learnt over the past four years, it was that patience had well-earned its status as a virtue, and Lady Evangeline of Raedonleith was worth waiting for.

"Evangeline?"

She tipped her head up to look at him.

"Will you dance with me?"

CHAPTER
29

King Lior closed the thick tome on his table and laid his head on top of it. He was trying to be present for Caralynne, Rose, and Mykah. He'd sat in his place between them at dinner these five nights past, clapped the loudest of all those present at Mykah's archery demonstration when she hit the center of all eight targets with barely a breath between them, and spent hours poring through correspondence searching for the right man to wed his Rose. He'd done everything right, but it still wasn't enough. His family was drifting away—Evangeline followed by his other two daughters—and he had no one to blame but himself.

He pulled out Manning's latest update, never far from his reach.

Evangeline was well, but she wasn't coming home. Manning told him to hold on to hope—that he believed the time was nigh when she would—but hope felt so small. And Lior was so tired. When once he'd clung to the knowledge that every day that passed was one day closer to the day his daughter would come home, he wondered now if she ever would.

He should have gone. It should have been him who'd been searching for Evangeline all these years. He'd been the one who'd driven her away. His pride had pushed him to refuse to apologize when he had the chance. And knowing where she was? It was all he could do not to storm Cavendish Castle and order her home.

But demands had been what made her run in the first place.

That and his foolish choice of a husband for her. How had he been so wrong about Waddingham? He'd known the man for years and shared a table with him on many an occasion. Had four years of waiting changed him so much? Lior should have had the man followed long before now. How many other ways would he fail his daughters before he finally got something right?

Lior lifted his head when a knock sounded against the door. Mykah had mentioned seeking him out this afternoon. He couldn't let her see him moping. Again. He forced a smile and a calm he didn't feel. "Enter."

But it wasn't his middle daughter behind the swathes of fabric that entered his private chamber.

"Caralynne."

He sighed, letting the façade go. He'd promised Caralynne on their wedding day twenty-three years ago that he'd never lie to her nor hide the truth. Of all the promises he'd made her, he'd not thought that would be the most difficult to keep. It would have been far easier to offer her a smile—forced as it was—than to see the long-suffering expression he'd come to know so well on her face.

Manning's note crumpled in his hand.

"You received word?" Caralynne asked, draping the fabric across one of the room's benches before walking to his side.

"Aye, but nothing new. She remains at Cavendish Castle. I shouldn't have let her go."

"She would have gone regardless. You couldn't have stopped her."

"I should have tried harder than I did. What if she thinks I don't love her? What if she was just waiting for me to fight for her?"

"You did."

He shook his head before dropping it onto the table again with a sigh. "Not hard enough."

Caralynne's hands came to his shoulders, rubbing them. For almost a minute, she was silent, before kneeling by his side. The hand she placed in his was as gentle as her reply, though he deserved neither.

"Lior, not one person in the entire kingdom could doubt the love you have for your daughters."

"Evangeline did."

"She won't once she comes home."

"What if she doesn't?"

Caralynne stood. Lior raised his head to see his wife, arms crossed, looking as fierce as any one of his knights.

"Then you tell her. Again and again. For the rest of her life if that's what it takes."

He appreciated her words, even if they weren't what he'd meant. Her faith in him too.

"No. What if she doesn't come home?"

"You told your knights to bring her."

"That doesn't mean she'll come," he argued.

"Then we'll keep praying, just as we have every day of her life, just like we do every day for Rose and Mykah. We'll pray for her safety. We'll pray for her future. We'll pray she finds joy, love, hope, and peace. We'll pray that, when she falls, she'll find the strength to get back up. We'll pray her heart finds home."

CHAPTER
30

H is caterpillar had come. Though she looked as skittish as a hare in the early morning light, she'd still come.

"Will you tell me about the scars?"

"I don't—"

"Evangeline." Darrek swept a piece of her hair back from her face, wishing he could rid her eyes of terror as easily. He kept his voice as gentle as he could when all he wanted to do was demand answers. "Trust me with them. Please?"

She ducked her head. "I wish you hadn't seen them."

He took her hands in his, cradling them, willing her to trust him.

The chapel was silent around them, not even the smallest breeze daring to break the reverence. It had been like this two nights ago too. He'd thanked Evangeline for their dance, seen her back to Maeve's side, and come directly here. He'd stayed until dawn peered through the stained-glass windows, turning the floor where he knelt to shades of rainbow. He'd tried to pray—all night, he'd tried—but every time he'd succeeded in quieting his spirit long enough to attempt words, he heard only Evangeline's.

I don't want to die, but the fight never ends.

He'd invited her to join him in the chapel yesterday morning. She'd declined. He'd just finished promising himself he'd keep asking, day after day until she said yes, when she told him she'd come today. He hadn't let himself believe it until she'd walked through the door, certain something—or someone—would stop her. The chapel was the only place he could think of to speak with her where they wouldn't be interrupted. And he had to speak with her. She'd had a new bandage on her arm the day after the dance.

"Please." His voice was a whisper of a plea. Though she shook her head again, she didn't pull away. Darrek waited, telling himself he could be patient for as long as she needed. Desperate for it to be true. "Evangeline?"

Maeve had said Evangeline did it to herself. Darrek had hoped the older woman was mistaken. He'd known the moment he'd seen Evangeline sobbing in the woods that day that Maeve was right. Though Evangeline had hidden the bandage from him, nothing could have banished the hopelessness from her eyes.

"Why do you do it?"

Her hands were still. His shook. The emotion, the wanting, the holding back… He trembled with it. Yet she might as well have been one of the stained-glass windows, still as she was. She barely even breathed.

"Caterpillar?"

The chapel was quiet. Beyond quiet. The two of them were alone this morning, and the elderly cleric was nowhere to be seen. Eva knew. She'd checked before slipping through the door. His words had stayed with her, haunting her in a way her nightmares never had.

You're far more valuable.

He was wrong. She wasn't valuable. Yet she couldn't ignore the ache of yearning for him to be right.

Darrek squeezed her hand. Waiting.

Eva wished she'd declined his invitation to come with him this morning, but he'd asked it in front of Maeve, who'd claimed she had a task she needed Arthur for. A long one. "Go," Maeve had ordered. "He cares about you. Let him." Eva had known as soon as she sobbed into Darrek's shirt at the dance that he'd not leave her words unanswered. She'd just hoped to postpone the inevitable for more than two days.

Preferably forever.

Darrek's hands felt like fire around her cold ones. She tried to tell herself that he knew everything she had to tell him already—he'd seen the scars and knew she was the one who'd inflicted them—but it didn't help. Admitting her failure was so much worse than having him know it.

She gripped his hands tighter. Where did one even start with such an answer?

"Please…"

Eva nodded. Sucked air into her suddenly dry mouth. Braced herself for his scorn, his disappointment, his judgment. And began the only place she could.

"I never wanted to."

Perhaps if he knew that—that it hadn't been so much a choice as a moment of desperation—the rest would come easier.

"I know how foolish a thing it is to do, and I hate it more than you ever could. But the pain inside me was too much. It was going to destroy me if I didn't find a way to let it out. You can bandage a physical wound and see it healing, but a wound within? It's just there. Constantly. Begging for an escape. It was too big. Too much. I needed to do something.

"One tiny cut on my hand. Easy enough to explain. And yet, it helped. I felt better. Almost like a little bit of the pain seeped out alongside the blood.

"I know, it makes no sense. It sounds so foolish to say it aloud, but—"

Her words caught, both hands going over her face. He would hate her now. Just as she'd known he would. At least he'd understand why going home wasn't an option. If it had only been Arthur holding her back, she would have left years ago. Arthur was her excuse. Shame was what chained her here.

Eva wished she could cry almost as much as she ached for a knife, but her eyes remained dry, and, as much as she disgusted him, she knew Darrek was too noble to let her anywhere near anything sharp right now. Perhaps he was her savior after all.

Bitterness roiled Eva's stomach. Sure. Like he was going to stay now he knew the truth. Darrek would discard her as quickly as

Cavendish had, and she'd be right back here, rolling in self-loath-ing as thick as clay. Why did she even try?

"Say it anyway."

Eva peeked between her fingers to see Darrek hadn't moved away. If anything, he'd come closer. And while his voice shook with barely controlled emotion, his hand was gentle as he pulled hers away from her face.

"What sounds foolish to say aloud?" he asked.

"You'll hate me."

"Seems you're doing a pretty good job of that already."

Darrek rubbed his thumb across the back of Eva's hand, his touch more soothing than she deserved. But he hadn't run. Hadn't even condemned her.

Yet.

Did she dare share the thoughts she'd barely begun to under-stand herself?

"You can trust me."

Could she? Truly?

"Tell me. Please? Let me in."

"It's—"

Emotion made her hands shake in his. She wanted to pull them free as much as she ached to tuck herself closer. Curl up in his lap, rest her head against his chest, hear the steadiness of his heartbeat, and pretend all this was another nightmare. In so many ways, it was.

"It's—"

His gaze held hers.

"It's okay," he whispered. "You don't have to tell me."

It was in the moment when he started to pull away that Eva realized how much she wanted to tell him.

"It's visible," she said in a rush. "A cut, that is. It's justifiable. I'm in pain because, look, I'm injured. There it is. Physical pain heals. It gets sympathy. People can see it. *I* can see it. What's in-side though? It's invisible. No one sees the fight or the pain, even though it's so much worse than anything physical. I'd rather cut my arm off altogether than have to deal with this pain."

"You don't mean that."

If only that were true. "Actually, I do. At least then, people would see."

Darrek recoiled as if she'd slapped him in the face. A muscle jumped in his cheek, right above the line of his beard, and he closed his eyes.

She wouldn't want to look at herself either.

"Evangeline, I—" His voice caught. He cleared his throat and tried again. "I should go."

She nodded, knowing this moment had been inevitable, even if it hurt so much worse than she'd expected.

"I know."

His gaze when he turned it back to hers was full of all the self-loathing she knew so well. "It's not you. It's me. I want to—have to—I…" Though he tried to soften the words, nothing he could have said could make them hurt less. He didn't try again, dropping her hands as he stumbled to his feet.

Eva's hands fell back into her lap, cold without his around them. "It's fine."

"No, I—" He ground out a groan before shaking his head and rushing the few steps to the door. He stopped, one hand on the wood, just long enough to whisper an apology before fleeing the chapel.

Eva closed her eyes. He'd run. Just like she'd known he would. He might have said it wasn't her fault and that she could trust him, but she knew the truth. She was too broken for any man.

She was too broken for herself.

For the second time in as many weeks, Darrek stormed his way through the forest, not caring who heard him or how many shrubs he destroyed in the process. Evangeline had given him the trust he'd begged for, and for what? So he could run away? Leave her to face the demons alone? He'd been so certain he could save her, but sitting there, watching her try to put words to the pain she fought—it was too much. If he hadn't run, he would have crushed her in his embrace. Crushed her like she'd crushed his heart.

She thought she was broken.

She thought no one saw her.

She thought no one cared.

She couldn't have been more wrong. About any of them.

But she'd been right about one thing—he couldn't fight this for her.

He'd been all set to challenge Cavendish—to the death, if need be—for her honor and pride. But while Cavendish might have compounded the problem, he hadn't caused it. This went so much deeper than one man.

He had to find that knife.

But first, he had to talk to Manning. Thankfully, Manning found him.

"I know you're angry, but you're making enough noise to bring out the whole of Cavendish's guard."

The relief Darrek felt at his mentor's presence and the fact that he didn't have to waste time trying to track the man was all but eclipsed by his anger. Darrek gritted his teeth. "I don't care."

Manning sat himself down on a fallen tree trunk, leaning back against another and crossing his ankles, as if he had all the time in the world to sit and chat. "Actually, I think that's exactly why you're so upset—because you *do* care."

Darrek picked up a rock and flung it. It hit the ground a foot from where he stood leaving a solid dint in the dirt. It wasn't enough. He threw another, and another, and another.

Manning watched until Darrek, chest heaving, fell to the ground.

"What happened?"

Two simple words. But behind them were far more compassion and far less condemnation than Darrek deserved when all he could think about was how he'd failed Evangeline. How they all had. He'd not told Manning or the other knights about Evangeline's scars, deeming the information too personal to do so. And, if he were truly honest, he'd still been hoping all this time that there was another explanation for them. He couldn't do that anymore.

"Evangeline has scars all over her arms. Self-inflicted. She's so broken inside that it's the only way she can keep going. But it can't be, Manning. She says she doesn't want to die but she'll kill herself trying to stop the pain. I have to save her. I have to find the knife and stop her before she takes it too far. There has to be another way."

Manning was silent. Darrek was anything but, pulling stones from the ground before pegging them back into it, time and time again. If he'd had his sword, he would have felled several trees by now. Or shattered his blade beyond repair. Whichever came first.

"Nothing?" he asked Manning, becoming almost as angry with the older man as he was with himself. How could he just sit there, knowing what Darrek had told him? He should have been rallying the others, storming the castle, shouting his anger, or scheming a plan to do so at the very least. Evangeline might die. And yet here Manning was, sitting on a log, barely even moving.

"I don't have time for this," Darrek said after several more minutes had passed. "I have to find that knife."

He'd stalked three whole steps back toward the castle before Manning's words stopped him.

"It's not about the knife."

Darrek spun back, throwing words like weapons.

"Of course it is."

Manning didn't even flinch. "No, Darrek. It's not. Taking the knife off her won't change anything. She'd find another. It's about why. Discover the why, solve that, and the physical wounds will stop too."

"She wants help."

"Then help her."

Help her. The advice was so simple, yet the execution was more of a challenge than Darrek had ever known. Help her. How? He couldn't fight her or her mind. Even if he took her away from here, there was no guarantee it would help. Evangeline carried her shame like a trophy. But Manning was right. Taking the knife would only stop her until she found another.

"I don't know how."

"Perhaps you're not supposed to."

"Manning…"

"Some demons can only be fought by the Almighty. It seems to me that this is one of them."

Darrek scoffed. "The Almighty doesn't care. If he did, he never would have allowed Evangeline to suffer this pain."

"Would he not? Even if she chose it?"

"She didn't know what she was doing. He did. He could have stopped it. Any moment, any time. He didn't. Not once. Show me one way he cares."

"You still don't see it, do you?"

"See what?"

"Darrek, he sent her you."

CHAPTER
31

Sparring with Spencer, Adam, and Landon for the rest of the day helped rid Darrek of his energy but not the frustration boiling inside him. Nor the guilt that he was with them while Craig watched over Evangeline. It should have been him. He should have stayed. But staying when he had no answers for her and could do nothing other than watch the woman he loved fall apart was too much. His friends gave up trying to reason with him and pull him out of his bad humor after an hour and took turns trying to outdo him instead. He won every battle but not the one he wished to.

Darrek couldn't fight Evangeline's.

Craig returned just before dusk claiming Evangeline had sent him away. She'd be working in the kitchen until retiring, she'd told the boy. Though she was a princess and her words a direct order, Darrek wondered if Craig would have been so quick to obey had her order not come with a handful of pastries the squire was trying to hide.

Darrek should return anyway. Work would be piling up for him, quite literally, in the stables.

A tiny butterfly floated past, a ray of late sunlight making its wings glow for an instant before fading back to white. George might have called it a sign. Darrek changed direction and walked in the direction of the clearing George had shown them instead. There wouldn't be any butterflies there this late in the day, but it wasn't to see them that he was going.

It was in that clearing that he'd told Evangeline, full of faith, that there was hope. Like the caterpillars, she'd one day make it through this and fly. He'd started calling her his caterpillar for that reason.

This time, it was him who needed the reminder.

It took only a few minutes to reach the clearing. He pushed through the branches to see an animal—a doe, perhaps—sleeping on the far side of it. He should leave it be.

But then, the animal moved, just enough to see it wasn't a doe at all but—

"Caterpillar."

She looked up at his whisper, the breeze having carried it to her. He was almost to Evangeline's side when he saw the knife clutched in her hand. The blade was clean. Her face was not.

How long had she been out here, tears mixing with dirt as she wept alone? What if an animal had found her? Worse, what if a man had?

His horror must have shown on his face because she lowered the knife to her skirt.

"I didn't do it," she said, quelling at least part of his fear. "Not—yet."

Not yet. The words made Darrek want to cry himself.

Evangeline— Almighty—

He placed a hand over hers on the knife. He didn't know which of their hands were trembling more.

"You can't keep doing this."

"I don't want to." Her voice was quiet, cowed, like she'd been that first time he'd seen her.

"Then stop, please. I beg of you."

Her shoulders drooped. A tear of defeat dripped down her face. "I wish it were that easy."

"I can't make you stop. You have to want to do it. But I can help."

"How?"

Darrek looked from their clasped hands to the clearing where they sat. The sun had gone, leaving a dusky purple sky above them. A few more minutes and it would be dark blue then black. Would the stars come out? It almost seemed wrong that they might shine when Evangeline—and Darrek himself now—was in so much pain. How could there be such beauty and wonder in the world when, alongside it, was such horror and pain? How could the Almighty orchestrate both?

He sent her you.

Was it no accident that butterfly had flown across his path, sending him here when Evangeline wept? Could he be the answer he sought?

"Evangeline." He waited until she met his gaze. "You said no one could see your pain, and you're right. We can't. You have to tell us. You have to ask for help."

She shook her head, despair written in every tear that still dripped down her cheeks. "I don't know if I can."

"You don't have to shout it from the rooftops, but during those times when the pain is too much, tell one person. Tell me. Tell Maeve."

"Maeve? I couldn't do that!"

Darrek rubbed his thumb across the back of her hand. The skin was so soft. "She already knows."

"What? No."

"No one is that clumsy. She cares, Evangeline. It hurts her to see you hurting yourself. Talk to us. Trust us. We want to help you."

"I talked to you. You walked away. Ran, actually."

"I wouldn't have been able to keep my distance if I'd stayed." The words were low, more than he should have said. Yet she'd been so honest with him, and something about the beauty of the clearing invited intimacy.

A star came out above.

"What do you mean?"

"I mean I care, more than I should. More than is wise. I care about you. You're—you—" He sighed. "You were so upset. I wanted to hold you."

"I would have let you," she said shyly, her gaze bravely holding his.

"I know. That's why I ran."

The urge to kiss her came like the blow of a sword hilt to the stomach. The shape of her lips, the way they turned up just that little bit at the corners of her mouth and parted when she noticed the way he stared. His face heated and, with no small amount of strength, he dropped his gaze.

And saw the knife.

"Caterpillar…"

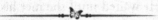

Darrek hadn't run out of disgust. He hadn't run because he hated her. He'd run because he cared. Eva touched a hand to Darrek's beard, smooth yet wiry, just like the man himself. Beneath the strength and fury raged a man who fought for honor. Her honor.

"Come to me next time you're tempted."

And yet, he asked too much of her. "I can't do that." Wasn't all she'd already told him enough? It was more than she'd told anyone. More than she'd even admitted to herself before that moment.

"Why? Because I'll talk you out of it?"

"No. Because you'll see."

Darrek's hand moved to her arm, his thumb stroking it, as if his touch could heal the scars beneath the fabric of her sleeve.

"I want to."

"Believe me, you don't."

His gaze captured hers. Time, fear, uncertainty, shame—for one drawn-out moment, all of them stopped. There was silence in the clearing and in Eva's mind. But, as if they'd all simply moved, her heart raced.

Was this what it felt like to be in love? To be so wholly accepted that even her scars couldn't scare him away?

"May I?"

At first, Eva didn't know what Darrek was asking. To kiss her? Hold her? Yes. And yes again. But as his fingers moved to her wrists, she blanched. He wanted to see her scars.

Her heart could have led an army into battle the way it thudded.

She closed her eyes and nodded.

She barely felt the fabric move as he pushed it up past her elbows, but she felt every trail of his fingers as he touched the scars, running a finger lightly along first one then another. With a gasp, Eva tried to tug the sleeves back down again. Ugly scars. She couldn't have looked Darrek in the eye if she'd tried. Not now, not ever. If he needed proof of how far she'd fallen, here it was. Permanently etched on her arms.

Darrek's warm hand stilled hers.

"Don't hide them. Not from me."

He was the one she most wanted to hide them from. Darrek was everything good in this world—pure, noble, honorable, strong, kind. The type of man who wouldn't even balk for a moment at being sent on a mission to find a king's wayward daughter. Even if it took four years, kept him away from family, friends, and battles, and ended up being disappointing.

This wasn't the first time he'd tried to help her. He'd offered a hand once before, when she was fifteen and tipsy from the ale she'd had at dinner. Her own, Mykah's, and Rose's. She'd almost fallen as she attempted to climb the steps to her chamber. He'd appeared at her side and put out a hand to steady her before offering to escort her back to the dining hall. She'd laughed in his face.

"You? A knight? Escort me? Thank you, but no. I have standards, you know, and glorified servants who stink of sweat and horse do not even come close to reaching them."

She'd thought herself so far above him back then. Above them all, really. She'd even thought him a lovesick fool for following her up the stairs and safely to her door anyway, despite her derision.

She felt nothing but shame now. For that moment, this one, and so many others.

Darrek lifted her arm and kissed the longest of the scars running across it.

"We'll get through this, Caterpillar. I don't know how, but I promise you this. We'll find a way. Together. You're not alone anymore."

CHAPTER
32

Dinner had been finished and preparation for the next day begun when Eva slipped in the back door of the kitchen. Though many of the servants looked her way, Maeve was the only one who looked concerned. The others all seemed annoyed. Likely wondering where she'd been all this time while they covered for her. Taking the spoon Maeve offered, Eva took over stirring one of the jelly pots and ignored them all. She didn't owe any of them an explanation. They rarely said more than a word to her anyway. Arthur and Maeve—they were all the family she needed.

Or so she told herself on the lonely nights when memories of giggling with her sisters and of her mother's embrace assailed her.

She'd shared a bed with her sisters until Rose's twelfth birthday, and rarely had a night gone by when they hadn't gotten in trouble at least once for giggling together too long past bedtime. Mykah had been quite the storyteller, her tales becoming more and more absurd the later the hour got. Eva had made herself sick one night laughing over a tale Mykah told of fruit coming to life and riding jelly horses into battle. Rose had tried her best to calm them both but had been laughing too hard herself to be much use.

Eva wondered what her sisters were doing now.

Both married, no doubt. Maybe even mothers themselves a few times over. Did she have nieces? Nephews? Did Mykah tell her own children those stories now? Darrek would know, if Eva dared to ask.

Darrek. Eva swallowed back a wave of emotion. He'd forced his way into her life and refused to leave. Eva couldn't decide if she was thankful for that or furious. She'd been fine before he came. Not happy—far from happy—but content enough with her lot. And then Darrek had come along, offering more, making her believe she could have it. Showing her how much better life could be. He gave her hope but, like the beauty of the chapel, what she *could* have only served to illuminate what she didn't.

"Who is he?"

A hard bump to her shoulder made the bubbling jelly spill over onto Eva's hand, scalding her. She gasped and grabbed at the closest cloth to wipe the liquid, succeeding only in smudging soot into the orange mess.

"Sorry," came the slightly muffled voice of the maid who was trying too hard to suppress her laughter to sound even a bit sorry. "Oh, give it here. You're making it worse."

Before Eva could answer Rhea, or Flaire waiting just beyond her friend's shoulder, she was being tugged past maids, cooks, and servers to the other end of the kitchens. A cool, wet cloth was thrown unceremoniously over her hand by Rhea while Flaire pushed Eva into a chair.

"Now, who is he?" Rhea demanded, crossing her arms.

Eva wiped the cloth across her still-smarting hand and wondered how much trouble she'd be in if she dunked her whole hand in the closest water bucket. Likely a lot. And she'd have to refill it herself. Then again, that would not only cool and clean her hand but get her out of the stifling kitchens and away from her two torturers for a few minutes, so it might well be worth it.

"You know him," Flaire said, crossing her arms as she stared down at Eva. "Tell us. Who is he? A spy? A guard? He's clearly not the simple stable boy George told everyone he was."

The liquid had cooled somewhat but still coated the burn trapping heat under her skin. Eva dabbed at it with the cloth, trying to clean it off without tearing the tender skin. The two women glaring at her weren't helping.

"*I* heard him say he'd fight as long as it took to bring you home. Maybe we should be asking who *you* are," Rhea added.

Eva stilled. They'd seen Darrek. With her. How long had they been watching? Had they seen him bring her hand to his lips?

"He's no—"

Flaire slapped her across the face.

"I asked you a question, girl. Tell me now. Or I'll tell Lord Cavendish you tried to escape again with that boy of yours."

"He's—"

Rhea leaned forward, blocking Eva's view of the kitchen. "Yes?"

"A knight," Eva whispered, hating herself for giving in so easily. But she couldn't lose Arthur. Not again. Darrek would understand.

"Sir Darrek." Rhea stretched the name out until Eva was ready to break. What was this angst inside her? Regret? Fear? Surely it wasn't jealousy. That would be ridiculous. Darrek wasn't hers to claim any more than George or Sir Manning. There was only one person in the world she called hers. His name was Arthur, and he was sleeping under the table where Maeve worked.

"Is he your brother?"

What? Eva's hands stilled as she looked up at Flaire. "Arthur?"

"Darrek, you fool. We all know Arthur's your by-blow. Darrek, what is he to you? Your brother? Friend? Lover?"

Heat rushed into Eva's cheeks along with the memory of how Darrek's arms felt around her. Of the times she'd thought he was going to kiss her and the way the world around her had ceased to exist when he whispered her name. The way he stayed, even when she ordered him away. Or showed him her failures. Whatever this thing between them was, it definitely wasn't brotherly.

"He's no one."

"Then who are you?"

Eva shook her head, the answer painful to say even though it was the truth. "I'm no one either."

"You think we're fools?"

This time it was Rhea who slapped Eva. The force was so hard the pain sent spots dancing across her vision. She blinked against the tears that followed, refusing to allow the wetness to fall.

"We don't believe you. And we don't think Lord Cavendish will either. Not when we tell him what we know."

Eva gasped. "No, you can't." Cavendish would kill Darrek.

"No?" Flaire grinned before elbowing Rhea. "And how do you plan to stop us? Bribe us with jewels? Oh, but wait, you can't because you don't have any. You don't have anything. Or did you plan on stabbing us with that knife of yours?"

Bile rose in Eva's throat, threatening to spill out over her attackers. The sting in her cheeks, the burn on her hand, the spots filling her vision—they were nothing compared to the horror stabbing through her heart at Flaire's words. The shame.

"No—" she whispered. Her head spun with the effort.

"Oh, yes, we know about the knife you try so hard to hide. We've seen you sobbing in that tree. Pitiful, you are. Playing with a knife as if it could ever slay your demons. Maybe one day you'll accidentally fall on it and not come back. It's not like any of us would care. Or miss you. Although, we'd happily take that man of yours. If Lord Cavendish doesn't get to him first. I can only imagine how *appreciative* Lord Cavendish will be to the maid who tells him about the *enemy* in his castle. Sir Darrek... Another of King Lior's knights, I suppose. Come to, what, rescue a *servant*?"

"No..."

The lamps behind Flaire's head bobbed. Swirled. Faded.

Went black.

CHAPTER
33

"Darrek, Darrek, are you there?"

Darrek dropped his shovel, the panic in Maeve's voice worrying him far more than her words.

"What is it?" he asked the frantic maid. "What's happened? Evangeline. Is she well?"

"No."

Darrek's heart stuttered.

"Two maids, they hit her before I could— She fell, and—" A sob caught Maeve's words. She shook her head and tried again. "Darrek, she won't wake. I'm afraid it's more than the fall. That she— That she—"

She didn't need to say more. He knew what Maeve feared. It was the same thing he did. The same thing that had tortured him since that first night he'd seen them. The scars. The bandages. Infection. A body too tired to fight it.

"Where is she?"

"The kitchen. She—"

He didn't wait to hear what else she had to say, not even bothering to check for guards or who else might be in the castle grounds before running across them.

He burst through the kitchen door, earning himself several gasps from the twenty or so maids who swiveled toward him. A cluster in the corner didn't move. He pushed his way toward them, barely remembering to apologize to the few he knocked aside in his rush.

Evangeline lay as still as if she were dead. Darrek dropped onto the ground, gritting his teeth as he fought to hold back a wave of fear he didn't have time to deal with. He touched a hand to her forehead. Hot but not burning.

"Water," he croaked before letting his head fall. "Eva…" His voice broke as he brought her hand to his lips. "Please… I need you."

Her eyelids flickered. Darrek's relief was swallowed up in the press of a cup of water to his side. He took the cup and helped Evangeline rise just enough to drink. She managed a few sips before shaking her head against any more.

Maids muttered around him, doors opened and closed, feet scuttled, two of them tripping over him. Darrek ignored them all. Nothing mattered but the woman in his arms.

"Caterpillar, please."

Her eyes fluttered again, this time opening. Her hand lifted to stroke his hair slowly. "Darrek. You're here," she said, as if she didn't quite believe it.

Darrek swallowed three times before managing to get a word out. "Always."

She'd never touched his hair like that before. Never touched him at all as much as she could help it. Heat filled his face, and he felt a little faint himself as her hand continued to play with the ends of his hair.

"What…happened?"

"You fainted."

"Oh." Her hand dropped, fear—horror?—written across her face. "Darrek, stop. The maids—"

"I don't care if they hear me."

"No. Rhea. Flaire." She pulled herself upright, pushing aside Darrek's offer to help. "Cavendish. They— Rhea—"

She was making no sense. Darrek was relieved when Maeve arrived at his side with a steaming cup of liquid she pressed into Eva's hand. Darrek hoped it tasted better than it smelled. From the way Evangeline scrunched her face and almost choked on the third sip, though, it was unlikely.

"How do you feel?" he asked when she thrust the cup back at Maeve.

"I'm well, Darrek, but—"

"Is it your...bandages?"

"No, Darrek. I'm fine. They're fine. But you're not. The maids, they know. About you. Cavendish knows. You have to go. Now."

Darrek caught at Evangeline's hands where they tried to push him away, cradling them against his chest instead. Against the heart pounding with relief. She was well. Alert. No fever. "I'm not leaving you."

"You have to. Please, Darrek. They know who you are. Cavendish too. He'll come."

"I'll fight him."

"No. Please. You can't. Go, please. Listen to me. I can't—can't—"

Lose you.

He heard the words she couldn't say, the words that echoed his own silent cry.

Seeing her lying so still on the floor like that had scared Darrek more than he cared to admit. He didn't know what Evangeline's nightmares consisted of, but lately his had been of her dying. Over and over again, in a thousand different ways. And in every one of them, he was too late to save her.

"Darrek..."

The words were swallowed up in the fabric of his shirt as Darrek pulled Evangeline into an embrace. "I'm not leaving you," he promised. "Not tonight. Not ever."

"It's true, then," an all-too familiar voice sounded behind Darrek. "Imagine my surprise when the maids told me who the supposedly simple-minded boy in my stables truly was. Sir Darrek Drew, knight of Raedonleith. I showed kindness in letting your friends go. I will not do it again."

Maids whispered behind their hands; all manner of food preparation forgotten as Cavendish guards stormed the kitchen to flank their master. Darrek's hand flew to his hip, but his sword was missing. He'd left it in the stable. He stood instead, drawing himself up as tall as he could to face Lord Cavendish.

"Take him to the dungeon," Cavendish said before Darrek could open his mouth. "He dies at dawn."

"No!"

Evangeline's cry wrenched Darrek's heart but did nothing to stop the two guards from gripping his arms tightly enough to make his hands prickle and forcing him out the door.

"Please, Lord Cavendish, if you have any mercy at all, let him go. He's a good man. He doesn't deserve to die."

"Mercy? You speak of mercy? After all your father has taken from me?"

"Please…"

The unmistakable sound of hand meeting skin hurtled through the door, followed by Evangeline's cry of pain. Darrek roared, pulling at the arms which held him. The man was going to kill her. He freed one arm but was pinned to the ground by three more guards before he could reach Evangeline. Though he struggled, it was no use. He couldn't overpower the four guards who held him nor the six more who waited for their turn. He saw the hilt of a sword swing toward him an instant before blackness crowded in.

Eva stood before Lord Cavendish in his solar, determined to neither cower nor cringe as he took his time looking her up and down. She'd done the only thing she could think of and offered herself in Darrek's place. One night, two, a week even, of Cavendish's touch. She could bear it, if it meant Darrek lived. But was it enough? Cavendish had told her once he couldn't bear to look at her. Had time softened his disgust enough that he might accept her now?

Her stomach felt like the storm at sea her father had once described. Her mind along with it. *Take the offer. Don't take it. Take it. Please, please, don't.*

She had to save Darrek, yet could she truly go through with what she'd offered in his place?

Darrek. Where was he now? The clang of a sword hitting his

skull would echo in her mind forever, as would the sound of the thud when his body hit the ground. The guards had dragged him away before she could find out if he was still alive.

He dies at dawn.

It was close to midnight now.

Take me instead. I'll give you anything you desire. Riches, jewels… myself. I'll stay. Be your mistress. Your prisoner. Whatever you desire. Just please, please, don't kill him.

Bile swirled in Eva's stomach, not helped by the taste of Maeve's horrid-tasting herbs lingering in her mouth. If only this were all simply another of her nightmares. She might wake hoarse and aching, but at least she'd wake.

Cavendish walked in a circle around her. Eva stared at the tapestry on the wall in front of her and focused her mind on Darrek. For him, she could do this. Whatever this was.

It felt like hours before Cavendish nodded. "I accept."

Eva didn't know whether to cheer or vomit.

"The knight goes free." He waved a hand at two of his guards, who bowed before walking out.

"Thank you, my lord."

"On Saturday's eve, you'll become my wife."

Eva gasped. "Wife? No. 'Tis not what I offered."

"You offered me yourself, to do with what I please. Would you rather the knight dies? My guards would happily oblige. I'll call them back, right now, and tell them, shall I?"

"No."

She couldn't do that. But marriage? To this man? To be joined with him forever?

Cavendish leered at her, his breath hot and rancid against her face. He ran a finger down her cheek, past her chin, stopping just far enough past the edge of her gown to leave no confusion as to where his mind wandered. Eva thought of Darrek's eyes and forced herself not to give Cavendish the satisfaction of squirming.

"You should be thanking me, *Lady* Evangeline. I saved you that day, fed you, clothed you. I made you my woman in every way but name. One need only look at your son to see the proof of that. Who else would take you now? That knight?" He scoffed. "You're broken, weak, scarred, ruined, nothing but a servant with a bastard child in tow. You should think it a miracle anyone would offer you marriage, let alone someone of my standing."

The words should have crushed Eva. Perhaps they might have, had she not already known how true they were. The day she'd walked away from her father's home, she'd thought she was gaining freedom. How wrong she'd been. She'd gained only heartache. At times, when love for Arthur overwhelmed her, she'd consider it all worth it for his smile and existence, but lately, all she'd been able to see was all the ways she'd failed him too.

It was her fault he didn't run and jump with the freedom of other boys. Her fault he didn't speak. Her fault he didn't smile. Her fault that, at merely three years of age, he knew more about collecting wood and keeping a fire going than climbing a tree or the joy of racing leaf boats down a river. Her fault he'd never known what it was to be free.

"You told me you would never marry and that, even if you did, you'd find a hundred women more appealing to you than me."

Cavendish laughed, though there was nothing but derision in it. "I could find a thousand. You are nothing to me, Eva, and you're a fool if you think otherwise."

"Then why marry me?"

"Because it will hurt your father." His hand moved to the side of Eva's neck, caressing, almost absentmindedly, though his gaze pinned hers like a sword to her chest. "Ever since the day he broke my sister's heart, I've been waiting for the perfect chance to break his. When I saw you stumbling along the road that day, I knew the chance was near. You were so trusting. All it took was the promise of food and clothes, and you were mine."

"You could have married me then."

"And have your father think you wished it? No. He would have been pleased to see you happy. He always did hope for a reconciliation between our families. Hope is so much more crushing when it's believed before being broken. Far better to take the time to woo you, ruin you, cast you aside, and break you. You've played your part admirably, I may add."

"My—part?"

"Aye. Pitiful. Far more broken than I could have ever imagined. Yet still your father's weakness."

She was her father's weakness? Eva almost laughed. She'd never been her father's weakness, not even when she was still at home. Rose was his treasure, Mykah was his joy, and Eva was the one he fought with.

"The time has come. What better way to break his heart than take his daughter from him when he thinks he's so close to getting her back? His daughter who is clearly in love with another man, if she's so willing to give up her life for him."

"I won't marry you."

Cavendish dropped his hand and took two steps back, his expression daring her to defy him further. "If you don't, I'll not only kill Sir Darrek but foster Arthur with a family far from here. You'll never see either of them again."

Tears bit at Eva's eyes. "You wouldn't."

"Of course I would. No one would even blink an eye at it. After all, I'm simply a father doing what's best for his son."

"You can't have him."

"I already do."

"But—" No. He couldn't. Arthur was with Maeve. He was safe. Wasn't he?

"Three days, Evangeline. And I expect you to come to me looking and smelling a mite better than you do now. Say goodbye to your knight, if you wish. Do whatever you like with him. I care not. But in three days, either you marry me or never see your son again. You are dismissed."

Eva walked out of the room, head held high and stomach roiling. As soon as she was out of Cavendish's sight, she ran. All the way to the stables.

Darrek. Darrek. Please be there.

He limped in not long after her, bruises already forming along his cheekbones. She threw herself at him, only realizing when he let out a gasp of pain that he likely had far more bruises than she could see. Still, he was alive. And he was free.

"Caterpillar," he said, voice muffled in her hair. "What did you do?"

She didn't cry. There would be time enough for that later. After she let Darrek go.

"Go home, Darrek." He'd said he'd stay, Cavendish had all but invited him to witness her pain—and their union—but she couldn't allow it. Better to send him far away than break him as Cavendish had her.

"Evangeline, no…"

"In three days, I'm marrying Lord Cavendish. Thank you for coming to rescue me, but I'm not going home. You've been—" A tremor stopped her voice. Darrek's heartbeat thudded against hers. *No tears. You have to do this.* She cleared her throat and tried again, talking into his neck lest she be undone by his eyes. "You've been everything to me, and I—" Love you, need you, want you. "—thank you. Live well, Sir Darrek Drew."

She wrenched herself from his arms and fled before he could say anything to make it worse. If not for the two guards who'd followed her and waited outside the stable door, she might have fled straight to the hollowed-out tree. Instead, they escorted her to the chamber beside Lord Cavendish's.

There, she threw herself across the tightly strung mattress and let the tears come.

Darrek watched Evangeline go, fury forcing aside the throbbing of his beating. She'd bartered her life for his. The guard who'd let him out of the dungeon had said as much, but he hadn't wanted to believe it. He still didn't, though the evidence felt like another punch to his gut.

His caterpillar had come to say goodbye.

Until now, he'd been willing—if unhappy—to wait for Evangeline to be ready to leave. He'd thought that if he only had enough patience, convinced her of her father's love and her own worth, she'd come home of her own accord.

Time had run out.

King Lior had to know. Three days wasn't enough time to get a message to Raedonleith and bring back an army, but this time, it would have to be.

He'd stall, and fight, and do whatever it took, but there was no way he was letting Evangeline marry Lord Cavendish.

CHAPTER
34

The feast was everything Eva remembered, everything she'd once loved—the minstrels swaying as they filled the room with music, the smell of honeycomb candles blending with roast meat and hot ale, knights and nobles dressed in their best, their elaborate hats and baubles bobbing as they conversed. Tables filled with steaming pies, yeasty bread, fruit, and—her favorite—ruby-red jellies that promised flavor unlike she'd tasted in years. It was everything she loved. And nothing she wanted.

The doors to the courtyard were open. Was Darrek out there on the bench they and Arthur had so often shared? She hoped not, for both their sakes. She didn't want Darrek to bear witness to this.

"Knights, nobles, ladies of the court, I bid you arise."

Eva waited out of sight as the noise of a hundred feasters rising to their feet filled her ears. She smoothed sweating hands down the sides of her burgundy gown and told herself to stand tall. It was strange to wear such finery after years of peasant clothing. Layers of thick fabric, a beaded belt, sleeves so wide and long Arthur could have hidden inside them, jewels at her ears and throat and braided through the intricate knots styling her hair. She looked like the princess she was.

She hated every bit of it.

"I have great joy tonight in announcing that three days henceforth, I shall be wed."

The murmur that passed through the crowd matched the one bubbling in Eva's stomach, threatening with every breath to burst out. No amount of deep breathing could calm the squall of nerves mixed with disgust.

"Allow me to present my bride, the future Lady Lissaria of Cavendish Castle."

Lissaria? He'd changed her name now too. Was there anything this man wouldn't take from her? Was it too late to run?

But no. If she ran, Darrek died, and she'd never see Arthur again. Unless the knights could save them both, or her father came, or—

Three days. It wasn't enough time. Raedonleith was too far.

Cavendish turned, his gaze finding her, narrowing just enough to send warning. He held out his hand, waiting. Even without looking their way, Eva knew the hundred-strong crowd would be straining their necks to see who Cavendish was gesturing to.

This was it. Too late to flee, here was the moment she'd been dreading. The first of many. On legs she was certain would fail her at any step, Eva walked out of the shadows, into the Great Hall, and up the three stairs to the dais. Cavendish's arm caught hers, hiding her stumble over the final one.

"Smile," he bit out. "Fail me and the deal is off."

Did he think she was here for any other reason?

"My name is Eva."

"Your name is whatever I tell you it is."

He touched a finger to her cheek, turning her face toward his before kissing her. Eva didn't even have time to gasp at his audacity before he was smiling at the crowd again.

"My bride."

Cheers and the clattering of mugs filled Eva's ears. She smiled, as instructed. Only those closest to her would be able to tell how forced it was. With a gentle nod of her head—one she'd seen her mother do countless times—she acknowledged the people. They cheered again, toasting her happiness.

"To Lady Lissaria!"

Eva clenched her teeth together behind the smile lest the bile climbing her throat win the battle she waged against the nausea in her stomach.

"Eat. Drink. Let us celebrate this wondrous occasion," Cavendish shouted, before sitting on the throne-like chair in the middle of the dais. Eva finally allowed her legs to collapse and fell into the matching one beside it.

"There now, that wasn't so bad, was it?" Cavendish said, handing her his cup of ale. Those still watching the two of them twittered behind their hands, likely giggling about love and romance and how besotted a bridegroom Cavendish was. If only they knew.

"They have no idea who I am."

"No, and see you keep it that way. You may tell everyone your true name at the wedding. It will be all the more pitiful when they realize who they've had in their midst all this time. Until then, you are Lady Lissaria."

"They'll find out."

"Do these people look like they have any idea who you are? Lady Evangeline, the king's daughter, *or* Eva, the maid?"

Eva let her gaze travel around the faces filling the long tables of the Great Hall. There was confusion on some of them—likely because Lady Lissaria was a stranger to them all—but no recognition. She, who'd been among them for years. She, who'd served them and washed their clothing. She, who'd emptied their chamber pots, stoked their fires, and cooked their meals.

New clothes, new name, elaborate hairstyle, a gold circlet on her head—she might as well have been a different person altogether.

"Pork, Lady Lissaria?"

Cavendish had cut her a piece of meat, holding it out for her to eat, every bit the besotted bridegroom. Eva's stomach turned. "No, thank you."

He pushed it toward her, forcing her to open her mouth or be covered in gravy.

"That wasn't a request."

She almost choked on it. Almost wished she had.

Dinner felt like it stretched longer than a week. Eva's head pounded with the pressure of trying to hold everything in—the fury, the nausea, the disgust, the defiance. Smile, Cavendish told her, every time she allowed herself a frown. The circlet on her head began to feel more like a chain, binding her to a life she'd never break free of.

The flickering candles began to swirl, faces blinking in and out like a dance. Eva put a hand to her head, willing everything back into place.

"Your lady doesn't seem well," someone on the other side of Cavendish commented.

Cavendish looked Eva's way, a drawn-out moment of concern touching his expression before a far more familiar smirk took its place. "Women in her condition get that way, you know. Queasy and such around rich foods."

The two men laughed. Eva's cheeks flamed, mortified at what Cavendish implied. Rumors spread faster at court than among the servants. By morning, the entire of Cavendish Castle would think she was with child. Darrek might believe it to be false, determined as he was to see the best in her, but would anyone else? After all, Cavendish had announced to everyone that they were to marry. Within three days. Even among peasants, weddings took longer than that to prepare.

"Perhaps you should take her to bed," the man replied. "To rest, of course, my lord." He grinned, leaving no doubt what he was truly suggesting. Eva put a hand to her mouth, certain any moment she was going to lose every measly bit of dinner she'd managed to force down.

Cavendish clapped the man on the shoulder, laughing as if he was more amusing than the court jester, before shrugging lightly. "She can find her own way. She's too ill to be of any amusement to me anyway." He turned to Eva. "Go now, *dear*. I'll see you in the morn."

With as much of a smile as she could muster—one likely closer to a grimace—Eva clutched her skirts, ran outside, dropped to her knees, and vomited what felt like the entirety of her insides onto the dirt. Tears drizzled down her cheeks with every painful gasp. When her stomach finally stopped heaving enough for her to stand, she wiped a hand across her mouth, took one last look at Cavendish Castle, and strode through the gates toward the hollowed-out tree.

She couldn't marry Cavendish, no matter what he said. But he held power, and she didn't. Except for one thing—he couldn't marry her if she were dead.

CHAPTER
35

D arrek had been outside when the announcement was made. He'd stood by the window, watching as Evangeline, dressed like royalty, had walked forward and taken Cavendish's arm. She'd smiled, and Darrek had walked away, unable to watch anymore.

He'd gone to the stables and flung punch after punch at the closest hay bale until his chest was heaving, his bruises throbbing and his arms like flopping fish. It hadn't helped. It wasn't a hay bale he wanted to punch.

George promising Darrek that the Almighty would protect Evangeline didn't help either. If forcing her to wed the man who'd ruined her as well as emotionally abused her to the point that she hurt herself to find peace was protecting Evangeline, then Darrek wanted nothing to do with it.

The Almighty wasn't saving Evangeline, no matter what George said.

King Lior wasn't likely to arrive in time either, despite Adam and Landon leaving the minute Darrek came with the news and promising they'd ride through the night to reach Raedonleith.

Manning would be killed on sight. Spencer too.

Darrek was her only hope.

Her only hope. And he was wearing himself out punching a hay bale.

When Darrek had calmed enough to see, he'd come right back only to find Evangeline gone from her place at the raised table. Thinking she'd returned to her room, Darrek went back to his.

Sleep was a long time coming. Especially knowing she'd bartered her life for his.

He woke to an intruder standing over him with a knife.

Darrek grasped his sword and scrambled away and to his feet before realizing the person wasn't trying to kill him.

"Evangeline?"

It was dark in the stable, but the light from the lamp George left burning was enough to see the way the knife shook in her hand. A hand covered in blood.

"I couldn't do it."

Darrek glanced behind Evangeline, checking for guards, knights, squires—anyone who might have hurt her. Anyone who still might. She was alone, as far as he could tell. There might be guards waiting outside, but he wasn't leaving her long enough to check.

Evangeline didn't even seem to notice Darrek there, caught up in her torment. He wasn't so far from it himself.

Waking to find any woman standing over him, holding a knife dripping with blood, was terrifying. Having it be the woman he loved would haunt him for the rest of his life.

"Evangeline. Put down the knife."

Her fingers were white where she gripped it. Shaking but white. Had she even heard him? Did she know he was here? A tear dripped off her nose.

"I couldn't do it."

Darrek took a step closer then another. They were slow steps, cautious and as unthreatening as he could make them. Even while his heartbeat pounded in his ears. One step more and he'd be close enough to take the knife from her. Then he would see where the blood was coming from. If it was her wrist, as he feared—

"I couldn't leave him. It's so selfish. He'd be better off without me. Any mother would be better for him than me."

Darrek eased the knife out of her hand, dropping it unceremoniously behind him, forcing his voice to come out gently despite the roar building in him. "That's not true."

"It is. I love Arthur, but I'm barely with him, and when I am, he wants to help, and I get frustrated with how much more effort it takes to let him and wish he'd leave. Which only makes the guilt worse. What kind of mother would wish away her own child?"

"A tired one."

Eva blinked unfocused eyes as more tears fell.

"Every day, you're up before dawn and you work, without ceasing, until long after the sun has set. You do the work of three women, and your son knows that. He doesn't love you any less because of it. He adores you."

"I have nothing for him. Nothing to give him. Not even the respect of a name. I'm broken. Ruined. Just like Cavendish said."

"Eva—" Darrek ran his fingers over her wrists, willing himself to keep going and do what needed to be done, when all he wanted to do was weep at her words. Had it truly come to this?

But no. She was here. She'd come to him. That was something, wasn't it?

He clung to that thought, a tiny spark of hope, as wave after wave of overwhelming helplessness threatened to drown him.

Almighty, help me—

There. Not her wrists. A cut across the palm of her left hand.

George appeared behind Evangeline, silent as he took in the scene. He tilted his head as if to ask whether Darrek needed him. Darrek waved a hand, hoping the man understood his wordless plea to stay hidden. Evangeline was both fragile and unpredictable right now, but he was fairly certain she wouldn't react well to another person witnessing her weakness. To Darrek's relief, George disappeared back into the shadows he'd come from. Far enough to give them privacy, close enough to help, should Darrek call.

"I'm ruined, don't you see?" Evangeline said. "I'd rather die than marry Lord Cavendish, but I'm not even strong enough to kill myself."

"Thank the Almighty."

"What am I going to do?"

Her plea was so quiet, barely audible over the hiccupping of her tears, but Darrek heard it. And it broke his heart.

"Caterpillar…"

He whispered the name as he drew Evangeline fully into his arms, needing the reminder himself that there was hope, even amid what felt like overwhelming darkness.

Almighty...

Evangeline shuddered against him, sobs drowning out whatever she tried to say. It didn't matter. She was safe with him. He'd vowed to King Lior that he'd find and protect her. Now, he made the vow to himself. He'd protect this woman with his life. Not because of her father or her standing as princess but because of who she was to him. A battered woman in desperate need of the hope he clung to. The woman he loved.

Almighty, thank you. You saved her. You didn't let her succeed. You brought her to me. Thank you.

Tears dripped down Darrek's nose and into Evangeline's hair as he held her in his arms. The Almighty had saved her. When he might have lost her tonight, the Almighty stayed her hand.

Her hand.

Darrek pulled back, just enough to pull free her bleeding palm. It was still seeping blood, though the cut didn't look as deep as he'd first thought. He tore a piece of cotton from his tunic, wrapping it gently but firmly around her hand until the bleeding stopped showing through. It would likely need stitches tomorrow—he'd ask Manning for advice with that—but for now, it was enough. He wasn't letting her out of his sight. Or his arms. For the few hours that remained of this impossibly dark night, Darrek was keeping Evangeline right beside him.

She'd not marry Lord Cavendish. He wouldn't allow it. He'd fight Cavendish for her, even to the death, if that's what it took. The time for waiting patiently for her to come home was past. It was time to act. He wouldn't give the despair another chance to try again. He couldn't. Not when, next time, she might just succeed.

"This isn't the end, little caterpillar. There's more to life than what you see today. You have a life and a purpose beyond here."

"You keep saying that."

"Yes, because it's the truth. We—*I*—came to bring you home, and the knights of Raedonleith don't fail. *I* don't fail. I will get you and Arthur out of here."

"I know you want to, but Darrek, what if you can't? You say that's the truth. Here's another—Lord Cavendish owns me."

"No, he—"

"He is the father of my son. Nothing you or anyone else say changes that."

"Come with me," he said. "We'll leave. Now. George will help us. We'll take a horse."

"No."

"Evangeline—"

"I can't. He'll kill you. He'll take Arthur. I can't— I won't— Darrek, no. Don't—"

Her arms flailed, hitting at his chest, pushing at his shoulders as she tried to get away. Panic stuttered her breathing. She swayed, almost falling.

"Caterpillar, stop. It's okay." He pulled her back in, bracing her against his chest before she could do herself more harm. "Breathe. It's okay. We won't go." Her flailing stopped, but her heartbeat still raced. He could feel it pounding against his chest. "We'll stay. You and me. Right here in the stable. You're safe here, with me. I'm here. You're not alone. Not anymore."

Whether she heard him over her sobs, which began again at his words, he didn't know. But perhaps the words were more for him than her anyway. Another vow. Not to himself, not to the king, but to this brave woman who had so much more to give than she could comprehend right now. One day, he hoped she'd see. One day, he prayed she'd see herself through his eyes. As a woman worth loving, worth caring for, infinitely precious, made only more beautiful by what she'd been through. A mother who'd given everything for her son, time and time again. A beloved daughter.

"You're not alone," Darrek whispered again.

CHAPTER 36

The sun beat down on Darrek, sending sweat down his back and neck. Fitting, that after two days of rain, today was clear. The perfect weather for a tournament. Any other time, Darrek would have been thrilled at the forecast. Today, even a sky of brilliant blue couldn't make Darrek smile. He fisted hands at his sides before forcing his fingers loose again. Though the grandstands were set with colorful pennants and the field cleared for battle, the tournament wasn't what the scores of nobles arriving at Cavendish Castle had come to see.

They'd come to see the lord of the castle's wedding.

Evangeline's wedding.

A clash sounded as two lances met. A cry went up from the assembled crowd. No thud of body hitting the sand followed, so both knights must have kept their seats. Good for them. The longer they dragged out this competition, the better.

Darrek swore under his breath before stalking to the other end of the field where Manning, Spencer, and Craig waited. Mud flicked up at his boots with every step. He kicked at a rock behind the tent, stubbing his toe when it didn't move like he'd expected. Must have been deeper in the ground than he'd thought. Typical. He kicked it again for good measure.

Any other time, his friends would have laughed and teased him for his frustration. Any other time, he might have grudgingly laughed along with them. But none of them felt like laughing today. Not with the quest they'd been throwing their all into for the past four years about to end in failure.

Bring her home, King Lior had said.

Not sit by while she married the enemy.

They'd scanned every guest who'd walked through the gates. King Lior hadn't been one of them. They were running out of time. With such short notice on the tournament, fewer knights than usual were competing. Half an hour—maybe less—and it would be over.

The wedding vows would follow.

"He'll be here."

Darrek smiled grimly at Manning. "I know. But he's not now."

Darrek strapped on his breastplate and picked up his sword and helmet. Another clash of lances. Another cry from the crowd, this time followed by a collective gasp and a thud. Another competitor down.

His back was wet. Any minute, steam would start rising from his armor, cooking him inside.

Twenty minutes to go.

Adam and Landon had left for Raedonleith within a minute of Darrek bringing the news of Evangeline's engagement. They'd promised to ride through the night and not stop until they spoke with King Lior. Darrek didn't doubt them. The last time he'd seen them so serious was the day Evangeline went missing. They'd get the message to King Lior. But would the king make it back in time?

"You don't have to do this," Manning said, though they both knew he did.

He'd vowed it to his king, Evangeline, the Almighty, and himself. If it took his life, he'd not break that vow. Darrek didn't know if he could beat Cavendish in a sword fight, but he could certainly buy Evangeline time. Hopefully, it would be enough.

Another competitor fell.

There were only two left.

"Darrek—"

Lances clashed, but neither cracked at the first run. "Not now, Spencer."

Spencer stayed anyway. "I just wanted to say what an honor it is to serve with you. You are a man of great strength and even greater courage, and King Lior couldn't have chosen a better man to fight for his daughter's freedom."

Darrek scoffed, rubbing sweat from his forehead. "Even if I lose?"

Spencer clapped a hand on Darrek's shoulder. "You won't." He walked away before Darrek could decide whether to thank him or laugh at him.

Darrek was unsure what would kill him first—Cavendish's sword or his own heart exploding out of his chest. Spencer had faith in him. Darrek couldn't pretend the same. He was just as likely to lose as he was to win. But losing wasn't an option. Not when Evangeline's life and future depended on his winning. He kicked another stone.

The sound of hooves on dirt mixed with the thud of his heart as the jousting opponents completed a second run.

The crowd was silent. Then a cheer went up. Cavendish announced a winner. Darrek slid on his helmet.

The time had come.

Stalking out to where Cavendish sat at his place of honor in the middle grandstand, Darrek stopped. The noise of the crowd stopped with him, drawing Cavendish's attention more than any word or action could have. He stood from his throne-like chair as if pulled by the crowd's anticipation. Evangeline, beside him, put a hand to her heart. Darrek saw her swallow before forcing his attention back to Cavendish.

"Lord Cavendish, I challenge you to a duel."

Darrek's voice thundered in the silence. Silence that quickly turned to murmuring as the crowd looked between the two men. Darrek didn't need to be close enough to hear their words to know what they were saying. He was crazy. A fool. Filled more with pride than wisdom. They were likely right. But he couldn't stand by and do nothing.

"You, knight?"

"Aye."

"And you are?"

"Sir Darrek Drew, knight of Raedonleith."

A gasp went around the crowd. Cavendish alone seemed un-impressed. He hadn't asked Darrek's name because he needed to know. He was drawing in the crowd. Ensuring *they* knew.

It would make the moment he killed Darrek all the more momentous.

"You have heard, no doubt, that I am the best swordsman in the land?"

Darrek stood his ground. "I have."

"You yearn so greatly for death?"

"No, but some things are worth fighting for."

"And what, pray tell, may that be?"

"A woman, of course." Darrek tried to keep his voice light, entertaining the crowd, though neither he nor Cavendish were laughing.

"A man after my own heart, I see. Very well, knight. In honor of this day and the wife I am soon to wed, I shall take your challenge. Name your prize. Any maiden here. She's yours, should you defeat me."

"Lady Evangeline of Raedonleith."

Cavendish considered Darrek a moment before raising his chin. "I know not this woman."

"No? Surprising, when she sits beside you."

"Lady Lissaria?"

"You can change her name, but it will not change who she is—Lady Evangeline, youngest daughter of King Lior of Raedonleith."

A collective gasp echoed around the field at Darrek's proclamation, followed by a wave of whispers. Did they finally recognize the woman who'd been in their midst all this time?

"You said I may claim any maiden here," Darrek said. "I choose Lady Evangeline."

The whispers turned to a roar of noise. The crowd's reaction came as little surprise to Darrek. Claiming as his prize the woman the lord of the manor planned to wed on the day of their wedding was no small thing. The fact that she was the missing daughter of

King Lior only added to the amazement. Darrek waited until the roar settled back to a murmur before speaking again.

"And her son."

Cavendish glared. "*My* son."

"Lady Evangeline's son. If you were truly his father, you'd act like it."

"No."

"You offered me any maiden here. Surely you wouldn't go back on your word now, not in front of all these people."

"Evangeline is mine."

Just the thought made Darrek's stomach roil. He had to get Evangeline out of here. He hadn't been able to convince her to leave, but if he won the tournament today, she would be his to do with what he chose. The rules, though unwritten, were understood by even the greenest of knights—and the cruelest of masters. More than words, they were a matter of pride. If Darrek won, and Cavendish denied him his prize, Cavendish would lose more than his people's respect.

"Fight me for her," Darrek called. "Or do you doubt your skill?"

"I am the best swordsman in the land. Ask any man present."

Darrek didn't need to ask. He knew already that this would be no easy fight. He would no more walk away uninjured today than the sun would turn back time. But he had to try. He'd promised his king he would bring Evangeline home, and he would do it.

"Then you need not fear losing her *or* the boy."

"I fear nothing."

"Then fight me. After all, you are the best, so what have you to lose?"

Cavendish didn't want to give her up. That much was obvious. But where coercion failed, Darrek's goading worked. That and the attention of the crowd who watched, captivated by the surprise twist to a tournament they thought over. A minute passed as Darrek waited. Finally, Lord Cavendish nodded. "Very well. Winner takes Evangeline and the boy."

Darrek nodded back but felt no sense of achievement as he

turned and walked toward his tent. Though he had convinced Cavendish to name Evangeline as the prize, he still had to win. Or at least make the battle last as long as possible.

"I don't think the lady appreciates your challenge," Spencer said as Darrek stroked a hand down his horse's neck. "She looks a little upset."

The words had barely lined up in Darrek's mind when an un-horse-like huff came from behind him. He turned to see what had Spencer hiding inside the tent. Evangeline stood, hands fisted at her waist. If she'd been a dragon, he would have been incinerated on the spot. How had she gotten down here so quickly? Not that he minded. At all.

Beautiful.

"You're a fool," Evangeline said.

Beautiful and furious.

Darrek checked his sword, running a practiced eye up and down the blade as he tilted it this way and that in the sunlight. "Perhaps."

"Don't do this. I'm not worth your death."

He barely kept the smile off his face. She worried for him. Evangeline, who'd tried so hard to convince him that she no longer cared. And here it was, proof of her affection, clear as the sky was blue. "You assume I'll die."

"Lord Cavendish is the best."

"So he's told me."

"More than that, he doesn't fight fairly."

Darrek had suspected as much. "I know."

"Please, walk away."

In the smallest, most human part of Darrek's mind, he couldn't deny he was tempted. Were it not for the prize, and no small amount of his own pride, he might have. No man in his right mind liked being hurt. Neither was it easy to walk willingly into a battle that would likely kill him. But for his king—for Evangeline—he'd do anything.

"I can't."

She bit her lip, brows pulling together as she tried to hold on to her composure. "Can you even fight?"

"My beautiful Evangeline, I wouldn't have challenged him if I couldn't. I would have found another way."

"I wish you would."

He wished he could have too. Without giving her the chance to react, he grabbed her hands, forcing her to stop worrying them. "Promise me you'll leave this place with us when I win."

"I want to, but—"

"Do you truly want this life for yourself? For Arthur?"

"I don't deserve any better."

"No one does. But nevertheless, the choice is there. If not for yourself, do it for Arthur. He should have the chance to know what it's like to be free."

Darrek's heart thumped against his armor. He was far more afraid of the emotions raging inside him than the enemy he was about to face. He had to tell her how he felt. He might not get another chance. "And for me." Darrek touched Evangeline's chin, raising it until she looked into his eyes. "I love you."

The crowd roared, knights talked strategy, and horses stomped their impatience. Darrek forced the noise aside, desperate for Evangeline's response.

"Evangeline?" She saw herself as weak, but she was the strongest woman he'd ever known. The most beautiful too. If he had to spend the rest of their lives convincing her of that, he'd consider his life well spent. "Did you hear me?"

Lord Cavendish called his name. A chant erupted through the crowd. Manning walked into view carrying Raedonleith's banner and, no doubt, more advice. Darrek ignored them all.

"Caterpillar?"

"I heard."

But she didn't smile. Didn't reciprocate. If anything, Evangeline looked even more worried. Was she afraid of him? Or for him?

"I wish you wouldn't do this. I don't want to see you hurt. But if you're determined, then let it not be said I allowed you to do it in vain. You win, and I'll come home."

She plucked a handkerchief from her sleeve and handed it to him. It was trimmed in blue, just like her gown. Darrek took it solemnly, knowing how much it cost her. Knowing he'd treasure it, and this moment, for the rest of his life.

A life which, he hoped, would extend far beyond today.

No matter what happened today, or how much it hurt, he had to win.

CHAPTER
37

D arrek was going to die. And it was her fault.

"I can't watch."

Eva put her head in her hands and tried to block out the sound of metal clashing against metal. At least if metal was clashing against metal, it wasn't searing through bone. Bile rose in her stomach at the thought.

A cleric had once told Eva that people could smell fear. She hadn't believed him then. She did now. Fear smelled like dust, heat, blood, and bile. Eva pressed a hand against her stomach. Why couldn't she have told Darrek she loved him?

She peeked at the battle through two fingers and one barely open eye. The two men still circled, both standing, though Darrek faltered more often than comforted her. She closed her eye again and tried to find the courage to watch.

The man was fighting for her freedom. The least she could do was give him the honor of watching him, even if it turned her stomach. Even if, with every strike of the swords, she was reminded that he was doing it for her. Her alone. And if Darrek died, which Lord Cavendish intended, his death would be for her. Because of her.

A gasp traveled around the crowd. Eva opened her eyes in time to see Darrek topple to one knee. He was up again, almost as quickly as he'd gone down, but too late to stop the slash of Cavendish's sword across his side. Darrek put a gloved hand against the wound. It had to be hurting—his whole body had to be—but he raised his sword again, determination to continue written across his face. He'd win her freedom or die trying.

Blood seeped down his armor, dripping onto the ground. How deep was the wound? How could he continue to fight when his side had to be burning with fire? Eva had cut herself with a knife enough to know how much it stung. How every movement pulled the wound apart and sent waves of fiery agony through every muscle in the body. She ground her teeth together, feeling his pain as if it were her own.

If only she could have been strong enough to fight her own battles. To stand up to Cavendish. None of this would have happened. She could have walked away years ago. Before a good man died because of her.

He was going to lose. Darrek didn't want to admit it. He fought against the admission as hard as he fought Cavendish's blade—coming at it first this way, then that, defending, striking, defending again against the man whose skill with a sword was so far superior to his own. Admitting he was going to lose felt too much like surrendering altogether. But it was getting more difficult to lift his arms each time they fell and to rise again each time he stumbled.

He was going to fail Evangeline. Fail Arthur. Fail himself. Still, at least he'd tried. He'd rather die as a fighter than as a coward.

Darrek jumped back, stumbling as Cavendish struck hard against his thigh. Though the armor protected him, the strike sent a shock of weakness down his leg.

He'd thought he could save her—from herself, her pain, her past, Cavendish. What a fool he'd been. Only the Almighty could save a person.

Forgive me.

Sweat dripped into Darrek's eyes. His arm shook with the struggle to hold his sword out straight. His side burned where Cavendish had sliced into it. His ears still rang from the hit to his helmet. Cavendish was slowing too but not enough.

Darrek saw the strike at his injured side coming a quarter of a second too late to block it. He barely had time to brace before hitting the ground hard enough to knock what little breath remained from his lungs. The tip of Cavendish's sword pressed against his neck.

Protect her, Almighty. Take her away from here. Bring her home.

The glare of the sun through the slit in his helmet made Darrek want to close his eyes. Honor forced them open. He flung off the helmet, needing to see the face of the man who would kill him. For Evangeline. His caterpillar. That finally she might be free from this darkness and fly.

Cavendish dragged it out, certain of his win, enjoying every bit of the power it brought, the way the crowd held its breath. He might have played to the crowd, but his sword never left Darrek's neck. Cavendish would kill him. Of that there was no doubt. Any breath now might be his last, and though he'd finally surrendered control to the Almighty, he had no intention of submitting to Cavendish.

Almighty, take me.

Darrek dropped his arms and waited.

And waited.

The death stroke never came.

Instead, gasps around the crowd gave way to murmurs. The pressure on his neck lifted. Cavendish took a step back. Then another, this time raising his sword in preparation to battle once more. Was he giving Darrek a second chance? Surely not. Lord Cavendish was not known for his mercy. But then—

A shadow fell over Darrek's face. He looked up, but with the sun directly behind the knight who stood over him, he could not make out anything beyond the silhouette of a knight in full armor. From his position on the ground, he couldn't even gauge the height of the knight.

Whoever the knight was, Darrek owed him his life.

Something he was all too willing to pay back in service—if the man lived.

"Who is he?"

The question echoed around the grandstand, from child to peasant to noble as, like one, the crowd rose to its feet, desperate to identify the knight who'd stalked onto the field. He rode no horse nor did his breastplate hold any insignia. It was as unmarked as the rest of his armor, with only the smallest slit across his eyes showing any hint of the man within. Even that was in shadow.

"For Evangeline," the knight shouted, raising his sword.

"He's challenging Lord Cavendish," Eva said in wonder, watching with the rest of the crowd as Cavendish and the knight circled each other, swords raised. Who was this man who would fight for her?

She felt humbled. And sick. She'd already had to watch one man almost be killed.

Darrek! Was he— *Don't let him be dead.*

But he was rising. Slowly, painfully, and relying heavily on the assistance of Sir Spencer. But rising. Was she the only one who watched his stumbling retreat? She pressed a hand to her heart, afraid its pounding might push it out of her chest. Darrek was alive.

She should have stayed to watch the ongoing fight, especially since the knight fought for her freedom, but she had to see Darrek. Pushing her way through person after person, she made her way to the knights of Raedonleith. One, in particular.

They crowded around Darrek, who leaned against the trunk of a tree. Sir Manning held a thick wad of fabric against Darrek's side to stem the flow of blood, while Sir Spencer worked at removing his armor. Standing beside Sir Spencer, Craig collected each of the pieces as they were removed.

"Darrek."

He turned at her voice. When he held out an arm, she didn't think twice before tucking herself in against his good side. Darrek wanted her near. That was enough.

"Evangeline."

Eva sighed, silent tears streaming down her face. She'd been so sure she would never hear her name in his deep voice again.

"What happens now?" she asked, uncertain she wanted to know. Darrek had fought for her freedom and lost. The two men who fought for her now were Lord Cavendish and a stranger. She didn't want Lord Cavendish to win, yet could she give her life to a stranger?

"We wait," Darrek answered. "And trust. The Almighty saved me today. I have to believe he'll save you too."

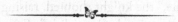

The fight seemed to last for hours, though Manning assured her it hadn't been more than ten minutes. Eva spent most of it helping Manning stitch Darrek's side and arm. The work was grisly and did nothing to help her stomach, but it gave her something to focus on besides the clash of swords behind her. The skill of the knight in black didn't match Cavendish's, but the lord was already weary from his first fight. Eva didn't know whether she wanted it to be over quickly or last forever. Either way, she couldn't watch.

But neither could she bear to look away for long, taking glance after horrified glance over her shoulder until she was dizzy from the effort. Tired as both men were, the fight went on, neither willing to concede.

Eva tucked herself in to Darrek's side, laying her head against his chest, and listened to his heartbeat, willing all else to disappear.

"Evangeline."

Darrek's words pulled her back.

"It's over."

Eva raised her head to take in the scene. Lord Cavendish lay on the ground while the mysterious knight stood above him, sword to Cavendish's neck just as Cavendish had done earlier to Darrek. The crowd was so quiet, Eva could hear the heavy breathing of both men.

She was certain they were all wondering the same thing—what would happen now? They'd come for a wedding, only to see the groom—their lord—be defeated. By who, they didn't know. No one did.

"My prize, if you please," the knight commanded Cavendish.

Cavendish turned his head toward the grandstand seat Eva had been in. The knight looked in the opposite direction—directly at her.

"Go to him," Manning told Eva, his voice low.

"I don't— I can't—"

"He fought for you and won. Go to him. It will work out. Trust me."

"But—" She looked from the unknown knight, to Sir Manning, to Darrek, the man she loved. "Darrek…"

He too nodded, a grimace of a smile on his face even as tears wet his eyes. "Go."

One word, yet her heart splintered like the wood of a lance struck soundly. Three men had fought for her, but only one man stood victorious. It wasn't the one she'd wanted. But, bound by the same honor code as the knights, the choice was no longer hers.

The knight had won.

She was the prize.

There was nothing else to say.

Eva stood and brushed mud off the skirt of her heavy blue gown as best she could before pulling back her shoulders, clasping her shaking hands together, and walking onto the field. A piece of her splintered heart fell to the ground with every step.

Had she truly believed even for a minute that she'd marry for love? That she, piled high with more regrets than memories, might one day be free?

With legs that threatened to send her to the ground herself, Eva held her skirts and dipped into a low curtsey before the man who now owned her. "My lord."

He held out a gloved hand. She took it, rising again.

And then stood, her hand in his. Waiting. For what, she didn't know.

"Who—"

The knight took off his helmet. Eva gasped. His familiar face blurred as tears filled her eyes. He was thinner than she remembered and his hair lighter—more gray now than the deep brown it used to be, but his eyes were the same.

"Father."

Her legs wouldn't move, nor would she have known where to run if they had been able to. Toward him? As far away as she could?

He'd come. And not only come but fought for her.

"You're free, daughter," he said, his voice shaking with emotion. "You and your son."

"Ho now, that's not—"

King Lior raised his sword to Cavendish's neck, silencing his protest. He held it there, just long enough to prove who held the power, before pulling a gasp from the crowd when he threw it aside and held out a hand to his enemy instead. When Cavendish didn't take it, King Lior crouched down beside him. Though he spoke too quietly for the crowd to make out more than a murmur, Eva heard every word.

"Before this crowd of witnesses today, I defeated you. And when I should have taken your life for what you've done to my daughter, I spared it. Though I regret the pain I caused your family all those years ago, I have done all I can—and more—in the years since to bring peace between us. My debt is paid twice over. Evangeline and her son leave this place today."

"Eva can go. *My* son stays."

"You would have claimed him as your own the day he was born if you truly wanted him. But, if he means so much to you, claim him now. Before this crowd of witnesses. Dress him in clothes befitting his nobility. Provide him the training and upbringing owed him. Give him the honor of your name, and be the father you claim to be." Lior swung his arm as he stood and gestured to the crowd. "Your people wait."

"No—" Eva's breath caught on the pain lodged in her throat. Her head spun as she tried to stay upright. A hand on her arm—Darrek's? Manning's?—steadied her. She leaned into it and forced strength into her bones.

"He's mute," Cavendish spat out.

King Lior didn't even flinch. "All the more reason to protect him."

Cavendish's gaze caught Eva's before moving to her side. She looked down to find Arthur. Horrified by the conversation happening between the two men, she hadn't even noticed Maeve arrive with him. She wished they'd stayed away. What if Cavendish took him, here and now? She'd not even get the chance to say goodbye. As if she could ever let go of the piece of her heart that walked around in the body of her son.

"The boy is clearly yours, Cormac," her father said, "and I'll not stand between the two of you should you wish to claim him as such. But I will not leave him a servant to be spat upon and downtrodden when he deserves so much more. Claim him now or let him go."

The pain in her chest as Eva waited for Cavendish to answer was physical, as if someone pressed the tip of a knife to her heart and held it there. She watched, blinking away the dots bouncing across her vision, as Cavendish reached for his sword and slowly stood. She moved between him and Arthur, relieved to see Darrek, Maeve, and Manning do the same. They were a wall, albeit a flimsy one. But together, they'd protect the boy. For as long as they could.

But Cavendish didn't come for Arthur, nor did he send his guards as he had the first time Eva had tried to leave. Instead, he laughed, low and bitter.

"Take the boy. I never wanted him anyway except to hurt you. And hurt you he will, Lior, because every time you look at him, you'll be reminded that I *ruined* your daughter, and that boy—as broken and useless as she is—is the proof."

With a sneer and a bow too defiant to be submission, Cavendish stalked from the field.

Somewhere in her mind, Eva registered the sound of the crowd talking, Arthur's hand sliding into hers, her father's loyal knights circling around them—protecting them both—but greater and louder than any of them was the shame. Her father had come for her. But instead of a princess, he'd found her.

"Evangeline."

I ruined your daughter, and that boy is the proof.

Ruined. Cursed. Broken.

Failure

"Evangeline."

Eva jumped when her father's hand touched her arm. She was surprised to see tears in his eyes.

"Come home with me today. You and your son. My men wait at the castle gates to escort us."

Home. It should have filled her with delight. She was welcome, wanted. Forgiven. Her father had come for her. Fought for her. For her freedom. And won. Yet the shame, the relief, the pain—it was too much, all at once. The emotion of the day threatened to fell her with every breath.

When she didn't speak, King Lior knelt in front of Arthur.

"What's your name, young squire?"

Eva's hand went to her mouth, holding back a dry sob. She'd never seen her father kneel before anyone, least of all a child whose life had the potential to ruin him. She swayed and felt a strong arm come across her back. Not enough to be called an embrace but enough to keep her standing. Darrek, protecting her when he could barely stand himself.

"Arthur," she whispered, overcome. "His name is Arthur."

The king laid a hand on Arthur's head, as if bestowing a blessing. "'Tis a joy to meet you, Arthur."

King Lior stood, leaning heavily on his sword to do so, and addressed Eva again.

"We leave for Raedonleith in an hour. It is my greatest hope that you'll join us, but if—" His voice cracked, the muscle in his jaw jumping. "If you find you cannot, even though you are free, then know that the gates are always open to you. Day or night, whenever you come."

He leaned forward to place a gentle kiss on her forehead. A tear dripped down his cheek and into his beard as he stepped away.

"I've missed you, daughter."

Lior turned and walked away without looking back.

Eva fell to her knees, grass pricking her hands as she tried to draw breath into a chest that felt far too tight. Dark spots danced across her vision. She closed her eyes, but the spots remained.

The crowd dispersed.

Maeve took Arthur away.

Manning ordered the knights to pack their things and see George about fresh horses for the king and his men.

Darrek stayed, his hand rubbing circles across her back.

"Breathe," he told her, "just breathe. Don't think of anything else. You're going to be fine. Just breathe."

His voice was soothing. The raging river of thoughts threatening to drown her were not.

Home.

She'd survived nightmares, abuse, loneliness, despair, and the derision of a man who threatened her son to keep her prisoner, yet it was freedom that brought her to her knees.

How could a single word cause such terror? And, more, what was she to do about it?

CHAPTER 38

"Once upon a time, there was a prince who lived in a huge castle. It was the grandest, sturdiest, most striking castle of them all."

Eva stared up at the gathering stars, determined to look nowhere else nor allow herself any other thought until she finished the story. She'd told Arthur this one several times before, but he didn't seem to mind the repetition. It was one of his favorites.

And her mind was far too busy trying to drown her in second thoughts and ignore the knight beside her to be creative.

Her father had left for Raedonleith four hours ago. Eva hadn't gone with him.

She'd packed her things, said goodbye to Maeve, and walked with Arthur to the back of the blacksmith's shop. She'd told Arthur she just needed to sit for a few minutes and that they'd go as soon as she gathered her strength after the exhaustion of the day.

They'd not moved since.

Darrek had found them two hours ago. He'd sat beside them and been as quiet as Arthur while Eva waged war with her thoughts. Manning had come not long after but left when Eva shook her head to his silent question. She wasn't coming.

The exhaustion was real, pulling at every step she took, but it wasn't why she'd stayed. The knights would have helped her where she struggled. Darrek and her father had been prepared to leave, even weakened as they were. It wasn't exhaustion that stopped her but fear.

Always fear.

Story, Eva.

"Tapestries lined the walls, down-filled mattresses sat on every four-post bed, every window was filled with glass. And then there was the gold. It was everywhere—knives, chalices, rings, bowls. Even the serving spoons were made of it. He should have been the happiest man in all the land, except for one thing.

"He was lonely. He had no family, no children, no wife, no one to share it with."

Eva tightened her arms around Arthur. Why did the words make her feel as if she was baring her heart? It was a story. She wasn't lonely. She might not be surrounded by family and loyal friends here, but she had Arthur. And Maeve.

And—

Darrek was looking at her from his place on the ground beside her and Arthur. Eva could feel it without turning her head to see for certain. He was waiting, no doubt, for her to continue. Or wondering, perhaps, why they were still here at Cavendish Castle when he'd all but given his life to free her. Her father too. She wished she had an answer for him. She wished she had an answer for herself.

"One day, a knock came at the door. The prince opened it to find, uh—"

He'd sat closer than usual tonight. Eva leaned against the forge-warmed blacksmith's wall, yet the whole left side of her body seemed to pulse with Darrek's warmth. If she put her hand down, it would land beside his. Close enough to lace their fingers, if she dared.

She didn't dare. Instead, she rearranged Arthur in her lap, leaning his head back against her chest and keeping both arms securely around him. She had to think of Arthur. He was the reason she'd stayed.

Eva closed her eyes. More excuses. It wasn't her health that had kept her here nor the best interests of her son.

It was fear—and fear alone.

Fear that she'd disappoint her father again. Fear of what her people might say about her if she came home. Fear that Arthur would be shunned or cast aside because of his birth and who his father—or worse, *mother*—was. Fear that Darrek might say again those words that she didn't know how to answer but wouldn't leave her heart.

I love you.

Those and her father's final words bounced between her mind and heart, tangling with the words so long etched there.

I love you.

Ruined.

I've missed you.

Failure.

Daughter.

Scarred.

I love you.

Broken.

"Two young bucks."

Eva blinked at Darrek, confused. "Young bucks?"

"At the door."

Oh. The story. Not that that made any more sense. "What would two young bucks be doing at the door of a castle?"

"I don't know, but they were the most handsome and energetic young bucks you'd ever seen. You said the prince was lonely. It sounds like he needed friends. Two young bucks would keep him entertained, don't you think?"

"I was going to say it was a person at the door." At least, she would have, if she hadn't been so distracted by the man beside her. And her father's words. And the fact that she was still sitting here, as if it weren't Cavendish that chained her to her failures but she herself.

"Well, that's not interesting."

Darrek definitely wasn't thinking of her.

"It makes more sense than two animals knocking on the door," Eva countered. "How would they even knock? They have no hands."

"They'd kick it, of course."

"Of course." Eva shook her head. She took a deep breath and determined to get her mind back on the story and the story back on track. Anything to avoid the battle inside her. "May I continue?"

"By all means."

"The prince went to the door and opened it to find—"

"A butterfly," Darrek interrupted again.

Eva gulped, her mind going to the clearing and the way Darrek had looked at her. The way he'd almost kissed her. And spun hope-filled stories of his own before promising he had enough faith for both of them. Did he truly believe she had a future? That *they* did?

The silence was stretching again. With a shake of her head, Eva again forced her thoughts back to the story.

"Butterflies can't knock either. And what would a butterfly be doing at a castle door?"

Except bringing hope. And wonder. And—

"It was lost. And it was magical. It could grant wishes."

"A magical butterfly? I'd prefer the young bucks."

"Who's telling this story?"

"Mama."

Time stopped. Eva gasped, head spinning as she tried to process the miracle in front of her. It couldn't be. She must have imagined it. Arthur didn't speak. She looked in wonder from her son to the man beside her whose stunned expression confirmed what she was too astounded to believe.

Arthur pointed his finger at Eva's chest. "Mama, tell story."

Her son had spoken.

"Mama?"

"Oh—uh, the—" Arthur had spoken. Every other thought flew from her mind as those three words repeated themselves over and over bringing a different emotion each time—first joy, then relief, wondrous awe, happiness. "—butterfly, uh—"

In an instant that couldn't have been explained, it was as if Eva saw into Arthur's future. Him as not a boy but as a man. Tall. Strong. Confident. Laughing and jostling friends' shoulders as they tried to outdo each other on the training ground. Everything she'd dreamed for him. Not a vision, as such, but a spark of hope.

"Changed into a princess before the prince's eyes," Darrek said, filling in the silence her moment of precious revelation had left. "The most beautiful princess he'd ever seen. He loved her on sight, and she him, and they married and lived happily together for the rest of their lives. And one day, they flung stars into the sky—one for each of them—so that anyone who ever felt lost or alone need only look up at the night sky and find their way home. The end."

Arthur snuggled into her and closed his eyes, content with the ending of the story, unusual as it was.

Eva was far more unsettled, the joy of the miracle and spark of hope that followed confirming a choice she didn't want to make. It was time to go home. Although walking out of here was so much easier to plan than put into action.

"Were those his first words?" Darrek asked quietly.

"Aye." Eva shook her head, wonder filling her again. "He called me *Mama*."

"He loves you."

She loved him.

"You know, if you needed more time, you could have told your father." Darrek's words were quiet, holding no condemnation, though no doubt she deserved it. She'd been given freedom and had chosen to stay imprisoned.

"I meant to come." Eva stroked her hand down Arthur's hair as she'd done so many times to settle him as a baby in her arms. The familiar action calmed her as much as it ever had him.

"But?"

"I didn't know how to leave."

The courtyard beyond was quiet tonight, as if the entire of Cavendish Castle was still in shock following their lord's defeat. Cavendish himself hadn't been seen since he left the tournament. Licking his wounds, Maeve had said. Eva thought it more likely he was planning how next to get back at her father. She knew him well enough to believe his revenge far from over.

"My father, the people of Raedonleith, they're expecting the return of a princess. But I'm not that person and never will be again. Here, I may be the cursed one and the broken one, but it's all I've ever been to them."

"It's not who you are."

"I don't know who I am anymore."

Darrek turned to face her, taking her hand in his. He lifted it to his lips and placed a gentle kiss against her knuckles before speaking.

"I do. You're Lady Evangeline, princess of Raedonleith. Nothing you've done can change that. You're not the girl they once knew, but that doesn't mean they won't love the woman you've become. You're strong, Caterpillar. And you're not alone."

Not alone. Sitting here, staring up at the stars, this man beside her when he should have given up on her years ago, Eva finally started to believe him. Manning, Spencer, and Adam had taken a beating for her. Maeve had loved her through her screams. Arthur had called her *Mama*. George had accepted her. Darrek had stayed time and time again when she gave him every reason to leave. Her father had fought for her.

"I'm scared," she admitted.

"Me too."

Eva turned her head to look at Darrek, incredulous. "You?"

"Did you ever think I might be scared too?"

"You're not scared of anything."

He laughed softly, shaking his head, his gaze never leaving hers. "I don't think I knew what fear truly was until the day we found you. But seeing you, hearing your nightmares, watching you battle so much more than anyone should ever have to face—I grew fearful every time you were out of my sight that I'd lose you or fail to be there when you needed protection. The night I woke to see you with that knife, I was terrified. I thought you'd succeeded."

Eva bit her lip. She almost had.

"I still fear you may. Or that I'll lose you another way. I've grown quite fond of protecting you."

Though Eva tried to smile, her lips trembled. "You haven't completed your quest yet. You still have to take me home."

Darrek touched a hand to her chin, and Eva's breath caught. His gaze softened as he looked at her.

"Aye, that I do, Caterpillar. And an honor it will be."

He stood before reaching down to take Arthur from her, balancing the sleeping boy against his shoulder and helping Eva to her feet. "Come, sleep at the stables tonight. We'll leave in the morning."

"What if I have nightmares?" The horses would stampede.

"I'll hold your hand, like always."

His face froze, realizing too late what he'd just admitted. With a grimace, he spoke. "Evangeline, I have to tell you—"

Eva shook her head, smiling as he tried to find the words. "Darrek? I know."

This time, she was the one who waited until he met her gaze.

"Thank you for all the times you've held my hand."

King Lior slid down from his horse and handed the reins to a waiting squire. Sir Cenah clapped him on the shoulder, welcoming him home. Sir John offered him a cup of ale. He accepted it with thanks, throat dry from the travel. Others milled about—maids, knights, and squires alike—waiting to take his cloak, his armor, his sword, to offer him trays of food or a cloth for his face.

He went through the motions, accepting their congratulations, their gifts, their service, but though he thanked them, he couldn't find the will to smile.

He'd waved in victory to the merchants and townsmen who'd lined the street to see him home again, their loyalty warming him better than any blanket. They made him feel like a champion. And, by all accounts, he was. He'd won his daughter's freedom from the man who held her captive. The tale would be recounted in story and song for years to come.

And yet, it didn't feel like a victory. She hadn't come home.

He and his retinue had waited two hours past the time he'd told her they were leaving. He would have waited days more if

Manning hadn't come to deliver the news the knight knew would break his king. Evangeline wasn't coming.

"Did you bring her? Is she here?"

Lior's gut clenched at the sound of his wife's voice. Though she stopped in front of him, squeezing his hands as she took them in hers, Caralynne's gaze skipped around him. He hated to disappoint her, yet what else could he say?

"No."

"But— The knights said you won."

"Aye. I did. But I can only make the way. She's the one who needs to walk it."

Caralynne's eyes filled with tears. "I thought—" Sobs took the words she couldn't find to say. Lior fought back tears of his own as the woman who'd held him, their family, and their kingdom together for the past four years fell apart in his arms.

"I know, my love. I know."

CHAPTER
39

There was Raedonleith, its castle standing tall atop the rise, towers reaching to the sky as they always had. It was just as Eva had imagined, just as she'd held in her heart during the long nights of wondering and denying the spark of hope that she'd ever see it again. Yet the catch in her heart, she hadn't imagined. The dread in the pit of her stomach. The trembling of her legs. The way air caught in her chest, as if she'd forgotten how to breathe. Perhaps she had.

"Caterpillar?"

She hadn't realized how much she'd slowed until Darrek turned his horse back to come up beside her. She stopped, dread swirling her vision along with her thoughts.

"Evangeline, what is it?"

His words were quiet, for her ears alone, yet the other knights had all stopped their horses too, waiting on her. Always waiting on her. It wasn't only Darrek who'd stayed behind when their king had left. Manning, Spencer, Adam, Landon, Craig—they all had. Just as they'd promised. She should have felt honored. Protected. Instead, she felt stifled. And guilty. It wasn't only she who was coming home. The knights were too. For the first time in years. Had they left behind family for her? Wives? Children? Sweethearts? She'd never even asked.

"Home."

It was a whisper of a breath but loud enough. Darrek slid off his horse before reaching to help her off hers. They stood there, tucked between their two horses, hidden from the other knights and her view of the castle. Darrek placed his hands on her shoul-

· 278 ·

ders, his strength—or perhaps his touch—more than she could bear. Tears fell down her cheeks, the weight of expectation, of shame, of hopes and dreams and disappointment, crushing her in their enormity.

"Evangeline…"

He pulled her close, wrapping arms around her trembling frame. The sobs came then, to her utter mortification, soaking into Darrek's cloak. When her legs refused to hold her, he carried her the few steps to a rock, cradling her against him as one would a young child. It fit. She was acting like one.

"Evangeline…"

She couldn't have spoken if she'd tried. The sobs made it impossible, along with the accusing voices inside her head. Home. She'd held the tears at bay while saying goodbye to Maeve. She'd held her fears at bay while riding a horse on her own for three days, even though Darrek had offered to share his. The attraction she felt for him had been far more terrifying than her fear of horses. They were almost home. She'd thought she was ready. She couldn't have been further from the truth. She wasn't ready. Maybe she never would be.

Three days' travel, riding slower than usual because she and Arthur weren't as accustomed to riding as the knights. It had felt like an eternity. Now, it didn't seem near long enough.

"Mama?"

Eva pressed her face tighter against Darrek's shoulder, hating that Arthur was seeing this. She wanted to assure the boy she was fine, but it would have been a lie. She was done lying. Even to Arthur.

A little hand that could only have been her son's joined Darrek's strong one rubbing her back. The sobs came harder as mortification mixed with the helplessness of failure.

Arthur, Darrek, Manning, Spencer, Adam, Landon, Craig—they were all watching her. They had to be. They wouldn't have gone on without her. All bearing witness to her collapse.

"Let's set up camp," Darrek ordered, his voice rumbling against her ear.

"But Raedonleith is only—"

Darrek kept speaking as if Spencer hadn't argued. "Collect wood, start a fire, feed the horses. We'll begin again at first light."

"But we could—"

"Do as the man says, Spencer," Manning said.

No more grumbles or complaints came after that, only the sound of horses being fed, food being cooked, and camp being made. When Landon asked if Arthur would help them, the boy happily went to assist. Eva stayed where she was. At first, it was because she couldn't move. Then, because she didn't want to. When, finally, she found the strength, Darrek let her go only as far as the rock beside him. He took her hands in his, as if he needed that point of connection as much as she did, before angling his body to shelter her from the others.

"What can I do?" he asked.

"Stay."

His hands squeezed hers. "Always."

"Even when we get home. Even when I tell you to go away."

"As long as the choice is mine, I'll be here. But why now? Why tell me this?"

"Because I know I will. And I'll be lying. I want you. Beside me. I just know it won't be easy for you, and I feel so guilty being a burden."

Darrek shook his head. "You aren't a burden."

"Tell me that too. Even when I refute it. Because it means a lot."

"I'll stay."

"Thank you."

"Was there something else?"

Eva shook her head. If she tried to put any more of her fears into words right now, she'd only cry again.

Darrek lay on his blanket and stared up at the stars. He should have been asleep. With the exception of Spencer, who'd taken the first watch, the rest of the men were. Their chorus of snores punctuated by the occasional grunt might have been what kept him awake, if not for how accustomed he'd become to sleeping beside them these past four years. He should have taken Spencer's place. At least one of them would have gotten some sleep.

But how could he sleep when Evangeline didn't?

She'd gotten up from her place by the fire over an hour ago. Expecting nightmares, Darrek had woken the second she stirred, watching as she walked to the flat rock the two of them had sat on earlier. She'd stood there for a few minutes before wandering over to the tree Spencer leaned against. They'd been too far away for Darrek to hear the words they exchanged. He probably wouldn't have been able to hear over the roar of jealousy in his ears anyway.

Then, she'd walked back to the rock and sat. She was so still that she blended in with the forest behind her, and he had to keep checking she was still there. She was. An hour later.

He wanted to give her space—he'd certainly invaded it enough earlier, sitting by her side for more than an hour as they'd watched the other men set up camp for the night—but how much space did one need? What if she fell again into the despair he knew she fought?

Almighty, please, let it not be…

Minutes passed as Darrek lay there wondering, praying, fighting fears of his own. He'd surrendered Evangeline and her life to the Almighty, finally admitting he alone couldn't save her. He wouldn't take that back. And yet, did that mean he could do nothing to help her? The Almighty used people to do his work, did he not?

Evangeline dropped her head into her hands.

Darrek gave in. He couldn't save her, but she didn't have to face this alone.

She started then sighed when he sat beside her. "I didn't mean to wake you."

"I'm glad you did."

"Why?"

"So I could be here now." He took her hand, wrapping it between his own. "What worries you?"

For a while, she was silent. Only leaves rustling in the breeze and the snores of the men filled the air. Then—

"We'll be home tomorrow."

"Aye. You'll see your mother and father and sisters, sleep in a real bed, be served and honored like the princess you are."

"I'm no princess. I walked away."

"Yes, and now you're coming home."

"But I'm not that princess, Darrek. I know you believe they'll accept me, but I don't know if I can. I have Arthur and—scars."

"They know about Arthur and where you've been."

"But they don't know about the scars."

Something in Darrek's chest ached at her words. He could tell her the scars wouldn't matter—not to him, nor her father, nor any other person who loved her—but he'd be lying. They'd tear her father's heart apart, just like they did his every time he saw them. But not for the reason she thought. Not because they were unsightly or shameful or made her any less cherished. Simply because she'd felt the need for them at all. He would have taken her pain on himself if he could have, just so she wouldn't have had to walk through it.

He lifted her arm and gently kissed the scars.

"They're beautiful."

Evangeline let out a short laugh, tugging her arm out of his and crossing both of them over her chest. "No, they're not."

Darrek rolled up his own sleeve, past his elbow, angling his arm to the moonlight. A thick corded scar ran across his bicep.

A gasp escaped Evangeline's lips. "What happened?"

"Sword strike. I didn't move fast enough."

That sleeve fell as he pushed up his other to reveal another scar. This one was thinner than the first but twice as long. "First joust. I have others too, as do Manning, Spencer, Adam, and Landon. Even Craig, young as he is. We all have scars, Evangeline."

"It's not the same. Yours came in battle. Through fighting an enemy."

"As did yours, Caterpillar. Just because my enemy was a person doesn't make it any less of a battle. I fight soldiers. You fight your demons. You could have given in, but you didn't. Neither of us did. Our scars are proof of that."

"Still, they hardly compare."

"I wish I could take them for you."

Spencer walked over to wake Landon, the men sharing yawns then grins as they conversed quietly before swapping places. Landon glanced over in Darrek and Evangeline's direction but didn't interrupt them. He waved to acknowledge their presence before leaning against the same tree Spencer had, sword laid across his lap.

Evangeline missed the whole exchange, staring down at her hands. Darrek took them both in his, turning them so he could run his thumbs across her palms.

She'd removed the bandage from the cut on her palm, but it still had a way to go before it was healed. Whether it would leave a scar remained to be seen.

"I hate it," he told her honestly. "I hate that you fight this. I hate how often it plagues you. I hate that you feel this is the only way to battle it. I hate that I can't fight it for you. I hate that you know this much pain and that I can't do a thing to take it away. But I will never, *never* hate your scars. They're part of you and your journey, and they're proof that you fought."

She stared at him, her thoughts too veiled to be guessed. Had he said too much? Too little? More than anything, he wanted her to know she was loved. Not because of her scars or choices, not even despite them, but simply because of who she was.

A light mist began to form around the camp, not enough to hide them from sight but enough for them to feel as if they were the only ones here. Darrek sighed. It was late, or early, whichever way one looked at it. Tomorrow would bring with it enough challenges without facing it on little to no sleep.

He opened his mouth to suggest they head back to their blankets before closing it again with an audible gulp. She looked so beautiful in the misty moonlight. The wetness of the air tugged at the ends of her hair, turning it to curls. He ran the pad of his thumb across her cheek, smudging the trail her tears had left. Her quick intake of breath had his gaze dropping to her mouth.

"Darrek?"

Surely it was the lack of sleep to blame—or perhaps simply her beauty—but he couldn't keep his thoughts inside. "I want to kiss you."

"Then why don't you?"

"Because you've had enough men taking what they want from you. I don't want to be another."

"What if I want it too?" Evangeline's voice was barely a whisper.

"Say that again?"

Evangeline raised a hand to his face, running her fingers gently down the scruff of his cheek. "I want you to."

Darrek's hands were gentle as they cupped her cheeks, far more so than she'd imagined a knight's being. His right thumb brushed across her lips, a tiny smile tugging at his own. He seemed content to take his time. Her thudding heart—felt in every one of her fingertips—wished he wouldn't.

"Evangeline," he whispered before closing the distance between them.

Darrek wasn't the first man she'd kissed. He wasn't the second, third, or even the fourth. But in this moment, held like a precious jewel, she wished—prayed even—that he'd be the last. She'd enjoyed the kisses of the other men, but none of them had felt like this.

With them, she'd always been trying to be someone else—older, more confident, more experienced, more everything. She'd wanted to impress them and had been all too aware of it. She'd been desperate to do everything right to hold their affection.

There was none of that with Darrek. He already knew how broken she was, how experienced, and how much she regretted being that experienced. He saw who she was rather than who she tried to be. She didn't have to guess with Darrek.

Didn't have to wonder.

Didn't want to leave.

Kissing Darrek was like coming home.

"Marry me," she asked. "Right now."

Darrek pulled back roughly, stumbling as he stood. Was that horror on his face at her plea? "No, Evangeline. You know I can't do that."

She had to try. "Please."

"Why?"

He frowned down at her for so long she almost decided to walk away herself. Instead, she stood to face it. To face him. He took a deliberate step backward. Eva felt it like a lance to the chest.

"Why, Evangeline? What is this about? You know I love you. I would do anything for you. But your father would never agree."

"Then we don't ask. We marry here. Before we leave. Sir Manning can perform the rites."

"Evang—"

"No. I know you keep telling me Father cares, but I just can't take the risk that he doesn't. What if he's just saying that to get me home so he can lock me up where I deserve to be? What if he doesn't protect me? What if he forces me to marry another man who turns out to be just like Lord Cavendish? What if he sends Arthur back and refuses to acknowledge him? He can't do any of that if we're married. It would be my husband who held that power. You, Sir Darrek. You said you'd protect me. You said you cared. Prove it by marrying me. Give me the protection of your name."

Darrek shook his head. His frown disappeared, only to have sorrow take its place.

"You have it already, even without my name. I made you a promise, and I will keep it. I *will* protect you, Evangeline. You *and* Arthur. I won't let anything happen to either of you."

"But you won't marry me."

"I can't. It wouldn't be right."

Eva looked toward the fire Arthur slept next to. He'd been so proud when the knights gave him the choice of where to lay his blanket, and he happily chose his place between Darrek and Spencer. Her little boy was in awe of the knights and their horses. But while he looked up to them all, he shadowed Darrek. No doubt because it was Darrek who'd first treated him like a child rather than a blight or mistake.

She had to convince this man to marry her. Not only for herself but for her son. The two of them could face any opposition if they had Darrek and the protection of his name.

"Please," she begged. "I know I'm scarred and used and not as beautiful as other maidens, but I would be a good wife to you. I would support you, and Arthur would—"

"You're beautiful."

"What?"

With a force that might have scared her had he been any other man, Darrek crushed her to himself.

"You're beautiful," he said against her hair. "The most beautiful woman I've ever known."

"No, I'm—"

"You are. And your scars only make you more so. You've struggled, and fought, and won time and time again. You're stronger than you believe and more beautiful than you'll ever understand. I couldn't imagine loving any woman more than I do you."

She didn't even bother to stop the tears gathering in her eyes at his words. The new dawn would bring with it so many unknowns. But this man loved her. Cared about her. Even her scars.

"Then you'll marry me?"

Darrek swallowed, his chest expanding as he took a deep breath, and stepped back. Though he placed both hands on her shoulders and gazed at her as if she were his entire reason for being alive, the distance between them was palpable. The cold seeping into her bones had nothing to do with the mist floating around them.

"Please…"

Though he tried to smile, it held no joy. Rejection rarely did.

"You, Lady Evangeline, are more important to me than anyone in this world, and there is nothing I want more right now than to agree to marry you, but as much as it pains me, I cannot. Your father—"

"Isn't here." Couldn't Darrek see that? Couldn't he see how much she needed this? She couldn't count on her father, but Darrek, she could. He was here. He'd *been* here. Tonight was the only promise she had.

"Your father loves you. I respect him. I won't take away his joy in seeing his daughter marry."

"Even if it would save him the embarrassment of seeing his unmarried daughter return with a child?"

Darrek pulled her close, pressing his lips against her forehead for a long moment before letting her go.

"One day, little caterpillar, you're going to realize that your mistakes don't define you, nor do they define your future. Only the Almighty can do that. When he looks at you, he doesn't see your mistakes or the shame you hold so tightly to. He simply sees his child. If only you could let the shame stop blinding you and see it too. He loves you, Evangeline, and I do too. But none of that matters if you can't see the treasure in yourself. You are worth far more than this."

"What if I can't?"

"Then stay close to those of us who do." Darrek held out his hand, waiting for her to take it before tugging her back toward the fire. "Sleep, Caterpillar. Things will look better in the morning."

Darrek had thought talking with Evangeline and assuring himself she was well would help him sleep. He couldn't have been more wrong. He could have taken every watch the whole night, wide awake as he was.

Marriage. She'd proposed marriage. Right after that kiss. His first. Only the thought of the disappointment on her father's face had kept him from agreeing to a lifetime of more. He couldn't do that to his king. Nor to her. If they were going to marry—something he yearned with all his heart, soul, and mind to be true—he was going to do it with all the honor he'd promised her.

He rolled over onto his side, unable to keep his gaze off Evangeline for more than a few minutes at a time. She faced away from him, so he couldn't see if she slept, though she was still, so he hoped she did. And that the nightmares that so often plagued her stayed away.

His job as a knight was to fight and protect. He couldn't do that for Evangeline. And it hurt more than he'd ever thought possible. In so many ways, it felt like failure. He could hold her hand through her nightmares, stand guard as she worked by day, and even fight Cavendish for her freedom, but when it came to fighting her greatest enemy, he was powerless.

But the Almighty wasn't. And so Darrek prayed until dawn crept across the camp and a new day began. For her life, for her protection, for her soul. He would have rather fought with a sword, but he had to believe this was just as powerful. More so. Far more than his sword could ever do.

Almighty, save her. Bring her home.

CHAPTER 40

"**D**arrek, will you—come with me?"

Darrek looked at Evangeline so sharply that she blushed, likely remembering her suggestion the night before. He remembered it too. Couldn't have forgotten if he'd tried.

Marry me.

"'Tis not that," she said quickly, wringing her hands together. "There's something I must do before I go home, and I don't want to do it alone."

He believed her—her face was growing redder by the second—but still, Darrek hesitated. It was becoming more and more difficult to keep his distance when he and Evangeline were alone. Even if she didn't bring up the topic of marriage again, he'd be thinking about it. And what that might mean. What came within its sanctity.

"We'll stay within view," she said as if reading his mind. "And not be long."

"I'll watch Arthur," Manning offered. "We'll leave as soon as you return."

Arthur grinned, playing with the two wooden horses Manning had whittled him. Darrek nodded and walked to Evangeline's side, wondering what had her so openly uncertain. Though he knew she often doubted herself, she rarely showed it.

She tried a smile when he reached her, only to have it fall.

"Caterpillar—"

She shook her head. "Not yet."

They walked in silence to the river. Eva followed it along until she reached a part that was too deep and too wide to cross as well as out of earshot of the other far-too-interested knights. Her hand trembled as she pulled a knife from her skirts and held it.

"Is that—"

She nodded. Darrek, finally realizing the significance of the moment, stayed silent.

The early morning sun glinted off the smooth metal of the knife's blade. A raven, Cavendish's emblem, was burned into the handle. It was a simple knife, one of hundreds like it, yet so much more. It was the representation of who she'd been, and—dare he hope?—who she no longer wanted to be.

"I thought my life was over the day Cavendish threw me aside. I didn't think I deserved any better. It was so easy to take that pain out on myself and make the outside match the worthless mess I thought I was inside. Time and time too many, I used this knife to prove that.

"But I don't want that anymore. I want to be better. A better mother for Arthur, a better daughter, better sister, better friend…" She looked at him, and Darrek nodded, recognizing it was him she meant. She blushed again, talking to her hands instead of him. "Maybe even a wife someday."

She turned the knife over in her hands, the movement seeming to bring her comfort. It took everything in Darrek to stay still and listen.

"This part of me, I don't want to take it home. I don't know how easy it will be to stop—likely it will be the hardest thing I've ever done—but I want to try.

"I know this is just one knife, but for years, it's been what I run to when I'm most upset. I don't want that anymore. I've carried it for too long, relied on it too much. When I go home, when I walk back through those gates, the knife stays here."

With a deep breath, Evangeline walked the few steps to the river's edge and threw the knife into the deepest part. Raging as the water was, it didn't take more than a second for the metal to drop out of sight. Eva fell onto her knees in the mud, face in her hands.

Darrek knelt beside her, knowing how much this moment meant to her. It was a death, of sorts, and with it, the choice to live. The decision to choose the pain of growth rather than the easy way out. A moment of realizing that, though others like her family, friends, and maybe even he would be there to support her, the first step had to be hers.

This was her surrender moment.

Darrek bowed his head. It was a miracle only the Almighty could have performed.

He placed an arm around her shoulders before realizing it wasn't enough and pulling her into his embrace.

They knelt there together, mud seeping into their clothes, for some time. Darrek swallowed against the thickness in his throat. How he loved this courageous woman.

"I'm proud of you," he forced out, his voice still catching on the words. "So, so, proud."

She didn't say anything. She didn't have to. He knew she'd heard. His caterpillar was growing her wings and breaking free.

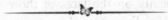

The gates to Raedonleith loomed before Eva, never before having looked so terrifying. Inside was home. Yet, was it? Could she truly find peace within them, as Darrek had promised? Stepping through them would change everything. No longer Eva, the servant girl, but Evangeline, daughter of the king.

Maybe.

Eva looked over her shoulder at Arthur, who was still sleeping in Spencer's arms atop the knight's horse, oblivious to his mother's angst. There was that small miracle to be thankful for, at least.

"Forward?"

"No!" The panic welled in Eva's chest. She couldn't do this. Not now. Not ever. This had been a terrible idea. She'd thrown herself at a man's mercy once before and had the scars and nightmares to show for it. She couldn't do it again. Not even for the man she once called Father.

"Open the gates!"

A bellowing cry came from inside Raedonleith's walls. If she planned to flee, this was her last chance. She wouldn't have time to wrench Arthur from Spencer's arms, but maybe that was for the best. He'd be safe here. Darrek would care for him. Spencer and the others too.

Only, that voice…

The gates weren't even fully open before the same man she'd disappointed time and time again pushed through them, running straight at Eva, pulling her from her horse and into his arms.

"My baby. My child. You're home."

Darrek brushed his horse, the rhythm too familiar to be a distraction for his depressed thoughts.

He should have married Evangeline when he had the chance. As expected, she'd been pulled away from him the moment they arrived, back into the arms of her father. It was a wonder King Lior hadn't crushed her ribs with the force of his embrace. There had been tears aplenty on the faces of those who watched the long-awaited reunion. Even Manning, stoic as he'd always been, had wiped a wet eye.

And then the party had gone inside.

Queen Caralynne had come running, hand to her mouth as she tried to hold back emotion of her own at the sight of her daughter. Evangeline had been sucked back into her world and family like she'd never left, while Darrek had taken his horse to the stables, unpacked the meager belongings that had traveled with him these past four years, and sat down to eat as if he'd never left either. It was exactly how it should have been.

He could have screamed with the injustice of it.

He'd taken the brush off a grateful squire not long after and started cleaning his horse just for something to do. Manning, Landon, Adam, Spencer, and Craig were enjoying a well-earned rest, but though Darrek's body craved sleep, his mind wouldn't allow it. His stomach protested the food too much to eat it either.

This was life. Again. It was the role he'd worked for, dreamed of as a boy, clung to as a squire when the days grew long and the work dull, been thrilled to give his vow to the day after his twentieth birthday. Being a knight was all he'd ever wanted.

Until now.

The biggest fools were those in love.

Perhaps there was still hope. Though she'd never said it aloud, Darrek was certain Evangeline cared about more than just the protection of his name. She cared about him. He'd seen it in the way she sought him out before anyone else. The way she trusted him with her most pain-filled secrets. The way she'd kissed. Perhaps he could talk to King Lior, confess his love for Lady Evangeline, beg him for her hand—

"Did you hear?"

Darrek's musings were interrupted by an overeager squire he didn't recognize. The boy couldn't have been more than twelve years of age, though he was bouncing about like a five-year-old.

"King Lior is throwing a banquet to celebrate Lady Evangeline's homecoming. It's tonight. And we're all invited. Even the servants and squires and pages, if the little ones can stay awake that long."

Tonight. Darrek closed his eyes. King Lior wasn't wasting any time. The kitchens would be a flurry. But he was glad. Evangeline deserved to be fussed over. Maybe with this, she'd finally comprehend how much her people, and father especially, had missed her.

"One of the maids told me that King Lior is going to announce her betrothal too."

"Her betrothal? No. Baron Waddingham broke the betrothal."

"Not that Waddingham fellow. Another man, although the maid said the king wouldn't say who the man was. She also said that, since everyone in Raedonleith is invited, that means I can come too. If I finish all my work. Can you believe it? I've never been to a banquet before."

Darrek handed the brush to the boy before stalking out of the stable. He couldn't let this happen. He'd thought he had time. He was wrong. He needed to talk to his king. Now. Before he lost Evangeline forever.

CHAPTER
41

Darrek waited outside King Lior's chamber for a whole hour before being allowed entrance. With every dressmaker, musician, cleric, and maid that walked in and out of the room, Darrek's confidence slipped a bit more. The squire had been mistaken, he'd told himself as he waited. It happened all too frequently. A servant heard a small part of a conversation and passed on their assumptions along with the rest as fact, each story growing with the retelling. There was a feast being planned, for sure, but a betrothal? Unlikely. King Lior wasn't about to say goodbye to his daughter so soon after getting her back.

And yet, a dressmaker with sweeping fabric of wedding-blue. A cleric with papers stamped with the king's signet. Jewels, entertainment, another cleric, Sir Manning—who either didn't see Darrek sitting there or carefully ignored him.

"Sir Darrek."

Darrek rose from his place and walked inside. She wasn't married yet. There was still time. Wasn't there?

King Lior sat on a chair draped with furs. He didn't often wear his crown except for official occasions. He wore it now. In honor of his daughter's return? Or something else. Darrek knelt before him, heart thudding as he considered his plea.

King Lior, I care for your daughter deeply. If you deem me worthy, it would be my honor to marry her.

And if you don't deem it, I'll prove how right you are by stealing her away before any other man can.

Probably best he leave off the latter.

"Arise, Sir Darrek."

Darrek did as ordered. He opened his mouth to make his request but closed it when King Lior continued.

"You have served me well these past four years and the years before that. You have always been a good knight, but today you did something I have only dreamed of. You brought my daughter home."

King Lior raised a hand to his heart and bowed his head. Darrek's palms began to sweat.

King Lior, I care for your daughter—

"It was my honor to do so, my king."

"Nevertheless, there is a reward I would bestow upon you, if you are willing."

Darrek shook his head. "Please, you owe me nothing." And the longer the king drew out this conversation, the more likely Darrek was to sweat through his outfit. *I wish to marry your daughter.* "I did only my duty as a knight in your service."

"You did far more than that."

"My king?"

"In the hours since you've come home, I've had two lengthy conversations—one with my youngest daughter and one with Sir Manning Beckett. Both mentioned you were instrumental in bringing my Evangeline home. They told me how, while the other knights kept watch from a distance, you laid down your sword in favor of a shovel and the work of a stable boy to be nearer her. And how you spent your nights beside her"—he held up a hand to stop Darrek's immediate defense—"*honorably*, to comfort her during nightmares, how you fought for her freedom against Lord Cavendish himself."

And lost, though neither of them mentioned it. "I would do all that again, my king."

"I hope so because I wish to reward you with her hand in marriage."

Darrek sputtered. "Marry Lady Evangeline? Me, King Lior? But—"

"Manning told me you care for her. He believes you may even have come to love her, these past two months. Is he correct?"

Marry. Evangeline. Him. It was everything he wanted. And he hadn't even said a word.

"He is, my king. I could not imagine ever caring for another woman the way I do Lady Evangeline."

King Lior rose from his chair and walked to stand in front of Darrek, placing a steady hand on his shoulder.

"You are a man of honor, Sir Darrek Drew, and a man who has proven that honor and love for my daughter many times over. I could not ask for a better man to love and protect her from this day forward."

Darrek blinked. Frowned. "Today, sire?"

"I believe it best, don't you?"

"Yes, of course, but what if Lady Evangeline doesn't agree?"

Darrek bowed his head, wishing he could take back the question as soon as he asked it. A knight didn't question his king, and the daughter of a king married whoever her father decreed. It was the way of the world.

"We'll ask her, shall we? Ah, here she is."

Light steps to his left had Darrek raising his gaze. His breath caught somewhere in his chest and, though he thought he might have made some kind of sound, his mind had become so garbled, he wasn't sure.

Evangeline had been striking as a young girl. As a woman dressed in servant's garb with dust streaked across her face, he'd thought her beautiful. But now—

"I do believe you've taken your knight's breath away, daughter," King Lior said with an almost straight face.

Breathtaking. Yes. That was exactly how Darrek would describe Evangeline as she stood there in the archway.

The peasant rags were gone, along with the mud from this morning, and replaced with a gown of forest green that skimmed her pale shoulders, tucked in at her waist with a thin gold rope, and fell to the ground. Her hair, the sides pulled back from her face in a series of intricate braids, tumbled down her back in a glow of sunset red. But it was her face that captivated him. She was smiling—not the forced one he'd seen so often but one that softened the edges of her brilliant blue eyes and made them almost glow with happiness.

"Evangeline…"

Darrek breathed out her name, first once, then twice, as he continued to stare at her, unable to pull his gaze away.

"Daughter, you've told me already, but your knight would like to hear it from you. Do you wish to marry Sir Darrek Drew?"

Her voice was a study of quiet confidence. "I do."

Darrek swallowed hard against the sudden lump in his throat. He was going to marry Evangeline. Eva. The woman he loved. The woman he'd cared for since the day he saw her, standing by that little cottage, and knew he'd finally found her. Not only the daughter his king sought but the woman he'd love for eternity. The woman he'd tried so hard to save, only to surrender to the fact that saving her had never been his job in the first place. The only woman ever to make him think that maybe writing sonnets about love wasn't so foolish after all. Not that he would do that. But he could understand why a man might.

Evangeline. His wife.

He couldn't get his head around it, even as she placed her hand on his arm and smiled shyly up at him. That smile. Those eyes. Brighter than he could have imagined against the green of her gown. She was radiant. And she was his.

Or, at least, she would be as soon as they were married.

Which, apparently, was happening tonight. His heart thudded even as his mind doubted such a gift.

"Are you certain, my king?"

"Would you rather I changed my mind?"

"No! Please, don't. That is—" Darrek looked aghast at King Lior to find the older man smiling. He allowed himself a wry smile in return. "No, my liege, I would not."

"Be at ease, Sir Darrek. I am certain. Any man willing to fight to his death for my daughter well deserves her. That she admires you makes my decision all the more pleasant. I only hope you'll forgive me the speed at which the marriage is occurring. While I trust you to keep your promises, I don't share the same faith in

Lord Cavendish. Though he was quite publicly defeated, it would still be in his best interests to come after Evangeline and young Arthur. Especially given the history between our families. The best—perhaps only—way to keep them safe is for her to be married and you to claim Arthur as your own.

"Please, do not think for a minute that I am forcing you into this union. If you do not believe you can love and care for Evangeline as a husband should, then I bid you walk away now. Marriage is not a commitment to be taken lightly. I remember well the struggle I faced in choosing my Caralynne when others believed I should have chosen another. I would wish you and Evangeline to be happy. You have a choice in the matter, as far as who it is my daughter marries. She must marry, but if you don't wish it to be you—"

"Yes," Darrek interrupted.

"You don't—"

"Yes, I wish it to be me."

Evangeline's quiet gasp pulled Darrek's attention from her father. Her eyelashes fluttered briefly as a tiny smile tugged at the corners of her mouth, so close to his own that for a moment he couldn't even remember what he'd been trying to say. Was her heart beating as quickly as his? Did she too feel full of wonder that this—any of this—was happening?

He wanted to kiss her. *Needed* to. She sucked in a breath as he leaned the tiniest bit closer.

A subtle clearing of King Lior's throat brought Darrek's head back around. Heat crawled along his neck and down his shoulders as his brain caught up to his body. Had he really been about to kiss Evangeline in front of her father?

Still, King Lior didn't seem too perturbed, if the crinkling around his eyes was any indication. Darrek cleared his own throat before meeting the older man's gaze directly. He was Darrek's king, certainly, but in this moment, he was far more a father. One who wanted assurance that he'd made the right choice for his beloved daughter, something Darrek was only too willing to give.

"I care deeply for your daughter, my king. Though, knowing

of her betrothal, I did my best to deny it, she captured my heart. It would be an honor beyond what I could dream to spend my life protecting her—body, heart, and soul."

It took every bit of self-control Darrek had to hold King Lior's gaze instead of looking back again at the woman holding tightly to his arm. When the king nodded, Darrek let out the breath he'd been holding.

"And Arthur?"

The boy who followed him around, trusted Darrek enough to speak to him, had the makings of a fine knight himself, and once had sat right under the heart of the woman he loved? There was no choice at all.

"It would be a privilege to give him the protection of my name. I hope one day he calls me *Papa* and is only the first of many to do so."

He could have sworn the king blinked back a tear.

"You are a good man, Sir Darrek."

"Only by the grace of the Almighty."

"Yes. By his grace."

The king nodded to one of his men, who walked out of the room, only to come back a moment later with something wrapped in fabric. He handed it to the king, who held it with reverence.

Darrek looked at Evangeline, but the question in his eyes was mirrored in hers.

King Lior cleared his throat.

"At the birth of each of my daugh—" His voice cracked with emotion. With a breath and another clearing of his throat, King Lior began again. "The day each of my daughters was born, a master goldsmith was tasked with creating a crown specifically for that daughter, which would be given to her on the day of her wedding."

Fabric fell to the floor as King Lior pulled from it a gold crown inlaid with gems. Evangeline gasped. Her hand went to her mouth.

"This is the one he created for Evangeline."

"But— I—" Evangeline's gasp turned to a sob. "I took it. Then lost it. And Cavendish—"

"I bought it back."

He said it so simply, yet Darrek, and no doubt Evangeline, knew how much that must have cost him. Cavendish wouldn't have parted with the crown cheaply. Lior handed it to Evangeline, whose hands were trembling so much she almost dropped it. Darrek put a hand under hers to support them.

"Darrek—"

Darrek saw it the same moment Evangeline did. Five white gems, in the shape of a butterfly. Right there on the front of the crown.

"I see it."

A white butterfly. Just like the ones they'd seen in the clearing. Just like the vision he'd had for her. Etched into the crown that had been made at her birth.

"Did you know?" he asked.

"I didn't— I never— No." She took a deep breath, fingering the diamond butterfly. "I had no idea. I never looked at the crown."

Darrek had never been interested in jewels before, but even he could appreciate the intricate craftsmanship of the crown they held. It was striking in its beauty and would have impressed Darrek even if it hadn't been for the butterfly.

The butterfly. He couldn't believe there was a butterfly etched into Evangeline's crown. It was like a promise and a fulfillment all in one. If ever he doubted the Almighty's hand on Evangeline's life again, he only need look to this crown.

With hands far steadier than Darrek's felt, Lior placed the crown onto his daughter's head before kissing her forehead. She closed her eyes.

"Daughter. Evangeline. It's so good to have you home."

"Thank you," she told her father.

Her gratitude, and Darrek's own, went beyond the crown. Beyond the welcome. Beyond her father's approval. It was as if, for that one drawn-out moment, the three of them stood in a world all their own. Three people, once far apart, now bound together by hope and the gift of a miracle.

A whoop from outside broke the moment, bringing them all back to reality and the realization that—miracle or not—life went on. And any moment, Cavendish could storm their reunion.

King Lior placed one hand on his daughter's shoulder and one on Darrek's. A benediction, almost. "Well, Sir Darrek. I do believe we have a wedding to see to and a feast to attend." He took his daughter's hand and kissed it. "Don't be longer than a minute." With a wink, he walked out, guards with him, leaving the two of them alone.

"A minute? What does he mean? Should we follow him?"

A minute. Darrek could have laughed with the joy of it. He would have, had the seconds not already been ticking down in his mind. He whisked Evangeline in against his chest, wrapping an arm around her waist. The other, he used to stroke her hair. Her beautiful, coppery hair. The crown tilted slightly as he pulled her closer.

"I believe he was talking about this."

The hand on her hair moved to her cheek, so soft against his calloused one. Her gasp was caught up in his kiss. *Evangeline.* It was all he could think over the thudding of not only his heart but what felt like every piece of his skin. She was so warm, so soft, so…perfect.

She pulled away, a frown on her face. "Are you sure? Maybe he meant something else."

His growl turned into a deep laugh at her grin. She was teasing him. Evangeline. Teasing him. Her eyes sparkled with life, where just hours ago, they'd been so wary. It was as if the years had been pulled back and she was the girl who'd never left. Only she had, and while with everything in him, he wished she'd never had to walk that pain-filled road, he was thankful for it because it had made her into the woman she was today.

He'd been amused by, stirred by, attracted to, and infuriated by that Evangeline, but he'd never loved her like he did the woman standing before him now.

"My butterfly."

A throat cleared from somewhere at the edge of the room. Darrek didn't have to look to know it was Manning checking on them, as King Lior had warned. He should pull away from Evangeline. The two of them would be married soon enough and he could sneak all the kisses he wished. For now, he simply stole one more. Though, the way she gave it up, it hardly felt like stealing.

"Thank you, Sir Darrek," Evangeline said, smiling up at him.

He frowned. "For what?"

She took his hand in hers.

"For bringing me home."

Later that day

"**F**ather missed your ball."

Mykah looked sideways at her older sister, wondering if Rose's thoughts on the matter were as tempestuous as hers. A cheer filled the Great Hall, carried on a wave of laughter and hooting from the crowd of guests hastily gathered to celebrate the king's youngest daughter's wedding. Mykah didn't need to look to know Evangeline and her new husband had kissed again. Sir Darrek would be grinning and Evangeline blushing prettily as the two of them accepted the congratulations—and obligatory teasing—of the room full of rowdy knights and ladies. It had been happening all evening.

"Rose?" Mykah tried again. Perhaps her sister hadn't heard her.

Rose took a slow sip from her goblet, her gaze never leaving their father. He stood beside the married couple, smile overflowing into tears that would have mortified him to shed in public any other day.

Of course, this wasn't just any day. This was the day everything he'd hoped, prayed, and almost died for had come true. His daughter had come home.

The youngest of his daughters, anyway.

His other two—she and Rose—had been here all this time, never having broken their father's heart as Evangeline had nor almost killed him with their selfishness. Of course, they hadn't given him reason to throw aside all decorum and weep in public out of sheer delight either.

"Yes," Rose said, her quiet voice barely heard above the crowd. "He did."

"And you're not angry?" Mykah asked, partly in disbelief and partly in wonderment. Rose seemed so calm, whereas Mykah's heart and mind roiled with such fierce emotions that she'd left most of her food on her plate. Anger. Hope. Resentment. Guilt. Pity. Disappointment. Happiness. Relief. Disdain.

She was happy for Evangeline and Sir Darrek, truly. How could anyone not be? Her beloved sister was home again. And not only had Evangeline come home, but she'd found love and a family of her own. It was the end Mykah hadn't dared hope for on the days stretching to months when she'd wondered if Evangeline were still alive.

And yet, Rose.

How could Mykah be happy for one sister when the other had lost so much?

And how could she respect the man who'd taken it?

Their father should have been there for Rose, at the celebration of her twenty-second birthday, to announce, as he'd promised, the name of the man he'd chosen for Rose to marry. Maybe he would have, if he'd been home to do so instead of riding off to rescue Evangeline. If he'd remembered to choose Rose a husband at all. It wouldn't have been the first promise he'd forgotten during the past four years.

"Evangeline needed him," Rose said.

"Yes," Mykah replied, with a tip of her head. "But so did you."

Acknowledgements

I always knew this book was going to be difficult to write. What I didn't expect was to be so broken and terrified by Eva's story that—for a time—I couldn't write it at all. It was too hard. Too painful. Too much. I wasn't qualified to write such deep topics. It was too close to my own story. I was going to fail—or worse, not do it justice—with Eva's journey *or* the incredible love of the God who never gives up on his children. I knew that this was the story God had given me to write, but I was too paralyzed by fear to put a single word to paper.

And then, listening to music one day while struggling over it yet again, my random playlist picked two songs. Or maybe (definitely) God did. "Love Moved First" and "One Awkward Moment," both by Casting Crowns. I honestly wonder if I might have ever found the courage to write this story without those two songs. One, about the immense wonder of a God who saw us at our worst, knew we could never save ourselves, and made the first move to save us. The other, asking if one awkward moment on our behalf is really too high a price to save a life.

I listened to those two songs on repeat for weeks as I finished writing this book.

So, before I thank anyone else, I want to thank the members of Casting Crowns for their music. For being willing to share their hearts, that I might find the courage to share mine, and hopefully in turn, encourage yours. I know, it's weird to thank a band, especially one who'll probably never even see these words, but their music was such a big part of the writing of this book that I couldn't leave them out.

Many, MANY thanks, as always, to my mum. I long ago lost track of the number of times I've turned up at her door, or on the other end of her phone call, in tears over a book I'm writing. Just as she's probably lost track of the number of times she's told me to pray over it, that God gave me this story for a reason, I *can* do it, and just to take it a day at a time. She gets the brunt of the frustration, which makes it all the more special sharing with her the finished book each time. And having her say, very nicely, "I told you so." Thank you, Mum, for your endless encouragement and prayers.

To my husband and kids. It's been a big year, overly full of change and challenges, but I wouldn't have wanted to do it with anyone else. Thank you. Times a million and a million more. For laughing with me, helping me brainstorm, giving me my Medieval Blacksmith Lego set (love it!!), letting me hide away for a few hours each day to write, and just being the most amazing people to share every day with. You make me smile and so proud to be yours. I love you guys! Special thanks (and credit) to my middle child for helping me write Arthur's stargazing stories. You have an incredible imagination!

To Roseanna and David White. You are truly amazing. Thank you for yet another absolutely stunning cover (Eeee!!! It's so, so beautiful!), the random "Hey, what about....!" emails, and for being bold enough to see a market and go for it. Yes, of course the world needs a publishing line just for royals! Your passion for reading, books, and the authors who write them shows through everything you do. Thank you! I still can't believe I get to be part of this.

Thank you to WhiteCrown's editor, Janelle Leonard, who has become so much more than just an editor over the course of the last couple of books we've worked on together. You've become a true friend. Thanks for believing in me, brainstorming with me, loving these characters as much as I do, and telling me I'm as good, if not better, an author than most of the ones who've inspired me. I still don't believe you, but I love that you think so.

And to Marisa, who had the fun (fun?) of doing this book's

final edit. This story reads so much easier because of you. Sorry about all the commas!

More thanks than I could ever put into words to those—family, friends, and sometimes even strangers—who, like Darrek for Eva, see me on my worst days, when I'm too tired to fight, and take up the battle for me. Who pray when I can't find the words. Who remind me of God's promises when my eyes are too wet with tears to read them myself. Who hold me when I fall apart, and don't leave when I stubbornly tell them I'm fine, and clearly aren't. Jeshanah, Karryn, Brett, Cherith, Mum, and so many others over the years. Thank you for fighting for me.

To you, my incredible readers! You are the reason I write. Thank you for reading my books, and for your encouragement, support, gorgeous photos, and words on social media. I love that I get to do this writing journey with you and thank God for you often.

And, above all, to God, the Almighty, whose love and grace is more, and means more, than everything else in my life. I couldn't have written this book without you. Not wouldn't, but couldn't. Only by your strength did a single word get on the page.

Thank you for being the God who takes the first step and meets me more than halfway. Every time. Who holds me through the pain but isn't content to leave me there. Who sees my failures, and still calls me his beloved daughter. Who makes a path to freedom but leaves the choice of walking it to me. Who gave me not only a story to tell, but the words to tell it.

To God be the glory.

Hannah Currie has loved royals—both real and fictional—for as long as she can remember and has always been fascinated by their lives. They started making their way into her writing somewhere around first grade, and never stopped.

While she never dreamed of being a princess for real (way too many expectations and people watching), she certainly wouldn't say no to the gorgeous gowns, endless wardrobes, chefs and cleaners that come with the job. A crown or two wouldn't go astray either. Or Belle's library. Where she'd just sit and stare at the books with a giddy smile on her face for hours.

Hannah lives with her husband and three kids in Australia, where they proudly claim Queen Elizabeth II and the royal family as their own. She is very honored to be one of the launching authors for the new WhiteCrown Publishing line with her Crown of Promise series full of faith, romance and—of course—royals.

LEARN MORE ABOUT HANNAH AND SIGN UP FOR HER NEWSLETTER
at
www.HannahCurrie.com

Also by Hannah Currie

Heart of a Royal
Daughters of Peverell, Book One

Brought to the palace as a newborn, the royal life bestowed upon Mackenna Sparrow was never meant to last forever. Like it or not, she must return to the birthright which should have been hers – that of a commoner. But not everyone at the palace wants her gone. When the truths she's based her life on start crumbling as fast as her future, will she find the courage to trust, both herself and the prince she's fallen in love with?

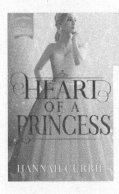

Heart of a Princess
Daughters of Peverell, Book Two

To the watching world, Princess Alina has it all— maids to serve her, a kingdom to revere her, a prince to marry her, and a wardrobe filled with enough frills, flounces, and shades of pink to rival a flower shop. But behind the smiles and designer clothes, Alina has a secret. She's barely holding it together.

Heart of the Crown
Daughters of Peverell, Book Three

The last place Lady Wenderley Davis ever expected to find herself after swearing off princes forever was living in a palace with two of them. She throws all she has into showing the royal family how to smile again, and she's loving every moment of it. Which is a problem. Because she's very quickly becoming attached, and – as the man she'd rather forget keeps reminding her—the one thing she can't do is stay.